W9-BWK-728

MAY 2016

THE DRINK AND DREAM TEAHOUSE

Also by Justin Hill

A BEND IN THE YELLOW RIVER

THE
DRINK AND DREAM
TEAHOUSE

A NOVEL

JUSTIN HILL

LITTLE, BROWN AND COMPANY
BOSTON   NEW YORK   LONDON

First United States Edition

The characters and events in this book are fictitious. Any similarity to real persons, living or dead, is coincidental and not intended by the author.

Library of Congress Cataloging-in-Publication Data

Hill, Justin.
The drink and dream teahouse : a novel / Justin Hill. — 1st United States ed.
p. cm.
ISBN 0-316-82400-3
1. China — Fiction. I. Title.

PR6108.I45 D75 2001
823'.914 — dc21   2001023497

10   9   8   7   6   5   4   3   2   1

Q-FF

Designed by Iris Weinstein

Printed in the United States of America

For the Shaoyang Tea Party:
Emma, Windy, Zoë, and SongQing

THE DRINK AND DREAM TEAHOUSE

For two weeks exploding firecrackers shredded the winter gloom at Shaoyang's Number Two Space Rocket Factory. The fourteenth and last night was the Lantern Festival: hopeful lovers carried their hearts in mothskin lanterns, bobbing like hooked fish on the ends of long canes. A river of stars flowed through the night, the candles burned steadily down, and after midnight solitary spirits wandered the streets with increasing desperation — searching for their perfect match, who might never come.

The next morning the radio announced the end of the holiday as children searched in the frost for the last unexploded bangers and detonated them in a ragged battle of irregular gunfire. At 7:45 A.M., Beijing Time, Party Secretary Li woke suddenly from a cold green dream that had stranded him back in the year 1967, and which had left him perplexed and nervous. It was the fourth time in as many weeks that the same dream had blown confusion into his sleeping mind, and this time he lay and shivered and thought hard, testing himself for any signs of private insanity.

Next to him Autumn Cloud, his wife, lay wrapped in cotton quilts, her head tilted back and mouth open, asleep. Party Secretary Li got up and opened the window to feel the frost on his skin. There was a chill morning breeze; firecrackers were sporadically shattering the silence. He rubbed his eyes as the smell of gunpowder smarted in his nostrils; opened them and saw the white snow sprinkled with the fallen petals of paper — cold and red.

Party Secretary Li tried to carry on his morning's activities as if nothing at all had happened. He cleared his throat into the toilet, then sat to empty his bowels in one long fluid motion, wiped away the excess with a strip of newspaper. He examined his old walnut-wrinkled face in the mirror and rubbed the chin of stubble that bristled defensively against the cold. He lit a cigarette and smoked; tried hard to be normal.

At breakfast Autumn Cloud steamed five bread buns full of date paste and poured out two bowls of sweet rice gruel, patterned with red jujubes and white tremella. She slurped expansively, and he slurped in reply. Slurp, slurp went their morning conversation. Next door, from her concrete balcony, Madam Fan was serenading the world with Beijing Opera. Her voice was shrill and beautiful, every note of the arias perfectly delivered. This morning she sang the young nun's soliloquy from *The White Fur Coat*:

> A young nun am I, sixteen years of age,
> My head was shaven in my young maidenhood

Party Secretary Li slurped, and his wife slurped back.

> My head was shaven in my young maidenhood.
> When beauty is past and youth is lost,
> Who will marry an old crone?

"She's been a crone for years," Autumn Cloud muttered. "Who does she think she is?"

Party Secretary Li looked up from his breakfast and stared at his wife. Her eyes held his then turned away. The words of the aria seemed to him very beautiful for an instant.

> They are not for my bridal chamber,
> These candles on the altar.
> They are not for my bridal chamber

He could picture Madam Fan with her sleeves blowing in the breeze, her shadow dancing on her concrete step next to her.

> From where comes this suffocating ardor?
> From where comes this strange, unearthly ardor?

The lonely words drifted across the skyline of gray concrete tenements and over the Shaoyang Number Two Space Rocket Factory's roof of corrugated iron; across the river, beyond the East and North Pagoda, to the hillsides of bamboo and pine, where the north wind whispered back. Party Secretary Li sat for a moment, eyes closed, breathing in circles, in and out, and felt for an instant a canyon-deep calm.

> A young nun am I, sixteen years of age,
> My head was shaven in my young maidenhood.
> For my father, he loves the Buddhist sutras
> And my mother, she loves the Buddhist priests.

Party Secretary Li laughed suddenly. He stood up and put on his army greatcoat and Russian fur hat.

"I'm going to the office," he said.

As he left, his wife shouted, "I thought you retired!"

He ignored her as he always did, and walked outside.

"What good's a husband who is always away from the house?" she cursed his footsteps, muttering as she cleared away the breakfast dishes. Party Secretary Li startled her so much by coming back and answering her this time that she dropped the blue bowl, which shattered, scattering shards across the white tiles, patterning them with fragments of blue and white. He stood for a moment in the doorway, sang to her the line "A young nun am I, sixteen years of age," and then turned and left.

Autumn Cloud hurried to the door to watch him. Who did he think he was? What if word got around that her husband was singing the lines of a young girl?

The offices were closed, so Party Secretary Li walked around the back of Number 7 block of apartments. He stood and surveyed the black soil of the allotments. Old Zhu was there, raking up dead leaves into a heap. His white hair, gap-toothed smile and skin of a baby.

"How was Spring Festival?" Party Secretary Li asked.

"Good!" Zhu answered. "Good!"

"Did your son come back?"

"No, too far. Too far. And yours?"

"No. Had no time off."

They stood in silence for a while. Young people never came back to Shaoyang, not even to die. There was nothing for them here, except memories. Party Secretary Li watched Old Zhu rake up another pile of leaves. There were now two piles of leaves, two tumbled mosaics of russet and black and brown. He lit a cigarette.

"Want one?"

Old Zhu shook his head.

Party Secretary Li lit his own, breathed in and then out in a long plume of smoke. It tasted stale. He threw it away, burrowed his hands deep into his trouser pockets. He watched Old Zhu rake up a third pile of leaves. The three piles made up the shape of a triangle. Three was a lucky number, but in each pile of leaves he could feel the chill of his dream: it was in the cigarettes he smoked, the food he ate, and it colored his sleep.

"Did you hear?" Old Zhu asked, as he straightened his back and leaned on his rake's shaft.

"Hear what?"

"They're closing the factory," Old Zhu said.

"They're doing what?" he asked.

"Closing the factory."

"This factory?"

"Yes."

"Impossible."

"It's true."

"It can't be."

Old Zhu looked up into the thicket of branches above his head that rained the leaves that he raked into piles. He thought of the factory, scratched his head, and said simply, "It is."

Party Secretary Li's seventy-eight-year-old heart palpitated as he hurried home. They couldn't close the factory, he told himself, not *this* factory. He opened the front door and called out to his wife. There was no answer. He checked in the kitchen; she wasn't there. He went to the bedroom door and opened it, but apart from the pale winter sunlight that stretched across the floor, the room was deserted.

The wooden chair creaked in protest as Party Secretary Li sat down at his desk, creaked again as he shuffled closer to the desk. He picked out his finest brush and squirted some ink from a plastic bottle onto a white chipped plate. The ink settled across one half of the plate, black and white, yin and yang. He dipped his brush into the ink and settled his mind. Madam Fan was still practicing her Beijing Opera, she had a tape player on in the background. Fan and tape mixed up so that he could no longer tell which was which. Outside he could smell the smoke that drifted up from Old Zhu's burning leaves, as they crumbled into ash.

Party Secretary Li leaned over a long sheet and the world went very silent, except for the whisper of brush on paper. He wrote the strokes of each character out carefully, stood back to survey his work. He took out his seal and printed his red square stamp at the end, then hung the first banner from his study window.

It read:

Our Leaders Are Drunk on the Taste of Corruption

He returned to his desk and drew another sheet of paper from the pile. He dipped his brush into the ink and wiped away the excess.

The Immortals Are Jealous of the Lifestyle of Our "Officials"

He stamped it with his seal of red.

The Privileged Officials Masturbate Over Blue Movies

And pulled another sheet from the pile.

Autumn Cloud spent the morning shopping in the market. She bought pork and spinach, bean sprouts and a square of tofu. On the way back she met Mrs. Cao, who invited her to go and play mah-jongg.

"We're betting," Mrs. Cao said with a wink.

Autumn Cloud screwed up her face.

"Come on, I'll carry your shopping!" Mrs. Cao insisted. "We need a fourth person."

They joined Madam Fan's husband and sister, who were playing mah-jongg in the kitchen. There was a brazier of glowing coals under the table that kept their feet warm, while their fingertips were still icy cold. Madam Fan sang on the balcony, occasionally casting disapproving glances at them through the window. Her arias and the clicking sound of the tiles being shuffled filled the morning. Autumn Cloud was nervous because she was starting to lose money. She pretended it was of no matter.

"I wish she'd give up on her rotten singing!" Madam Fan's husband cursed.

Autumn Cloud laughed louder than the rest.

"The factory's going to be closed," Mrs. Cao mentioned.

"Good," Madam Fan's husband replied.

"Good," Autumn Cloud echoed, not meaning to say good at all. They shuffled the tiles around the center of the table as she sat worrying. "What will happen to our pensions?" she asked at last.

"Oh, they'll still pay them," Mrs. Cao said.

Autumn Cloud nodded, trying to hide her relief. "And what about the workers?"

"I don't think there are any workers left, are there?" Madam Fan's husband replied.

"A hundred, I think," Mrs. Cao said.

Autumn Cloud nodded to back up this piece of information.

Madam Fan's husband was unconcerned. "Serves them right. They should have found another job. Set up in business. Have to move with the times. What about the Four Modernizations? What about the Open Door Policy? What about the Socialist Market Economy? Don't they know the world has changed?"

Autumn Cloud nodded. Yes, yes, serve them right. Have to move with the times.

She was still losing money when Peach, Madam Fan's daughter, ran in. Peach looked white, she was so white that she looked unhealthy.

"Mrs. Li, come quickly," Peach gasped.

Mrs. Cao scowled at Peach because she was on a winning streak.

"Mrs. Li, come quickly," Peach gasped again, then giggled and put her hand over her mouth. "There are bad words hanging out of your windows!"

Autumn Cloud went as quickly as she could, but her left leg was stiff and it didn't like to hurry. She went down the steps and followed Peach out of the door. Peach pointed up.

"Look, Mrs. Li."

Autumn Cloud looked up.

The Party Officials Are Screwing Our Daughters hung from the bathroom window.

The Fifth Modernization — Democracy was draped over the balcony railings.

Fuck the Communist Party wafted gently on the breeze.

"Oh, heavens!" she gasped, and held her left hand. "Oh, heavens!" she said again, and her left hand began to shake.

*T*he community gathered in Old Zhu's house to discuss what to do. Old Zhu held up a torn banner that he had managed to pull off the Li family's balcony. He held it up:

The Mercedes Benz Stops Nightly at the Red Light District

"What does it mean?" Peach asked.

Old Zhu cleared his throat. "It means Party Secretary Li is sick," he said. Everyone nodded.

"What can we do about this?" Madam Fan asked, moving forward into the center of the room.

"Yes, we don't want trouble."

Faces turned to Autumn Cloud, who sat in the corner, small and shaking like a frightened child in the arms of Old Zhu's white-haired wife. They hoped for a reaction from her, but she gave none. She just sat and shivered. Old Zhu's wife smoothed her hair back from her face.

"So what will we do?" Madam Fan asked.

Everyone turned to Old Zhu. He was the most senior person there. It was his decision. They looked to his white hair and gap-toothed mouth for the words of guidance.

"He's locked the door," Peach put in.

Old Zhu nodded at this piece of intelligence and everyone watched him think. Autumn Cloud shivered in the corner, as Old Zhu's wife held her close and wiped away the sweat from her forehead.

"Party Secretary Li has been upset by the factory closing," Old Zhu said at last. People held their breaths as they waited for more. Old Zhu scratched his head.

"He has worked all his life to build the Motherland. He was a shining light to all of us — we learned from his example." Someone cleared their throat. "All his life he has been an exemplary Party Member. And Autumn Cloud was a model worker too." People turned to offer sympathetic looks to Autumn Cloud, but she didn't hear or see anything in the room. "We have to help him. We must help him understand that the closure of the factory is good for the country. We must help build the Socialist Market Economy!"

Party Secretary Li hunched over his desk and looked into his cup of tea. A single jasmine flower swirled slowly on its surface, around and around. He could hear the crowd of voices outside his doorway. They were discussing what to do. Old Zhu was there, all of the neighbors as well. They discussed between themselves for a while, and then they resumed banging on his door. The thunder of all their fists on the metal door boomed through the apartment; then there was a moment of stillness, like gentle rain.

"Comrade!" Old Zhu called. "Comrade!"

Party Secretary Li didn't answer. He was out of paper, but he still had the bedsheets.

"Comrade Li! We have a doctor here."

"Neighbor Li!" another voice called.

"Brother-in-law Li!" So they'd got Autumn Cloud's sister here as well.

It's no use," Old Zhu told the conference that evening. "We will have to call his family. Where are his children?"

"Does she know?" Madam Fan asked, pointing to Autumn Cloud.

"Where are your children?" Madam Fan's husband shouted into her left ear. "Your children!" Madam Fan shouted into her right ear. Old Zhu took her hand, and looked her in the face. "Comrade. Autumn Cloud, where are your children? We are trying to help you. Where are your children? Your children? Children."

They'd given up on getting an answer, and some of them had actually left to go home when Autumn Cloud spoke. "Seven, six, five, two, two, eight, eight, eight."

"Can you say that again?" someone asked.

Autumn Cloud repeated. "Seven, six, five, two, two, eight, eight, eight." Old Zhu reached for a pen and wrote down her words.

"It must be a telephone number."

"Yes, but where?" Madam Fan said. "It's not a Shaoyang number. Her children aren't in Shaoyang. They've gone south."

"We'll try every city in China," Old Zhu declared with confidence. He smiled as he announced, "We'll save the duck by stealing her eggs!"

As the residents of Shaoyang Number Two Space Rocket Factory gossiped about the scandal of the Li family, Old Zhu sat on the phone and diligently tracked down each of

Party Secretary Li's four children. Two were in Guangzhou, one was working in a factory in Shanghai, and the fourth was a teacher in a nearby middle school. He confided to each of them that their father was seriously ill, and that their mother had had a relapse. They all packed immediately and set off on the long journey home.

Each banner Party Secretary Li hung from his window the residents of Shaoyang Number Two Space Rocket Factory had torn down by using long poles and canes with hooks on the ends. His neighbors had even managed to tear the flapping white blankets off the railings while he was trying to stop anyone from getting the banner that hung from the bathroom window. But Party Secretary Li was too old and wise for all of them; he still had one sheet left. It was enough for his final protest.

He walked into the bedroom and felt his hands tremble as he pulled the top sheet off the bed. It resisted for a moment, so he yanked violently. Its folds ripped out from under the mattress and it swirled in the air before falling prone across the floor, one end still clamped in Party Secretary Li's fist. He pulled it across the floor and jammed it under the bed leg so that it was rammed down tight, then began walking backward, step by slow step. He twisted the sheet around and around, determined hands continuing the torture till the sheet was a white cotton rope. He kept twisting till the fibers groaned in protest, then he twisted it one more turn and the end of the rope began to bend into a noose.

When he was satisfied, Party Secretary Li climbed onto the bed and reached up to tug on the fan shaft. It felt solid enough. He tied the rope onto the fan with a knot the size of a skull, then climbed down. There were four dirty footprints embedded into the cotton quilt, which still smelled freshly washed. He imagined his wife having to rewash the sheet, and silently rebuked himself.

Party Secretary Li's shaking hands patted out his last footsteps and smoothed back the hair from his head as he took a deep breath. His wife's face haunted him for a moment — she would understand, he thought, she knew what the factory meant to him — then he took another deep breath. It didn't calm his nerves. He looked around the room, on the desk lay his brush and the ink-smeared plate. Yes, that's what he had to do. He took the brush and wrote huge black characters across his bedroom wall, reaching up high for the top characters and bending down low for the bottom ones. As he wrote, the ink dripped one huge character into another, as if they were banding together for solidarity.

They were still dripping as Party Secretary Li washed the ink from his brush and returned it to its porcelain holder. He put the lid on the ink bottle and then turned to face the bed. He checked his cigarettes in his breast pocket, took off his shoes, neatly arranged them next to each other, then stepped up. The soft mattress swallowed his feet and he swayed like a man aboard ship, hanging on to the rope to steady himself. When he was steady he lit his cigarette and put the noose around his neck, and it lay on his shoulders like the arm of a trusted friend.

As Party Secretary Li smoked, his hands shook terribly. Halfway down he threw his cigarette away. Closed his eyes. Took a deep breath.

And stepped.

Off the bed.

The noose tightened slowly and Party Secretary Li gasped for breath, his fingers clawing at his neck. His feet kicked violently; his lips peeled back in a desperate grimace. His breathing became strangled gasps. Blood started out where his fingers had scratched. After a few minutes the violence of his kicking slowed to an erratic waltz. Urine trickled down his legs as his bowels opened. His gasps changed to gurgles. His open mouth gaped like that of a beached fish. His eyes bulged.

There was a brief moment when the throttling pain lifted:

the words on the wall swam together, and the last thing his strain-
ing eyes focused on was a single thread of ink, dripping down the
wall.

The ink dried to a thin crust of black on the white plas-
ter as a crowd gathered outside the door of Party Secretary Li's apartment. Old Zhu directed them as they brought up a
large hammer. Stand back, he shouted, stand back. The hammer
swung and the empty rooms echoed with shouting voices and the
thuds of the pounding hammer. Party Secretary Li heard nothing
as he hung above the bed, his sporadic twitches stilled, his feet
motionless.

When the metal door was bent and twisted it was kicked
open, and the residents of Shaoyang Number Two Space Rocket
Factory rushed inside. They spread through the apartment in a
panicked crowd while Old Zhu walked straight to the closed bedroom door and pushed it open. Party Secretary Li's body was sus-
pended from the ceiling, feet swaying slightly in the draft from
the door. Old Zhu stopped and shook his old head, felt shock
clutch his throat. He gasped and shivered, felt tears build up in
his stomach and start to rise.

Madam Fan's husband helped Old Zhu pull the body
down. They both flinched as the warm head flopped
unnaturally on the stretched neck, and the legs left a cold smear
of sewage on the bed. Madam Fan's husband closed the staring
eyes as Old Zhu wiped his hands in disgust. Madam Fan's husband curled his lip when he saw that shit had landed on both his
shoes. Old Zhu looked up through his tears and saw the black
characters across the wall, Party Secretary Li's final message:

Honor and wealth are gusts of wind
That blow for a while then disappear.

That night the pale moon rose in the eastern sky, before the storm clouds rolled over it. Thick soaking clouds that dropped anchor over the factory and started to rain. The first drops rang out loudly as they dashed against the windowpane. The individual rattles increased to a thunder like the firecrackers that had celebrated Spring Festival only fifteen days before.

As the rain fell Autumn Cloud sat alone, sniffing in the cold azure candlelight, grief turning slowly in her gut. Tears of sleet built up a thousand layers of cold, a cold so fierce it stunned the flesh. To Old Zhu the world seemed unbearably damp, and he took a candle to melt his melancholy with a cup of wine. Madam Fan struggled to sing her lines of opera, *A young nun am I, sixteen years of age; My head was shaven in my young maidenhood,* her voice drowned out by the noise of the falling water.

All night the truculent heavens poured their anger down on the factory, swamping the nearby paddy fields and the streets alike. The gutters burst, the river flooded; the streets were opaque with rain.

In the Li family apartment the ceiling sprang a leak. Water seeped through the roof and slithered down the shaft of the fan. It collected on the fan's underside, the water gathered and swelled up to a droplet, and jumped. Unseen in the empty room of Party Secretary Li's last lines, the water dripped that long night to pieces.

Old Zhu woke to a sky draped with black clouds and imagined he was submerged under water. Raindrops fell unceasingly, splashing off the roofs and windows like shattering jade. The sight of Party Secretary Li hanging by a stretched neck on a rope of cotton sheet came back to him. He felt winter in his bones like never before. He climbed stiffly out of the soft mattress and saw that all the leaves had dropped during the night. Madam Fan stepped out into the morning to sing her arias. She stood on her balcony, cleared her throat and the world held its breath, but all that followed was a silence that prickled the skin.

The stillness woke Autumn Cloud. She'd dreamed she was standing by a gray lake at dawn, watching a boat drift beyond the headland. She sat and for a moment wondered why the world felt so heavy, then remembered her husband's death, and it crushed her again. Her solitude was intensified by the relentless babble of memories, all their old regretted quarrels restaged. Autumn

Cloud sat down at the table and drank some cold green tea left over from the night before. It was bitter and thick, but she couldn't taste it. Water dripped in the empty room; the apartment was full of echoing footsteps.

Autumn Cloud clutched her cup for comfort as the rain-water stretched the windowpanes. The picture of the boat came to her mind again, drifting out to sea. The boat faded away without leaving even a single ripple, and her heart drifted after. She battled with a wave of hatred for the husband who had abandoned her, cast adrift on the far edge of loneliness; but hatred was too exhausting to sustain, all she felt was gaping loss.

Old Zhu went out rake in hand, but there were so many leaves he didn't know where to start. An icy gust combed the old man's bones and his organs shivered. The black trees rattled as he looked up and saw a light on in Party Secretary Li's apartment. In the square of the window was Autumn Cloud's face, staring down the path for someone who would never come again. He looked at the leaves and shook his head. They fell and grew again year after year while his body only got older. There was no sense to it all. Another icy gust rattled the branches, Old Zhu let out a long sigh, and began to rake the endless wet leaves off the path.

The rain seemed to lessen as a truck pulled up, white head-lights pale in the chill mist. A man smoking the wet butt of a cig-arette climbed out and walked toward Old Zhu. "Is this the place of Party Secretary Li?" the man shouted across, breath hanging in the air.

Old Zhu wiped the damp from his face as he looked up. "It is."

The man shouted back to the truck "Get to work!" and five peasants jumped down and began to unload bamboo poles that rattled on the gravel, shivered for a moment, then lay still. The men worked without the need to talk, tying poles together as the rain dripped from the trees and the last few leaves swung down to the ground. When the frame was up and steady they pulled a plastic sheet from the truck and threw it over the top. It billowed in the breeze like a bird taking flight, until they tied it down and weighed it to earth with stones and bricks. The plastic sheeting was striped red and blue and white. Red for the Communist Party; blue for the sky; white for death, winter snow and the unwritten page.

The peasants finished their work and climbed back into the truck. Old Zhu shivered in the damp. His clothes and flesh no protection against the cold, he felt: the cold of moonlight shimmering on his gravestone. He bent to his work, raking mounds of color up from the earth and felt a moment's warmth in his soul. He thought of Party Secretary Li's suicide and the factory closing, and tried to make it fit what he knew about the world.

"Where's the widow?" the truck driver shouted across as he gave the tent a final check.

Old Zhu nodded up toward the window where Autumn Cloud's pale face seemed half a ghost through the glass's reflections.

"What kind of funeral do you think she wants?" the man asked.

"The best," Old Zhu said.

"Is she rich?"

Old Zhu smiled. "No one here is rich."

"Does she work?"

"She's retired."

"What about the factory?"

"It's closed."

The man spat the stub of cigarette out onto the floor. "All the factories are closed."

Old Zhu didn't answer. Closed factories were something he didn't understand.

"Everyone in this shitty town's jobless." The man kicked a stone, then laughed suddenly. "Especially when you ask them to pay the bill!"

Old Zhu stiffened. "You'll get your money, don't worry about that."

The man looked at him and his gaze hardened for a moment. Then he turned back and walked toward the truck.

"Remember, we want the best!" Old Zhu shouted after him. White hair, old skin and terrible fear of death. The man made no reaction as he climbed into the cabin and revved the engine and pulled away. Old Zhu watched the truck disappear back through the curtain of gray rain. It left nothing behind but tracks in the mud, a swirling cloud of exhaust, and the funeral tent in the shadow of the trees.

Party Secretary Li's body was laid out on an old wooden table, covered with a red cloth. The body had been dressed in a blue Mao suit, buttoned close around the collar. There was a sash of scarlet and gold across the right shoulder and a gray uncomfortable expression on his lips. At the end of the table Old Zhu and the neighbors placed an old chest of drawers. The polish had been worn through by generations of hands, the brass fittings were black with age. Old Zhu dusted it down with his hand and spread a white cloth on top of it, and a photo of the dead man. No longer a chest of drawers, but a shrine.

No one could agree on what the traditional funerary offerings should be, so objects accumulated during the morning as they occurred to people. Autumn Cloud cooked pig's tripe and green chilies and put them on a plate on the tabletop. She lingered there looking at the soles of her husband's shoes, which made almost a right angle, and thought how much he liked that dish. She wished she'd cooked it for him every day — breakfast, lunch and dinner. She wanted to cook all his favorite foods, and imagined the mouthwatering smells might raise him from the dead.

Old Zhu's wife stroked Autumn Cloud's hair, and sat her

down near the body. She went to comfort Autumn Cloud as Madam Fan rearranged the offerings and put the incense pot at the front. Madam Fan fussed over the prominence of food and photo and pot, then cleared her throat, and asked, "Has anyone here got any matches?"

One of the neighbors' husbands gave her his, and she lit the two red candles as a squad of old women came hobbling up from nowhere and sat down in the middle of the tent. They had half a mouthful of teeth between them, and white rags wrapped around their heads.

"Wah! Red candles at a funeral," one of them hissed, "that's bad luck," and they all tutted and shook their heads at Madam Fan, who glared back and muttered loud enough to be heard, "Red or white — it doesn't matter."

The old crones got themselves comfortable and began to wail, encouraging one another's efforts, then losing concentration and falling away into conversation. They loudly discussed the cost of the tent, the extravagance of the funeral gifts, the life of the dead man and the bad luck his family would now have. Madam Fan tried as hard as she could to make them feel unwelcome, but they were not to be budged. They'd come for the day.

Autumn Cloud didn't hear the old women's comments. All she could see and hear was the past, locked into the present and turning over and over. People filed into the tent to present wreaths of colored paper, and Autumn Cloud looked up from her memories that were more real than their faces, and smiled briefly. As each person came the old women nudged one another and stopped talking to wail some more. Eventually Madam Fan tipped them five yuan, hoping they would leave, but they refused to be bought off and wailed a little louder instead. They rocked on their bony old buttocks and sucked their gums as sandalwood incense rose in the air; sobbing and falling away as black smoke swirled off from the red candles and the twilight shade deepened.

Eventually the file of mourners slowed for the day and the

onlookers got bored and wandered back to their dinners. One of them came back with some leftover rice to sustain the sad. The old women showed determined agility as they hobbled over to be first in line. They ate hungrily, polishing their bowls clean with their chopsticks. Then they considered their job well done, got up and walked away.

"What kind old women," Autumn Cloud said, watching them go.

Bloodsuckers, Madam Fan thought.

As evening fell a tangle of evening crows flew back to their roosts. Autumn Cloud shivered, not from the cold, but because she was exhausted by the voices in her head and because a night without her husband seemed unbearably long. She got up to go back to her apartment, but as she did so the crows flapped in the branches and croaked in disgust. Everyone looked pleadingly at the black birds, but they flapped and croaked again.

"I think I ought to stay," Autumn Cloud said.

"You'll catch your death of cold," Old Zhu's wife insisted.

Autumn Cloud refused to move. Old Zhu's wife fussed around her, but she wouldn't be budged. "This is the last hardship we'll share together," she said, so they brought quilts down from their houses, and Autumn Cloud wrapped them around her shoulders to warm her frail body. She sat and tortured herself by imagining going back to the morning of the Lantern Festival and stopping her husband from taking the path that slanted off toward his death. She fantasized ten thousand possible endings, and found herself back in this one, alone.

At around ten o'clock a group of tired musicians came stumbling out of the rain and stood in the candle flames. There were three old men carrying an amplifier and a heavy speaker.

They were stooped and their heads stuck out from their shoulders like three old tortoises. Behind them stood a young girl dressed in a white T-shirt and blue jeans who was cradling a microphone in a transparent plastic bag.

"Is this Party Secretary Li's funeral?" the girl asked the figure by the coffin.

Autumn Cloud answered, "It is."

The girl let out a long sigh and collapsed onto the bench, and the old men began to unpack their gear. One had a pair of symbols, another a drum, while the third sat down, tuned the strings of his erhu, began to play. The girl took her microphone out of its bag and began to sing. She sang the modern love songs she heard on the radio, full of love and loss and love again, which were amplified out into the dark rainy night. People sat in their cold apartments and listened to her beautiful voice: it was young and soft and caressing, full of the hopes they had lost over the years.

The girl sang to the spirits as the red candles burned themselves down, and then went out. The tent was plunged into darkness and the musicians stopped playing. All they could hear was Autumn Cloud's gentle sobbing.

"What time is it?" the girl's voice whispered.

A cigarette lighter spurted flame for an instant, yellow with a nimbus of blue, then one of the men said softly, "Nearly midnight."

"OK, let's go home," the girl said, and they left.

The musicians came back the second night: one girl and three old men walking out of the shade. They stood in the orange glow of the lamplight, silently unpacking their instruments as the girl coughed to clear her throat, ran her hand through her damp hair and took a deep breath.

People waited in their apartments, sitting silently until the girl began to sing the latest pop songs from Taiwan and Hong Kong. They were songs with heartbroken lyrics, words that took Autumn Cloud back to a time, fifty years before, when she'd sung love songs too — before love became bourgeois. She was still lost in the past when she heard a sniff through the music. The girl was crying as she sang; diamond-black tears wearing grooves down her cheeks. It was as if she were singing of all the sadness her life would hold — either that or the death of Party Secretary Li had touched her soul.

"Take her home," Autumn Cloud said. "She's too young to sing at a wake."

The old men shuffled forward into the candlelight, and she studied their worn tortoise faces and bright old eyes that sparkled with miniature candle flames. "We need the money," one of them said.

"Our granddaughter . . . ," another began, but Autumn Cloud cut them off.

"I won't tell the boss. Let her rest."

The old men followed her advice and went home. They didn't come again.

Incense burned in the tent for six full days as the red candles dripped the lonely hours away. During the morning people brought more wreaths, banners of yellow, and paper-cuts of white mourning. The paper-cuts were hung from the roof, while the wreaths were laid along the sides of the tent, and the banners were draped around the coffin. Others brought tinsel and fairy lights till the tent was a display of wreaths and sparkle that brightened a gray world, leached of color by the endless rain.

Friends and relatives took over from the karaoke band. Silhouettes without youth or age, they sat up playing cards to keep

Autumn Cloud and Party Secretary Li's body company as a tape recorder played military tunes through to morning. Sometimes Autumn Cloud would come and sit with the men playing mahjongg or cards, listening as they joked and laughed to raise her spirits.

On the fifth and last night the rain stopped. Autumn Cloud came out and stood over the body. She pulled back the red cloth and looked into her husband's face: his eyeballs had sunk into his skull, his lips were gray, and his body was so still. She looked at him for the last time, thought secret words of parting and recrimination, then pulled the red cloth back over his face.

On the morning of the funeral a truck bringing relatives from the countryside broke down and they arrived in tractors half an hour late; a party of invited officials overslept; the brass band lost their trumpet player; and a group of important old cousins refused to go by taxi and insisted on walking instead. There was pandemonium and confusion. Autumn Cloud shivered in the graveyard wind as noisy telephone calls were made and frantic messages were dashed around town.

When at last all was ready, the procession rolled out of the factory gates. There was a large crowd of expectant spectators who went silent as the procession began, led by a man carrying a banner that listed Party Secretary Li's achievements. He was followed by a crowd of fifty male relatives carrying the gaudy wreaths and the brass band who walked and played out of step with one another. There was a gasp of excitement as the spectators saw Autumn Cloud dressed in white with soot smudged down her cheeks. Approving comments were made on the cost of the coffin that was loaded on a bier carried by sixteen men. Next came a crowd of friends and relatives, many old and frail; a traditional band of pipes, gongs and drums; three part-time Buddhist priests who knew the Diamond Sutra by heart; and at the last a crowd of children who were running and playing and squealing with excitement.

The procession filled the streets and caused three-hour traffic jams throughout the town. Passersby wanted to know who it was; how old he was; how did he die. Angry car and truck drivers blared their horns and leaned out of their windows to shout get a move on; get out of the way! while traffic policemen took time off to smoke a cigarette.

The brass band answered the angry shouts by putting their instruments to their lips and giving a long blast. The traditional band was not to be outdone and struck their gongs and blew on their pipes and flutes, and the part-time monks at the end of the file added to the bedlam of noise by chanting their sutras and striking out an occasional *clok!* on their wooden blocks. Last man was the trombone player, who stopped to get a stone out of his shoe. He hopped on one foot, ran to catch up to the procession, and gave a wheezing blast to support his colleagues before the discordant noise faded away.

The funeral snaked its way through Shaoyang to the town's Number 4 Incinerator and ran into a number of other funeral processions going the same way. The bands competed with one another; grievers mingled in a blurred confusion of people; banners and achievements got confused and mislaid. Peach clung to Autumn Cloud, while Madam Fan cursed and blindly attacked the bodies around her. Old Zhu pushed through the confusion, and the men carrying the bier pushed after him. He fought his way through the crowd at the doorway, and managed to deliver the body to the correct official. He paid the hundred-yuan bill and received a stamped receipt for the ashes.

"Come back tomorrow," the official shouted. "Next!"

"What time?"

"Are you deaf? Tomorrow!"

"What about the wreaths?" Old Zhu asked. "Can they go in with the body?" The official turned around and pointed to a large bin where mourners were dumping wreaths. "Wreaths go over there!"

In the confusion around the town Number 4 Incinerator the grievers were split up and lost, and they straggled away alone or in small groups like troops retreating from a crushing defeat. Some dumped their wreaths on the road, where they were trampled underfoot, others went off for something to eat, but most just wanted to go home and shut the door. Old Zhu hurried through the streets with the receipt for the ashes and spotted his wife on the pavement a long way in front of him. He dodged cars and bicycles and caught up with her, desperately clinging to the ticket. She looked up at her breathless old husband, and squeezed out a smile, and they walked together in silence, stumping along together on their old joints.

"I'm hungry," Old Zhu told his wife.

"You're always hungry," she said, and heard the reprimand in her voice and relented. She looked again and said more softly, "Yes, so am I."

They walked together, Old Zhu feeling better because he was with his wife and they both felt hungry. Hunger was a reliable feeling; it had a simplicity love or grief did not.

Back at Shaoyang Number Two Space Rocket Factory a truck was parked under the trees and four peasants were dismantling the funeral tent. They had made a fire out of the remaining wreaths and paper money, white ashes rising on the flames.

"Make sure they don't steal anything," his wife whispered to him, so Old Zhu went to check inside the tent. He organized the removal of the chest of drawers and table. The green bronze incense burner was returned to Madam Fan, the food was dumped in a nearby trash can. He picked up a wad of paper money and the paper-cut of a television and dropped them into the fire. The paper-cut rose on the column of hot air and ashes, and then floated away on the breeze. He watched it sail away on the east wind, and turned to go home.

After they'd eaten dinner Old Zhu and his wife went to visit Autumn Cloud. The lights in her apartment were off, so Old Zhu knocked gently. There was no reply, so he knocked again, and listened to the stubborn silence.

Nothing.

"She must be asleep," Old Zhu told his wife. She nodded. They walked back down the stairs and went to bed, and that night Old Zhu slept as deeply as a stone dropped into the ocean.

Over the evening skyline of Shaoyang burned the dot of a Buddhist lantern in the Monastery of Universal Purity. From a distance it looked no more than a bright grain of white sand, but under its light a monk was chanting the Lotus Sutra for the soul of Party Secretary Li, dispelling the aura of death. The monk diligently read the words, and struck a gong each time he turned the page. In the early hours he reached the final stanza and stumbled over the last line, repeated it, then struck his gong three times, the echoes fading to memory.

The monk looked at his watch and swore, "Shit!" It was too late to go home. He curled up under a blanket, and slept dreamlessly.

While he slept the lantern flame burned low, and the statue of Guanyin watched the hungry mice gradually emerge from their holes, her serenely painted eyes full of compassion. As the mice nibbled her holy offerings the moon rose high in the branches and turned the dew to a snow-white frost.

*S*now fell during the night, smudging the factory's straight lines and imposing quiet upon the world. Madam Fan disturbed the white silence when she stepped onto her balcony a few minutes after sunrise. An icy sharpness cut the air as she stood and cleared her throat, but the fine snow floated aimlessly on the breeze, undisturbed. She stamped her feet for reassurance, coughed, and then blew steamy breaths over her fingertips. Snowflakes drifted down like blossoms, burying the world. She wiped her eyes and shivered, not from the cold but from the oppressive authority of the snow.

Madam Fan decided she would no longer sing the nun's soliloquy from *The White Fur Coat,* but the wife's song from *The Upright Official*. She stamped her feet again; the muffled echoes were soaked up by the blurred world as she wiped a few melted snowflakes from her face with her sleeve, let her breath condense in front of her, and began:

Common folk suffer when kingdoms rise,
Common folk suffer when kingdoms fall.

Old Zhu's wife got up to find the room an unnatural color and the windows fish-scaled with frost. She shivered as she dressed, then rubbed a hole through the ice and saw the outside world was just a white blur of buildings that had melted during the night. She stamped her feet and flapped her arms against her sides and, cursing the cold, completed three circuits of the apartment before she felt ready to start cooking breakfast. As she heated the soup she heard distant singing, then heard the words and stopped stirring. She turned to her husband as he blundered out of the bedroom, a worried look on her face. Old Zhu sat very still and listened.

"She can't be," his wife said.

"I think she is," Old Zhu replied.

The singing continued as the soup went around and around in the pot.

Laws that govern are slack,
Laws that punish harsh.

The soup boiled and his wife poured it out with an old aluminum ladle. She put a bowl of egg-and-spinach soup in front of Old Zhu. He nodded, then lifted his spoon and began to slurp. His wife sat down opposite him and dredged up thick green spinach leaves, stirred them back in. She was listening too hard to eat.

Why are we ruled by these barbarians?
These arrogant and corrupt barbarians

Old Zhu splattered his soup over his wife. He choked till his face went red and then sucked in an enormous breath and coughed ferociously while the aria continued:

These fucking corrupt officials
Who killed our children
And destroyed the hope of Ming?

There was the sudden sound of shouting and the singing broke off. Madam Fan's voice snapped short; a man's angry voice rising above Madam Fan's.

Old Zhu peered around the curtain to see what was happening. He rubbed a hole in the frost-patterned window and peered through. It was Madam Fan's husband, trying to drag her in off the balcony.

"Stop that noise!" Madam Fan's husband bellowed, and Madam Fan struggled to get free.

"Curse the day I married you," he spat as she scratched his arm.

"Have you no face?" he demanded. "Shaming the family?"

Old Zhu watched the Fans arguing on the balcony, and tutted softly. "Poor Peach," he said. "It's not right for a child to have parents behave like that."

"Yes," Old Zhu's wife said as she wiped spinach-and-egg soup off her sweater. "It'll upset Autumn Cloud if she hears it."

Old Zhu watched as Madam Fan was dragged off the balcony. Distant doors slammed, the building shook with echoes that faded away to nothing. Old Zhu was left staring out into the snowy landscape that looked blankly back. He listened hard but he could hear nothing more of the Fans' argument, nothing except the hungry silence.

Old Zhu leaned his forehead against the cold window. "What has happened?" he said at last. "What has happened to us all?" His words condensed onto the cold pane of glass and froze. His wife sat in silence, then crossed the room and stood behind him. She moved the curtain back an inch so that she could see as well. The balcony where Madam Fan stood every morning was empty, except for footprints in the snow. The lights at the house of Party Secretary Li were still out, even at this time. Autumn

Cloud must still be asleep. These little changes were so disconcerting.

Old Zhu's wife put her left hand on his shoulder and leaned her weight on him, and the old man felt supported. They stared out through the chink between curtain and window frame at a world they no longer recognized or understood. People went about their daily business: to market for the vegetables, to a friend's house for cards, to see the snow, to go down to the allotments to think about planting next year's vegetables; but all of it seemed unreal.

We must try harder to understand, Old Zhu thought. This is the world we live in.

"When are you going to collect the ashes?" Old Zhu's wife asked as she began clearing away the dishes.

She'd disturbed his line of thought, and he frowned for a moment and then said simply, "Today."

"Have you got the ticket?"

"Yes."

"Where is it?"

"I don't know."

"You've lost it?"

"No."

"Where is it?"

"I don't know."

"You have lost it."

"It's not lost," Old Zhu said, "it's *somewhere*."

His wife was unconvinced and she went to the kitchen to vigorously batter pots and plates together, then stormed back through the door.

"Have you decided how you're going to bring the ashes back?" she demanded.

"I'll put them on my bicycle," he told her, hitting the table with his palm as if that were the final word.

She stared at Old Zhu's rounded shoulders as he sat at the table, then went over to the pot of tea on the shelf and lifted it up. There was a thin wad of ten-yuan notes, folded over in half. She took one of them and put it in his breast pocket. "Get a taxi."

"I'll cycle," he said, and took the money out and put it on the table. The note lay flat for a moment, then curled back in half.

"When was the last time you cycled?"

He didn't answer.

"It's too dangerous. It's snowing." She stood above him for added authority. "All those cars and motorbikes. It's not safe!"

Old Zhu didn't answer. He put on his coat and went into the bedroom. His wife watched as he searched through the drawers for the ticket. He found it under an empty packet of cigarettes, clenched it between thumb and forefinger and then put his whole hand with ticket into his pocket. Her eyes followed him as he walked out of the door into the snow.

"Wah!" she said after he'd walked out. "Trust my luck — being married to a stupid old goat."

O ld Zhu spent the morning walking around with the ticket for Party Secretary Li's ashes in his pocket. He went down to the allotment behind Building Number 7, but the leaves were buried under snow so he decided to go for a slow walk around the factory compound instead. He set off along the tight rows of drab gray tenements, then turned down past the dance hall and the old communal restaurant, where they'd smelted all their pots and pans into iron in the summer of 1959. An old woman with a knitted mask across her mouth was sweeping a black path through the snow. The slag that had come from their homemade furnaces was bubbled and shiny like meteorite.

Old Zhu thought of the stars and the moon, the day when Vice-President Zhou Enlai visited the factory. We will take Communism to the Moon and Ten Thousand Stars! he'd proclaimed, and they'd renamed the factory Shaoyang Number Two Space Rocket Factory in his honor. Party Secretary Li had been in charge then. Had run the factory till he retired in 1990, after the troubles.

The path led him further back into his memories, to the time just after liberation when he was fierce with youth and the determination for change. They were going to build a new China, sweep away the old. He'd been assigned as a leader of teams of volunteers, and together they'd imagined the factory was the country. They'd all let that dream dominate their lives. For many of them it had proved fatal. Now the new leaders had decided it was time to sell up and move on.

Old Zhu looked up as he approached the snow-draped factory. There was an unnatural quiet about the place: the windows were dark, solitary ghosts lingered where crowds had once marched, and there were even birds nesting in the chimney stacks that had once proudly poured black industrial smoke into the heavens.

At the far end of the factory hall a team of peasants were dismantling the New Block. They had stripped down the roof tiles and beams, and were now removing the bricks one by one. The peasants passed them down a chain of hands, down to the floor where the bricks were piled up in squat square blocks.

Old Zhu remembered building the New Block in 1978. He'd stood on the roof and caught each brick as it was tossed up, and then he'd tossed it to the next man, and so on until someone laid it in a bed of mortar. They'd built up the walls brick by brick. Watching the peasants dismantling the New Block was like seeing his memories unravel. He no longer felt sure of the past or the present, knew nothing about the future.

The demolition workers lived in a tent of plastic sheeting, sleeping in bunks of twenty men, crammed in tight for warmth.

They worked split shifts, one group worked days, the other nights. They took it in turns to cook. They did not make food in the local way, but made thick wheat noodles with eggs and tomatoes; or toasted flat breads on the inside of oil barrels filled with charcoal. Old Zhu's friends blamed the rise in crime on these migrant workers, repeated insults they read in the newspapers under headlines about the "Rushing Tide" or "Blind Fish."

"It's cold," Old Zhu said to one of them as he passed, a young boy maybe eighteen or nineteen.

"Yes, it's too cold." The boy shivered. "But it's colder at home."

Old Zhu looked at the boy and nodded with a half smile. His white hair stood up and his eyes were bleary in the biting wind. "How old are you?" Old Zhu asked.

The boy struggled to understand the old man's accent. "I was born in the Year of the Dog," he said uncertainly.

Old Zhu nodded. "And where are you from?"

"Shanxi."

"My ancestors were from Shanxi," Old Zhu said. "Their hometown was at Ruicheng."

The boy didn't answer.

"Have you ever been there?"

The boy shook his head because he didn't know what the old man was saying and didn't know how to answer. Old Zhu looked at him.

"Paying you well, are they?" he asked.

"Hmm," the boy said.

"When I was your age I was in the army. Fought against the Japanese, I did. And then against the Guomindang. And then we built this country up."

The boy shivered and rubbed his hands, which were blue and white and chapped with blotches of red.

"Enough handfuls of earth, and you have built a mountain!" Old Zhu exclaimed from the past, and then it occurred to him that this boy was being paid to tear his mountain down. He grinned for a moment, a grin that felt heavy and awkward on his face, then said "Good work" and walked on.

Old Zhu tried walking down to the river. There had been a time when you could count the stones through the crystal-clear water, but now the water was black and sickly, sheets of algae matting the shore where ice plates of frost started out to cross the river. The inky water reflected the factory, trees lapped the bank, rainbows spread on oily patches. A gust of wind blew holes in the reflections. Old Zhu watched the rainbows dance for a moment and decided it was time to go and collect the ashes of Party Secretary Li.

Old Zhu cycled, and regretted it as soon as he'd set off. The streets were so noisy and chaotic, so many people, so many cars and motorbikes, so many bicycles and crazy cyclists, so many hawkers jostling the pavements and spilling out into the road, so many people and peasants and thoughts in his head where there wasn't enough room for them all. The snow had melted to black slush that splattered and sprayed up from car wheels. It was a long way. And uphill too.

Old Zhu pedaled slowly and the joints of his bicycle creaked in protest as the chain ground its arthritic way around and around. It took him nearly an hour to navigate his way back to Number 4 Incinerator, where other funeral processions were washing up bodies like flotsam, and then washing away again. He pushed his bike through the crowds and noise, the tires drawing straight lines across the fallen wreaths that were being trampled into the snow. The colors ran and mingled, making patches of blue and pink and indistinct brown, all crisscrossed with footprints and cycle tracks. He looked back but couldn't trace which way he'd come, just knew that he was there.

Old Zhu rested the bike against the wall, and it leaned heavily. The lock was rusted shut, so he let it be and went inside. No one would steal it, surely.

Inside the Number 4 Incinerator Office there was a confused line of people trying to get in and get out all at the same time. The wintry weather had frightened everyone, they were in a rush to get home and hibernate. Hands and shouting mouths loomed all around, the air was filled with curses and names and was humid with the grief and desperation of so many people. Old Zhu felt fear spread from his gut like warm tea; he clutched inside his pocket and found the ticket, and with head low he slowly pushed through to the front, ticket clasped in his hand.

The counter was besieged by a tight army of desperate relatives and friends who fought off intruders with elbows and fists. Old Zhu tried to force his way in three times and failed each time. He had reached the end of his endurance when a yellow-skinned girl with gloves knitted in every color of the imagination took his hand and gave him her place. He was so grateful he forgot to thank her, forgot all about her until well after the event. He pushed into her niche and enlarged it, then pulled himself forward and held up his ticket for inspection.

"I've come for Party Secretary Li," he called out, but the attendants took no notice.

"I've come for Party Secretary Li," he said again, waving the ticket. People were trying to push past him and he elbowed them back. He felt he was trying to ride the waves, and that they were crushing him instead. An old gray-haired woman with sinews of steel embedded herself into the front row. He was using his elbows to shove her back, without success, when he felt the ticket being snatched from his fingers.

"Name?" the attendant snapped.

"Zhu Zhonghua," he said quickly.

"ID card."

He produced it.

"Receipt?"

He panicked and felt inside his jacket pocket, found it and held it up. The man took it. "Number eighty-seven!" he shouted over his shoulder. "Next."

P arty Secretary Li came out of Number 4 Incinerator in Old Zhu's arms, carried carefully in a brown cardboard box that rattled. The rattling had startled Old Zhu.

"There's no ghost in there," the attendant had shouted so everyone could hear. "It's just bones!"

Everyone had turned to laugh, but they had stepped away from him as well and Old Zhu had taken the box, rattles and all. Just bones.

Old Zhu tied the box to the back of his bicycle, and Party Secretary Li took his last ride down the long hill between here and the Number Two Space Rocket Factory. Old Zhu didn't need to pedal going back, but kept his hands pressed down on the brakes that squeaked and grated as the wheels spun around. His white hair flew back in the wind, and he felt quite exhilarated for a moment as he swept down on the world like a rush of wind. Exhilaration for a moment long enough to remember a tune from the early years after liberation, and hum it along. He hummed and sang odd words about green hills and workers' solidarity and their new socialist paradise, and the wheels spun around and around and the bones rattled for the joy of cycling downhill, and a snowstorm of white dust raged inside the box.

O ld Zhu cycled through the factory gates, and parked his bike next to the staircase that went up to Party Secretary Li's apartment. He took the box in his arms and trudged up the stairs, then knocked on the door. There was no answer. He knocked again, louder this time. Silence.

"Autumn Cloud!" he shouted, and banged again.

Nothing.

Old Zhu checked the floor number, and checked the door. It all fitted. This must be the right apartment. He tried again, but still nothing.

Old Zhu looked at the door and shook his head. One more knock.

Nothing.

He tried knocking on the neighbor's door opposite, and a voice shouted from inside.

"Who is it?"

"Old Zhu!"

The door was opened a crack and a face peered out.

"That's the apartment of Party Secretary Li, isn't it," he said, pointing behind him.

"Yes."

"Do you know where Autumn Cloud is?"

"She's gone away."

"Where to?"

"I don't know. Gone to stay with relatives. She's got a child who works in the country."

"She's gone away?"

"Yes."

But I've got her husband here in the box, Old Zhu thought; but said, "Ah — thank you."

The door closed.

Old Zhu stood between the two closed doors and wondered which way to go. It was a strange position to be in — with the bones of a man whose wife has gone off to the country. In the end he went down, carrying Party Secretary Li in his arms. He took the box back to his apartment and put it on the table, made himself a cup of tea and sat down, exhausted. When his wife came back she was just about to ask him how it went when she saw the brown cardboard box on the table. "What have you bought?" she demanded.

"Nothing."

She took one step forward. "What's this then?"

"It's the ashes."

She gave him a dangerous look. "Ashes of *what?*"

"Party Secretary Li."

She screamed. "Aya! What's he doing on my table? Get him out of here. You can't bring dead bodies in here! What luck will it bring us?"

They argued and shouted, just to fill the apartment with noise. The box was picked up and put down, shouted at and shouted about. It was thrown onto the balcony and brought back inside. At last they reached an impasse.

"I'll go back to my parents' house if you keep that box!" Old Zhu's wife threatened.

"Your parents are dead!" Old Zhu shouted in exasperation, red-faced and breathless.

His wife didn't answer. They stood and stared at each other, then she bit her lip and turned and walked into the kitchen. She picked up the chop and slammed it down onto the chopping board. It quivered. She hit the pot against the wall, kicked the gas stove, and considered smashing a plate. Old Zhu let her rail and carried the box into the bedroom. It wouldn't fit under the bed, so he opened the wardrobe and slid it in at the bottom; put a pair of shoes on top of it, made it look as if it belonged.

That night his wife insisted she couldn't sleep with a dead man in her wardrobe, but she did. It was Old Zhu who couldn't sleep. He thought of everything that had happened, and thought of their son, who had left home to work in the Special Economic Zones. He woke up the next morning and found the world was still smudged by white snow. Sitting alone Old Zhu's thoughts were still of his son, who had gone away. He checked on his wife, she was still snoring wistfully in her dreams, so he closed the door and went to the phone, picked it up and dialed a number in Guangzhou.

The line was crackly and faint. Only his voice seemed loud as he shouted down the phone. "Da Shan!?

"Da Shan? I can't hear. It's a bad line.

"Good. We're well.

"You'll have to shout.

"I think so.

"Yes, she's well. She's asleep at the moment. I don't like to wake her. She misses you."

Old Zhu cleared his throat and took a deep breath. "Listen, your mother thinks you ought to come home.

"She's not well.

"Yes. I think so too . . .

"OK, I know you're busy," Old Zhu said at last. "When you can get away."

*D*a Shan retraced the journey back to his hometown as if he were returning to childhood. He'd left seven years before, on a spring day when wisteria flowers weighed heavily on the branches and afternoon butterflies danced in the sun. It had been a beautiful warm day, and he'd left never thinking he'd return.

His mother had cried. For her leaving home was like falling in with bandits on the road. She'd been silent the days before he left, then at the station she'd tried to argue him into staying.

"Who will care for us if you go?"

"I'll come back," Da Shan had said.

"If you come back we'll be dead," she'd said, and regretted it straight away. It was an unlucky thing to say. It tempted Heaven.

"I can get a job in Guangzhou."

"Why not work at the factory?" his father had said. "In a few years' time the leaders will have forgotten."

Da Shan almost laughed in exasperation. "What's the point?

I can get a good job in Guangzhou. Maybe even Shenzhen or Hong Kong."

His father had warned him sagely, "Other hills always seem taller than this one."

"Yes, Father," he'd answered, without listening.

Da Shan had left home and found that the hills on the horizon really were taller, they were steeper and more beautiful as well, and on the pale afternoons they looked sapphire blue. He'd written to tell his father this; continued to write deliberate and infrequent letters listing things he had achieved, friends he had met, and giving reasons for what he'd done. His father never answered, he'd been upset that Da Shan hadn't stayed on to work at the factory. Upset that his son was a capitalist. It was even more unlucky than being a counterrevolutionary.

D a Shan checked the battery on his cell phone, but it was dead. He sat and looked out of the train window. Two days of the world passing by, a film of daily life, from dawn to dusk, in minute detail. Winter deepened with each mile, taking him deeper into the snow-clad limestone hills that rose up like camel humps all around. Here and there frigid black rivers slithered between white slopes and thatched villages; peasants moved like hungry scarecrows through fields of broken stubble; ragged children looked up and waved, while young boys ran and tried to jump aboard, before giving up and throwing stones.

"Coca-Cola, beer, cigarettes, noodles," shouted the cabin guard, moving slowly through the carpet of bodies, kicking those who slept, and barging past the slow.

"Any meat?" Da Shan asked when the man reached him.

"Beef jerky," the man said.

"How much?"

"Six yuan."

"OK, give me two."

Da Shan chewed the beef strips slowly as the train chugged through each minute of the forty-three-and-a-half-hour journey. His jaw slowly ground the meat into threads and then the threads into something he could swallow. He washed them down with a sip of cool green tea. It had been a long time, he told himself. Returning home gave him a cold feeling in his stomach. He'd tried to bury the past, left it to molder under a cold blanket of moss, but in quiet moments fragments came back to him. On dull wet days he could still hear the ghosts sighing.

On the second day Da Shan started to recognize the landscape of hummock hills, paddy fields, village roofs and icy lakes. This was almost home — Hunan Province, where the people were as hot tempered as the food they ate. Men like Mao Zedong and the Pioneering General Cai E, who fired his pistol and toppled the Qing Dynasty. And home to Shaoyang, where Da Shan had abandoned all of his childhood dreams.

He looked out at the black trunks streaked with winter mist and poor farmers scattering handfuls of manure on the frozen soil. Their only dream was to leave the land and go to the big city and stuff their fantasies with hot food and crisp bank notes. Every day more of them setting off, spilling out again at places like Shanghai and Guangzhou. Seduced and confused and trapped in the modern world of cars and neon. Supermarket shelves stacked high with extravagances they could never afford. Unable to return to their villages, and unable to master the new drugs of wage and profit. No better off than they were in the dynasties past. Exploited.

Laws that govern are too slack, he thought,
but the laws that punish stern.

The hills and forests of pine and bamboo continued until late into the afternoon of the second day, when Da

Shan started to recognize the contours of the land. There were place names he knew and accents that were close to home. The skyline of Shaoyang city edged out from behind the curves of the land and he could see the North and East Pagodas, stacked chimneys and thousands of gray concrete blocks of apartments. He recognized the old monastery crouched among the trees on the white hill, sat up and felt his heartbeat quicken. The landscape was as familiar as scenes from his childhood, but the snow-clad hills and trees had no reason to act familiar. They watched his train approach with cold disinterest.

Train Number 516 trundled into Shaoyang Railway Station with a blast of its horn and a curt announcement on the station loudspeaker, came to rest with a long sharp hiss of steam and hydraulics. Platform Number 8 was full of waiting peasants and unemployed workers who were migrating with the geese, in search of work and money, seated and sleeping figures that burst to life when the train arrived, like bean sprouts searching for the light. They ran with sacks tied to their shoulders, up and down the train in search of an open door or window. People inside the train kept the windows and doors shut, which caused a rush of panic along the platform; panic, and the fear of being left behind in their towns and villages, where the hours and days silently devoured their lives.

Battle raged around the train for five full minutes. Windows were forced up, hands pulled people through or clenched into fists and tried to fight them off. But eventually doors were forced open and the migrant workers scratched, kicked and clawed their way onto the train.

Only a few passengers got off. Da Shan was one of them, fighting against the funnel of humanity who wanted to get on. His shirt sacrificed a button to the crowd before it let him go and he wrenched himself out of the press.

"Fucking peasants," he muttered.

A whistle blew, a flag waved, the brakes eased and the monolithic train moved off, carriage after carriage, till the last one passed and sped out of sight, hurrying to keep up. It dragged a swirling gust behind it and Da Shan shuddered at the vindictive cold. He was home.

He left the station and hailed a taxi. "Where to?" the driver asked.

"The Space Rocket Factory," Da Shan answered, and almost laughed.

The man turned on the radio and hummed along to a string of Hong Kong pop tunes. His voice was flat and tuneless as he sang. His Cantonese accent was terrible.

"You come on the Guangzhou train?" The man raised his voice over the music.

"Yeah."

"Working there?"

"Yeah."

The man nodded. He pulled a pack of cigarettes from the dashboard and offered one to Da Shan. They weren't foreign cigarettes, but he took one anyway. "Thanks."

They smoked with the windows open to the night as the driver negotiated the traffic lights and rotaries, swerving through the sprawl of itinerant salesmen who sold yesterday's fashions from their rusty rickshaws.

"Had the taxi long?" Da Shan asked.

"A year," the man said. "Cost me forty thousand yuan. Borrowed it off my brother. He works in Guangzhou."

"What does he do?"

"He's in a factory there. Makes clothes for export. Good money."

"And you?"

The driver laughed. "I get by," he said. "I get by."

As they drove Da Shan saw that Shaoyang had changed.

The old wooden houses were gone, replaced by concrete right angles and flashing neon signs. The driver drove along the river and turned in through the factory gate. It had sprouted a crown of grasses and a bent sapling clung to the red brickwork. The painted characters had been chipped and eroded by time, but they were still legible:

Shaoyang Number Two Space Rocket Factory, down the right column.

Work to Build the Four Modernizations, down the left column.

We Wel Come Your In Vest Ment, written in English across the top.

It was so tragic he almost laughed. The taxi pulled in under the gateway with its optimistic slogans, and braked. Da Shan climbed out.

"How much?" he asked.

"Twelve yuan."

Da Shan gave him fifteen. "Keep the change."

"Thanks," the driver said and stuffed the money into the glove compartment. "Thanks."

Da Shan took in the scene before him. The factory windows were dark and lifeless; they looked and felt deserted. It didn't match his memory at all. This was the ultimate tragedy, he thought, the traveler who comes home to find that home is no longer there.

Da Shan walked up the stairs, two hundred and sixteen, if he remembered correctly, taking two at a time. He would have been proud of that once, when a step seemed a mountain and taking two at a time was a trick only grown-ups could perform. But now it barely crossed his mind as he retraced his way back into the past and heard the shrill sound of a woman singing Beijing Opera. It was something about a nun, and being sixteen. Half listening, Da Shan found it difficult to make out the words. He passed a few people coming in the opposite direction, but it was too dark to see their faces. He counted the blocks of apartments as he passed them by, found his way up the three flights of steps to his parents' door. He knocked three times, bang, bang, bang — and waited in the shadows. The door opened and the angle of light widened to an arc.

"Hello, Mother, I'm back," he said.

She looked at him, and squinted. The voice was familiar; he called her Mother.

"Mother, it's me, Da Shan."

"Da Shan?" She peered. "Da Shan!" she exclaimed. "Da Shan! I hardly recognized you! My own son!"

D a Shan's mother hobbled around the room and smoothed back her gray hair all in a fluster. She'd cultured her anger each day he'd been gone, tended it and kept it alive and growing through all the years, but when she saw him she was so surprised she forgot to be angry. "Come in," she fussed. "We weren't expecting you. You must be tired. Come in, sit down. I didn't know you were coming. Why didn't you warn us? You should have said you were coming home. You've given me such a fright."

She gestured him to sit, and he tried to stop her from going off and making tea. She pushed him back to the seat and pressed him down, then went off to get the thermos flask and a cup. She put them on the table and turned to get the bowl of sweets reserved for special guests.

"Mother, please!" Da Shan said. "Sit down. You make me feel like a guest in my own home."

"Why didn't you warn us you were coming today!" she said,

and put the sweets in front of him. "Have some tea," she told him, and poured steaming water from the thermos into the cup. She composed herself and began to return to her usual self. The first thing that returned was the anger.

"You should never have left — look what it's brought us all here!" she hissed out of the side of her mouth.

"What?" he blurted.

She looked straight at him then. Hard, furious eyes and hard, furious words. "The factory's closing, and everyone is killing themselves over it," she spat. "And I have a dead man in my wardrobe! How can I live with a dead man in my wardrobe? And all because you go off to the ends of the world and leave us here all alone!" She wiped away the tears that were welling up. He wanted to get up and say something, but he knew it would make her even more mad.

"Don't think I'm crying," she told him as she cried. "Drink your tea." She leaned down and took a sweet and unwrapped it and put it in front of him. "Have a sweet."

Da Shan sipped and looked at the naked sweet he didn't dare eat, and didn't dare not eat — and remembered why he had left home in the first place.

*D*a Shan's return warmed Old Zhu's old bones, defrosted his marrow. He lay in bed and forgot that the box with Party Secretary Li's ashes was still in the bottom of the wardrobe, under a pair of leather shoes and an old blanket embroidered with tiny blue flowers. "It's right that our son should be back at home," he sighed. Winter had passed.

His wife sat in front of the mirror combing back her steel-gray hair, raking through the thousand tangled strands and pulling out each knot. She looked at her husband lying in bed in his white vest. The man she had married all those years ago; who had given her the son who'd left and gone beyond the edges of her world, then suddenly reappeared.

"Wife," Old Zhu cut through the silence, "we are lucky to have such a filial son, and a rich son at that."

She frowned and put her comb down, turned to Old Zhu and said, "Are you really so stupid?! How can you keep a tiger in the backyard! Whatever he's come back for — he's not going to stay!"

Old Zhu looked across the room into her hard eyes. He'd not thought Da Shan would leave. Not so soon.

Da Shan got up early that first morning, but his mother was up earlier and she told him to go back to bed. The second day the exhaustion of the journey hit him and he lay in till past breakfast time. His mother banged around the house and the fury of her passage shipwrecked his dreams and cast him adrift in daylight. He dressed and ate and watched TV and she banged and stamped even louder.

"Why don't you go and catch up with your old classmates?" she told him at last, and so he went out, but when he came back home through the dark, she was sitting up, waiting for him.

"You're late," she accused.

"I'm sorry."

"Your father couldn't wait up."

"Don't worry. I was only out with my classmates."

"How do we know where you were? You've been gone seven years."

He nodded and said nothing.

The next morning Old Zhu was sitting at the breakfast table, smoking. There was a pile of hard-boiled eggs on a white plate, salted pickles, a mound of steamed bread buns and a large pot of noodle soup.

"Morning," Da Shan said as he sat down.

Old Zhu smiled and nodded through the threads of cigarette smoke.

"This is a lot," Da Shan said. Old Zhu didn't answer. "Where's Mother?"

"She's eaten."

Da Shan waited while Old Zhu finished his cigarette, stubbed it out and then picked up his chopsticks. "Eat!" Old Zhu told his son. "Eat!"

Old Zhu tapped a hard-boiled egg on the table, shattering the shell into a thousand islands in a delta of cracks, then gave it to his son. Da Shan nodded and picked the filigree of cracks apart. When he had finished eating the egg Old Zhu took the ladle and filled Da Shan's bowl with noodles. Da Shan put his head down to the bowl and slurped, loudly. He kept slurping as he sucked up the noodles and slippery green seaweed — then drank down the pale green broth.

"More?"

Da Shan shook his head. Old Zhu nodded and put the ladle down.

"It is good to have you back home," Old Zhu said after a long pause, then stopped and reached inside his jacket pocket to pull out his cigarettes. He lit one, sat back and took the first few puffs. His face relaxed and he smiled at his son. "You know," he said at last, "I always hoped that you'd bring your wife and come and live here."

Da Shan took a deep breath. "But my wife and I are divorced," he said. It was something he'd written to tell them about, he was sure. He wondered for a moment whether his parents had ever read his letters.

"Yes," Old Zhu said, "I know," and then fell silent. Da Shan was about to say something, but Old Zhu looked up. "The stream of life is an endless river," he said solemnly. "It should not be left to run dry."

D a Shan was by the television, staring at the picture of his wife and daughter, when his mother came home. He quickly put the picture down, and sat down and stared at it across the room. His wife was dark with full lips and a lopsided kind of smile, his daughter the same. She didn't look like him, she could be anyone's, he thought and stopped. Now he was away from them it didn't matter much. The not caring was what surprised him most.

He turned on the TV with the remote control and flicked through a few channels, then turned it off again. Da Shan's mother scrubbed around him, banged and clattered, but he was too stubborn a stain to shift.

"I'm cleaning today," she told him, "and you're in my way." He picked up his feet, but she refused to give in. "You're young. Go out," she told him, and continued banging cupboard doors and clearing her throat till at last he got up and went out.

Da Shan borrowed his father's bicycle and pedaled down through the factory gate toward town. He looked around, thoughts drifting away to pictures and thoughts with no particular order or connection: a day he'd sat to eat noodles in the street; the disappointment when he saw the others off to Beijing; a birthday when he was young and his mother made Long Life Noodles, and he slurped them up without breaking them. It was a lucky sign, his mother said, and he was young enough to believe her.

Da Shan stopped at a red traffic light and waited. The city had changed so much now he hardly recognized where he was. This was the road that led to the Eastern Park. As he pedaled along he saw the road that led to the front gate and turned down it, past people selling chewing gum and popcorn. There was a new brick wall around the outside. A slogan was written across it in large red characters: *Foster a correct spirit,* it said. *Resist corruption!*

Da Shan went to the side gate, but it had rusted irrevocably shut, so he had to go back to the front gate and pay two yuan to get in. The park was overgrown with weeds and discarded bits of metal. He pushed through them toward the lake, on the way stubbing his toe on the frame of a cast-iron Flying Pigeon bicycle that had lost both wheels to the years.

Da Shan remembered the times he and his first love had come here. He shut his eyes and pictured her: her narrow black eyes and smooth yellow skin. The terror as he plucked up the courage to ask her out, which was nothing to the terror he felt when she said yes. Later they'd found places closer to home. The surer they became in each other the less shy they'd been. But the first months had been played out around the lake. The first time he'd kissed her had been in the autumn. Her lips were cold but her mouth was warm.

Da Shan tried to remember the taste of her mouth, the thrill he'd felt as they kissed, but the image wouldn't come. All his mind saw was the place as it was now: paths smothered in weeds, water thick with half-rotted leaves, and a rusted tin can stuck to the shore.

Da Shan opened his eyes. All he had left was his parents. Even the ghosts of his past had gone.

When Da Shan came home his mother accused him of being deliberately late for dinner. She kept up her assault for ten more days. If he stayed at home she drove him out, and when he came back she was waiting for him with a rebuke. On the tenth day they sat down to lunch. Old Zhu helped himself to the dishes. He picked out some roasted liver, put it in his mouth and chewed and reached for another piece.

"You're not eating," Old Zhu's wife said to his son.

"No," his son said.

Old Zhu reached for another piece of liver and looked up at them both.

"Why are you doing this?" Da Shan asked.

"What?" his wife said.

"This."

"I'm not."

"Yes, you are."

"I don't know what you're talking about."

"Yes, you do," he said.

Old Zhu watched them as they stared at each other. He didn't know what either of them was talking about. The world was only their eyes and the sound of his chewing.

Da Shan looked at his mother. Her gray hair and tired old face, the wrinkles eroded around her eyes, the puckered look of her lips. She tried giving him that punishing look, but it no longer worked; Da Shan smiled.

"Why don't you eat — is my food too poor for you now?" she asked.

"No. But it doesn't taste as good as it used to."

"What are you trying to say?"

"I'm not trying — I'm saying it."

Old Zhu blustered for a moment, wanting to assert his authority and trying to swallow and speak at the same time.

In a dangerously low voice Old Zhu's wife said, "Are you *ashamed* to be my son?"

Da Shan looked at his mother's cold eyes and opened his mouth. Old Zhu blustered even louder, but no words came. Da Shan looked and opened his mouth and started laughing. Long, loud and excessive laughter that built to a peak, and dropped off, and then built up again.

"Have some respect!" Old Zhu demanded, but Da Shan laughed even more. His mother glared, but he bent double and wept tears. She put her chopsticks down onto the table, stood up and turned and walked slowly out of the room, into the kitchen and shut the door.

Old Zhu followed her into the kitchen, where he stood behind his wife, hands by his side, doing nothing. The sounds of Da Shan's hilarity were undiminished and Old Zhu started snickering too, though he didn't know why. The old man tried to suppress his humor, thought it might be dangerous to stay in the kitchen and retreated into the dining room and let himself down onto a chair, let it flow.

Old Zhu's wife looked for something to smash. In the cupboard there was an odd collection of plates and bowls that she'd put together over the years, but there was nothing that she loved enough. She'd already smashed everything that was precious to her. She picked up the cutting board, a thick slice of tree trunk. It was heavy in her hands as she raised it over her head and threw it through the kitchen window. The glass exploded into the night: a flower of glittering glass with a center of wooden chopping board that hung for a moment before it felt the pull of gravity and fell down out of sight.

Da Shan checked himself, and Old Zhu stopped as well. Da Shan coughed and blinked his eyes, and Old Zhu sat up hopefully, wanting his son to break out laughing again so he could join in, but he didn't.

"What was that noise?" Old Zhu asked, hoping to prompt another outburst.

Da Shan pointed into the kitchen, where his mother stood scratching the back of her left hand with the nails of the right. She scratched till a thick stream of blood began to flow. A thick and viscous ruby line that clung to her like a leech. She licked the blood away, the metallic taste in her mouth.

Da Shan came into the kitchen. He saw the blood on her left hand and wiped it away. She let him clean her hands under the tap. He looked at his mother and the smashed window.

"Let's go out for a meal," he said. "I'll take you for the very best!"

"Don't waste your money."

"No problem — I have lots of it."

"My food is better," his mother said.

"I don't want to trouble you."

"Your father should have thought of that when he got me pregnant."

"He didn't." Da Shan smiled. "But I am thinking of it now."

"Then you should never have left."

"I've come back."

"I don't want to go to the restaurant."

"Don't be so polite," Old Zhu urged her.

"Come on, I'll take you to the very best."

Old Zhu grabbed his wife and pulled her out of the kitchen.

"Don't you read what it says in the newspapers?" she protested as they stumbled down the stairs. "We'll be poisoned!" But Old Zhu pulled her along after their son, who strode on ahead and hailed a taxi.

"Where's a really expensive restaurant?"

"The Cultural Revolution Commune Restaurant," the driver announced.

"Good," Da Shan said, "that's where we're going."

Old Zhu dragged his wife through the car door, and Da Shan shut the door behind her.

"Take me back home!" she insisted.

"She's just being polite," Da Shan told the taxi driver, and the driver looked in the rearview mirror at the old pair in the back.

"My mother's just the same." The driver smiled. "Always thinking of other people." He drove the taxi back along the dark street into the crowded town, through the flashing neon lights, the throngs of people and bicycles and cars. Out of the gloom a neon sign flashed Cultural Revolution Commune Restaurant, and the taxi pulled over and they climbed out and slammed the doors shut.

"Ten yuan," the driver said through the open window.

Da Shan gave him fifty. "Keep the change."

Old Zhu wanted to go back and get the change but didn't want to make Da Shan lose face. He saw his son for the first time: rich and well dressed, confident and complete.

"Mother, Father — here we are!" Da Shan announced with a flourish.

A posse of pretty young waitresses dressed as peasants came running out to the taxi. Da Shan led the way as the girls shepherded Old Zhu and his wife into a room decorated like the inside of a log cabin. Chairman Mao's picture hung on the wall, his sayings were written out in red strips of calligraphy that hung on all the walls. A midi-system played tunes from the Cultural Revolution: "Chairman Mao Is the Red Sun," "The Red Sun Lights Our Lives," "Our Chairman Is the Great Helmsman," "The East Is Red."

Da Shan chose a table with Mao's poem "Re-ascending JingGangShan" hanging over it:

> Nothing is hard in this world
> If you dare to scale the heights.

And pulled out the chairs for his parents to sit.

"Aya! This is too expensive!" his mother said.

"Can you really afford this?" Old Zhu whispered.

"To love others without first loving your parents is to reject virtue," Da Shan said.

Old Zhu nodded in respect: this was his son.

A waitress came over. She had her hair cut short, and an army cap on her head. Her eyes were almond shaped and light brown, her skin was white.

"The table's dirty," Da Shan said.

The waitress blushed, pricks of blood in her white cheeks. "I'm sorry," she said, and bent low to wipe it.

"Here," Da Shan pointed. And she wiped there as well.

"Would you like drinks?" She blushed.

"Mother?"

"Hot water."

"Have tea."

"No. Water."

"Have tea."

She didn't answer. Da Shan told the waitress "Tea." Then he turned and said, "Father?"

"White spirit."

"What spirit do you have?"

The waitress smiled. "Sorghum Wine, Rice Wine, Plum Wine, Chrysanthemum Wine."

"Which is the most expensive?"

"Sorghum Wine."

"OK, two bottles."

She wrote it down. "And food?"

"Fatty Meat and Red Cooked Fish. Fried Chicken, Grass Fish, Smoked Tofu, Lotus Root, and Three Flavor Soup."

"Anything else?"

"We should have dumplings," his mother said, "because now we are together again."

"A kilo of dumplings," Da Shan said, and the waitress smiled dimples into her two red cheeks as she wrote it down.

"Anything else?"

"Marlboro cigarettes."

"And?"

Da Shan stared into her almond eyes and said, "No. Thank you. That's it."

When the wine came Da Shan poured it into three cups and declared a toast, "To an unfilial son!"

"No, no," Old Zhu corrected. "To a parent's joy."

They drank the wine down; it was fierce and ruthless. Old Zhu and Da Shan drank two more glasses before the dishes arrived. Their cheeks were red with the alcohol, their talk expansive. They laughed together, Da Shan lit a cigarette and gave it to his father, then turned to his mother and said, "Eat! Eat!"

She didn't. Da Shan picked out the choice piece of fish and put it on her plate. He picked out the chicken's head and put it next to the fish, pulled a rich hunk of grass fish, and piled it on top. Body parts collected on her plate, but she didn't eat them.

"Eat! Eat!" Old Zhu said.

She didn't eat.

Da Shan called the waitress over. She came willingly and smiled.

Da Shan pointed with the hand holding his cigarette. "This food is no good. My mother can't eat it. Take it back."

The girl's face dropped. She nodded once, then ran off to the manager. The manager came over. He was a smiling man with a worried look.

"This food's shit," Da Shan declared. "My mother can't eat it."

The manager looked. "I'm very sorry. I'll fetch the cook."

The cook came, wiping his fingers on his stained white coat. He was a loud-laughing man, till he stood in front of Da Shan, when he desperately smothered his bemused look.

"What's this rubbish you've cooked?" Da Shan shouted. "My mother hasn't eaten anything. Who taught you to cook? A dog?"

The chef apologized.

"I don't want fucking apologies. I want food my mother can eat!" Da Shan raged, red-faced and spittle flying.

The manager stepped forward and addressed the gray-haired old woman. "Please, lady, what would you like to eat?"

"I want to go home."

"What's the most expensive thing on the menu?" Da Shan demanded.

The manager asked the cook, "What have we got in?"

The cook gave a shrug. "Crayfish, Turtle Soup. Snake's Gall, Fried Scorpions."

"Bring them all!" Da Shan shouted, and Old Zhu joined in as he poured more sorghum wine. The wine spilled over in Da Shan's cup, he missed his own cup altogether.

"Bring them all!" Old Zhu shouted. "The most expensive things on the menu!" He drank his cup down in one, and Da Shan handed him another cigarette.

"More cigarettes!" Da Shan shouted.

"More wine!" Old Zhu chorused.

"More food!"

The table groaned under the weight of the bill that was presented to Da Shan. As he counted out the money the kilo of dumplings cooled and stuck together. A bestiary of animals lay uneaten. Old Zhu was drunk and replete. His wife hadn't touched a thing. Da Shan watched her with red, baleful eyes. She put a hand to her gray hair as if she were a young wife. "Have you both had enough?" she asked gently.

Old Zhu burped. Da Shan took a scorpion and crunched it in his mouth, and spat it out half eaten. He was drunk and confused.

"If you have had enough, then I will eat a little," his mother said, and took a dumpling. She dipped it in red chili paste, and put it in her mouth, and chewed slowly. Da Shan watched her eat with dull satisfaction. He poured another toast for his father and himself. "To your wife, and my mother!" he declared. And they drank.

Old Zhu looked at his wife and son. "Filial piety is the source of civilization!" he declared.

"A husband is Heaven. You can't leave Heaven, nor your husband," his wife corrected.

Da Shan silenced them both. He poured out the last of the wine and gave them cups to drink. He stood up and quoted Deng Xiao Ping — To be rich is glorious! — and then fell down laughing.

When the sun rose Old Zhu's wife was already up, making breakfast. The sound of her chopping shallots echoed through the whole block, pulling Old Zhu back from sleep. He lay and wriggled under the quilt, then stood up, stretched his old limbs and found his old body as stiff as a gnarled tree. Outside it was raining, warm spring rain soaking green back into the landscape.

Good for the peasants, he thought as he got dressed, good for the soil.

It's raining," Old Zhu said to his wife as he walked past her into the bathroom.

"It's always raining," she said. "All this place ever does. Rain in winter and rain in summer. It's like living in a piss pot."

"It's early, should be good for the peasants," he said optimistically.

"Since when have you been a peasant?" she asked, stirring the soybean milk. "What do we care about the peasants? They're all right," she muttered to herself. "What about us?"

She stood and watched the soy milk till it boiled, then she ladled it out into one large bowl and called out, "Come! Eat!"

Old Zhu was on the balcony smelling all the damp odors of soil and spring. He heard her call and came back in. "I think I'll do some planting today," he declared to no one in particular.

"Come! Eat!" his wife shouted toward Da Shan's room. "Food!"

D a Shan woke to the hangover that had patiently waited in his head all night. He forced himself upright, dressed, then came out and slumped down at the table. His mother cleared her throat as she filled each person's bowl, set steamed bread buns out on the table. The two men ate and drank in silence while she kept talking.

Da Shan wasn't hungry. He swirled his soy milk around the bowl clockwise, and then counterclockwise, and his mother watched him. She cleared her throat again, but he ignored her. She cleared her throat, louder this time, and Da Shan looked up. Not at her, at his father. "I was thinking," he said, "what ever happened to the Family Genealogy?"

His mother heard the kettle boil and jumped up, pushing back her chair with a loud scrape as she hurried to the kitchen. Old Zhu carried on eating his soup, spoon by spoon.

"Father."

Old Zhu looked up with tired old eyes.

"What happened to the Family Genealogy?"

Old Zhu lifted a spoonful of soup to his lips and then put it back into the bowl, and looked down. "What do you mean?" he asked.

"The Zhu Family Genealogy. What happened to it?"

Old Zhu looked toward the kitchen, where his wife was pouring the water into thermos flasks. The stream of water from kettle spout to thermos an arc of steaming water.

"I want to know where that book is," Da Shan said.

"I burned it."

"When?"

"In 1967."

"Why?"

"You know why."

His mother came back, looked at her husband's face and then her son. Da Shan sat back and stared at her, arms folded.

"What's wrong with you two?" she asked.

Old Zhu ate his soup and Da Shan stared.

"You're like a pair of old bulls," she scolded, "with no cows to fight over." Neither of them responded. "Serves you right for drinking like a pair of village dogs."

Old Zhu cleared his throat. "He wants to know what happened to our Family Genealogy."

Her eyes flickered from one face to the other.

"I've told him I burned them," Old Zhu said.

"You did," she agreed.

"Why?" Da Shan asked again.

"We had to," she told him.

They finished their breakfast in silence, thoughts chattering in their heads. When Old Zhu had scraped his bowl clean he stood up and went to the bathroom. He hawked and spat noisily, then flushed the toilet with water from the bucket. He came out humming the national anthem, and bent to put his boots on.

"Where are you off to?" his wife demanded. "It's raining."

"It's not heavy," he said.

"You'll get wet."

Old Zhu tied the lace of his left shoe first, and then started on his right. "I'll take a coat."

"Why do you have to go out now?"

"It's time to plant the onions."

"Onions indeed! Why did I marry such a crazy old man —
always planting vegetables."

Old Zhu pulled out an army surplus raincoat, thick and
green with a large hood that he pulled over his head, then turned
and walked out.

"Where are you going?" she demanded of Da Shan as he
stood up.

"Nowhere."

"Why not? I don't want you here cluttering up the house."

"But it's raining," Da Shan said, and she muttered in reply.

Da Shan brushed his teeth and then opened the door of
his father's study and walked in. The air hung heavy
with memories and the smell of books. Da Shan had stood here
as a child reciting poetry. By the age of ten he'd learned all the
classics, the Words of Mao Zedong and Karl Marx too, but the
Ancient Classics were the hardest. They were full of strange ref-
erences, characters no one used anymore, and his father had
beaten him for each mistake.

"These stupid poems don't even rhyme!" he'd said to his
mother one day, and his father had overheard.

"How dare you say that! You treacherous little bourgeois!"
his father had shouted as he hit him. Old Zhu hadn't been a
white-haired old man then; and Da Shan had only been a child.
"People have studied these poems for a thousand years!" his father had raged before putting pink stripes all over Da Shan's hand
with his bamboo cane. Da Shan's childhood was layered with
beatings. Each thrashing made him more convinced that any
problem in China was intimately linked with her poems, and the
fact that her greatest poetry no longer rhymed.

Now he stood and weathered the images and memories,

scarred over by time. He scanned the bookshelf for the book he was looking for, pulled it out, and then sat down to read.

Da Shan's mother washed up the breakfast pots and began cleaning the apartment, moving in a regular pattern — a wide circle around the bedroom. When she had swept the kitchen, toilet, main room and porch, she went into the bedroom and quickly cleaned around the wardrobe. She cleaned the whole apartment except the study, where Da Shan sat reading. It annoyed her that he was in there because she was used to having the apartment to herself.

Morning passed as she walked past the doorway at regular intervals, peering in to see what he was up to, but Da Shan didn't look up or say anything, even though she was sure he'd seen her. In retaliation she turned the radio on, loud; began chopping pork and eggplant for lunch; smashed cloves of garlic with the flat of the chop, then shredded the remains. She banged and clattered in the kitchen till making noise became an end to itself, and carried on banging even when she'd forgotten why she'd started. The radio reception slowly wandered till there was more crackle than words, so she tuned it in again and turned it up when the hourly bulletin came on. All the news was good, but the world she lived in was so wrong.

When yin and yang are poorly mixed
the world is muddy.

It was certainly true in Shaoyang, she thought, what with all this rain.

D a Shan came out of the study only as she was heating the oil in the wok for lunch.

"We're eating early today," he commented.

"How would you know when we eat? We eat when the food is cooked, that's when we eat."

Threads of smoke curled up from the oil as he stood in the

kitchen doorway with a book of poems in his hand. He held it up. "Father never made me learn this one." He laughed.

She gave him a sidelong glance but didn't answer. The spine of the book read *Ten Thousand Tang Dynasty Poems.*

"Since when did you like reading poems?" she said. "You always hated poems."

Da Shan ignored her and read out the title: "Li Bai's Poem to Du Fu."

She looked at him as he held up the book; scowled as he chanted the lines, reading quickly and nonsensically. Then Da Shan stopped and repeated the last two lines:

> Du fu, how come you've grown so thin?
> You must be suffering from too much poetry.

His mother didn't laugh. "Does your father know you're going through his books?" she asked.

"I was looking for something."

"And did you find it?"

"No."

"Wah!"

Da Shan lowered the book, let it hang by his side. "What did happen to the Family Genealogy?" he asked.

"Your father burned it."

"In 1967?"

"Yes."

"Why?"

"It was from the past," she said, turning the heat up. "It was dangerous to keep it."

"Do you think he can remember any of it?"

"I don't know," she said, the oil smoking. "Ask him."

"How about you?"

"What about me?"

"How about your family?"

She looked at him.

"Where did they come from?" he asked.

"Why are you so interested in history?" she retorted as she lifted the pan from the flames. "How can I remember all those silly things? It's all past and finished."

Da Shan stayed in the doorway, flicked through a few pages, came across a poem or line; flicked forward again. His mother put the pan back on the heat, tipped the pork into the oil, which hissed and spat as malevolently as a cornered cat, then stepped back for a few seconds until it was safe to reach out and turn the gas down. Da Shan watched her stir the meat shreds around and around till all their raw redness had turned to a cooked pink.

"I don't remember where they were from," his mother said suddenly. "I think it was Suzhou."

Da Shan looked up. "Your family?"

"Yes."

"What did they do there?"

"Police."

"Not for the Communists?"

She didn't answer.

"Were they Guomindang?"

"Maybe."

Da Shan continued flicking through the book of poems. After a long pause he asked, "So how did you get to join the Communists?"

"I can't remember," she said. "It was all a long time ago."

They sat and ate lunch in silence, waiting for someone to speak; but no one did. Old Zhu scraped his bowl clean of rice and then swilled a glass of tea around his mouth to dislodge food from between his teeth, which he swallowed before getting up and going back to his allotment.

Da Shan watched his mother as she cleared away the plates and bowls, tipping all the uneaten food onto one plate that she cleaned off into the bin. When he'd first seen his mother she'd looked so old. Noticeably so. But since his return her wrinkles were filling out and her stoop was straightening like a bent bamboo that springs effortlessly back.

Da Shan had a cigarette on the balcony, looked down to the allotments, where his father's frosty white head bent and rose and dipped as he dug the soil. When Da Shan had finished he came back in and he went and stood in the kitchen doorway, leaning against the door post.

"Have you ever been to Suzhou?" he asked his mother.

"No," she said, rolling up her sleeves and beginning to scrub the pots, "not since liberation." She continued scrubbing and he watched without speaking.

"What was your father like?"

She glanced up at him, and smiled. "He was very kind. You look like him."

"Do I?" Da Shan said, surprised, and folded his arms.

"He was a very well educated man," she said. "He sent us to the best school in the district, even though we were girls."

"And your grandfather?"

"I never met my grandfather. We lived in the city. He was a businessman, I think. Traded in silk. Everyone in the village traded in silk. It was exported as far as America and India, they said."

"Why did your father join the Guomindang?"

She laughed humorlessly. "He wanted to liberate China from all the imperialists. That was all."

"But he was in the police."

"Yes."

"What happened to him at liberation?"

"He went to Taiwan with Jiang Kaishi."

"Did you ever hear from him again?"

"No."

Da Shan nodded. His mother wiped the stove top. "What did he think of you being a Communist?" Da Shan asked.

"Oh, he didn't know for a long time. Such a long time. I was a spy on my own father!" She laughed. "What a terrible daughter I was!" She held the cloth in her hands and looked for something else to wipe but couldn't find anywhere, so she wiped the side again. "I told the Communists who he was meeting, what he was doing. After 1980 we were allowed to write to people abroad. I wanted to apologize to him, tell him I was wrong. But the letter came back; he'd died, of course."

A thoughtful quiet filled the room.

"When did you meet Father?" Da Shan asked.

"Oh — just before liberation."

"What was he like then?"

"Very handsome."

"He was a Communist."

"Yes, oh yes. He was a teacher, that's how we met. He was my teacher and he introduced me to socialism and patriotism."

Da Shan stayed silent as he watched his mother empty the washing bowl and wring the cloth dry. She wiped the sink then hung the cloth up to dry.

"So what was it like in 1967?"

"Don't you remember?"

"A bit. But I was only little. It's not very clear."

"Wah! It was chaos."

"That's when you burned the genealogy."

"Is that what your father said?"

Da Shan nodded; his eyes followed her as she wiped the taps and the rim of the sink, then inside the sink, wringing out the cloth again, and hanging it up once more.

"Isn't it true? When did he burn them?"

"I don't know."

"Did you ever see them?"

"No."

"So he burned them before he met you?"

"Why so many questions?"

"I just wanted to know our history."

"Your father knows."

"Really?"

"Of course, he had to learn it all when he was a child."

"And he still remembers?"

"Did you come all this way to ask me silly questions?" she said and pushed past him, out into the sitting room. Da Shan followed in her wake and began another question, but she scowled as she wiped the table and he stopped. The phone rang and they both made a move for it, but his mother got to it first.

"Hello?" she shouted. "Yes. He is — who is it?" She listened then held out the receiver to Da Shan and said, "It's for you."

He took it from her hand. "Hello!" he said, and his mother began to patrol the room, looking for dust. "Who is this?" There was a moment's silence before Da Shan spoke again. "Fat Pan!? I know, it has."

As Old Zhu's wife looked for dust she listened to the half conversation.

"This afternoon? OK. Sure. At five fifty. Great!" she heard Da Shan say before he put the phone down.

"That was Fat Pan," he told her.

"I know." Under steel-gray eyebrows her eyes stared hard.

"Oh, he just asked me out for a meal. Just heard I was back. Got a banquet organized."

"What's he doing now?"

"He's still in the army. Runs one of their karaoke bars."

"He was a good friend to you," she said like a warning.

"I know," he said, "I know."

Da Shan decided to get a taxi to the Number One Patriotic Karaoke Night Club. As he walked through the factory gates he thought he heard a man shouting.

"Heh!" he heard again and half turned to see who it was.

"Yes!" the man shouted. "You!"

Da Shan stopped.

"Da Shan?" the man asked. He had gray bristly hair and his left eye was larger than the right, which drooped. "Good to meet you." The man smiled. "I'm Wang Fang."

His smile was too ready, there was something unpleasant about him — more than his eyes or familiarity or sweaty palms. "I don't think I know you," Da Shan said.

"No," the man said, "but I know you."

"Really?"

"Really."

Da Shan waited. "I am in a hurry."

The man smiled. "I know all about you."

"Congratulations."

"No — I know all about you and," the man thought of the right word to use, "all the *things* you've done."

"Good."

"You don't seem to understand."

Da Shan took a step forward. He couldn't tell if the man was trying to get money or what. "Understand what?"

The man held out his hands. "I don't want any trouble."

"Then what were you trying to say?"

"I'm not trying to say anything. I've said it."

"Good," Da Shan said, "then you can go back to wherever you've come from."

The man adjusted his jacket and ran a hand over his hair. "I just wanted to warn you," he said. "Don't get involved again. Not if you know what's good for you."

"Thanks for the advice."

"That's all I wanted to say."

"Now you've said it, you can go."

"Remember!" the man said, as Da Shan pushed past him; called out again. "Remember!"

It took fifteen minutes by taxi to get to the Number One Patriotic Karaoke Night Club. An awning of fairy lights was strung above the door, a neon sign flashed out the name of the place, and the English word "OK — OK — OK" flashed repeatedly in blue, red and green. At the door two statues of smiling girls in traditional robes of embroidered silk imperceptibly nodded their heads as Da Shan walked in. He stood in the lobby and looked around, and was wondering what to do next when a short, frail girl appeared from the dark. She had a white powdered face and blood-red lips that parted to reveal a smile of yellow teeth.

"Can I help you, sir?"

"I'm Da Shan. I'm meeting Commander Pan."

"This way." She nodded and showed him up the carpeted stairs to a private banqueting room at the end of a long corridor. She stopped by the door, gave him one quick look with half-moon eyes, and said, "Please, sir," and opened the door.

The room was small, wallpapered in red and gold; lined with blue sofas and a wide-screen TV. In the center of the room was a round table with a revolving center. There were six army officers reclining on the sofas. One of them was singing karaoke into a microphone. All stood up and came forward as Da Shan stepped inside. At the front was the smiling face of Fat Pan.

"Da Shan!" Fat Pan said, holding out a pudgy-fingered hand to shake. "Da Shan, my old friend, you look well."

"And you," Da Shan said. "How long has it been?"

"Too long, too long," Fat Pan said, still shaking Da Shan's hand. "Meet my friends: this is Driver Zhang, Officers Song, Wan, Deputy Guo and Vice-Commander Jiao."

Da Shan introduced himself, shaking each hand in turn.

"How do you know Commander Pan?" Vice-Commander Jiao asked, while Driver Zhang offered Da Shan a Marlboro cigarette.

"We were at university together, then I became a teacher and Fat Pan joined the army."

Fat Pan lit his cigarette then announced, "Teaching is the most honored profession under the sun."

"If only," Da Shan said. "I was more like a candle — illuminating others, but burning myself out."

They all laughed, ha-ha-ha!

"You were always the joker," Fat Pan said.

"No."

"Look, my friends," Fat Pan said, "so modest."

"Too much modesty is the same as pride."

Ha-ha-ha! They brayed. Ha-ha-ha!

Fat Pan coughed. "You see," he said. "What did I tell you?"

"Come, let's sit down," Fat Pan said, and gestured Da Shan to the seat opposite the door. "Please."

Da Shan took the chair offered, and the other men sat around the table according to rank. Fat Pan sat next to him and Vice-Commander Jiao sat directly across the table. Three girls came in with starters. They were dressed in matching red cheongsams, high heels, and high, ornate hairdos that threatened to topple every time they bent forward. Da Shan watched them balance their coiffures on their heads as they slid dishes of cold roast meat, pickled tofu skin, crispy vegetables and boiled peanuts onto the table. When they'd finished they slowly left the room, walking backward, and reentered moments later with more food. When the table was buried under expensive dishes, the waitresses took up their places against the wall, and waited.

"Where's the wine!" Fat Pan shouted across the table. "Wine!"

The three girls blushed and the shortest giggled, a glimpse of crooked white teeth as she quickly shuffled out backward, covering her mouth with her hand. Fat Pan shifted uneasily, and then laughed, ha-ha-ha!

They all laughed with him. Ha-ha-ha!

Da Shan joined in, Ha — Ha — Ha, then stopped, while

the others continued. They were all still laughing when the girl came back with a bottle of plum wine; kept up a tired chuckle as she struggled with the screw top, finally got it open and then poured the wine into a green patterned porcelain teapot. At last the girl handed it to Pan, who smiled at his guests. The chuckling stopped and the waitress shuffled backward to the wall.

"Good!" Fat Pan announced. "Now let's begin!"

When all the cups were full Pan announced the first toast. "To the return of a long-lost friend!" he declared, and they downed their wine.

Vice-Commander Jiao came in with the second: "To wealth and prosperity!"

Fat Pan came in again: "To the success of our joint venture!"

"Cheers!" the army officers shouted, and drained their cups. No sooner had they begun the cold dishes than they were whisked away and replaced with hot and aromatic meats and fried vegetables.

"Sweet and Sour Lotus Root," Fat Pan declared. They all tasted it and ummed in appreciation; then it was snatched away and another dish set down. "Red Cooked Pork!" Pan announced.

"Steamed Egg."

"Phoenix Wings."

He looked up at the waitress. "What's this?"

"Ants Climb the Bamboo," the waitress said softly.

"A-ha!" Pan declared, and put a spoonful in Da Shan's dish. "Ants Climb the Bamboo!"

"Umm," said Da Shan, "delicious!" and reached to try another dish only to find it had been replaced already.

"West Lake Fish," to the left.

"Beef in Syrup," on the right.

"Three-Colored Tripe," right in front of him. "Coral Red Cabbage," to replace the West Lake Fish.

When everyone was utterly confused what dish was what the three waitresses descended in a swirl of arms and smiles and cleared them all away. They came back carrying in a large copper hot pot between them, which they set down on the table.

"The house speciality," Fat Pan declared, gesturing with his chopsticks, "Three Dog Hot Pot!"

"Very good for the blood!" Vice-Commander Jiao said.

"It'll keep you warm in the winter!" Driver Zhang agreed.

"Just like a wife!" Da Shan said.

Ha-ha-ha! they chorused. Ha-ha-ha!

"So how's business going?" Da Shan asked.

"Good, very good," Fat Pan said. "In Shaoyang the People's Liberation Army owns both nightclubs, the top restaurant and most of the karaoke bars."

"Excellent."

"And we thought we'd move into real estate. Which is where you come in," Fat Pan said, resting a hand on Da Shan's knee. "I heard you've done very well down in Shenzhen. We need some capital, and I thought you might be able to help introduce us to some people you know."

"I hope I can help you."

"I'm sure you can," Fat Pan said, and helped himself to more of the hot pot, "because we're such good friends."

"We are," Da Shan said, and felt everyone scrutinizing him, except Fat Pan, who continued talking expansively.

"You know," Fat Pan announced, "who'd have thought it that my friend here was in prison less than ten years ago? Look at him now — so successful!"

All the eyes turned to him.

Da Shan smiled. "I was young and foolish," he said, and the officers all smiled with him.

"It's all over now. All over," Fat Pan assured. "No one cares about that now."

No, no one does, Da Shan thought, but everyone cared about it then. And he smiled back at them all and gave a little humorless laugh, Ha.

The rest of the meal slowed down as people dropped out and stopped eating. When everyone had finished they stood up.

"It's been good to see you again, Da Shan," Fat Pan said, showing him down the stairs.

"I've enjoyed every minute," Da Shan said.

"A successful evening," Vice-Commander Jiao said.

"Very," said Da Shan.

The posse of green-uniformed officers herded Da Shan toward the car as Fat Pan stuffed a packet of cigarettes into Da Shan's pocket.

"Oh, Pan," Da Shan said at the door. He put his arm on Fat Pan's shoulder and drew him close. "I just want you to know," he said earnestly, "I'm not here to get involved in anything. Really. That's all behind me."

"Of course, of course." Fat Pan nodded. "Don't worry about that now!"

"Good," Da Shan said. "I don't want any misunderstanding." He gave Pan a look. "You know, I had a strange conversation on the way here," he said, and stopped, let the silence speak for him. "I don't know if you have any friends in the police."

"I see." Fat Pan pursed his lips and nodded slowly. "There's a man I know. He's a good friend. I'll talk to him."

Da Shan shook Fat Pan's hand, kept shaking it for a long time as everyone beamed at one another. "To our future venture!" he called out, and climbed into the car.

The officers all lined up under the fairy lights and stood back to wave him off. "Go safely!" they called out as the taxi pulled away. "Go safely!"

The driver hawked and spat out of his open window, as Da Shan closed his eyes and groaned.

"Been for a massage?" the driver asked.

"No."

"No?"

"No."

The driver turned on the radio; a phone-in about the crime rate.

"This is crap," Da Shan said, and the driver turned it off, then looked over to Da Shan and grinned. "I heard they've got some lovely Miao girls in there!"

"Really."

"Too expensive for the likes of me."

"Listen," Da Shan said, "I just went for a meal."

"Oh," the driver said, and braked sharply as the lights turned red. "Friends with that lot, are you?" he asked.

"No," Da Shan said, "I owed one of them a favor."

"Oh, yeah?"

"Yeah."

The driver pulled out a pack of cigarettes from the dashboard and gave the pack to Da Shan, who took two, lit them both and gave one back to him.

"Yeah," Da Shan said again.

The driver inhaled and rolled up his window halfway as he drove slowly through the empty streets. Da Shan stubbed his cigarette out, rested his head against the window, the cool of the glass sobering him up. The air was too hot, the city dark, except for blurred neon streaks in the corner of his eyes.

"Are you all right?" the driver asked.

"No."

"You gonna be sick?"

"Yeah."

The driver pulled over, and Da Shan opened the door halfway, vomited into the road, retched and then vomited again. The driver rested his elbow on his open window, smoked and watched people across the street stumbling home on the broken pavements. The night air was neither cold nor warm. The driver blew his smoke up into the air toward the clouds, and Da Shan groaned.

"Feeling better?"

"Much," Da Shan lied as he closed the door.

"You sure?"

"Yeah."

The driver tossed his butt out into the night, and pulled off down the road. "Where did you say again?"

"Along the river," Da Shan said. "The Space Rocket Factory."

When he was dropped off at the gate Da Shan ignored the steps that led up to his parents' home and walked around and around the factory till the world steadied under his feet. Long after midnight he stumbled home, opening the door quietly in case his mother was sitting waiting, but she'd given up long ago and gone to bed.

Da Shan slumped down on the sofa, and rubbed his scalp. He smoked a cigarette and massaged his temples. After a cup of tepid tea he got up and opened the door to his father's study, and walked across to the desk. He hesitated for a moment, then pulled out the chair and sat down. He pulled a piece of paper out of the top left-hand drawer, which jammed as he pushed it closed, pulled it out again, and it slid in smoothly this time. Da Shan let out a long sigh, massaged his temples with his fingertips. Above the desk two scrolls of calligraphy hung down.

If you would know the true character of the pine, they said, You must wait until the snow melts.

Wild geese flew low over town, heading west. Da Shan heard them calling to one another as he took a brush from the stand and held his book open on the desk. There was a squeezy ink bottle and an ink stone. He steadied himself against the table as he squirted out a pool of ink and dipped the point of the brush in it. A cold apartment, a sheet of white paper and the black tip of the brush. The beginning of spring.

He lowered the brush tip to the paper, and began:

"My name is Da Shan. I was born in 1960, in the Year of the Rat. I am writing in the 48th Year of the Communist Dynasty."

He checked the amount of ink on his brush. Dipped it in a little bit more. The geese flew away from the neon lights and busy streets, over the empty hills and the Temple of Harmonious Virtue.

Da Shan carried on writing:

"For each man that Heaven produces, earth provides a grave. My ancestors reach back throughout eternity. I am of them and will follow where they have gone. The only one I know is my father. He was an official in the Communist Party. My mother was also an official. The line stops with me. I have one child, a daughter called Little Flower. Her mother and I are divorced. There will be no more sons to continue our line."

Da Shan wrote out the details his mother had told him about her family: checking the ink on his brush, writing the characters on the page with clean brush strokes.

"Stories are just like families," he wrote on another sheet. "They only have beginnings in books. Tracing your ancestors is like trying to count the stars, this is just a beginning."

Da Shan heard the geese honking as they flew across town. He stood close to the window and spotted them flapping away westward, calling out to the pale stars.

*I*n the old town a mother and son watched the wild geese fly by, low over the rail tracks where the grass was tall and dry. Little Dragon shivered and Liu Bei looked up into the night sky, pointed to where the black clouds were racing to hide the moon.

"Look!" she said.

"What?"

Liu Bei's outstretched arm and finger led to where the evening star was twinkling above the mountain ridge. "Can you see that star?"

"Yes!" Little Dragon clapped.

"It's a planet."

Little Dragon sat in silent and ignorant awe of the white sparkle on the horizon, and wondered what a planet was. Liu Bei rocked him on her knee, bounced him so he giggled. "Who's a big strong boy?" she said.

"I am!" he snapped.

"Who is?"

"I am!"

"Who is I?"

"Me!"

She looked around, a sweep that included everything except him. "Who said that?" she called.

"ME!" Little Dragon shouted and stamped his foot, then fell back laughing. "ME-ME-ME!"

They sat and looked out of the window at the crescent moon. Her fingers traced familiar paths through his silk-soft black hair; scratched his scalp, rubbed his hair smooth again. The west wind trawled up inky black clouds that blotted out moon and stars till Liu Bei and Little Dragon were looking up into a black night sky with no way of knowing which way was east or west. At last Little Dragon spoke in a hushed voice. "The moon's gone, Mother."

Liu Bei leaned down and whispered behind his ear, "That's because she's shy."

"Why?"

"Because you're staring at her."

"If I don't look will she come out?"

"Maybe."

Little Dragon put a hand over his eyes, and peeped between the crack. "She's not there!" he protested.

"You have to give her longer than that."

He hid his eyes and peeped again.

"I can see you!" his mother said.

His fingers closed like scissors.

"I can still see you!"

"I'm not looking!"

"Yes, you are!" She tickled his ribs. "You're looking!"

They spent the evening sitting up, watching a dance show on the TV. Pop stars came on to sing Hong Kong and Taiwan pop songs, and Liu Bei sang quietly along. Little Dragon listened and laughed, and his mother rubbed her hand through his hair and kept singing softly. She kept singing until all the celebrities came on together at the end, and the orchestra began the first bars of the national anthem.

"Come on, young man," Liu Bei said, picking him up, "time for bed."

"Can't I stay up?"

"But then you'll be so tired!"

"I want to stay up!" Little Dragon pouted and his lower lip trembled.

"Who's a strong young man?" she asked, her fingers moving in to tickle. He shoved her hand away, as his eyes filled with tiny teardrops.

"How about I take you kite flying tomorrow?"

"I don't want to go kite flying. I want to go to Grandma's house. I hate stupid kites!"

"Oh dear," she said taking him to his bed. He punched her, fingers curled into a miniature fist. "Heh! Who are you hitting?"

"You!"

"Why?"

He turned away and didn't answer.

"Heh?"

The back of his head was rigid and silent.

"Heh?!"

He stayed silent.

"Oh dear!" Liu Bei said, tidying his hair. His little face was twisted in a scowl. "Come on, then, you can sleep with me." She tickled him softly behind his ear. "How's that?"

He wrapped both arms around her neck and buried his head into her neck. She carried him into the bedroom and laid him on the bed, tugged off his shoes and socks.

"So — who wants to go to the toilet first?" She managed to smile.

"Me!" he said, jumping down and pattering off on bare feet.

Liu Bei sat on the bed and turned to look in the cracked mirror. She stared at the broken reflection of her face as the wind began to build outside. If she hadn't had him, her reflection wouldn't be looking so worn and weary. She wouldn't be single either, she thought. Outside a gust blustered in the trees and made them sing. She suddenly wondered if he could hear it too, wherever he was.

Little Dragon came running back in, and jumped up onto the bed. He yanked the quilt back and flung it down over himself, peeping out.

"Have you cleaned your teeth?" she snapped.

He nodded solemnly and Liu Bei took her turn in the bathroom. When she came back she stood in the doorway for a moment, turned the light off, then undressed. There was a whisper of clothes dropping to the floor; she felt the cool touch of air as she stepped toward the bed. She dug a T-shirt from under the pillow, pulled it on, and climbed in next to her son. He was small and warm, curled up like a fetus. He shifted when he felt her near and buried his face into her side; uncomfortable but comforting.

The bed slowly warmed up, and Liu Bei lay with her eyes open, stroking her son's soft hair and listening to the wind in the trees.

Little Dragon's voice came from under the sheets. "Mother?"

She absentmindedly traced a finger behind his ear. "Hmmm."

"What does Daddy look like?"

"He's tall and strong," she said.

"Does he look like me?"

She tried to smile. "Oh yes. And he likes kite flying and reading books."

There was silence as she stroked his head. Then Little Dragon spoke again. "I thought he liked basketball and karaoke."

"Oh, he likes that too." She could hear the impatience in her voice and wished she couldn't.

"Mother," Little Dragon began again, "when is Daddy coming home?"

"I don't know. Go to sleep."

He shuffled closer and she squeezed him. "Go to sleep," she said, softly this time, voice blending into the measure of a lullaby as she repeated, "Go to sleep," and his breathing slipped into the soothing and predictable rhythm of dreams.

As Little Dragon dreamed of soldiers, Liu Bei listened to the rain outside just beginning to fall and remembered how she and Da Shan had sworn to each other that whatever happened they'd wait for the other. It had been raining that night as well. She tried to work out how long ago that had been now and stretched her toes under the quilt. She wondered where he was, what he was doing, and whether he was thinking of her at that moment.

Like she was thinking of him.

*T*he spring rains continued from gray dawn to gray dusk, through black night and back again to dull wet day. The streets and paddy fields were flooded with acres of water pockmarked by unforgiving rain.

Behind Number 7 block of apartments Old Zhu dug over the heavy soil of his allotment feeling his feet sink further into the yellow mud of his Motherland, as if the soil were claiming him already. He dug harder, but the effort exhausted him, so the harder he worked the less he got done. At last he leaned on his spade handle and wiped his white hair, felt his pulse flutter flirtatiously and curiously thought of the day of liberation, October 1, 1949, when Chairman Mao Zedong had stood at Tiananmen Gate and announced the founding of the People's Republic of China. Mao had waved to the millions and declared that the Chinese people had stood up; then spent the next twenty-five years kicking them to the floor again. Old Zhu looked at his vegetable plot and didn't know why he bothered, nor why he should have remembered Mao's speech now of all times, when it was raining.

As Old Zhu thought of Mao, Da Shan caught a taxi to the center of town. The driver forced his way through the confused traffic, his hand pressed down onto the horn the whole way. At the crossroads next to the Main Post Office the traffic had welded itself into an irrevocably solid mass. Policemen in dark sunglasses gathered like vultures and added more tangles to the chaos by blowing whistles and issuing contradictory orders. The taxi driver slammed to a stop, and rammed his hand down on the horn. Beep! Beep! Beeeeeep! He began punching his steering wheel — Beep! Beep! Beeeeeeeeeeeeep!!!

The policeman blew a whistle and motioned the driver to go forward, but he couldn't. Beeeeep! Beeeeeeeep! The driver gesticulated and the policeman blew his whistle again, this time at the jostling crowd, which took no notice at all.

"Forget it," Da Shan said. "I'll get out here."

The crush on the pavement swallowed Da Shan up, squeezed him tight like a long-forgotten friend. He cursed the confused jam of peasants and salesmen and shoppers as they hugged him closer, and finally managed to push himself across the pavement. He edged a short way up the street, then turned down a side alley that ran between two mirror-fronted shopping arcades.

The alley took him back into the old town of crooked alleys and cluttered houses, of courtyards walled off from the main road and barricaded with old wooden gates. He found the shop he was looking for through a round moon gate. Inside was a paved courtyard with buildings on three of the four sides. A family was moving out; everything they owned was piled up in the middle of the courtyard: there was an old writing desk, a box of clothes and shoes, a red plastic bucket with the family's wok and chop.

"I'm looking for the Meng Family Number One Antiques Shop," Da Shan said.

A woman pointed across the courtyard.

D a Shan stooped under the door lintel, then he straightened himself up and looked around. The room was cluttered with objects that dated back to the Old China, before liberation in 1949. Rare treasures and commonplace things that had managed to survive the years of starvation, poverty and the destruction of the Red Guards. In the middle of the dusty paraphernalia was a little boy, sitting watching TV and eating chocolate. He saw Da Shan and jumped down and ran out of the door shouting "Grandpa! Grandpa! Grandpa!"

An old man with a young face appeared and found Da Shan studying a fine porcelain cup. On it there was an exquisitely painted young girl, sitting under a cherry tree of pink spring blossom.

"It's from the Ming Dynasty," the old man said, taking it from Da Shan's hand and slowly turning it upside-down. There was the potter's stamp in red on the bottom, but it wasn't clear. "Made in the time of Emperor Wang Li," the old man said.

There was a tiny porcelain teapot to match. "It contains only three cupfuls," the old man told him, "for luck. Made from Red Sands Clay. Came from the West Lake. Highly valued. It's been in my family for generations."

There were lines of characters that went down the side of the pot:

> If there were no cherry blossoms in the world
> Then I could find peace.

A Song Dynasty poem, Da Shan thought.

"Where did you get all this stuff from?" he asked.

The old man smiled. "My father gave it to the government after liberation. He gave everything to the government. Then twenty years ago I found the receipts inside the mattress and claimed it back. Some of it had been lost, but this is what remained."

"You were lucky."

"I know."

"My father had an ancient coin collection he'd had since childhood."

"Did he get it back?"

"Did he hell," Da Shan said.

The television churned out excited chatter as Da Shan examined the cup and pot. "They're beautiful," he said at last.

"They're from the Ming Dynasty."

"How much?"

"Seven hundred yuan."

"For the pair?"

The old man laughed. "Each."

Da Shan put them back and moved on. The TV kept talking to itself as he paced through the room. He turned his concentration on to objects from the past and the TV's noise turned to silence. Carved wooden panels with gold paint still sheltering in the deep grooves, porcelain pots and vases, a copper kettle, a beautiful copy of *The Classic of Filial Piety* and the first volume of Ban Zhao's *Admonitions for Women*.

Da Shan picked up the *Admonitions*; the brown paper was still soft and clear. He lifted the book and sniffed the open pages: there was a faint air of rose perfume that clung on in spite of the years.

Each life has its limit

but sorrow has none.

Da Shan put the book down. "I want the cup and the teapot," he told the man.

"Good."

"How much did you say again?"

"Seven hundred each. That makes one thousand four hundred yuan."

"I think you said it was cheaper than that."

"How much cheaper?"

"Much cheaper."

"Because we are friends — one thousand for the pair."

"Six hundred."

"My friend, these are from the Ming Dynasty."

"Five hundred."

"Nine hundred."

"Too much."

"Eight hundred and fifty — I can't sell for any less. I have my grandson to care for."

"Where are his parents?"

"They work in Shanghai."

"Then you must be rich."

There was a moment of silence as they looked at each other, both of them smiling.

"Seven hundred."

"Eight hundred and fifty. Really, that's my very lowest."

"Eight hundred."

"OK."

The old man wrapped the cup and teapot in a sheet of *China Daily,* and put them in a white plastic bag, cultivated an air of sadness as he counted the money. "Look after them well," he said slowly. "They've been in my family for generations."

"Then you shouldn't have sold them."

The old man smiled. "If Heaven lets a plum fall, then open your mouth."

Da Shan smiled back. "If you eat too many plums you'll get the shits."

D a Shan stopped at all the antique shops he could find hidden in the winding streets of the old town. At one shop, owned by a young boy with a squint, he bought an old scroll of *The Venerable Scholar* that was torn and ripped. At another shop, run by an age-pickled woman, Da Shan found a dragon ink stone from the late Qing Dynasty. The ancient woman wobbled about on bound feet the length of his forefinger, and when she got close she stank of piss.

"My husband was a businessman," she said when she took his money. "That's how I got these things."

Da Shan took the bag and moved away from her.

"I was the most beautiful courtesan in Shaoyang. You wouldn't believe it to look at me now, would you!"

"No."

"It's true, though. He bought me for ten thousand yuan, but we were never happy." She sniffed. "I only gave him two daughters. He always complained: that's a woman's gratitude!"

"Where's he now?"

"Oh — he's been dead for years. They shot him. He was a capitalist, you see. Into all kinds of perversions." The memory of his perversions made her laugh out loud, but she didn't elaborate. "But we're all capitalists now," she said, "aren't we?"

"Yes," Da Shan said, and turned to walk back into the street.

As he left she called out to him, "Does sir like to play in the flower garden himself?"

Da Shan looked around and saw her coming toward him with a grotesque smile. "If you want to play the butterfly, then I have some things to make the flowers taste sweeter," she cackled. In one hand she held some silken ribbons, and a book in the other.

"What are those?"

She held up the ribbons. "Shoes for bound feet! Only three inches long!"

"And that?" He held out his hand and she put a set of bound books into it: *The Most Noble Dong Xuan's Thirty Heaven and Earth Postures.*

"I used to use this with all my customers!" she whispered.

Da Shan turned the title page; there was a picture on silk, with accompanying text:

Leaping White Tiger: the Master prepares to introduce his new bride to the pleasures of Clouds and Rain. He turned to the next page.

Hovering Butterflies: the Jade Stem awaits the Flower's Heart.

The Mule in Springtime: the Turtle Head dives into the Golden Gully.

The hag took the book from him and turned to a familiar page.

"This is the best," she said.

Da Shan studied the detail of the painting: it showed two lovers in the bamboo grove entwined in the agony of love.

Offering to the Male Warrior, read the caption. *Recommended methods: Before penetration move the Yang Peak slowly and steadily as if refining one of the Five Elements. After penetration: Float and sink in the same movement, like a duck on the ripples of a lake.*

"Are you married?" the smell asked.

"I am."

"You can use it with your wife!"

Da Shan turned to the next page, looked, and then shut the book. "No," he said, "we're divorced."

"Divorced, huh?" The smell moved closer. Her breath washed over him; it had a different, more unpleasant odor. Da Shan looked down into her gap-toothed mouth, at the gums that had receded so far her few remaining teeth were like the irregular stumps of fingers, clawing for food. "A wife is never as sexy as a mistress," she giggled close to his face, "and a mistress isn't as exciting as an affair." He stepped back, but she kept coming forward. "And the troubles of an affair are easy to handle compared with love for an unattainable beauty."

"I don't know how you know," he said, pushing past her back into the street.

"I'll give it to you for six hundred!" she called out, but he kept on walking. When he was almost out of earshot she shouted, "And I know where the sweetest flowers grow!" but he kept on walking around the bend, where her words could not go.

When Da Shan got home his mother was waiting, with all the food for dinner chopped and ready. "Where've you been?" she demanded, wanting to be angry but just feeling relieved he'd returned.

"Shopping," he said.

She smiled and ran a hand through her hair, training it back. "Now you're home," she said deliberately, "I'll start cooking dinner."

He ignored her and said simply, "I found these," took out the pot and the cup, the scroll of *The Venerable Scholar* and the dragon ink stone.

His mother picked them up one by one. "Wah — we used to have these when I was a child," she said. "So many things like this."

Da Shan watched his mother feel their weight. "I don't know where they all got to." She slowly turned them over in her hand, the cup, pot, and the heavy ink stone with its carved dragon. "They were smashed or stolen during the Cultural Revolution. We smashed and burned so many things — and then when the Red Guards came to take your father they destroyed everything else."

"I remember," he said.

"You can't," she told him. "You weren't very old."

"I do remember," Da Shan stated flatly. He was young, but how could he forget? The Red Guards had come day after day to search and destroy, and they had taken his father away, leaving a father-sized hole in the middle of their family. And then one morning in the early hours they'd taken his mother away too. He'd run away to a neighbor's house. The next day he'd come back to his house only to find the door locked and a red seal on the door and a banner with characters he didn't understand. He'd stood on tiptoes to peer in through the window, saw smashed furniture and scattered clothes and wandered the streets crying.

In the weeks and years that followed, Party workers had told him, Chairman Mao is your father. Da Shan had tried ever so hard to love The Great Helmsman with all his heart, but he'd secretly loved his mother and father, even though they were enemies of the state. In that long five years with no news and no letters Da Shan had learned that a mother-shaped hole and a father-shaped hole were almost big enough to swallow the world.

"You were too young," his mother repeated, and put the cup down. "Anyway, how much did you pay for these?"

"Over a thousand," he said.

"Wah," she declared as she stalked off. "So much for old rubbish!"

Da Shan watched her walk into the kitchen: despair, desolation, hope, love, loss and now an excess of riches — so much in thirty-six years. He drew up a chair and sat down, pulled up his trousers and idly picked up the cup. It was cool and light and fragile.

There were two characters in neat black brush strokes on one side and the picture of the girl on the other. He turned it in his fingers, stared at the girl. She was sitting next to a rock, a bamboo fence behind her. There were blooms of red azaleas to either side, all sheltered under spring blossoms. The girl's hair was plaited, the curl tied up on top of her head. She wore a pale blue coat — hugging herself against the cold, he thought; then decided no — not at springtime — she must be hugging herself against loneliness.

Da Shan reached over and slid the scroll of *The Venerable Scholar* across the table toward himself. The paper was stiff as he unraveled it, torn in places. The painting showed a man sitting at a desk, copying a text, a pile of books on his right and a candle on his left. But he was looking up and away from the desk and the books, reaching for inspiration in the top left corner of the scroll.

Da Shan laid the scroll out next to the cup. Now the scholar was thinking of the girl, and she was longing for him. If they were both in a story then there would be a happy ending, Da Shan thought, but only in stories.

Men dream of the Past, the ancients had written, because only Heaven understands the future.

That afternoon Old Zhu came back from his allotment on a trail of muddy footprints, which stopped at the door, where he took his shoes off and put on slippers. He found his wife steaming grass fish with chili and shallots, and his son standing on the balcony, talking into his cell phone. It'd been a good day — he'd dug over the whole plot and planted most of his seeds. He wanted to tell someone about his day, but there was no one to listen, so he walked around the room in little circles, and stopped at the table. "What's this?" he called out to no one in particular.

"He's been out wasting money," his wife shouted through the kitchen door.

"Why does he want all these dirty old things?" Old Zhu called out.

"He's stupid."

"We should throw them out," Old Zhu shouted. "They've probably got diseases."

"I'm not touching them."

"Well, we can't leave them on the table."

"You ask him what he wants to do with them."

"I will," Old Zhu said, but he walked into his bedroom and

sat down on the bed and smoked a cigarette instead. He breathed in and out, as he had always done, as if the world would never end; tapped the ash onto the floor and then stubbed out his cigarette. His son was still on the balcony talking into his phone. Old Zhu watched him and tried to think of something he could say to his son, but couldn't, so he went into the kitchen to tell his wife about the day's gardening.

"I've planted the shallots," he said. "And the eggplant."

"Umm," his wife said, lifting the lid on the fish and checking it.

"Looks like it could be a good year."

"You always say that," she said, closing the lid. "It never is."

They sat and ate the fish. Old Zhu chewed the fish bones out of his mouth and let them drop onto the table, his wife sucked the bones free of meat, Da Shan ate the fish, bones and all. Old Zhu spat, and slurped his soup, scraped his bowl free of rice, then sat back. No one looked up from their bowls of food. Old Zhu stood up and farted and walked back into the bedroom for a smoke.

When he'd left the room Da Shan picked at the last piece of fish and went to put it on his mother's plate.

"No, you have it," she said, and pushed away his hand. "I'm old. I don't need it."

Da Shan ate it silently. He helped his mother clear away the pots and began washing them up.

"Don't do that," she protested.

"I'm not a guest," he said, "and besides — you're old."

She let him have his way, but took each plate from his hand with care and dried them and put them back onto the shelves. She dried faster than he could wash, always waiting for the next dish. When he'd finished she brought the teapot and cup and ink stone in carefully.

"These need a wash," she said.

"Let me do it."

"No," she told him. "You're too clumsy."

Da Shan watched her fingers curl around the porcelain surface, unwrapping the color from the layers of dirt and age that had settled on them. She cleaned each one with infinite care, and set them sparkling wet next to the washing-up bowl. They glittered with water, a string of rough-cut gems.

"There were many bad things in Old China," she said, "but we had such pretty things too." Da Shan and his mother stood and watched the teapot and cup and ink stone for a moment. She remembered something and went off into her bedroom, rummaged around in the wardrobe, and came back holding a small mirror, speckled as an egg and rimmed with tarnished silver.

"The only thing I have left is this — do you think it's worth much?"

Da Shan laughed. "No."

She held the mirror, unsure what to do; stung by his laughter, a still-born smile fading from her old face. The mirror was too loaded with memory to hold for long, too precious to put down.

"But let me have a look," he said. "I could be wrong."

She put it down next to the porcelain cup, teapot, ink stone and scroll — now a set of five objects.

"It was my mother's," she said as Da Shan examined the silver edging, "and I think it was her mother's before that. Your father tried to make me destroy it, but I wanted to keep this. I always have. Don't ask me how I stopped it from getting destroyed."

He looked up into her face. "I'll look after it," he said. "Don't worry."

Da Shan lit his father's cigarette, and they sat back together, exhaling long funnels of smoke into the air.

"How are the vegetables?" Da Shan asked.

"Good," Old Zhu said, sitting forward and scratching his white hair. "The soil is light this year."

Da Shan nodded. "Good."

Old Zhu tapped the ash of his cigarette. "It's reassuring to have you back, son."

Da Shan began to say how it was good to be back, but Old Zhu just carried on. "When will your wife come back?"

Da Shan stopped. "She won't," he said. "We're divorced."

"It's not good to split a husband and wife up, that only brings trouble."

Da Shan looked at his father. "Yes, you're right," he said.

"It'd be good to have some grandchildren around the house."

They sat and smoked, tapping their way down to the butts.

"Father, actually there's something I wanted to ask you."

"Yes?"

Da Shan hesitated. "I'm curious about our family."

"Oh, that stuff." Old Zhu laughed. "I'm sure you're not very interested in all that."

"Yes. I am."

"It's all very boring," Old Zhu said. "I had to learn all the names of the ancestors — I got beaten if I forgot the name of a father or son, or if I forgot the rank of the ones who passed the civil service exams." He laughed at the memory. "It's very stupid information — never helped anyone."

"Don't you think it's important to know where you came from?"

Old Zhu rubbed his nose and suppressed an old smile. "It's important to not know."

After his parents had gone into their bedroom to sleep, Da Shan sat watching TV and smoking. His book lay in front of him, the ink making the paper crinkle, the creases flattening themselves as the ink dried. He knew a few things that relatives had told him. He had a list of names, all beginning with the surname Zhu, but he had almost no idea of events. Was it his great-grandfather or great-great-grandfather who'd come south from the famine? Which one had joined the Taiping Rebellion, his eldest great-uncle or the next eldest?

In front of Da Shan was his mother's old mirror. He turned it over in his hand and saw his own reflection covered with liver spots of rust. How many lives had the mirror swallowed? — smiles, expressions, moments of hope, all disappearing from the world. Smashed or burned or stolen; Red Guards, foreign invaders, the government.

His mind wandered as he put his feet up and lit another cigarette. It meandered awhile, took him back to 1985 — was it, or 1984? — anyway, it was when he first met her. She had been young and hopeful, had an energy and zeal for tomorrow that had made her inspirational. It was natural that they'd fallen in love; almost natural that they'd been driven apart again. Unfulfilled love is infinite, the poets had said, and it was the poets' job to know such things. Da Shan stubbed his cigarette out. There was no point sitting at home and thinking; tomorrow he would go and see her.

The next day Da Shan left after breakfast and found the house he was looking for in the center of the old town. It stood halfway up a hill that was tunneled through with bomb shelters the people had used to shelter in from Japanese bombs in 1943. The slopes had once been emerald with bamboo groves but were now littered with toilet paper, addicts' used syringes and neat piles of shit.

Da Shan stood on the top step and knocked. The door wobbled under the impact, but the wood was too old to make much sound. He tried again.

"Yes?" came a woman's voice.

He knocked again.

"I'm coming — I can't run, you know!"

He stepped down back to the path and waited as bolts were slid back.

He didn't expect to see her but was still disappointed when she didn't appear. Instead he was met by a skinny old woman with skin the color of tobacco and gummy eyes shriveled like peas.

"I'm looking for Liu Bei — or her mother. They used to live here," he said.

The old woman shouted over her shoulder, "There's someone here to see you!"

Da Shan clenched himself, held his breath; but the figure that stepped out of the shadows wasn't Liu Bei but her mother; not much changed except her hair had gone gray and the fan of wrinkles at the corners of her eyes, which had opened a little wider.

"Hello," he said.

"Is that you, Da Shan?"

"Yes."

She didn't answer but put one hand on the door frame and rested the other on her chest.

"I was back in town and I thought . . ."

The two women looked down at him standing at the bottom of their steps. They waited for him to finish his sentence, but he didn't. They both wondered what it was that he thought.

"I thought I would come and say hello," Da Shan managed at last.

A gust of clear wind rattled the bamboo poles at the side of the house, carried on over town, till they could no longer hear its rustle. Liu Bei's mother's eye traced it as it passed on, then she turned back to the man on her doorstep.

"Is Liu Bei around?"

"No," Liu Bei's mother said. "She's not."

"They let her out, didn't they?"

"Yes, they let her out."

"Good," Da Shan said, stepping back. "Is she OK?"

"Yes. She lost her job, of course. Her work unit chucked her out. I think she went to Changsha."

"She moved away from Shaoyang?"

"Of course she did. She couldn't stay here. Not after what you two did. She's got a job there now."

"Excellent," he said, even though he knew it was the wrong word to use. "Does she need money? Do you need money?"

"Of course we do!" the tobacco-faced old woman put in suddenly. "Of course we do!"

"Thank you, Da Shan," Liu Bei's mother said.

"Maybe you can pass some on to Liu Bei," Da Shan told her as he pulled out some money from his pocket and counted it — not note by note — but by the thickness of the wad, which he put into her hand. "And tell her I came to see her."

"I will."

"Thank you," he said ánd turned to go, then hesitated. "I'm staying with my parents — at the factory."

"I know," Liu Bei's mother said. "I heard you were back."

Da Shan smiled briefly, then set off back down the hill. The two women watched him go, and Liu Bei's mother put the money inside her top without counting it.

The old woman squinted her beady eyes as she turned around to go back inside. "How much did he give?"

Liu Bei's mother shut the door and bolted it. "I don't know."

"Well — count it!" Aunty Tang said.

"It's not for us," Liu Bei's mother said. "And it's not for Liu Bei. I'd burn it if I could, but when you're poor you can't afford ideals. I'll keep it for Little Dragon. He'll need it."

Aunty Tang grumbled. "Where's Liu Bei, anyway?"

"She's working."

Aunty Tang gave a low humorless cackle, like grinding

stone. Liu Bei's mother ignored it. "I don't want Liu Bei to find out he's come here," she said sternly.

"Won't she find out anyway?"

"Maybe," Liu Bei's mother said, "but not from me, and not from you."

Young people who left to go south never returned to Shaoyang, not even to die, so the news that Da Shan had come back, and more important, that he'd come back rich, kept people gossiping for weeks. People broke off gossiping to turn and have a look when he passed by, and when he was nowhere to be seen they talked about him anyway. The old women circulated rumors between themselves. One swore that Old Zhu's son had come home to save the factory; another that he had come to retire here.

"How can he retire!" one demanded. "He can't be forty yet!"

"Well," the woman said in her defense, then stopped.

One of the factory's nurses, a woman whose husband had gone to Guangdong and never come back, went to see Da Shan one evening to see if he'd heard of her husband.

"What was his name?" Da Shan asked.

"Li DongPing," the woman said earnestly.

Da Shan squeezed his eyebrows together in concentration

and then shook his head. "No, I'm sorry," he said. "If I met some-one from Shaoyang I know I would remember."

The woman pursed her lips and nodded. She wasn't so bothered about getting her old husband back if she could get a new one. The next morning she put on a red lipstick smile and a short summer dress that showed off her legs and waited around, not so much in the hope of seeing Da Shan as being seen. She didn't meet him that day, nor the next, and by the third day she began to feel like she'd been abandoned all over again. On the fourth she sauntered past his parents' apartment and saw Da Shan sitting on the steps in slippers and shorts.

She stared at him, her red lips kept tightly shut in concen-tration. He looked straight through her, turned back to his news-paper. She stopped a little way off and turned around to watch him. His eyes kept flicking down to the newspaper, then up at the faces of people walking past. She watched him flick through the paper to the last page, fold it up, stretch out his legs and pull out his pack of cigarettes from his pocket. The nurse decided to try again. She walked up until her shadow lay at his feet. "Hello." She smiled. "Have you eaten?"

"Yes."

She waited for more. "I was going to cook some extra today," she began. "My son isn't back from the school till late."

"I didn't know you had a son," Da Shan said. She blushed. "Yes."

"Thank you." Da Shan smiled. "But unfortunately I've got to meet a friend."

"Oh," she said, "of course."

Da Shan watched her pass away, her legs and the sway of her dress as her buttocks moved. He smoked his cigarette slowly — eyes following the blue smoke as it curled up into the sunlight and then disappeared. He'd always expected to find Liu Bei when he came back; it didn't seem right that she should have left.

Madam Fan's husband was playing mah-jongg with a group of friends when he brought up the matter of Da Shan's return. "Old Zhu's son has come back," he announced with feigned disinterest.

"And he's been throwing money around since!" said one of the neighbors. "Everyone's talking about him. Especially the matchmakers!"

"If there was enough money in it you could persuade a matchmaker that even a pig was attractive," Madam Fan's husband said. "From the way people talk you'd think that even his farts smell good!"

"Money is money," Madam Fan shouted from the bedroom. "And you don't make any." There was a pause as Madam Fan's husband raised his eyebrows to his mah-jongg partners and they sniggered. "All you do is lose it!" Madam Fan shouted through the doorway, after a long pause.

"It's true," the other players agreed. "Which is very good for us."

Madam Fan's husband shook a cigarette out of the box, picked it up and lit it, all one-handed. "I tell you why I don't win," he whispered loudly. "I've got no yang energy left."

"You're not telling us that you're frying beans in a cold pan!" One of his friends laughed.

"I am!" Madam Fan's husband grinned as he puffed the cigarette to life, wreathed his face in fumes that curled and licked the air. "The heat's off when you're around, but turn the lights off and my wife's as excited as hot oil!"

Peach stood up and left the room.

The mah-jongg players watched her go.

"Like mother like daughter, heh!" One of them sniggered.

Madam Fan's husband leaned forward. "I don't know how I deserved both of them in one life!"

"She's pretty enough!"

"What can you do with a flower that refuses to go to seed?" he asked.

"She could marry my son."

"She's not a dog." Madam Fan's husband laughed, and the others laughed too. "That son of yours couldn't even mount a bicycle!"

Peach closed the door of her parents' bedroom, and stilled the voices. The house seemed to be full of voices; ever since Party Secretary Li had killed himself. Her parents had hardly stopped arguing. Madam Fan sat on the bed with a blanket over her legs. She was knitting a pair of baby's trousers.

"Are you all right, Mother?" Peach asked.

Madam Fan looked up and ignored the question. "When you get married and have a child, then you'll need these," she said, holding up what she'd knitted so far. "I'll embroider a dragon and a phoenix on them — for a boy or a girl!"

Peach sat close next to her mother. "Are you all right, Mother?"

Madam Fan smiled a tight smile as she patted Peach's knee, but inside she was reliving the latest row with her husband. With each stitch she felt every blow, on the head and arm and back. And the kick in her stomach. White bruises on her white skin; invisible and unforgivable. She was thinking so much she missed a stitch. Peach didn't notice and lay back on the bed. Madam Fan missed another stitch, and swore.

"I wish I'd learned to do this as a child," she said.

"Why didn't you?"

"Nobody was interested in Old China. We had political studies. We were getting rid of all that."

Peach nodded. She'd learned all about Old China when she'd been a student. In Old China women had their feet bound, the country was under attack from all kinds of foreign countries, there were drugs and prostitution, and the life of the people was very bad. But there were drugs and prostitution now, Peach thought.

"Was it very different then?" Peach asked.

"When I was your age," Madam Fan said, "we'd been liberated. The Communist Party officials were honest and good men. They worked hard."

"But didn't they do some bad things?"

Madam Fan looked up and returned her daughter's stare. "Like what?"

"Like shooting Father's father?"

Madam Fan looked back down at her stitching. It was good her husband's father had been shot. Madam Fan would have shot him herself if she'd known what his son would do to her. "In those days the officials were hard but honest. They shot people because they were the people's enemies. But now they just shoot anyone." Madam Fan stitched. Peach looked out of the window to where the factory chimney no longer smoked. "It's all the fault of Deng Xiao Ping. Mao should have shot him first of all."

Peach lay back again. The room next door was full of the rattle of mah-jongg tiles and the dull banter of her father and his friends. Their chatter made her mother seem quieter, and more real. She'd never talked to Peach like this before. Peach wanted to ask her about the past. Things she didn't understand, that she'd never dared ask before, because questions had always seemed such dangerous things.

"Is life better now?" Peach began.

There was a long silence filled by the creak of the bed and the rattle of tiles in the other room. "No, it's not," Madam Fan said at last. "Things now are much, much worse than they've ever been."

"Why?"

Madam Fan counted out the stitches. "Stop asking questions. Don't you have anything to do?"

Peach picked at her fingernails, easing out the dirt, then

looked up at her mother. Madam Fan was still concentrating on her knitting.

"When you were my age you were married, weren't you?" Peach said.

Madam Fan screwed her lips together and thought. "How old are you now?" she said.

"Nineteen."

Madam Fan hummed a snatch of opera.

"Well?" Peach said.

"Well what?"

"Were you married at my age?"

"No," Madam Fan said.

"I thought you married Father when you were sixteen."

Madam Fan stopped humming and bit her lip. "Your father never married me," she said with stone-hard coldness. Her eyes began to fill with the tears she had protected and nourished all these years. She let one curl down her cheek; a pearl in the light that shone for an instant and then slipped out of sight.

Peach watched that teardrop disappear, and felt it land on her hand.

"Your father never married me," Madam Fan repeated slowly, making sure she said it calmly, knowing there was no way back. "Your father never married me — I sold myself to him for his monthly rice ration." There was a long gaping pause that stretched on. "I sold myself to him. My father was landlord class, we had no food, we were starving. Everyone tried to make me leave him afterward. Our backgrounds were too different. But I wouldn't."

Peach looked away; Madam Fan patiently stitched and let one more tear roll down her cheek. It landed on the same spot as the first. Right on Peach's heart. Madam Fan stitched, and kept on stitching. She only looked up when Peach had dashed out of the house and slammed the door. And then she hummed her line of opera.

The hills inhaled the last of the cold sunlight and night fell, as cold and sharp as icicles. The moon rose silently through the black branches as Peach ran down toward the factory gateway. She ran and sobbed as she went. Tears for her mother and her father, and most of all for herself.

Heaven and earth are not kind, she thought,
For them we are all disposable.

The moon looked down with soundless contempt as Peach cried. The past was behind her, waiting to chain her down as it had chained her parents. Above her head the stars glittered like her dreams of the future — beautiful, bright and impossibly distant.

Peach wandered out of the factory gate, under the words *We Wel Come Your In Vest Ment*, and off into the darkness of her thoughts. Past the pool tables where young men were laughing and through the empty stalls where the peasants had left piles of rotting cabbage leaves and plucked chicken feathers on the road. A street-sweeper was brushing the garbage together into a pile. There were a few shops open and their owners sat amid their sacks of rice and boxes of milk powder and watched TV. Peach walked and walked through her thoughts, down past the film rental shop and down to the river, which flowed as dark and silent as death.

In the video shop Sun An was shoveling the last of his dinner into his mouth when he saw Peach lean over the lip of the bank. He tipped up the bottom of the bowl and cleaned away the last flecks of rice.

"You'll get a zit for every piece of rice you leave," his grandmother had warned him when he was a boy. Since then he'd always eaten all his rice, but it didn't seem to help. He was twenty-three and still felt pimply. Sun An watched Peach for a while, her willowy waist and tenuous figure. He watched and imagined, till he was frightened she'd feel him watching her, and he cleared his throat. "Heh, Peach," he shouted. "Have you eaten?"

Her pale moon face turned to him through the dark. "Yeah."

"You want some more?"

She didn't answer, but slowly reeled herself toward him, kicking stones as she came.

"Look — there's plenty! Have some!" He picked up the lid of the pot and let it steam the smell of cooked food. She leaned against the door post.

"I'm not hungry. I've eaten."

"Don't be polite, I'll get a bowl for you!" Bits of rice flew out when he spoke. "If you don't eat it, it'll just go to waste. Here, I have a bowl, sit down!" He forced her to sit, and dug out the rice using the bowl, and then handed it over to her. "And here — the dishes," he said, gesturing to the plate of fried egg, and plate of pork and green chili. "Eat!"

Peach sat and picked threads of pork out of the chilies.

"How's your mother?"

"Fine."

"And your father?"

"Fine."

"Good."

She looked up and caught him watching her. "Eat! Eat!" he said. "Don't waste it!"

Sun An beamed too much. Peach chewed a strip of pork. "I'm really not hungry."

"I cooked it myself."

"It needs more salt."

"I'm not a very good cook."

Peach sat staring at the food, but not eating. At last she asked, "What time is it?"

"Nearly eleven."

"I think I should go home."

"It's not safe. Let me walk you back."

"I don't want to trouble you."

"It's no trouble."

"What about the shop?"

"Oh, it's too late for customers now. Come on, let's go."

Sun An and Peach walked back through the deserted streets. Nocturnal beggars were picking through the day's rubbish, eating scraps of rice with their fingers, and then hurrying out of sight in case they were recognized. A few taxis rattled around potholes as they looked for customers; karaoke singing echoed through the streets and buildings, then faded off into the empty heavens.

Da Shan sat at a roadside shack, eating a late snack of cold beef and rice wine, chewing. He watched Sun An and Peach walk past, but only saw Peach. White skin and black eyes. She caught him staring at her, and stared back till she passed and looked away; but after she had walked on, her beautiful black eyes stayed there in the middle of the street, looking into him.

Da Shan thought of his wife, and his daughter, and all the women he had ever seen and loved. And those beautiful eyes.

> Love's troubles are not to be numbered,
> Just one evening scars the soul.

He sipped the wine; spiced with sadness and the petals of chrysanthemums.

At the Mists and Dew Pavilion, Fat Pan was making love to a whore. He ejaculated with a grunt and rolled to the side, his penis leaving a wet trail as it slid out, and he dropped again into the deep loneliness of strangers. Fat Pan reached for a cigarette with one hand while his other hand cupped her breast. He absentmindedly massaged it with his left hand, rubbed the nipple until it was erect, then tweaked it between his fingers.

Fat Pan let go of her breast to light his cigarette; smoked as the girl tore off a piece of toilet paper and wiped herself. The cigarette's red ember was like a red eye watching him in the darkness. The girl tore off another piece of paper and dropped it onto the far side of the bed. There was a wet *splat!* as it landed. Fat Pan decided to pay her less for that. He didn't pay good money to fuck peasants. Next time he'd go to the teahouse and drink tea.

The red eye glared at him as he inhaled, then the glow dimmed as it watched him from the shadows. He thought of Cherry, next time he'd go and see her. It took a couple of cigarettes before his energy returned, the rhythm of the girl's hand hastening his erection. At last he was firmly erect again, and he stubbed his cigarette out and rolled on top of her and kissed her neck.

After midnight Fat Pan washed himself and dressed. His footsteps echoed on the wooden steps, filling the house with the dull thuds of his descent. Outside the spring air was warm, the brothel courtyard was empty except for a bonsai cherry in a terracotta pot turned gold by the yellow light that came from an upstairs window. As Fat Pan walked away the light was turned off, and the darkness rushed in. Over the silhouette of the tower blocks, little by little, the crescent moon appeared. Before dawn, in the silver moonlight, a cherry bud opened up in a slow and silent explosion of petals.

*T*he next morning was clear and bright. Da Shan got up early and set off along the road that went into the center of town, which was clogged with peasants and beggars. He struggled through the melee of bodies, pushed himself free of a tight clam of people and got onto the scrubland between the pavement and the river. The river had stopped years before; now it lay dead and stagnant in the long trench of the riverbed. Leaves floated just under the surface, there were pale gray smudges where plastic bags had drowned, and flecks of green algae made up a lurid scum on the surface. In the middle floated a fishing boat, anchored to an unseen net.

"Heh — what have you caught?" Da Shan shouted across the water.

The man waved to him, thinking it was someone he knew.

Da Shan shouted again. "Caught any fish?"

"No," the old man said, "no fish."

"I caught a grass fish as long as my arm when I was a child."

"I've never seen a grass fish in this river."

"Well — you've never fished here then."

"I've fished here for forty years."

"It was as long as your arm."

"Grass fish don't grow that long in this river."

"I tell you it's true."

Da Shan waved and the old man waved back, and a polystyrene cup bobbed on the black water.

D a Shan walked through the town, down roads awash with liquid mud, and up the hill toward the Temple of Harmonious Virtue. There were steps of granite laid up one side of the hill. Untouched by the passage of feet and years, the steps were as rough as the day they were chiseled out of the mountainside. Da Shan's feet left no mark as they carried him up and away from the desperate chaos of the streets.

As the slope leveled out, the steps were replaced by a path, long buried under grass. He found the groove feet had worn into the earth and followed it. It led to the temple door, which exhaled a cool breath of air spiced with sandalwood incense. Da Shan stepped into the candlelit gloom of the shrine and felt strangely as if he were entering a living body. He took a sheet of yellow newspaper from a pile and spread it out on the floor, then sat down. The statue of Guanyin smiled as it had always smiled, and in front of her knelt two old apprentice nuns chanting the Lotus Sutra. They were his mother's generation, old, with their hair beginning to fade from gray to white. One had thick glasses and the other needed them. She squinted to focus, squinted so hard her eyes were almost closed.

Da Shan tried to cultivate his mind as they massacred the Lotus Sutra. The text was full of characters they didn't recognize, meanings that had been lost to them through time. They chanted without understanding, mispronouncing words and then correcting each other, and the plastic statue of Guanyin looked down on them, half-moon eyes full of compassion and hands raised in a gesture of inner peace.

He sat at the back of the temple for a long time. In the blundering chaos of the women's worship he shut his eyes and tried to imagine that there was no past or future; but all he could hear were the two women chanting and stopping and correcting each other, and then striking their blocks as they turned the next page.

Shaoyang was soaking up the evening twilight as Da Shan returned to town through Li Family Village. The mud path wound down between brick houses; a smell of burning hung in the air. Da Shan stopped and saw lots of small fires burning in the village. The closer to town he got the stronger the smell. Threads of smoke veined the skyline; the smell of burning had a melancholy taste; and above his head a tall pine sang in the breeze.

The path wound between the houses, and Da Shan turned a corner and found a man in a cheap suit squatting by the roadside. He was squinting through the smoke as he fed a small fire with bundles of paper. His face was flushed red by the dancing flames, a cigarette perched between his lips as he shuffled back to watch the flames dance.

"Has someone died?" Da Shan asked.

The man tossed the last wad of paper on the fire and looked up, still squinting. His chin unshaved, his voice high-pitched. "It's Qing Ming tomorrow," he said with peasant simplicity.

"Of course." No one had celebrated Qing Ming when Da Shan was growing up, certainly not in the cities. Not the educated people. It was a peasant superstition.

Da Shan and the man stood back and watched the flames fight one another in their eagerness to consume the wads of paper, burning themselves out in their struggle; leaving only crinkled shreds of white ash that took nervous flight. Da Shan shook his head: he wouldn't even be able to celebrate Qing Ming if he wanted to. He didn't know how.

Old Zhu was playing cards with one of his friends when Da Shan came home. There was a half-smoked packet of cigarettes on the table and a half-full ashtray. They were talking of 1950, the year after liberation, when they had been sent to Shaoyang to set up a reeducation center for prostitutes. They'd called it the Reeducation Center for Shaoyang Prostitutes. On the first day they held a parade through town with drums and banners to proclaim the benefits of the new Communist society and to call all the town's whores for reeducation. None came. Undeterred they'd begun to plan out the camp. They'd staked out an office block, residential quarters, a clinic and a kindergarten on the crest of the hill. When they had finished, the rain came and washed away their plans, but that didn't matter. The next day they just started again.

"I came across a peasant burning money," Da Shan said as he sat down. "He said it's Qing Ming tomorrow."

The two old men looked at him as if he were an unwanted memory disrupting their conversation. Their smiles flagged, they looked down at their fingers. They sat in silence for a moment. "The Grave Sweeping Festival already?" Old Zhu's friend asked.

"I remember the fuss we made when I was a child," Old Zhu said. "Days of fuss and worry. All the food we used to leave on their graves. Better than we had ourselves, and they were only dead people!" Old Zhu gave a short laugh, but no one else joined in. He shook his head in the silence. The past felt more immediate than the present, more real than the future. It worried him. White hair, white face and fear of death.

The scrape of Da Shan's chair broke Old Zhu's concentration. He watched his son get up and walk to the balcony and reached across for the pack of cigarettes.

"How are your grandchildren?" Old Zhu asked his friend, and glanced to see if Da Shan was listening, but Da Shan quietly closed the door behind him.

On the balcony the air was damp and cool, thick with the scent of smoke. Other fires were burning across the town, overhead the stars were red. Da Shan remembered the time he had gone to the Zhu Family cemetery to bury his grandfather. There was a field of gravestones low to the ground, grass growing high around them; and under the grasses all the generations of the Zhu clan — dead in their terrible graves. On that day they'd left a few steamed bread buns, made with millet flour because times were hard. There had been no paper money to ease the pain of parting or to bribe angry ghosts. Instead an uncle had read a list of achievements and honors, hollow praise for a dead man, and they had closed the soil on top of him. As the men of the family dug the soil back in, Da Shan had cried, not because his grandfather was dead, or because his parents were in prison, but because of the fierce Mongolian winds flaying the flesh from his bones.

*A*bout a week after Qing Ming, Old Zhu sat at the lunch table, waiting for Da Shan to come home and fill the empty third seat.

"He didn't say he would be late," Old Zhu's wife said.

Old Zhu nodded.

"Eat up, or it'll just go cold."

Old Zhu didn't move.

His wife looked at him then and at the three steaming dishes that were steaming less and less the longer they waited. "Come on, they won't taste so good if they're cold," she said.

Old Zhu took a sliver of pork and put it on his rice. He added a slice of tomato and then raised the bowl of rice to his mouth and began to shovel the food in. His wife sat opposite him and watched her husband eating, thinking of her son. "I'm worried," she said at last.

Old Zhu scraped his bowl clean with his chopsticks.

"Husband," she said.

He looked up, after picking a last grain of rice from his bowl.

"I'm worried," she said again, a table's width away from her husband, looking into his eyes. "You don't think he's getting involved in all that again, do you?" she asked.

"No," Old Zhu declared, "he's just catching up with old friends."

"But how about that girl?"

"What girl?"

"That girl," she said.

Old Zhu scratched his white hair as he thought for a long moment, and finally remembered. "Oh — no," he said, "you're just worrying."

She gave him a long look, testing him for his resolution, and he stared back. "That's all over," Old Zhu assured her. "No one cares about that now."

When they were finishing the rice there was a knock at the door that broke the silence of chewing. It was Madam Fan. Her entry caused a little swirl of activity as Old Zhu dragged her to the table to sit down and his wife fetched a bowl and a pair of clean chopsticks.

"Have some food," Old Zhu's wife insisted.

Madam Fan shook her head. "No — I've eaten."

"Have some — Da Shan hasn't come back. It'll just go to waste."

Madam Fan held her hands up in refusal. "I couldn't."

Old Zhu's wife gave her a bowl of rice. "Go on, eat!" she said. "Eat!"

"No, no," Madam Fan insisted, then relented. "OK, I'll just have a little."

Goaded on by Old Zhu's wife, Madam Fan picked at a few

dishes, managed to eat just over half her rice, then put her chopsticks down and sipped her glass of green tea. Old Zhu smiled encouragement before he stood up and went to the bedroom for a smoke and a snooze.

As Old Zhu slept through the long slow hours of afternoon, Madam Fan and Old Zhu's wife gossiped about the closure of the factory, the rising crime rate, how dangerous it was in Shaoyang these days what with all these migrant workers. There was a sign up by the factory gate thanking all the workers of the factory, past and present, for their contribution to the Motherland. There was a rumor they were going to build a bowling alley where the factory had been. Another that the company that had bought the land to build the hotel was owned by the brother of the present factory leader, and that the land had been sold for nothing.

"Aya!" Old Zhu's wife exclaimed. "There's no order anymore, these days are so wrong."

"I know," Madam Fan said, "I know."

They both thought of Autumn Cloud's going away, but said nothing. From the bedroom came the sound of Old Zhu's snores; interspersed with a creak of bedsprings as he turned over into a new dream. When the usual rounds of gossip had been exhausted Madam Fan sat forward and politely asked a hundred questions about Da Shan and the outside world, and Old Zhu's wife smoothed back her gray hair, primly answered them all, recounting what had happened since the night when he turned up on her doorstep unannounced.

"You must be so glad to have him back," Madam Fan said.

"Yes," Old Zhu's wife told her, "we are." There was a pause and Old Zhu's wife felt the need to show a reciprocal interest. "And how is Peach?" she asked.

Madam Fan gave an exasperated smile.

"Still no boyfriend?"

She shook her head.

"Don't worry, she shouldn't have any trouble," Old Zhu's wife said. "She's got your looks."

"Oh, you're flattering me," Madam Fan said.

"Don't be too modest," Old Zhu's wife told her, as the sound of prolonged coughing came from the bedroom.

"I'd better be going," Madam Fan whispered.

"Don't worry."

"I don't want to be any trouble."

"You're not."

"Well, I promised my brother I'd go and see him today."

Their chairs scraped on the tile floor as they both stood up. Old Zhu was still coughing in the bedroom as his wife escorted Madam Fan to the door, saying how nice it was to see her again, when Madam Fan stopped by the antiques and exclaimed, "Oh — how beautiful!"

Old Zhu's wife blushed. "Oh, they're just some dirty old things."

Madam Fan ignored the old woman's words. "They're so beautiful," she said. "Where did you find them? They must be so expensive."

"They're our son's," Old Zhu's wife said, wishing she'd put them away, knowing how easily gossip spread. "He likes that sort of thing."

"He must be doing well."

"Only so-so."

Madam Fan laughed. "Then I wish I was doing 'only so-so.'"

Madam Fan took the Number 11 bus across town. When she got to her brother's house and knocked on the door she was faced by her brother and sister-in-law, who shared the surprise at seeing her on their doorstep.

"Come in, come in," they insisted, but Madam Fan refused to come in. "I'm sure you didn't come all this way to stand on our doorstep," her brother said as he dragged her in through the door. "How can I leave my elder sister outside like a stranger?"

Madam Fan refused the seat she was offered and perched on the edge of the hard sofa. Her brother brought her a cup with a generous pinch of tea leaves, which he filled in front of her with water from a blue plastic thermos flask.

"Please don't be so formal, you're treating me like I'm a guest," Madam Fan said, but her brother took no notice and put a bowl of sweets in front of her, then began peeling an apple; the skin unspiraling from the white flesh. There was five minutes of tight formal chatter till Madam Fan's sister-in-law finally asked, "How is your family, how is Peach?"

"Very well."

"And your husband?"

Madam Fan composed herself but said nothing.

Her brother grunted. "You should have divorced him."

Madam Fan's eyes began to well with tears that she forced back down.

"Here," Madam Fan's sister-in-law said, handing her a tissue.

"No, thank you, I'm fine."

"Why go bringing all that up again," Madam Fan's sister-in-law chided her husband, who closed his mouth and folded his arms. Her sister-in-law apologized to Madam Fan.

Madam Fan blew her nose. "Thank you. It wasn't that I was crying about. It was Peach."

"What's she done?"

"She hasn't done anything. It's only fair that I should suffer — I did choose him as my husband, after all, but it seems so unfair on Peach. How can a child choose its parents? Why did she have to have such a terrible father?"

They sat and listened to her in silence, concerned expressions on their slowly nodding faces.

"Doesn't she have a boyfriend?"

"No. How can she? What future does she have? Ever since she left school she does nothing."

They nodded in sympathy.

"She's pretty, though," Madam Fan's sister-in-law said.

Madam Fan smiled weakly. "She is. But the factory has closed. She has no job, and there are so few men with reliable jobs these days. It's so difficult for a young girl to find a good man."

"And there are so many bad men around," her sister-in-law added.

"Why doesn't she go to Shanghai or Shenzhen?" Madam Fan's brother asked.

Madam Fan looked tragic, her sister-in-law cast her husband a dark look. "How can you ask such a stupid thing?" she scolded. "What do you think would happen to her?"

"I would worry so," Madam Fan said. "You hear such terrible stories."

"And what do you think she would do with her only daughter in Shanghai or some other such place?" Madam Fan's sister-in-law continued. "And her living with that beast?"

He shrugged.

"Don't worry," Madam Fan's sister-in-law soothed, getting up and going into the kitchen, and coming back with a rusty old tea tin in her hand, "we'll help you out."

Madam Fan sat forward onto the edge of her seat again. "No, please, I don't want you thinking I came for money."

"Don't be silly."

"No, I can't."

"Take it," her sister-in-law said, counting out and then handing over a hundred yuan.

"Are you sure?" Madam Fan said, stretching out a hand to take it, then trying to give it back.

"Put it away," her sister-in-law said. "It's nothing."

"You're blood," her brother said. "Hush!"

"Ten thousand thanks." Madam Fan sniffed, humility and gratitude squeezing tears out. "Heaven does not miss a good deed," she said, "even when men have forgotten."

When Madam Fan got back her husband was out playing poker. Peach was in her room playing pop music and singing along. When she heard her mother she opened her bedroom door and turned the music down, but Madam Fan smiled and said, "It's OK."

"Are you all right, Mother?" Peach asked.

"Of course."

Madam Fan hummed along with Peach's music, and it put Peach off the song, so she turned it off altogether.

"Where have you been all day?" Peach asked.

"I went to see Old Zhu's wife, and then I went to see my brother."

"How were they?"

"Very well."

The cheerfulness disturbed Peach.

"And how about you?" Madam Fan asked. "What have you been up to?"

"Oh, nothing."

Madam Fan gave her a long look over the rims of her glasses. "You should get out more. Meet some friends."

"Mother — please!" Peach groaned.

"You mother me now, but . . ."

"Mother!"

Madam Fan felt Peach's embarrassment; began to nurture a little plan in her head that made her smile.

*P*each got up and shivered in the dawn cold, pulled on clothes over her underwear and stepped into her slippers. She filled the kettle and lit the gas stove, a hot flower of blue petals in the dim room. Her eyes were gummed with sleep, her face bruised by the pillow, her hair confused. She washed in a bowl of cold water, clearing the last of the night from her mind, then stood in front of the mirror and combed her hair till it hung black and glossy past her shoulders. Her mother was still singing and her father still snoring and the kettle was starting to bubble with life. Peach stood in the kitchen and hummed and gazed out of the window down to the people as they went walking by, driven with purpose.

When the kettle whistled she turned it off, pouring half into the aluminum pan and half into the teapot. She set a pinch of green tea leaves dancing on the water, put six bread buns on the pan to steam. Apart from the singing and the dripping and the snores and bubbling pan — the world was quiet.

The tea leaves sank.

Peach dipped a quick finger into the pot to swirl them around. Then put on the lid.

Her father's snoring had stopped about ten minutes earlier, replaced with the smell of cigarette smoke when Peach finished her breakfast. She listened as her mother sang the last notes of her aria, and then Madam Fan came back through the balcony door.

"I've already eaten," Peach told her.

Madam Fan nodded.

"And I'm going out."

Her mother looked up. "Where to?"

"Shopping."

"I was going to take you to buy some new clothes today."

"I just wanted to go by myself," Peach said.

"Why not go with me?"

"No reason, I just wanted to go by myself."

Madam Fan sat in a pool of disapproval. "Anyway — I was going to say it's raining again."

Peach sat down opposite her mother. Madam Fan pulled strips of hot bread off her steamed bun, dipped them into her tea and nibbled. She sipped her tea loudly, and pointedly ignored the sounds of her husband getting up and coming out and grunting on his way to the bathroom. Peach sat, the air between them heavy.

"If you're going to go you ought to go," Madam Fan said at last.

Peach smiled.

"I don't suppose you have any money, do you?"

"I have the money I got for Spring Festival."

"That's not enough, take some more." Madam Fan looked around and pointed with a strip of bread bun. There was a pile of old notes all folded over; Peach took fifteen. "Get yourself something nice to wear. Something pretty."

Peach nodded.

"Will you be back for lunch?"

"I'm not sure."

"Well, be careful. And don't get wet."

"Thank you," Peach said.

"Off you go!" Madam Fan said, almost smiling.

Peach opened her umbrella and sauntered out of the factory. The street was full of umbrellas: so many shapes and colors — red, blue, green and yellow. Umbrellas walking deep in conversation, umbrellas selling and haggling, umbrellas milling around, moving closer or going away. Under her own umbrella, Peach turned left onto the road that went toward the town center.

The town was busy with street hawkers who had risen early and set up stalls. They filled the pavement with their goods, forcing everyone to walk on the road. There were people who'd tied lines between the lamp posts and hung their clothes on them, a Uiger from western China with a pointed white beard and embroidered skullcap selling Mare Nipple raisins; a local Muslim grilling lamb kebabs; and then a long line of stalls selling electronic knick-knacks and cigarette lighters that had smiling portraits of Mao and that could play any one of a number of revolutionary tunes. Horns blared and people swore; bodies mixed precariously in with the angry traffic.

Peach stopped at a woman selling candy.

"How much?" she asked.

"Eight yuan for a half kilo."

"Too expensive!" Peach said, and walked off. The old woman tried to call her back — "Six yuan!" she shouted, then "Five!" — but Peach kept on walking. She didn't want the stupid sweets. She pushed into shops and down ragged markets but didn't find anything to spend her money on. She walked around till lunchtime, when her footsteps led her back toward the Space Rocket Factory, past the piles of books and magazines, past the funeral tent, where the women were still banging on their wooden blocks, and then she found herself at the factory gateway — looking back over her shoulder into the crowd of colorful umbrellas. And she felt for a moment that the town had never existed. All there was was the walk there and the walk back, and then the waiting to return.

Peach stood under the factory gate and decided she didn't want to go back home yet. The rain had stopped, she saw the hills and the green bamboo and set off.

The path led around the back of the factory. In the flooded paddies there were rows of peasants planting rice seedlings. On a wall was written a slogan in red characters:

Grow Rich Through Apricots

Peach walked on till she had to pause for breath. She stood by a field and watched some peasants planting rice seedlings. They were bent over, arms dangling in the mud, moving through the fields, seedling by seedling; living their hard life, chained to soil and the passing seasons.

Peach started walking again, her thoughts drifting aimlessly. When spokes of setting sunlight broke through the clouds she started back along the path to town. The umbrellas were gone now, but not the chill of home, so Peach continued along the river, looking down into the black water.

"Heh! Peach!" Sun An called. "Heh!"

She turned and smiled to see him half silhouetted in the light.

"Have you eaten?"

"No," she said.

"Want to eat?"

"OK."

"Come on then."

Sun An put a film on for Peach and started cooking. He put a bowl of peanuts in front of her, and she picked them out and cracked open the shells, rubbed off the brown skin, and slid the smooth white nuts into her mouth.

Sun An washed the rice and put it to boil. He chopped shallots and smoked pork, mixed it with soy sauce and a little dried red chili, then fried them up over the kerosene stove. The oil spat as he stirred the food around and around.

"Good film?" he asked.

Peach ummed.

Sun An smiled and stirred, watching her strip peanuts, the action in the film, and then watching her again. When the meat was done he checked the rice, but it was still wet. Shit, he thought, and worried whether to turn up the heat. He stabbed the rice with a chopstick, too wet, he thought, and replaced the lid.

Sun An put the pork on the lowest setting and chewed his lip. Peach was loving the film, she was laughing hard, almost too hard. Sun An counted out the seconds until the rice would be ready, waiting for the good part of the film to stop so he could interrupt her. He decided he'd interrupt her when he reached fifty, but carried on counting. He swore he would stop at eighty, but reached eighty-five, and then ninety, ninety-one, ninety-two, ninety-three, before he shouted, "It's ready!"

Peach turned and grinned at him as he opened the pot of rice and stuck the chopstick in again. Again it came out wet. Shit, he thought again.

"It's a good film," Peach said.

"Yeah!" he said putting the lid back on the rice and thinking, Ninety-four, ninety-five . . .

"I'll get two bowls," Peach said, and put them down in front of him. "Umm, looks delicious!"

"I hope so," Sun An said, torn between the terror of overcooked pork and undercooked rice.

"Shall I serve?"

"No, I'll do it," he said, and unmasked the rice, which steamed innocently.

Sun An filled a bowl of rice for Peach, set the dish of pork in front of her. "I'm sorry, this food isn't very good."

"It smells great."

"You're too polite."

"No, it's true," Peach said. "Really."

They sat and ate, and Sun An glowed red with humiliation for his sticky rice and dried-out pork.

"Do you cook for yourself every day?" Peach asked.

He nodded because his mouth was full, then started speaking anyway. "Every day. For me and my sister."

She nodded and started shoveling the rice into her mouth. "Where are your parents?"

He swallowed quickly. "In my village."

"They're peasants?"

"Yeah." He nodded his head, unsure what to say next. "They're very hardworking. My mother makes rice wine, and my father works in the fields. I send them money every month."

Peach smiled. Sun An stuffed his mouth with rice and carried on talking. "It's a very hard life. Now my brothers help them, especially at this time of year." He shoved more rice into his mouth. "My family's not very rich. I borrowed money from my relatives to start this shop. They are very kind. I must work hard."

Peach kept on smiling, and thought how she had once wanted to be a peasant, and laughed. Sun An thought she was laughing at him for some reason. "Don't you like the food?" he worried.

Peach put her hand over her mouth and waved her chopsticks as she gasped for air. "No — it's just so silly!"

"What?"

"I was just thinking when I was little I used to wish my parents were peasants."

Now it was Sun An's turn to laugh. "Why?"

"My mother was the landlord class and my father's father

was a counterrevolutionary. It made life very difficult, even when I was a baby I knew we were different, all those years I wanted nothing more than to be a peasant."

He smiled. "Those times are gone now."

"Yeah. I can't really remember them. My mother's told me," she said, and remembered what she was trying to forget.

"Times are much better now," he said.

"Yeah, except all the factories are closing."

"Yes, but apart from that."

"Yes, things are much better now."

They smiled, he nodded and she looked away. Peach waited till he'd finished and gathered up the pots and started washing them.

"No, please!" Sun An said.

"Don't treat me like a guest!"

He felt too awkward. "Don't be polite."

"I'm not being polite at all."

"Then let me do it," he said.

Peach looked up and disarmed him with a smile. "No," she said. "Sit down, I'll wash."

Sun An washed his mouth out with green tea and spat out into the street. "I do good business here, you know," he said. "I send my parents twenty yuan every month."

Peach looked up from the bowl of washing, rubbed a lock of hair back from her cheek with her shoulder. "You're a dutiful son," she said. "Your parents are lucky."

Peach got up early again the next day, was out with her kite before her mother could stop her.

"Where are you going?"

"Out," she shouted back.

"Where out?"

"I'm going to fly my kite."

"Where?"

But Peach was out of earshot.

"Will you be back for lunch?" Madam Fan shouted, but Peach kept walking away, off into the rain. "I thought you would help me with my singing," Madam Fan said, as a final recrimination, then sat down and felt teary.

At ten o'clock Madam Fan's husband got up and ate the breakfast that was left on the table for him. He brushed his teeth then went out to play cards at a friend's house. She watched him leave with cold satisfaction, the rain sounding like the splatter of footsteps taking him away. Forever. She sat humming snatches of opera and knitting baby clothes, listened to the falling rain. With time the slow and irregular patter of water became regular and predictable.

If an east wind blows . . . she sang, then hummed and stitched. In the quiet of the moment she stitched and listened to the water and forgot to remember her past.

> If an east wind blows,
> Then send me your fragrance on it.

Peach spent the morning walking muddy paths in the hills looking for the wind; but she couldn't find it anywhere. The rain slowly failed and then stopped altogether, and she sat down next to a giant clay water pot that was as wide as her outstretched arms. The water was black and still, above it swirled a column of midges. She sat and watched a peasant woman pull green clumps of coriander out of the soil, wash their roots free of dirt, then head off to market; saw a husband and wife talking in the distance as they slowly inspected their rice seedlings; a little girl in bright green trousers and a red T-shirt playing next to the field her mother was laboriously weeding. Figures came and worked, then went. The air was still too quiet for kite flying.

"Hello!"

She jumped up.

"Don't you live at the Space Rocket Factory?"

Peach turned and looked up and saw a man, then blushed.

"What are you doing sitting here?" He laughed. "It's dirty!"

He stretched out a hand and pulled her up.

"I came to go kiting, but there's no wind," Peach said.

"Why not go up to the temple?" the man said. "You can usually get a breeze up there."

Peach looked down at her kite. She didn't know what to say.

"You're Old Zhu's son, aren't you?" she said at last.

"Yeah," the man said. "Da Shan."

"Oh," Peach said.

"And you're?"

"Madam Fan's daughter."

"Madam Fan?"

"The one who sings opera."

"Ah. I know." Da Shan took the kite out of her hands. "Come on then, I'll help you up."

Peach followed, making heavy going, hoping he'd turn and help her up, but he didn't. "You came back," she called out. "To Shaoyang, I mean."

"Yeah," he shouted. "It's changed a lot."

"I'd never come back if I'd left!"

Da Shan laughed and carried on up the hillside, and Peach followed.

M y father taught me how to fly kites," Da Shan said, holding the strings that let the kite dance in the wind. "When I was a boy."

"You're very good."

He laughed. "No, not really."

Peach watched him pull and feed the kite more line, then roll it back in. Da Shan was concentrating on watching the wind so much he forgot to speak. Peach tugged at the grass at her feet, wound it around her finger, then looked up into the sky, where the kite was flying to heaven. She looked at him and decided he was so entranced with watching the wind that he'd forgotten her. She twiddled some grass between her fingers, looked up at the kite, then up toward the temple.

"Does your mother love your father?" she asked suddenly.

Da Shan turned for a moment, and laughed. "What a strange question."

Peach looked down on the city, the roads and buildings where smoke and the ranting blare of car horns drifted up to her. In the grass there was a carved tortoise that had once been part of the temple, the stele it had supported now lying in fragments, grass widening the cracks. She sat down on the tortoise's head, folded her legs against the breeze, put her chin on her hands.

"I bet they do. You have such kind old parents," Peach said. "Not like mine. All my father does is gamble and all my mother does is knit. And they're *always* arguing."

Da Shan nodded, all his attention skyward.

"My mother's knitting baby clothes for when I get married."

He nodded again.

"Don't you think that's strange?"

"A bit."

"I mean, I haven't even got a boyfriend."

"Don't worry."

"I'm not."

"There must be lots of boys who are just waiting for an introduction," Da Shan encouraged.

"No there aren't."

"I'm sure there are."

Peach looked off, her profile turned toward him. "Who wants to marry a girl from Shaoyang? No money, no nothing."

"Don't worry, you'll be fine," Da Shan said, turning around and handing her the strings to the kite. "OK. There you go, she's up now, you should have no trouble."

Peach felt so clumsy as she took the strings off him, apologizing for nothing. The kite seemed to sag with her touch, lose its tautness.

"Oh, I'm so stupid!" she said.

"Not at all, just keep her high in the wind. That's it, you're doing fine."

He held her hands as she spun out more and more line, then he stood back and talked her through it. She learned quickly. "That's it," he said, "good," and fell silent.

Peach concentrated hard on getting it right. After a few minutes of silence she turned to see what he was doing, and saw with irritation that he was walking on up the hill. The fact that he wasn't there to watch took the joy out of what she was doing. She felt bored, wanted to talk with someone, and could only think of Sun An. It was getting late anyway.

Sun An was in his video shop, playing with his sister.

"Hello, Aunt," the girl said when Peach arrived. She was short and thick waisted, had pale brown hair held down with cheap wire hair clips.

"Go and do your homework now," Sun An told her, and his sister nodded solemnly, picking up her books and taking them into the back room. Sun An wiped a seat for Peach to sit down, put some lotus seeds out in front of her, poured water into a glass. "Is hot water OK?" he asked.

"You don't have any tea?"

"Little Sister! Can you bring the tea!"

Peach waited while he got her tea, munched on a few lotus seeds for something to do. Sun An served a customer, then came back to where she was sitting.

"Do you think love is important in a marriage or not?" Peach asked him when he came and sat down.

He opened his mouth for a moment, then said in a soft voice, "I think it is very important."

Peach realized what she'd said and how he'd understood it and blushed red. "Oh no, I mean, do your parents love each other?"

Sun An nodded and Peach pursed her lips, hmmm.

"Do you want to watch a film?" he said quickly.

"No," Peach said, and they sat in silence.

Sun An looked at her fingers and her hair falling over one ear, and her thirsty eyes that drained his in an instant and made him feel ashamed, and he looked away. He rubbed a spot on his trousers that wasn't there, and could bear it no longer because it would drive him insane if he didn't speak. "Do you want to come out sometime?" he blurted. "With me, I mean? We could do something, like go to the park, or maybe see a film."

Peach held his eyes as he spoke, leaned back, away from him, said, "OK. If you like."

He grinned a lopsided grin and hunched forward on his chair as if he were about to pounce.

"But I think I have to go home now. Will you walk me back?"

For Sun An the walk was too long and too slow, because his nerves were on edge trying to decide whether he should put his arm around her or not, and if he did whether he should kiss her. The ripe melon tastes sweeter than one that is picked too early, his grandmother had always said.

He tried walking up close to her, brushing her arm with his, or bumping into her occasionally, and she didn't seem to mind; so he counted to ten and put an arm around her shoulders. It hung there uneasily, half touching and half not touching too much. She hasn't pulled away, he told himself, a consolation that failed to calm him down.

They turned right up the road that led to the factory gateway. The street was strewn with market debris. Sun An took her hand and led, guiding her through the dark and muck as if he were a tightrope walker in a circus. When they got to the gateway he was almost disappointed to let go of her hand.

"So," he began, "when would you like to go and see the film?"

"Oh, I'm not sure," Peach said.

"OK, no problem." He smiled. "I'll find out when there's a good film on and tell you. Is that OK?"

"Yeah," she said. "Good night," and turned and left without looking back.

When Peach came home the rising moon was already leaning low on the horizon, its light set in a halo of glittering stars. She opened the door quietly, and saw with dread her mother — sitting by the window, glasses on her nose, knitting and singing to herself. Peach paused in the doorway, taking off her coat and hanging it by the door.

"You're making a draft," her mother said without looking up.

Peach shut the door and came in and sat down at the table. Madam Fan kept stitching. "Your lunch is in the kitchen."

"Thank you."

"And your dinner."

"Ah," Peach said. "Sorry."

Madam Fan held up a pair of baby's blue trousers. "Look!" she said with a bright smile. "I've nearly finished them. And when they're finished I'm going to knit a hat to match."

Peach looked into her mother's icy smile and hard eyes and nodded.

"You'll need them when you get married, and have children."

"Child," Peach corrected.

"Child."

"But anyway," Peach said, "I'm not even married."

"But you will be."

"I don't even have a boyfriend."

"Why not? How old are you?"

"Nineteen."

"I know that. So it's time you found someone. I'll look out for someone suitable. I told your uncle as well, if he knows any nice boys with good jobs."

Peach sighed again.

"If there's only one suitable boy in Shaoyang, don't worry — we'll find him."

Peach pinched the skin on the back of her hand, dug her nails in to see how much it would hurt. "Maybe I've already met one," she said.

Madam Fan sat up. "Who?"

Peach concentrated on nothing.

"Who?"

"No one."

"Who?"

"Oh — I don't know!"

As the darkness gathered itself over Shaoyang, Da Shan stopped writing. He'd written the names of his mother's family as far back as the second half of the Qing Dynasty: their ranks, their children, their achievements in life. His parents had gone to bed and now he sat up smoking a cigarette, wondering how much more his mother would remember. This was probably it, he told himself. His father didn't seem to be able to remember anything.

Da Shan thought of any more stories he could record, and then he smiled. Maybe he could write the history of Shaoyang. He knew it well; Shaoyang was an ancient city. First mentioned in the *Annals of the Historian*:

"Where the Zijiang and Shaoshui Rivers meet," he'd learned as a child, "Earl Zhao held court under the gantang tree."

In the Drink and Dream Teahouse, Liu Bei waited until she heard the door click shut then reached across and locked it from the inside. She swung her legs off the bed and winced as she pushed herself up, and winced again as she walked to the bathroom. The water in the bucket was cold; she used a cloth to wipe away the sweat and damp. Her skin shrank protectively against the cold as she wiped her body. She bent over and rubbed the white powder from her face. It stuck to her fingers like the scales of a moth's wing, floated on the surface in a gray scum.

When she felt clean Liu Bei wrapped herself in a blanket and crept along the wooden balcony to the toilet. There was a chill in the air, replaced by the stink of ammonia when she stepped into the toilet room. Down the deep hole she could see the creeping action of ten thousand pale-white maggots.

Liu Bei squatted and squeezed, heard the tinkle of urine splattering on maggots below.

"Heh!" came a voice from outside.

"Coming!" Liu Bei shouted, and the knocking stopped. She squeezed out another drop, wiped herself with toilet paper. The paper tumbled in the air as it dropped. Liu Bei pulled another handful off and wiped herself again and let it fall into the darkness. The door rattled again.

"Come on!" said the impatient voice.

"Finished!" she called out. "Finished."

It was dark when Madam Fan's husband came home, stumbling through the doorway, half drunk.

"Our daughter is in love," Madam Fan declared abruptly. "And if you weren't such a bad father we wouldn't be in this position."

He slumped onto the sofa, turned on the TV. "What now?"

"Our daughter has been out all day again — with some man!" Madam Fan's voice was taut with anger.

"What man?"

"Any man!" she shrilled.

Her husband sat and stared at the TV.

"She's got a lover!"

"Who says?"

"She says."

He didn't respond.

"I say!"

He sneered, "So what?"

"Won't you do anything! Damn your ancestors!"

"Why did I ever marry you."

"Any fucking peasant's bastard!" Madam Fan shrilled, standing up and dropping her knitting. "Fucking your daughter, you bastard!"

Madam Fan stood still for a moment quivering with rage, demanding an answer that he wouldn't give, snatched up her knitting, too angry to speak. She ran to the bedroom and slammed the door, collapsed on the bed and lay back, took in great long slow breaths and tried to sing her lines:

> A young nun am I, sixteen years of age,
> My head was shaven in my young maidenhood.

but her throat was too tight, and tears came out instead. She curled over onto her side and tried to force the lines out, but her face contorted and she sobbed the words incoherently:

> For my father, he loves the Buddhist sutras
> And my mother, she loves the Buddhist priests.

Peach lay awake and heard her mother shouting, doors slamming, and then the TV filling the silence. She heard her father get up and go to bed, then she lay and watched the nearly full moon rising in the window. She lay alone in the dark and before she fell asleep she resolved to run away, knowing that she wouldn't, but resolving to run away regardless.

Madam Fan slept badly because of the worry for her daughter. Next morning she was out early doing her shopping.

"Heh!" the bean sprout seller called out. "Was that your daughter flying a kite yesterday?" Madam Fan was too angry to answer. "Out with Old Zhu's son!"

"She can't have been." Madam Fan snorted indignantly, but when she got home she put away the shopping and began humming as she boiled the kettle. Instead of going to sing on the balcony she went into Peach's room and sat down on the bed. The moonlight had dried the tears from Peach's sleeping cheeks; her breathing was slow and shallow. Madam Fan touched her dreaming daughter's hair. Peach stirred, saw her mother and closed her eyes again.

"Good morning!" Madam Fan said.

Peach didn't answer.

Madam Fan said nothing, just sat stroking Peach's hair.

"I've cooked Eight Treasure Soup if you want some," Madam Fan tried.

Peach opened one eye, then the other, wondering what she'd done to deserve her mother's Eight Treasure Soup.

"Come on, get up," Madam Fan continued, "I've got a special day planned for us today. I'm going to take you shopping, and then I have a surprise for you."

"What's that?"

"If I told you then it wouldn't be a surprise, would it?"

Madam Fan said, throwing back the sheets. Peach muttered in protest as Madam Fan sailed out, humming loudly. She poured out a bowl of soup for Peach, put it on the table, then went to the balcony and sang:

> I'll leave the monastery
> And all the gongs and prayers

Peach came out and sat down and bent to suck up her Eight Treasure Soup from the spoon.

In the apartment opposite, Old Zhu's wife looked out of the window; told Da Shan to come and have a look at Madam Fan dancing on the balcony, her sleeves fluttering in the breeze.

"No shame," Old Zhu's wife said. "You'd think it was her needing to get married, not her daughter!"

Da Shan nodded and sat down to his breakfast again as Madam Fan's shrill voice echoed across the yard and through the apartment:

> I'll go and find me a handsome lover.
> Let him scold me and beat me,
> Kick me and ill treat me,
> But I'll not become a Buddha!

*A*utumn Cloud returned to Shaoyang on a sunny Saturday morning, when the skeletal trees were green again with budding leaves. Looking out of the bus window she saw a world that was no longer gray, but full of color and life. The sky was blue, young lovers walked hand in hand to admire the pink plum blossoms, and in the window her own half reflection seemed to smile back at her.

The driver edged his bus through the excited crowds as Autumn Cloud sat and peered out of the cracked window. She remembered spring days from her childhood, when the blossoms had mottled the pavements and she had had someone's hand to hold. Fear and joy twined inside her like two sudden lovers. Tears began to bubble up in her throat; it seemed that Shaoyang had never looked so colorful. There would be more springs, she told herself. The world was full of memories still waiting to happen.

It took nearly an hour to reach Shaoyang East Bus Station, through chaotic streets packed with people. At last the driver swung the bus around through the station gate, the bus juddered to a rest and the hydraulics let out a soft sigh of exhaustion. Autumn Cloud lined up to get off, stepped down into oil-black puddles of mud, looked up and saw white puffs of vapor floating across the blue sky. It was an auspicious day, she told herself, and confidently set off for home.

She pushed through the streets of milling crowds until she came to a food stall set along a street wall. She was tired and there was no particular hurry, so she pulled a bamboo stool from under the table and sat down in the cool, damp shade, reached inside her bag and pulled out her fan, and gently fanned herself as she gazed into the endless struggles of the crowd. Pushing and pulling, and getting nowhere.

Two bodies tore themselves out of the crush, two men, who came to sit down at the table next to her. Autumn Cloud smiled and moved her knees to the side to let them in. They were tall and strong, with a week's worth of stubble on their chins, and dirty faces, hands and nails. One had a thin face and bulging eyes, the other high, prominent cheekbones jutting out under his skin. They both had tall stuffed sacks that they leaned against the wall, then sat down at the same table. She kept smiling at them, but neither smiled back.

The owner maneuvered his way around the tables to them. "Yeah?" he asked.

"Two egg fried noodles," one of the men said.

"And you?"

"Nothing," Autumn Cloud said.

The owner stared at her with one hand on his hip and the other slipped halfway into his trouser pocket.

"Don't worry. I'm about to go," Autumn Cloud told him gently. He nodded and waited. Autumn Cloud fanned herself a little more, stood up and walked into the crowd, disappearing without a ripple.

It was just after lunchtime when Autumn Cloud arrived back at the gate of Shaoyang Number Two Space Rocket Factory. She let out a long sad sigh, looked up at the familiar gateway and suddenly remembered her front-door key. She panicked for a moment, then found it at the bottom of her left trouser pocket, although she didn't remember putting it there.

The whole factory compound slept in a dream-soft silence, so the only person who saw her return was an old man who spent each day sitting outside his front door, smoking cigarettes. He sat and smoked and watched as Autumn Cloud took a deep breath and started up the stairs that led to her apartment, tried to calm the fear that flapped frightened wings inside her stomach. She paused for a moment to wipe away sweat from her forehead that wasn't really there, took a deep breath and calmed her nerves before continuing up the stairs.

When she stood and looked at the front door, still bent and dented, the fear inside her was almost too much. Her imagination paraded ghosts and demons through her mind, rotting bodies hanging from the neck, cold unseen hands touching her skin. She clenched her jaw tight and put the key into the lock and turned.

From the gloomy interior of the apartment there was a soft exhalation of cool air and a stale smell of dust. Autumn Cloud's hand reached inside and groped for the light switch. She turned on the light and looked and found the room was unsettlingly normal — just as she'd left it — and not at all what the months of nightmares had led her to expect. She paced slowly around the apartment till she reached the bedroom door. Then she paused, then pushed the door open, and inside the bedroom she found there was nothing strange except the damp smell of tears that had permeated the walls. She walked around the apartment again, resisting oppressive details in the house that pointed to her dead husband — and fighting the urge to just sit down at the table and cry. When she had walked around and around she carried her bag to the bedroom and began to unpack. Inside she found the tape she was looking for, and put it into the tape recorder and turned it on. It was Buddhist chanting.

Nan wu guan shi yin pusa, the voices chanted, *nan wu guan shi yin pusa* — as she swept the dust back up into the air.

Nan wu guan shi yin pusa — Autumn Cloud hummed along as she hung a black-and-white photo of Party Secretary Li on the wall, arranged a black cloth around the top of the frame so that it draped down both sides.

Nan wu guan shi yin pusa — as she threw back the curtains and opened a window to the outside world, let fresh air and sunlight back into her life.

Nan wu guan shi yin pusa — as she lit three sticks of sandalwood incense and bowed three times; continued humming as they burned their lonely way down into nonexistence.

Madam Fan heard the news when she was out shopping with Peach. Peach said she'd heard it from a friend of the hairdresser, who had said that he'd seen Autumn Cloud in the street that very morning.

Madam Fan handed Peach the shopping and set off immediately to tell Old Zhu's wife. On the way she passed Old Zhu himself, who was sitting next to his allotment behind Number 7 block of apartments, dressed in a white vest and old gray trousers. He was smoking a cigarette in the dappled shade of a green tree, his white head and smooth old skin, nodding softly to himself in some private conversation.

"Autumn Cloud's back!" Madam Fan shrilled across the neat furrows of tended soil, and Old Zhu looked up and squinted at her. "Eh?"

Madam Fan was in too much of a hurry to delay. She dashed to the block of apartments. Ran as quickly as she could, her heels tapping out an accelerating beat as she clattered up the stairs.

BANG! BANG! BANG! she beat on the metal door, and Old

Zhu's wife came rushing to the door in a state of panic. Madam Fan rushed past her, across the room to the window. "Look!" she said breathlessly, and Old Zhu's wife looked everywhere and nowhere in particular.

"Look!" Madam Fan said again, and Old Zhu's wife followed Madam Fan's finger to the balcony of Party Secretary Li in the block opposite.

"What?" she said.

"She's back!" Madam Fan said.

"Who?"

"Look! Can't you see the light's on?"

"Where?"

"There!"

Old Zhu's wife stared in disbelief. "She's back?!"

"Yes."

"She's come back?"

"Yes."

"Good!" Old Zhu's wife said and strode into the bedroom and threw open the wardrobe doors. "I've got something for her!"

Old Zhu sat and smoked another cigarette under the green tree and watched catkin fluff drift like summer snow. A deranged cockerel crowed suddenly, and at the edge of hearing he could just make out from across town the temple's bell, muffled by haze. The spring had been good so far, he mused, the warm rains had dyed the trees green, the peasants had planted their rice.

Old Zhu pinched the butt of the cigarette between his fingertips and smoked the tobacco down to the stub. Madam Fan's progression came back to him; he hadn't really been listening and her words sounded something like "The cloud's slack." He looked up at the blue sky and wondered what she'd meant.

She must have meant something, he reasoned, stretching

out his legs, thinking of the summer heat when his tomatoes would ripen. He was still ruminating on this when he saw his wife and Madam Fan, and wondered what they were doing crossing the yard. They didn't have any friends on that side, as far as he knew, and why was his wife carrying a box?

Old Zhu sat and wondered; felt his organs inside him warm and snug, truly warmed through for the first time since autumn of the previous year. Spears of sunlight stabbed down through the fresh spring leaves, and a delicate trail of black ants climbed a tree trunk behind his back. Thoughts slowly trickled down to the roots of his mind, nourishing them after a long hibernation.

Why the box? he thought, stretching again, feeling sunlight dance on his skin.

Old Zhu opened his eyes and stood up suddenly. He squinted up into the sunlight and looked to the apartments opposite, to a certain apartment in particular, and saw that the balcony door was open. On the same balcony where banners had once drifted in the wind.

Oh dear, that could only mean one thing, Old Zhu thought as he stumped across the yard on his old legs, that could only mean one thing.

Autumn Cloud was sitting on the sofa having a moment's rest when Old Zhu's wife burst in through the door with Madam Fan in close pursuit.

"Aya!" Old Zhu's wife shouted. "Aya! Where have you been! How you've worried us! We haven't slept a wink since you left! Why didn't you tell us you'd gone!" she screeched, and held out the cardboard box and shook it, rattles and all. "And what were we supposed to do with this!?" she shouted. "It's *him*," she enunciated slowly, as if Autumn Cloud were deaf and simple together, "his ashes. He's been in my wardrobe all this time! We've been looking after him for you. What have you put me through with a dead man in my wardrobe — I haven't even been able to get undressed in my own bedroom!"

Madam Fan quickly sat next to Autumn Cloud and took her hand. "Now why did you go and leave us at a time like that? We all wanted to care for you, we were so worried. Imagine how we felt! It was terrible!"

"It's not responsible to go off like that," Old Zhu's wife reasserted herself. "It'll bring you and your children bad luck. It will bring all of us bad luck! You should never had done it!"

Autumn Cloud nodded slowly with each litany that was presented to her, admitting her guilt. When she began to cry they relented and Madam Fan went to put the kettle on and searched the cupboard for some tea and cups. While the kettle boiled more people arrived, and soon the factory was like an ant's nest — everyone was running around in a hurry, either coming or going.

Old Zhu arrived in the middle of it all, in time to see Autumn Cloud sitting on the sofa as the neighbors berated her for going off so irresponsibly. Such was the sense of grievance that when one young woman shouted, "No wonder the factory is closing — if people like you contradict the laws of Heaven!" — no one thought to correct her.

Not even Autumn Cloud, who sat and nodded, yes you're right. There were so many of them shouting so loudly — how could they be wrong?

Now Autumn Cloud was back the local neighborhood committee decided that the period of mourning for Party Secretary Li should come to an official end. A small delegation came to her house the next afternoon and she gave them tea, which they didn't drink.

Faint plumes of steam softly waved to each other as the tea cooled, and the neighborhood committee chairman told Autumn Cloud how much the meal and supplementary activities would cost. She gave them the money and agreed that it was best if they organized it all.

"You are very kind," the neighborhood committee chairman said, "and I'm pleased to tell you that the neighborhood committee has decided to contribute thirty yuan to the costs because of your husband's fine contributions to the Party and the factory."

Autumn Cloud smiled politely, thank you.

There was a moment of silence, then the committee leader nodded and stood. The rest of the delegation stood up as well, as their leader declared how good it was to have her back.

"Thank you. It's so kind of you all to take the trouble," Autumn Cloud told them as she stood in the doorway. "It's good to be back home. I feel like I'm back with my family again. Thank you."

The next week a blue truck arrived at the factory, and a party of retired factory workers assembled a yellow-striped tent. There wasn't much to show this was a religious ceremony, except for the three part-time monks, who came back and chanted for a few hours, before they gave up and started a game of poker with Madam Fan's husband. He had nominated himself as de facto organizer because a friend of his had promised to bring a film projector and screen.

"An American film tonight," Madam Fan's husband had announced to everyone. "A friend of mine. Yes, the newest film there is. Rambo and Madonna together. The best!"

The coming film meant the inhabitants of the Space Rocket Factory had something new to talk about other than the fact that the new leaders were going to build a hotel. It gave them something to look forward to. When Autumn Cloud arrived they peered over one another's shoulders to get a glimpse of Party Secretary Li's widow, who looked creased and worn, like an old shoe. She sat down with the head of the neighborhood committee, he insisted that she take his seat.

When the film projector did arrive Autumn Cloud explained to the neighborhood committee that she was feeling a bit weak and went upstairs to burn incense. Her absence did nothing to dampen the excitement as the inhabitants of Shaoyang Number Two Space Rocket Factory sat down on neat squares of newspaper they had brought with them, and felt the warm evening air snuggle down between them. Their excitement increased a little when they found out the film wasn't American at all, but a scratched old copy of *The Upstanding Night Soil Collectors Visit the East in Red Commune,* which they'd all seen before, Peach included.

She sat at the front of the crowd on a tight square of newspaper, her chin resting in her cupped hands. She hummed along to the opening song, sung by a band of marching peasants and workers with broad Communist smiles. There was a round of comments and chatter, people suddenly remembered how the film ended, who got punished and who went off with who; and after reminding their friends they all began to settle down and watch.

Five minutes into the film Peach whispered to the person next to her, "What time is it?"

"Seven thirty."

"Thanks."

She sat for a little longer, then got up, picking up her newspaper behind her, and hurried away.

Sun An was waiting for Peach by the factory gates. He had a nervous look on his face, which was replaced by something approaching a smile when he saw her coming.

"I was worried you'd change your mind," he said. Although she smiled, her estimation of him dropped a little because he'd admitted something so silly.

"Why would I do that?" she asked.

Sun An shrugged. Then he said brightly, "I've got the tickets!" pulling them out of his pocket to show her.

"Good," she said. "Let's go."

They started walking down the street along the river. Peach lagged behind. "Which cinema are we going to?"

"The one on Dongfeng Street."

"And we're walking?!"

"Yes." He blushed because she made him feel so stupid. "Unless you want to get a taxi," he said, and started worrying in case he didn't have enough money on him.

"It's such a long way to walk."

Sun An checked his money, and Peach watched him count his scruffy wad of notes. He looked up and smiled when he saw that he had enough. "Yeah, let's get a taxi," he said. "Good idea."

The film was a Hong Kong kung fu epic, with protracted fight scenes interspersed with rapid-fire dialogue and the incessant babble of the audience. Peach and Sun An were holding hands, hearts pounding as the light off the silver screen reflected in their eyes.

After ten minutes Sun An cleared his throat and leaned over to whisper in Peach's ear, "This isn't very interesting, is it?"

He was going to suggest that they go for something to eat, but Peach turned to him, her eyes bright crescents — half reflecting the light of the screen, half in shade like the dark side of the moon.

Sun An's breathing stopped while a man on screen was getting beaten up and spitting blood. In the bedlam of shouting and punching he closed his eyes and leaned in so close he could feel the heat of her skin. Peach barely moved her head or lips in response. He pressed his lips against hers. Her lips were slightly parted. He tried to put his tongue into her mouth but came up hard against the ridged wall of her teeth.

Sun An opened his eyes and sat back, and bristled. The fighting on screen was almost frenetic. Sun An sat and watched and bristled. Felt even more angry and guilty because he was bristling.

Peach squeezed his hand encouragingly. "Not here!" she whispered in his ear. "Let's go outside."

"You want to go outside?"

"Yes."

"OK."

Sun An and Peach walked back through the dark streets, bursting full of kisses they had for each other. His hand was damp and hot, her heart was disco dancing. They walked slowly, took a half step and slowed, and he bent to kiss her again. She leaned her head back and he looked down into her face for a moment, her lips half parted and this time she opened her mouth, and their tongues met.

Sun An pulled her into a doorway. Hands wrapped her waist. He bent his head down to hers, concentrated all his effort; felt the warm inside of her mouth and the rough surface of her tongue, which filled the whole world. His hands explored the contours of her body through her clothes. She rested her arms around his neck so that he couldn't escape.

At last Sun An pulled his mouth away gasping for breath, pressed his face into the dark tangles of her hair, whispered into her ear, "I love you, you are so beautiful, I've always loved you, I think about you all day every day. I love you so much, I can't even begin to say how much I love you."

He whispered into the dark, hardly knowing himself, and

Peach held her breath and squeezed her eyes shut and pressed her head against his heart. She felt tears of wonder fill her eyes as again he said, "Peach, I love you, I love you, I love you I love you I love you." She rested her head on his chest and squeezed him close, wanting him to say more.

*L*iu Bei's mother was sitting on her front steps, peeling garlic. Aunty Tang was sitting with her, basking in the heat like a cold lizard warming its blood. She squinted at the sparkling sunlight, a clear stream of mucus was welling up from her tear ducts and dribbling down the wrinkled fissures of her cheeks. She occasionally picked up a clove of garlic and sniffed it, then positioned it between the few molars she still had and took a bite, gave it a gummy chew.

"She'll have to know," Aunty Tang said at last, as Liu Bei's mother continued picking up the cloves of garlic and stripping them, and putting them in the bowl at her feet.

Aunty Tang burped a garlic belch. Her gums worked rhythmically, slowly reducing the garlic to a pulp that she could swallow. "She'll have to know."

Liu Bei's mother glanced at her and took another bulb of garlic.

"What are you going to tell her when you give her the

money? She'll think you've been out working again!" Aunty Tang said, and let out a slow croak that was laughter. "Out working again!" and more laughter.

Liu Bei's mother wiped back a graying lock of hair and crushed the bulb in her fingers, unconsciously seeking out the fattest cloves to start work on.

"Money doesn't just come from nowhere," Aunty Tang sighed, almost to herself. "You have to work for it. Whatever you do . . ." She trailed off, the silence making her world feel empty suddenly. "Unless of course you're a beggar," she added.

"My family are not beggars," Liu Bei's mother stated. "I worked and my daughter works too. The money is for her son."

"Bastard," Aunty Tang corrected, "bastard." She bit another clove and began to masticate it around her mouth. "No one in this world loves a bastard. Nor a whore."

"Nor old bags," Liu Bei's mother told her.

Aunty Tang didn't hear the retort; her hearing was like her manners, she could turn them on or off at will. In ignorant bliss she smacked her gums and her tongue roamed around the rim of her mouth. Liu Bei's mother watched her: Aunty Tang's tongue was the only thing about her that hadn't wrinkled and withered with the years. It was stubby and pointed, and the absence of teeth made it look big and sluglike. It slithered from one side of her lips to the other, wetting her gums, and then Aunty Tang sighed again.

"Poor child," she said, and Liu Bei's mother looked away. "Poor child."

Liu Bei's mother picked up the bowl of garlic and took it inside and set it down next to the stove. There were some fragrant chives that needed washing, she brought them back out with her and set them down on the floor and sat and rubbed her hands in the sunlight as if it were a fire to warm her bones.

Aunty Tang was still sighing and murmuring, "Poor child."

"No father," she exhaled after a while. "Poor bastard." She

turned her half-blind eyes to Liu Bei's mother. "How can a boy survive in the world without a father? It's unnatural."

Liu Bei's mother ignored her and took in a deep breath that reached down to the pit of her stomach, it stretched her ribcage, and then she let it slide back out of her body.

"A child could do worse than have Liu Bei as a mother," she stated.

"But no father."

"She might find someone. I did."

"But that was under the Communists," Aunty Tang said. "And anyway," she scolded, "it wasn't our fault. We were all abused by the Old Society. But now . . . ," she said, and left the sentence hanging open. Liu Bei's mother picked up the fragrant chives and began to pick through them, discarding the wrinkled leaves. "But how can a bastard do well now?" Aunty Tang asked. "Just look at your family. Your ancestors must have done something terrible. You a whore," she said with almost wistful melancholy, feeling her way back along a friendly and familiar list. "Your daughter a whore."

Liu Bei's mother scowled because she knew what was coming next.

"And your grandson's a bastard."

Liu Bei's mother took a deep breath and wondered why on earth she put up with this. Aunty Tang rubbed away a dribble of mucus as if it were a tear, wiped her nose, and her tongue crept out for a quick lick. She was relishing the new ending she had found for her daily diatribe, which she built up with theatrical slowness.

"You a whore," she sighed again. "Your daughter's a whore, and your grandson is a bastard. Whore, bastard, whore. There's nothing you can do about it," she reiterated slowly with melancholic glee, smacking her lips and licking them one more time. "Heaven hates you all!"

*P*each was up before her parents and went down to the river, found the letter under the stone Sun An had shown her. It was intricately folded into the shape of a heart and her name was written on the outside, not in the usual Biro but in the black brush strokes of calligraphy. She wiped off the few bits of grit that had stuck to it; wrinkled her nose up because the writing wasn't very good, then slipped it under the edge of her bra, next to her heart. She started walking and the sharp folded corners stabbed into her flesh, so she took it out again and held it tightly in her hand; walked down to the factory, which was washed in sunlight and rectangles of shade.

She sat down under a tree and opened out the petals of paper, till the heart was a ridged square of paper in her lap.

"Dearest Peach," it began. "Last night I could not sleep because I was thinking of you. I watched the moon rise and set, and shivered with cold. Just because you are from the city and my family are peasants doesn't mean we can't get together. Chairman

Mao once wrote we should 'dare to struggle and dare to win' — you and I — we dare to love each other. Other people may try and stop us, but I know we will win because we love each other. I was telling myself this in the shop today, and I felt very sad. You haven't come to see me for three days. I miss you so much. I took a brush and wrote a poem. It is not very good."

Peach flattened out the paper:

> Life is like a winding path
> Surrounded with flowers
> Butterflies and delicious fruit,
> But I was only looking at my feet
> Until I met you.

She giggled at the silliness of his poem, but her heart began to dance again.

"Please do not look down on me because my handwriting is so bad," the words read. "My family are peasants and my education level is poor. I hope that when we are married you can teach me how to write better! I love you, Sun An."

Peach turned the page over, the characters continued, "I love you, I love you" over and over, all the way down the page. She folded it back up and put it in her purse with his other letters; went back to the house, enjoying the dry smell of spring.

Old Zhu saw her go and thought to himself: what a beautiful young girl. Just seeing her walk past swinging her arms and smiling to herself made him feel young again, if only for half a minute.

After singing and breakfast Madam Fan took the hundred yuan that her brother's wife had given her and called out, "Peach, come on, it's time to go!"

There was the sound of footsteps from her bedroom, and then Peach came out and smiled softly. Her cheeks had a blush to them this morning, the pink looked good against her pale skin and black hair. Madam Fan wondered that her husband could have given her such a beautiful child. But it's me she looks like, Madam Fan thought as she opened the front door. She's *mine*, not his.

"Come on, you take *so* long to get ready!" Madam Fan repeated, as Peach followed her out the door, then Madam Fan closed it behind them, and the lock clicked shut.

Madam Fan and Peach spent the morning in the street market searching for clothes, but found nothing nice, and ended up in a new salon on Liberation Street that played loud disco music and where the assistants all wore matching red T-shirts. There was an initial problem on what style of clothes they were looking for.

"How about this?" Peach asked.

"Too modern," Madam Fan said. "Why not try this one?"

"Mother, you're so old-fashioned!"

"What about this?"

"It's ugly."

"Well, that's much too short."

"Times are changing," Peach insisted. "Everyone's wearing these now."

"OK," Madam Fan relented, "try it on."

When they'd decided on a pair of jeans and a cut-off T-shirt a shop assistant came over and Madam Fan said, "We want these. How much?"

"Forty-five yuan."

"They're not worth any more than twenty-five."

The assistant sighed. "We don't bargain here," he said. "If you can't afford the clothes then get out."

Madam Fan stared at the boy. "Where are you from?" she demanded imperiously, but despite her haughty tone he replied simply, "Changsha."

"Well." She snorted. "Indeed!"

"Do you want the clothes or not?"

"Of course we want them!" Madam Fan hissed. "What do you think we're doing here? We're not on a sightseeing trip, you know!"

The assistant shrugged and walked to the counter, rang in the price and took the money, handing the clothes back in a blue plastic bag. When they were outside in the street Peach expected her mother to unleash a torrent of abuse, but she didn't. "Come on," Madam Fan said. "Let's go."

They stopped off at an ice-cream bar on the way back, and sat at a table with fixed molded chairs. "Ice cream," Madam Fan told the waiter.

"What color?"

"What color have you got?"

"White, brown, red and blue."

"We certainly don't want white," Madam Fan said. "How about red. That's luckier. This is going to be a lucky week, I can tell."

They sat and ate their red ice cream with plastic spoons, and Madam Fan talked and talked. "What a year!" she declared. "It's too much. Really!"

Peach put the ice cream into her mouth, felt the spoon's plastic surface and the cold melting on her tongue, and thought of Sun An.

"So many things that go against nature," Madam Fan continued. "All this business with the factory closing; Party Secretary Li, Autumn Cloud disappearing and reappearing. It's unlucky. I don't like it at all."

Peach swirled the melted ice cream around in her mouth, squeezed it between her tongue and the roof of her mouth, was aware of her mouth like she'd never been aware before.

"Oh dear," Madam Fan said, and looked up at Peach and smiled. "Oh dear," she said and scraped up the last of her ice cream. "So many things."

Peach felt Sun An's arms crushing her ribcage and imagined his hands on her breasts.

Madam Fan peered across at Peach's bowl. "Have you finished?" she asked.

"Yes."

Madam Fan nodded absentmindedly as she looked for her purse, then said, "Oh yes — do you know what else I heard?"

Peach wished she could summon back the daydream she'd just been enjoying, but couldn't, and shook her head instead.

"I heard that Old Zhu's son, Da Shan, is *divorced*," Madam Fan whispered. "He's left his wife and daughter. And with all that money he's got too!" Peach looked at her mother as Madam Fan sat back and let out a half smile. "You could do a lot worse, you know."

"What do you mean?"

"I mean you could do a lot worse than catch him."

Peach blushed and Madam Fan smiled again. "Such a successful young man," she said. "Just think."

Peach hardly heard, she looked down and away and felt her cheeks blushing very red. Madam Fan watched her for a moment, then ran a hand through her hair. "I think it's time I had a haircut," Madam Fan said at last. "And you should come as well."

Peach was tired of shopping, and of her mother. "Mother, isn't all this too expensive?"

"Listen," Madam Fan said, taking Peach's hand, "remember what I told you about your father and me?"

Peach nodded. Her mother's eyes were very wide.

"I don't want that to happen to you, understand? I want you to have the best you can possibly get. I want you to have what I never did. Can't you see what's happening here — this country's going backward. All the factories closing, all this corruption and all these peasants killing and stealing! You have to get out. Get married to someone strong and upright. Not just any old worker. Not a gambler like your father. Someone successful."

Peach listened to her mother and nodded: yes, I understand.

"You're my only daughter," Madam Fan insisted, "my *only* child."

Sun An sat and wrote another letter. It was the third one he had written that day, and he gave it to his little sister. "Here you go," he said.

"I don't want to go," she protested. "I've been twice already. Why don't you take it?"

"Because I have to look after the shop. And you have nothing to do."

His sister pouted and took the note and walked off down the street toward the Space Rocket Factory. Sun An stood in the doorway and watched her go, imagining Peach looking under the stone and finding his letter there.

When his sister came dawdling back half an hour later Sun An was still waiting in the doorway. He'd half hoped that Peach would come back with his sister. Or even beat his sister back. But she hadn't and he'd have to wait. He stood and watched the clock hands claw their way around the clock face, going as slowly as possible.

After a few hours had been stretched impossibly thin with worry and anticipation he turned to his sister and demanded, "Are you sure you put it under the right stone?"

She folded her books closed and piled them up and walked into the back of the shop. "I've got homework to do," she said.

Peach arrived later that afternoon, when the waiting had reduced Sun An to a slumped figure in the doorway, eating his way through a bowl of salted melon seeds. He saw her coming and energy spread through his veins like a stiff shot of adrenaline. He stood up grinning as she came into the shop, slightly breathless, wearing jeans and a red cut-off top that showed her stomach.

Sun An said "Hi!" and for a few moments they both stood laughing and smiling at each other. After so many days of letters — almost astonished to find each other so close as to reach out and feel the other. He tried not to look but found his eyes continually drawn to her pale white stomach, its soft curves and the shallow indent of her belly button.

I just have to, he thought, or I'll go mad.

Sun An closed the front door of his shop and told his sister to go for a walk. He and Peach stood and chatted in the half shadow of the room. He was holding her hand, stroking it rhythmically with his thumb. He could smell her perfume and see light glitter off her teeth when she smiled or her eyes moved; could see the pale moon of her stomach that glimmered in the dark. As they talked and held each other's hands her voice suddenly dropped to a whisper. He smelled her fragrance draw close and then she was in his arms and he was kissing her mouth. He kissed her again, spoke soft words in her ear as he stroked her body. Her stomach shivered at the touch of his fingers tracing invisible hearts over her skin. She felt his hands edge slowly underneath her top till her clothes were ruffled up and disheveled and then the fingers of his right hand smoothed up and under the cloth of her bra and he held one of her breasts in his hand.

Peach pulled back and kissed his cheek. "Tell me," she

whispered, and he told her how much he loved her as he kneaded her breast. He crushed it too hard. Peach winced and moved her body so he couldn't reach her there anymore. He tried to kiss her lips, but she turned her head and rested it against his, their skulls pressing together as his free hands now stroked her rigid back and buttocks.

"I love you," he said, "I love you, your beauty, your laughter, your music. I love you, I love you." His hands were insistent and powerful. Peach felt them desperately searching her body, squeezing and pressing, one hand stroking her neck while the other worked a handful of buttock.

"I love you, I love you." His breathing was heavy in her ears, and she realized she was sucking air in and out as well. "I love you, I love you, I love you." His fingers stroked around her buttocks moving forward to her hips, and the ridge of her bones that led down — and a knot in her stomach suddenly tightened. His hands kept moving, almost tickling the sensitive skin of her stomach. They reached the front of her jeans and fumbled for a moment; then she felt the release as her button burst free. The chill in her stomach turned cold, very cold.

Sun An pulled her zipper down.

"I love," he was struggling to talk because he was so entranced; "you," as he pulled her jeans down off her hips — and reached one hand down into her underwear. He slipped his finger inside her, felt himself stiffen as he explored her insides. Her precious and hidden insides, that were intoxicatingly warm and wet and shapeless.

Sun An moaned and kissed Peach's neck: a wet kiss that left a cooling patch of saliva on her skin. He started to wrench his own trousers open, took her hand and pushed it down.

Peach didn't know how to stop this from happening. She opened her eyes and concentrated on what and where he was taking her hand, wanting to stop.

Sun An kept pulling the front of his pants open. His penis

flopped against her skin. It was hot and throbbing and smooth. Peach flinched.

She pushed away; tried to step back but he pulled her close again. "I'm sorry," he told her as she tried to pull her clothes back over her body. "I'm sorry," he said, "I love you."

Peach tried to pull her clothes straight as her throat tightened like a screw, twisting out tears, but Sun An hugged her close and she found she could hardly move.

"I'm sorry," Sun An said.

Peach wrinkled her face up. Froze. This isn't happening, she thought.

His voice kept saying "I love you, I love you," and she was thinking, This isn't happening, this isn't happening. This is *not* happening.

Again Peach tried to push away, but he held her tight. This is not happening. She felt his hand moving in rhythm with his voice. "I love you — I love you — I love you — I love you —" He pressed her even closer, his hand moving up and down and his breathing harder. She remembered going to the ice-cream parlor with her mother. The ice cream in her mouth. Her mother's face when the man told her there was no bargaining in the shop. I don't want to have my hair cut. She saw Da Shan flying her kite. His fingers.

Peach pushed back again, but Sun An held her fast and she was too frightened to shout or scream, just wanted it to be over and willed herself away from here as he moaned in her ear. She thought of the kite. Flying. "I love you — I love you — I love," between gritted teeth then clenched up and Peach felt something warm and wet squirt onto her hand and she screamed.

He let go, but now she was free she didn't move. This isn't happening, as his *thing* spurted four more times.

Sun An's eyes were closed, his face was tortured.

This isn't happening.

She wiped the stuff off with her other hand and smelled it

and felt sick because it wouldn't come off. Wanted to feel a breeze in her hair and to fly her kite up and up.

Sun An looked down at the stain that lay in his lap, seeping into his clothes; felt exhausted and guilty. He stood up and took Peach in his arms, and his trousers fell down to his knees. He pressed her close into a hug from which there was no escape. His white underwear against her unzipped jeans. His wet patch against hers.

"I'm sorry," he mumbled, his voice calm as he squeezed her tighter and kissed the soft skin behind her left ear. "I love you." His voice so reasonable. So calm.

What had she done?

He looked down into her face. "I love you, Peach," he said, and she stared at him.

Flying a kite.

"Do you love me?"

Peach didn't know what to say, didn't care what she said. Didn't want to stay here, didn't understand how it had all happened.

Did this happen?

"Do you love me, Peach?" he asked, so reasonable.

This never happened, she tried to believe it, even though she couldn't.

"Yes," Peach said, saying anything to get out and away, and wash that stuff off her clothes and hands. "Yes, I do."

The next morning Da Shan woke with relief from a dream where he was back inside his ten-year-old self, trying to avoid the future by changing what he did and said; but his ten-year-old self made the exact same mistakes he'd made in his own life. He lay in bed and shuddered, there was no way back. Outside Madam Fan was singing:

> When beauty is past and youth is lost,
> Who will marry an old crone?

and Da Shan stood up, tried to shake the dream off, but it clung relentlessly to him.

"Why do you sleep all day?" his mother cursed when he came for breakfast. "Why do I deserve such a lazy son? You must have been switched at the hospital!"

"I have your eyes," he told her.

"You stole them as well!"

Da Shan sat watching his mother. He saw the wrinkles that spread from the corners of her eyes like fish tails, her hair almost entirely white. He was glad he'd come back home while his parents were still sharp, but it made it more difficult to ever leave again: if he did it would probably be for the last time. He could always come back to Shaoyang, but his parents would probably be gone.

"What are you staring at me like that for?" his mother demanded.

"Nothing."

She didn't believe him.

"Actually," Da Shan said, "I was thinking about the time I was given the picture of Mao as a prize, and how I couldn't put it on the wall."

"And?"

"And everyone said I was a counterrevolutionary because I wouldn't put his picture on the wall."

"And?"

"And that was all." He smiled innocently.

"Hmm!" she retorted.

Old Zhu came home before lunch carrying a large terra-cotta pot and a hopeful smile. His wife stared, as he tottered through the apartment to the balcony.

"What are you doing?" she called out, and there was a muffled response.

She stomped through to the balcony and repeated her question.

"I've got a plant pot," Old Zhu said.

"I can see that," she told him. "Where's it from?"

"There," he said.

"Where?"

He pointed down toward the factory gate. She followed his finger and saw a crowd of people and an old green army truck.

"They said they're closing the Number Eight Army Base, and they're selling the pots," Old Zhu said. "I managed to get one."

"Who are selling pots?"

"I don't know."

"And you believed them?"

"Of course. Does it matter?"

She wasn't sure it mattered or not, but she knew she didn't like having new pots on her balcony. "What are you going to do with it?" she demanded.

"Get some flowers," Old Zhu said.

"What happens if it falls off and kills someone — what will happen then?"

"Stop tempting Heaven," Old Zhu told her, and for once she was stumped for a reply. Her mind came up with a thousand retorts, but the moment had passed, it was too late. The next day Old Zhu returned with a chrysanthemum plant, put it next to the terra-cotta pot, as if he were arranging a marriage. The flower nodded and the deal was done.

As he potted the plant Old Zhu's wife watched him from the kitchen and shook her head. Stupid old man, she thought as the phone went, and she paused to see if her husband would get it. He didn't even react. Hmm! she thought to herself.

When she'd put the phone down she waited, but Old Zhu didn't even look around to see who it was.

"That was Fat Pan," she told him.

Old Zhu took another handful of soil and dropped it into place.

"He wanted Da Shan."

Old Zhu sat back on his heels to admire his plant.

"Which angle do you think is best?" he asked.

That afternoon a notice was posted on the factory notice board saying there would be a meeting in the Revolutionary Hall the next day to discuss the future of the factory. People stopped to read it as they passed by, and then walked on and thought: what was the point? The factory had closed already. There was nothing to discuss. Old Zhu heard about it but decided not to even go: he looked around him and decided to spend the afternoon tending his vegetables. His beans were starting the long climb up the bamboo poles, purple eggplants were beginning to curve like ox horns, the garlic shoots were dark and green. It was a summer garden bursting with life.

The matchmaker saw the notice on the way to visit Old Zhu's wife. If it meant more people losing their jobs then it was bad news for her. She stopped and tutted for an appropriate amount of time, then moved on.

She'd been meaning to visit Old Zhu's wife for quite some time: she couldn't have single young men in her neighborhood without feeling the urge to see them happily settled — for their own good, their parents' good and, she reasoned, the good of the Motherland. The urge was even stronger when the young men were rich: a matchmaker had to make a living somehow — and it was easier to find girls for rich men. In fact it was more a job of picking the right one from the crowd of hopefuls.

Old Zhu's wife rose late: the night had been perforated by rain and she'd felt cold during the night. The sky was a hammered gray, it crushed down upon the city, made her feel like eating mutton-broth noodles. She was thinking of where she could get sheep meat from when there was a knock on the door.

She saw it was the matchmaker and felt relief and disappointment at the same time. The two emotions tussled inside her, and disappointment soon won.

"Come in." Old Zhu's wife smiled, and the matchmaker came in, sat down.

"I hear the factory is closing," she announced.

"It is."

"Well," the matchmaker said, and then stripped Old Zhu's wife clean of gossip, taking in every piece of gossip about family rows, arguments and children come of age.

"And how is Madam Fan and her husband?"

"Just the same."

"Tut! She should divorce him," the matchmaker said. "I could find her a good husband, a nice old one — they're easier to manage."

Old Zhu's wife thought about Old Zhu and his plant pots and wasn't sure that was true at all.

"What has happened to Party Secretary Li's widow?"

"Oh, she's back," Old Zhu's wife said. "But I don't think she's interested."

The matchmaker made a mental note to check this out. When she had outstayed her welcome she stood up to go. Just as Old Zhu's wife was seeing her off from the door, her son arrived.

The matchmaker gave him a warm smile. "Your son is so handsome," she told Old Zhu's wife. She shooed the compliment away as if it were a bad smell, but the matchmaker stood wedged half in the doorway and half out, suddenly unsure whether now was the right time to leave, now that Da Shan was back. Her thick body wobbled in indecision and ended up outside the door.

"Well," she said, wistfully, "I suppose I'd better be off."

"You're always welcome!" Old Zhu's wife smiled too hard, felt it set solid on her face. "Go slowly!" she called out, "Go slowly!" and tried to stop smiling.

Despite the general apathy, about half the remaining workers did turn up to the meeting, to see if there was any chance to save their jobs, while a smattering of residents arrived to find out what was going to happen to the factory they had worked in all their lives.

When the room was a third full the leaders filed up to the stage, led by the Factory President and Party Secretary. There was a scruffy uniformity about them: suit trousers, open-necked shirts and sleeves rolled up to the elbow. They all sat down together and assumed dignified postures as the President cleared his throat and checked the microphone was working.

"Hello, hello," he said, tapping it with his right forefinger. The crowd's conversation rose a degree in response. The President looked up, and the crowd ignored him.

"Good afternoon," the President began, clearing his throat. "Comrades, workers — good afternoon," he said flatly, "on behalf of the Communist Party, Shaoyang Space Rocket Factory Sub-branch, greetings. This meeting is called to discuss the future of the Shaoyang Number Two Space Rocket Factory. . . ."

Da Shan sat at the back and watched the President begin to read through the pages of his speech. No one in the scattered audience seemed to be talking, but the hum of conversation stayed constant, occasionally rising or falling in response to the words of the speech.

"As we know, the factory was founded in 1952, three years after the liberation of the country from the Guomindang and Foreign Imperialists. The factory started its long and glorious life affiliated to The Number Three Correct Thinking Establishment Reform Camp for those abused by the Old Society and became an independent work unit in 1955, under the name Shaoyang Number One Steam Engine Factory. Great efforts were made to build the factory, under the wise leadership of the Communist Party and the guidance of Mao Zedong and the local leadership of a number of key workers."

There was a murmur, and Da Shan heard the name "Party Secretary Li" whispered among the older people present. The drone of the President's voice continued.

"The factory had a glorious beginning making steam engines for the industrialization of the country. How they carried the fame of Shaoyang to the four corners of the country! From corner to corner workers and comrades knew the name of Shaoyang. The whole country was united in love for our steam engines!

"In the Great Leap Forward the workers of the factory won high praise from the Provincial Government for their contribution to the effort to produce steel. In the food shortages of those same years, caused by natural events and the intervention of certain counterrevolutionary elements who wished for a return to the Old China . . ."

On and on the speech went, gliding through history with the guile of a snake. Not truth, that most shifting of absolutes, but a distorted reflection.

". . . and in the Cultural Revolution we supported the endeavors of the patriotic youth by making Chairman Mao badges, which were distributed free to all the young people who volunteered to go to the countryside to learn from the peasants . . ."

Da Shan sat and listened as the entire history of the factory was illuminated and titillated and smudged with facts. A final burst of glory before it was sold off to building contractors and the leaders retired on their bribes.

"And of course we were host to the great revolutionary, Zhou Enlai, who visited this factory in 1958, as part of the Bringing the Great Leap Forward to the Masses Campaign. And it was in his honor that the factory was renamed the Space Rocket Factory, carrying on steam engine production as well as making valuable contributions to the Chinese Space Endeavor. The factory was awarded Gold Prize twice for Revolutionary zeal and Silver for . . ."

Da Shan lay back and closed his eyes as page after page was read out, listing awards and events and praise won by workers of the factory for their participation in national campaigns.

". . . and from 1979 until the present day the factory has

striven to help build the Socialist Market Economy that was be-gun with the correct and wise implementation of the Open Door Policy."

A decade disappeared in a sentence of doublespeak. At the back of the hall Da Shan sat up — "What about June fourth?" he said, half laughing with anger and incredulity. A few people turned around, but most continued talking to one another as the President read from the page.

What about all those people?

What about Liu Bei?

What about me?

Da Shan had to get outside. Away from this world of illu-sions: allies, enemies, good and evil. His feet scuffed the bare concrete steps as he climbed back out into the warm daylight, stood in the speckled shadow of a beech tree. He took a deep breath, a flutter of birdsong made the meeting seem very far away and he looked up: white clouds floating past like a succession of dead friends.

*I*t rained for a week, a curtain of water that hid the world outside the factory, hemmed people in, restricted their imaginations. Da Shan and Old Zhu spent their time playing chess, trying to outfox each other with apparent displays of simplicity. On the fifth day the rain stopped and fringes of sunlight began to show around the clouds. It was their twelfth game of chess, each was still trying to outdo the other in modesty and guile. Old Zhu scratched his white hair, as thin as autumn grass, and acted as if he had no idea what to do next. Da Shan shrugged and admitted defeat with every move. It was a game of bluff and counter-bluff so complicated that neither of them knew that the end had come, till Old Zhu suddenly grinned and slapped his castle down on the table, the wooden counter clapping the table in surprise.

"Hmm!" Da Shan sat back. He looked at the table, but staring didn't make the counters change position at all. "Well, you won," he admitted. Old Zhu scratched his old head, acting as if he couldn't understand how.

"Another game?" he asked, offering his son a cigarette.

"It's time for dinner!" Old Zhu's wife intercepted.

They sat and ate a light supper of boiled rice and pickles, then Da Shan said he was going out. He hailed a taxi at the front of the factory and the driver pulled up against the curb and turned the lights on.

"Where to?" he asked.

"Three Happinesses Night Club."

Da Shan climbed in and the driver pulled away from the curb, missing second gear and making the car shudder. "Sorry," he said. "It's new."

Da Shan looked at the peeling plastic on the dashboard. "What do you mean it's new?"

"I mean," the driver said as he adjusted the clutch, "that it's new to me."

It was difficult finding the place in the center of town, so many buildings had been knocked down, rebuilt, and knocked down again over the years that each street started to look and feel the same. It wasn't the vague feeling of unfamiliarity that was so disconcerting, but the sense of dislocation.

At the Black Dragon Bridge the driver turned right at the traffic lights, drove down alongside the river. It looked black and bottomless, held the reflections of streetlights in silent suspension. The lights polished the surface clean of rubbish, but even through the closed window Da Shan could smell the stagnant water. The driver filled the silence with a story about how a peasant had gathered enough aluminum cans to send himself to university. Da Shan nodded at the appropriate moments, just enough to keep the story going as he scanned the neon signs ahead. It was strange that there were so many lights these days, when no one had any money. The whole city center was full of them, flashing sapphire, emerald, ruby red.

The driver seemed not to care that he was lost. Maybe it was something he was used to, Da Shan thought, as he checked his watch. He was going to be late.

At last they pulled up and asked an old man with a neatly ironed shirt and greased-back hair. "Over there." He pointed, and the taxi nosed its way down a back street Da Shan had forgotten was there. A small blue sign flashed apologetically: Three Happinesses Night Club. The driver smiled. He'd gone past this turn twice already and missed it completely. The fact left him strangely reassured. When life went too smoothly he got suspicious; it was as if fate were saving something big up for him.

Concrete stairs led up off the street, plain and unadorned. They led up to a carpeted landing where a piece of calligraphy hung in a red frame. The Limitless Nothing, it said in a swirl of black on white.

Da Shan pushed through the padded door and stepped into the teahouse lobby, a room dimly lit with red lights. He stopped for a moment to let his eyes accustom themselves to the gloom. A girl in a gold-sequined dress flickered like a flame as she glided out of the shadows to greet him: her skin was pale mauve, she smiled a pink smile.

"I'm here to see Fat Pan," Da Shan said.

The girl blushed a deeper shade of red. "Brigade Commander Pan?"

"Yeah. Is he here yet?"

"No," the girl said, leading him into the salon. She wore heels and flesh-tone pop-socks. Apart from the candles that flickered on the tables, there was no other lighting except the glitter of her sequined dress. It curved away in front of him, around the candlelit tables, like a comet negotiating the constellations. He followed her across the room to his table, sat down in an armchair. She left a menu on the table, then walked back through the night sky to the lobby, pop-socks and all.

Da Shan hunched forward into the candlelight to read the menu. There were four pages of teas listed. He flicked through them: Tibetan Flower, Iron Buddha, Peony, Pu Er, Jade Dragon Snow Mountain, they led like a trail to the last and most expensive: Jasmine White Tea, at two hundred yuan a pot.

"Jasmine White Tea," Da Shan told the girl when she returned, and she nodded.

"Anything to eat?"

"Sunflower seeds and aniseed plums."

"We don't have any aniseed plums."

"What do you have?"

"Haw Fruit Jelly and Brazil Nuts."

"How much?"

"Twenty yuan."

"No thanks."

The water was too hot so Da Shan took the lid off and a tail of steam floated up from the opening, kept hanging in the air as the tea steeped. After a few minutes Da Shan poured himself a cup of almost clear liquid. The flavor was so delicate it dissolved in his mouth. All memories are in the nose, the saying went, and the smell of jasmine always gave Da Shan a satisfied feeling.

Under an illuminated Fire Exit sign a black door swung open, and a thickset man in a white suit stepped out and walked to the stage. He turned a spotlight on, illuminated the piano a brilliant white. Da Shan checked his watch as the man sat down, adjusted the seat, and began to play.

The notes came singly at first, vibrating in the air; then they built up into strings and waves that rose and fell, tossing the pianist's torso from side to side like seaweed. He swayed and played and Da Shan could feel his breathing quicken toward the crescendo. At last the man lifted his fingers from the keyboard and the tune faded into silence. Da Shan clapped.

The pianist nodded once, put his fingers to the keyboard and began again: a patriotic song from the 2000 Olympic Bid. Da Shan had just about forgotten that he was here to meet Fat Pan when he heard his name being called and turned to see his friend's grinning face, one hand extended in greeting.

"Pan." Da Shan smiled as he stood up. "I thought you weren't coming."

"I wanted you to see this place, and enjoy it for a while."

"It's quite something."

"Yes, it is, isn't it." Fat Pan grinned, sitting down on the other side of the candle flame, the darkness of the room as a backdrop to his face, lit from underneath, that made his fat features exaggerated and sinister. "We've had this a few years now. It's one of our more classy places. It's actually the kind of place we want investment for. You know what I mean."

"I see." Da Shan smiled. It was too early to talk business.

They sat and chatted about inconsequential things, chancing haphazardly on mundane topics and opinions before Da Shan looked into Fat Pan's eyes and smiled. "I had no idea you were so high up in the army," he said. "That's pretty quick work."

"It was luck."

"You must have impressed someone."

"No." Fat Pan looked down bashfully. His flesh was too heavy on his face, losing the battle with gravity. "I always thought you'd be the high flier," he said, "but Da Shan, you got involved."

"You're right — I was stupid."

"If the wind's blowing east then go east."

"You're so right. Cigarette?"

"Thanks," Fat Pan said. He leaned forward to suck at the candle flame, then sat back and took a long drag. They continued talking, avoiding the topic of investment with neat turns to neutral topics of conversation. Old friends, things they remembered from their youth, news about the Space Rocket Factory. At last Da Shan sat forward and said, "Oh yes, about the project we were talking about," as if it had just crossed his mind. "I've spoken to some friends of mine," Da Shan continued, "and I'm glad to say they're happy to put up the money."

"But?"

"No buts."

Fat Pan looked with surprise at Da Shan. He'd never expected him to be able to come up with so much. Had his friend been that successful? Maybe he should have sailed west after all — the earth was round: you never knew what lay over the horizon.

When it was time to go Fat Pan and Da Shan came to blows over who should pay. Fat Pan pushed Da Shan back into his seat, tried to set off to the counter, but Da Shan grabbed his hand and pulled him back. They jostled for a few moments, and Da Shan's height gave him an advantage as he pushed Fat Pan back into his seat.

"Let me pay!" Pan insisted, but Da Shan would hear none of it.

"Don't be so formal," he said. "Sit down."

Fat Pan sat, but as he watched his friend go and pay he felt increasingly uncomfortable, as if he'd been somehow outmaneuvered.

The bill came to over three hundred yuan.

"What's that?" Da Shan asked, checking the list of numbers.

"That's the candle," the girl said. "They're twelve yuan each."

Da Shan nodded and handed over the money. On the way out he took hold of Fat Pan's arms and drew him aside, away from the shadows. "There was something else I wanted to ask you about," he said. "Have you spoken to your friends in the police?"

"Yes."

"And?"

"There will be no problem."

"Good," Da Shan said, shaking his hand for about ten seconds, "good. You know it's good to have friends you can rely on." He smiled. "And you and me, we go back such a long way."

"We do," Fat Pan said, turning away. "We do."

*I*t was an early summer's day when Fat Pan knocked on the door of the Drink and Dream Teahouse, stood back and fiddled with a brass button on his jacket. Swallows were swooping under the eaves and plucking insects out of the air as he fiddled and tapped his foot in mild irritation. He hadn't been here for a while; a long while at that, and to his surprise he could feel a little nervousness in the flutter of his heartbeat. Being nervous irritated him, and made him a little more nervous as well.

It was a long thirty seconds before the door opened and Mistress Zhang smiled out at him. "Hello," she said, her body cut in half by the partially open door, "have you come to drink tea?"

Mistress Zhang's steel-gray hair coiled up on her head like a snake, her narrow eyes sparkled with humor as she stepped back to let him in. She made Fat Pan feel slightly ridiculous, so he walked around in self-important half circles. A piece of Qing Dynasty calligraphy hung on the wall opposite the door; it was a large piece, written in seal script: *Advice to Men Visiting Brothels*. Fat Pan looked at it in surprise: it looked genuine. He had no idea how Mistress Zhang had kept this piece, through all the convulsions of the past. It was very much part of the Old China.

Fat Pan glanced at the first few admonitions: *Do not boast of your prowess as a lover. Do not make excuses for your failures,* and tried to look away. *Do not perform your toilet in the girl's presence. Do not spit on the matting.* He cleared his throat, turned to face Mistress Zhang and stated bluntly, "I'm thirsty."

"What tea would sir like?"

"What tea have you got?"

Mistress Zhang's mouth twitched at the corners, the beginning of a smile. "Well," she began, her face resisting humor's pull long enough to say, "we have Water-Spirit Flower; Cherry, of course Jade Lotus," without smiling.

"Ah." Fat Pan turned and took a few more steps so he could hear his heels clicking on the floor. *Do not believe her flattery or loving words. Do not flatter her with poems unless they are sincere.* He paused to peer into the fish bowl. The curved glass bent the goldfish into a ludicrous shape as it fanned itself with its voluminous fins. Fat Pan leaned forward from the waist and tapped the glass with a single forefinger. "Hello, beautiful!" The goldfish shot forward through the water, then stopped and stared back at him, resumed fanning itself. He tapped the glass again, the goldfish shot forward and Fat Pan laughed. Ha!

"I know Cherry has missed your attentions. Shall I see if she's available for you?" Mistress Zhang asked.

"No, not Cherry."

Mistress Zhang waited. Fat Pan completed his circuit of the room. "I want Pale Orchid," Fat Pan said.

"She's very busy today."

"Surely not so busy."

"I'm not sure she's in . . . ," Mistress Zhang began, but Fat Pan took her hand and patted it. It had a fifty-yuan note in it. She looked at the note, curling in her palm like a fortune fish, then closed her fingers upon it, turned to go.

"And," Fat Pan said, "I have this for her."

Mistress Zhang took the package and raised her fine painted eyebrows, as delicately curved as willow branches. Inside was an antique dress of blue silk and embroidered willows.

In the Studio of Contemplative Recline, the soft sofa cuddled Fat Pan's body. He tried to sit forward, had to push himself out of the cushions and sit on the hard edge. He absentmindedly pulled his trouser legs up to his knees, picked up the microphone and used the remote to turn the karaoke video on. It showed a Western city in winter, snow, clusters of naked trees decorating the horizon. He scratched the back of a calf as the title came up on the screen: *The Girl Opposite*. Fat Pan shuffled forward and cleared his throat. The tune began, strong and rhythmic, a bouncing ball showed when to sing the words.

The girl opposite looks at me, looks at me, looks at meee . . . Fat Pan tapped his knee as he sang off-key and loud, *The girl opposite looks at me, looks at me . . .*

Mistress Zhang hurried up the back stairs to where the girls sat, playing cards. "It's Fat Pan," she said, and Cherry winced. Mistress Zhang patted her head. "Don't put on airs," she told the girl, "he's tired of you long ago. Why do you think he stopped coming? You putting on all kinds of pretensions. No, today it's Pale Orchid's turn." She ignored the groans of protest and handed her the package. "And put this on."

Liu Bei refused to move.

"The stream of men is an endless river," Mistress Zhang quoted, "and whores have no right to be fussy where they land!"

Still Liu Bei didn't move.

"Get up!" Mistress Zhang snapped at last, pulling her from the chair and pushing the bundle into her arms, "his money is as good as any other's!"

Fat Pan was still singing pop songs when Mistress Zhang came in and found him on the sofa. *Your heart is far too soft, far too soft . . .* he sang, and from the doorway she cleared her throat. "Pale Orchid is ready."

Fat Pan stopped singing and stood up. Sunlight filtered through the window, absentmindedly casting shadows across the floor. He passed through the yard, where a leaf swung down to the ground and a black rook flapped overhead. The people on the video kept moving as Fat Pan started up the stairs, his footsteps echoing through the timber building, summoning ghosts from a hundred years. On the TV screen the ball bounced silently along the words, in the back room the girls looked up and listened as the footsteps came closer. Cherry shuffled the cards then paused, wrinkled up her nose.

"I can smell him from here," she spat.

"Are you sure he isn't coming for you?" Water-Spirit Flower teased, and Cherry punched her on the thigh.

"Ssshh!" She kept on dealing the cards as Fat Pan's footsteps moved along the balcony. Premonition wrinkled her spine, she heard a door open, held her breath, pictured Fat Pan in the doorway, licking his lips, then heard him step inside and shut the door. Then she smiled with pleasure.

"Poor Orchid," Lotus whispered.

"Pa!" Water-Spirit Flower said. "She gets all the old men, spends most of the time making them tea! It's about time she did some work."

"Yeah," Cherry sniggered, "serves her right!"

Liu Bei reclined on a black-lacquer bed, striped sheets over the mattress, a matching quilt rolled up at the end of the bed. Her face was powdered white, her eyes lined, her black hair pinned up behind her head. She wore a red dress with embroidered flowers, clip-on butterfly earrings, a plastic-pearl noose draped around her neck. Light perforated the closed shutters, giving the room a cool twilight feel. In the darkness a red light bulb on a shelf illuminated a cheap plastic statue of Guanyin, gazing down at the bed; her hands raised in an expression of inner peace.

"Pale Orchid." Fat Pan had a hint of a smile. "It's been a long time."

Liu Bei nodded, her face too made up to betray any expression.

"How are you?" She didn't answer, but he could feel her stiffen as he sat near her on the bed, put a hand on the bed between them and leaned forward into the gap. "OK, don't talk to me." He took off his army cap and put it on the bed behind him, then slipped off his shoes. "I was only being polite."

Fat Pan held her eyes with his own, as his hand scuttled across the bed and onto her dress. "It has been a long time," he repeated, slower than before. His hand crawled into the hollow of her dress, found the warm softness of her thigh. "I've been very busy," he said. "Otherwise I could come and see you more often."

His hands unbuttoned her dress, let her breasts spill out. "Ah." He smiled and she tilted her face away, eyes averted as his hands moved over her body. In her mind she tried to turn the stabbing sunlight into fingers of moonlight tracing the walls; to think of her mouth full of winter melon soup; of anything but the present. She focused on the statue of Guanyin, felt herself looking down: saw Fat Pan take off his jacket and shirt; pull his belt open, lift himself up high enough to pull his trousers down, and push his y-fronts down his legs. His y-fronts caught on one of his feet, then fell to the floor in an abandoned heap of clothing: an army officer costume.

His legs were hairless, except for the shins, which had thick wiry curls. Guanyin watched him smooth the embroidered silk over Liu Bei's pale flesh, massage her thighs, push the red silk up her legs, pull her underwear off. Fat Pan positioned himself between Liu Bei's legs and slipped a finger inside.

Liu Bei struggled to concentrate on the statue's gaze but couldn't keep it up. She could feel the rough stubble on his chin and his hot, smoky breath panting over her skin. She closed her eyes as he licked her breast, moved up her body to nibble her ear.

"I see your temple is ready," he said, his voice cracking with excitement as he lay on top of her, then sent his bald-headed monk in to worship.

He moved in and out, she could feel him filling her again and again. She felt no pleasure. "Is this how you were for him?" Fat Pan's voice came soft and insistent like groping hands. "I want to hear," his voice was hoarse, "that moan."

He licked her neck and shoulder, tried to kiss her lips, but she turned her face away to the side.

"You want to turn away," he whispered, "then turn away." There was a moment's silence then he pulled himself out; instructed her: "Fire Behind the Mountain," and turned her over onto her side. Liu Bei tried to concentrate on the memory of a leaf on a pond: imagined it was a lone flake of sail floating away across the sea as his hands spread her buttocks and the memories faltered. She could feel his finger trying to find her anus, leading himself in. She gasped as he pushed deeper. Squeezed her eyes shut. Flinched.

Fat Pan grasped Liu Bei's hips and thrust till she moaned. "Is that good?" he asked her. "Is that good?"

Liu Bei bit her finger harder.

"I'm going to fuck you so hard." Fat Pan was breathless. He thrust in; pulled out; thrust again. "Is this how you were for him?" His rhythm speeded up. He relished each twitch she gave until he ejaculated inside, then tried to keep going.

Liu Bei felt his thrusts fade to nothing, like ripples on water, and reached behind. His penis was small and soft, like a child's. It slipped out.

Fat Pan's face was over hers. He kissed her neck and Liu Bei stared up at Guanyin on her high shelf, hands still raised in a gesture of peace and pink cheeks blushing with shame.

It was late afternoon when Liu Bei left the teahouse and got back to her mother's house. An afternoon shower had settled the dust, a few errant leaves lay scattered on the dirt. Aunty Tang silently watched her approach, she didn't need to say anything, she just licked her lips with her tongue and squinted. Liu Bei ignored her, marched inside and found Little Dragon sitting at the table, drawing with straight, deliberate pencil strokes: an airplane.

"Come on," Liu Bei snapped before he'd even noticed her, "it's time to go home."

"Grandma's going to cook winter melon soup," Little Dragon protested, his pencil poised.

"No time for soup. Mother has to go."

"But I want the soup," he said and started crying.

Liu Bei yanked him off the seat. He started crying so much his legs stopped working, so Liu Bei swept him up into her arms and carried him out of the house, past Aunty Tang and through the winding streets of the old town, where people stared and shook their heads. When they got home Little Dragon had cried himself almost to exhaustion, and he was still sniffling and glaring through his tears as his mother went outside to get the washing in.

The clothes were flapping angrily on the line, it looked like it was going to rain. A pair of Little Dragon's trousers were fully inflated by the breeze, she grabbed a kicking leg, tore off the pegs and threw them into the basket.

"Stop crying!" she snapped when she came inside, and Little Dragon did, long enough to take a breath of air and begin again. Liu Bei ignored him as she cooked him a dinner of greens and reboiled rice. Slowly his tears ebbed away and he got up and walked across to his mother, held on to her leg.

"I'm sorry," she said, lifting him up. "Mother is sorry." Outside the wind grew stronger, bringing the dust to life and sending it around the yard like a crowd of starving ghosts. On the horizon the clouds gathered in force, then rumbled in over the city. The temperature dropped, the wind stilled and they ate in silence, listening to the crunch of food between their jaws. There was an angry clap of thunder. "Eat up," she said.

"I'm not hungry," Little Dragon told her. There was a flash of lightning, which seemed to back Little Dragon up so Liu Bei clicked the TV on and let him watch while she gathered up the pots and put them on the shelves. There were only ads, ads or another Beijing Opera. He turned on to the ads.

Liu Bei boiled water for the thermos flasks and tried not to think of the afternoon with Fat Pan, as outside stars were picked off, one by one, by storm clouds that turned the heavens black.

*T*here were a few more days of rain before the impatient summer settled in for good at Shaoyang. Cold weather staples of lotus root, cabbage and white radish disappeared from the market. In the fields the rice stalks grew tall and emerald green, and in the market all people could buy were piles of lettuce hearts, bamboo shoots or bulging purple eggplant. Trucks rumbled into town from the outlying towns and villages, their tip-ups full of bloated watermelons that dusty men sold by the pair. Earthworms hid deep underground, and in the country whole villages slept, waiting for harvest.

In the city, people began to view summer like a visiting relative: a pleasure at first but increasingly unwelcome. It got too hot to lie-in in the mornings, too hot to stay awake in the afternoons. New high-rises blocked the cool hill breezes, lonely people wandered streets of neon signs and concrete that they no longer knew. In the Space Rocket Factory people snoozed off the hottest hours of the day and woke to find flies crawling up their noses or investigating their ears; when they lay down at night they watched the moon rise, and after hours of tossing and turning they watched it set as well. It was only by sleeping on the concrete floor that people managed to get any sleep at all; dreaming of winter as they simmered gently in sweat.

At the beginning of the sixth month the first truckloads of lychees arrived from Hainan Island, priced at nine yuan a half kilo. Old Zhu's wife pushed through the crowd at the back of the truck, then turned the salesman down in disgust. Nine yuan — too much! It wasn't even worth bargaining. She continued prowling around the market, hungry for the new summer foods but bitter at the price she would have to pay. She walked up and down, then decided she needed an umbrella to keep the sun off.

At the factory gateway a group of workmen with ladders and distinct Sichuan accents were removing the signs that had been there so long people couldn't remember what was there before them. The wooden board that said Work to Build the Four Modernizations lay in shreds at the side of the road. Two men were levering Shaoyang Number Two Space Rocket Factory off with crowbars and across the top half the sign had been ripped away, so it now said *r In Ve t Ment*.

Old Zhu's wife squinted up into the sunlight, trying to pronounce the foreign writing, letter by letter, but couldn't. When she'd been at school they'd learned Russian; everyone had learned Russian until Khrushchev had become a revisionist, then all the Russians had left, abandoning their socialist cousins. Now the newspapers said there were Russian whores in Beijing. Spreading diseases.

Old Zhu's wife was still squinting up at *r In Ve t Ment* when she felt someone grab her hand, and jumped. It was the local matchmaker, back again.

"How's your son?" The matchmaker grinned, and Old Zhu's wife couldn't answer. She didn't want a matchmaker getting involved. They only put a couple together, they never cared what happened in the rest of their lifetimes.

"I have a girl who's ideal for him," the matchmaker continued. "She's an 'elder unmarried youth.'"

"What does that mean?"

"She's just turned thirty-one."

"Is she divorced?"

"No, no, nothing like that."

"Then what's wrong with her?"

"She's just a little bit slow, you know how girls are now — they go to university and get ideas. Not like us."

Old Zhu's wife didn't know what the matchmaker meant by "us." She'd been a cadre, she was educated, well educated and married; the matchmaker was a lazy busybody!

"Your son was born in the Year of the Rat, yes?"

"Yes, but he's divorced," Old Zhu's wife said, trying to fend the woman off.

The matchmaker was unperturbed. "Divorced is OK these days," she assured, "especially if you're a man."

"He won't marry any 'elder unmarried youth.'"

"Who then?"

"It seems he won't marry anyone," Old Zhu's wife said, and started away. She was sweating, and the sweat made her feel more uncomfortable. How should she know what her son got up to — she was only his mother.

When Old Zhu's wife got back home she found Da Shan and Old Zhu sitting in front of the TV with a bunch of lychees, spitting the glossy brown nuts onto the floor and filling the table with cracked red shells. It was too hot to play chess these days, and anyway Da Shan had started to win: it took the fun out of playing for both of them.

"They're good," Da Shan said, wiping his chin, moving over to give her room to sit.

"Where did you get those?"

"In the town center. Fresh from Hainan." He held a lychee up for her, but she didn't move.

"How much did you pay?"

"Eight and a half yuan a kilo."

"You were robbed," she told him. "You ought to bargain."

Old Zhu's wife went to the kitchen and set down her shopping. She tipped her minced pork into a wide bowl, took her cleaver and began to shred the lettuce. When she'd minced the gingerroot she squeezed the juice out of the lettuce, tipped it all into the bowl.

"Come and eat!" she heard her husband call, and throttled the pork mixture between her fingers. Come and eat indeed, as if she had the time to come and eat when she was making dumplings. She kept squeezing as she thought about the matchmaker. The phrase "Elder unmarried youth" kept coming into her head. Is that what her son had sunk to? There was a time when he had so much ahead of him: he could have been leader of the factory by now, she told herself, if that girl hadn't got him involved. She blamed Liu Bei for everything that had gone wrong in her son's life, whether it was her fault or not. She blamed Liu Bei for many other things as well, just to stoke her indignation. If it hadn't been for Liu Bei her son wouldn't have gone off to Guangdong, got married and got divorced. If it hadn't been for Liu Bei she would have a grandson: here, in Shaoyang — and not a granddaughter she'd never met in Guangdong. She thought of her granddaughter like a Missing Person. Investing love in a Missing Person was like watering your neighbor's field, there was no sense in it at all.

It was all Liu Bei's fault. But what could you expect from a whore's daughter? Things like that ran in the family — the sunflower cannot stop itself, it always turns toward the sun. That was the nature of things. Whoever heard of a pig giving birth to a goose?

"There aren't many left," Old Zhu called out from the other

room, but she couldn't go and eat when she was making dumplings; and besides, lychees that cost so much would make her sick.

After her afternoon sleep, Old Zhu's wife got up and walked, bleary-eyed, to the toilet. She squatted and wiped herself with some toilet paper, turned the tap to flush away the yellow puddle. The dry pipe croaked back at her. She hoped a spout of water might follow the noisy rush of air, but instead the sound faded away; diminishing as it disappeared down the building. She checked the taps in the kitchen: they gave dry and malevolent hisses as well.

Old Zhu's wife looked out of the window and saw the blue sky and the sharp divide between sunlight and shadow. It was too hot to be without water, so she went into the cupboard and took the two buckets out, and set off down the stairs, the empty buckets flapping excitedly at her sides.

Outside the afternoon cicadas' shrill had thickened to an incessant scream. One tree-load would fade away, then another would start up: a whole orchestra of insects playing the same interminable note. People were waiting at the standpipe, standing in the shade with their buckets. Old Zhu's wife joined them, and turned to find a young girl take her buckets to fill them up. Old Zhu's wife thought the girl was trying to steal her buckets, so she shouted in alarm and tried to snatch them back.

"Let me help you," the girl said, but Old Zhu's wife didn't listen. The girl fought back, so they struggled for a few seconds before Old Zhu's wife realized what was happening and gave in. She stood, feeling foolish, watching the girl put the bucket on the floor and turn the tap on full, checking she got it right. The water gushed noisily into the buckets, spraying up at first then charging around and around in a foaming whirlpool. The girl left the tap on as she switched buckets, splashing water everywhere and making Old Zhu's wife's feet squeak in her plastic slippers.

When the buckets were full the girl tried to carry the buckets, but Old Zhu's wife would have none of it. "I'll take them," she said. "Don't be so polite."

Halfway home Old Zhu's wife wished she hadn't said that, or that the girl hadn't filled her buckets so full. She wasn't as young as she used to be, and water was heavy. Old Zhu's wife set them down and changed hands, although it didn't make much difference as she tottered along. The buckets bumped against her legs. She'd spilled half the water, but now they felt heavier than before. She rested under a shrilling cicada tree, saw a swallow swoop down in front of her and pluck a hovering dragonfly from the air.

A flash of turquoise, gone to bird food.

The water-cut struck all of Shaoyang. There was no news as to why it had happened, and no one cared, they just picked up their buckets and tramped to the nearest standpipe. Standpipes never ran out, they were something you could rely on, like the coolness of autumn. Liu Bei was filling up her buckets when the old man in front of her said, "This always happens when the weather is at its hottest, never when it's cold."

Liu Bei was thinking of something else. She half listened, half nodded.

"Never when it's cold," the old man repeated, "nor when it's dry. But only in the summer, when it's at its hottest."

"Yes, it's true," Liu Bei said just to shut him up.

She watched the water splashing into the buckets and thought it was the same with the teahouse. Men never came to drink when it was at its hottest, they only needed warmth when it was cold. It was at this time that she began to feel lonely. As she shuffled closer to the standpipe the idea made her smile to herself: a lonely whore!

The drought lasted for two whole days; gurgling pipes gasping for water. When the water did come back Old Zhu's wife was out buying bean sprouts. Old Zhu heard the sound of splashing water, ran to the kitchen, and saw rust-colored liquid and lumps of dirt drip-dribbling out of the tap. He turned it on full, even turned the tap on in the toilet and let the filthy water wash out. It took over an hour.

When the water was clear Old Zhu filled all the buckets, just in case, then put a kettle on to boil. It took more than an hour to cool in the heat, then he tasted it, still warm. It tasted salty, he decided, and turned the taps on again. They were still on when his wife came back from Autumn Cloud's house. She put a bag of bean sprouts down on the side and then went into the bedroom for a lie down. Old Zhu watched her come into the kitchen and then go out again, and decided to water his chrysanthemum. It needed daily water now it was hot. He usually watered it in the evenings, but his wife had been watching him the last two days.

"Don't think I carry water in buckets for you to water your flower!" she'd told him.

Old Zhu didn't know what to say then, he watered it with the water he carried. Not hers.

Old Zhu's wife lay thinking of her unmarried son and tried to think who she could turn to for help. Autumn Cloud came to mind, but Old Zhu's wife dismissed her. She was too old to know girls for Da Shan, and what did old people know of affairs of the heart?

She thought about Mrs. Cao. Even worse. May as well put it on the national radio news.

At last Old Zhu's wife decided on Madam Fan. Her daughter, Peach, must have some friends who could be suitable for Da Shan. Not too pretty, nor too clever — it didn't make for a happy marriage — but not an idiot either. And not "elder unmarried youth."

When Madam Fan listened to the old woman's problem she was so excited she wanted to clap her hands together. "Your son needs a girl," she laughed, "and my girl needs a son!"

"I didn't mean your daughter," Old Zhu's wife began, but Madam Fan cut her off.

"I was joking," she said, "but why not? Let's invite you all for a meal, then they can meet each other. They're both adults, they can decide."

Old Zhu's wife nodded and then Madam Fan did clap her hands: Heaven *was* kind!

All her daughter needed was a little encouragement, and you never got oil without applying a little pressure.

*M*adam Fan stood on her balcony and tried vainly to suppress a long, slow yawn. Dawn was still half an hour away: the world was pale and colorless. She shivered briefly and cleared her throat, and thought of all the food she had to get for lunch. It was too early for singing, she decided, better to go shopping.

Madam Fan pulled the door behind her as quietly as she could, and fumbled across the dark room. Her purse was on the shelf by the door, she thought, and her hand crawled along the shelves until she found it. She slipped it into her pocket as she unlocked the front door and stepped out into the cold light of dawn.

Madam Fan caught a flicker of movement on the edge of her sight as she walked toward the gate. It took a moment for her eyes to adjust to the shadow under the trees, then she could see the man dressed in white practicing tai chi: the scrunch of gravel as he moved his feet, his arms and legs moving with the slowness and elegance of a dream. She didn't stop, but kept on walking down to the gate. The dawn sky had a green sheen, it seemed to be an auspicious sign for the day ahead. Nothing would go wrong today she decided as she walked under the factory gate. Nothing.

The first peasant Madam Fan came across wore a Russian hat with sticking-out earflaps that made him look half man half dog. She picked through the pile of cucumbers at his feet while he rubbed his blue hands against the dawn chill, and stared down at her.

"How much a kilo?" she demanded, turning cucumbers over and squeezing them.

"One yuan," the man croaked.

"For this rubbish?!"

He nodded.

"Wah!" she said and walked on.

Madam Fan stopped at the next, but the price was the same. These days everything was so expensive: it was too difficult to treat friends. Prices were like floodwater, she thought, they just kept on rising.

At the end of the row the chicken seller had filled his bamboo crate with clucking fowl. Madam Fan lifted the lid and reached a hand inside. There was a surprised squawk as her fingers closed on a chicken, then the sound of flapping wings. She felt the bird's breast for meat and then let it go and searched for another, sending off another flurry of startled squawks.

The stall owner squatted behind, warming a pot of water on a coal stove as he watched her. "Native chickens," he declared as he lit his cigarette, and blinked away the acrid smoke.

Madam Fan was still rummaging inside the crate with her hand. "How much a kilo?" she called out.

"Twenty yuan."

"Too expensive!"

The man took no notice, but crouched by the coal stove and sucked in his first drag of the cigarette: complaints were expected.

Madam Fan's fingers soon closed on a chicken that felt right. She pulled it out of the crate and held it up. The chicken blinked a reptilian eye at her. She massaged its legs and breast and it let out a long nervous squawk. Another squeeze and she dropped it back in the crate and reached for another. Too thin.

"Native chickens," the man said again, standing up. "Good for the blood. Keep you warm."

Madam Fan took no notice. He irritated her, what with his black-stained teeth and promiscuous familiarity. The fact that he annoyed her annoyed her even more, because today was such a special day. *No one* was going to irritate her today.

Eventually Madam Fan pulled out another chicken. It struggled and flapped its wings for a moment, then gave up. Its legs were fleshy and soft, the breast full of meat. She checked its gullet wasn't full of grain, ran finger and thumb down the legs just to make sure and then handed it to the man and said, "I'll take this one."

The chicken let out another curious squawk as the man tied its feet together and hung it on his scales. "One and three quarter kilos," the man said, picking up his knife.

Madam Fan nodded.

"Do you want the blood?"

"Yes, please."

The chicken squawked as its throat was pulled back. The note of tentative protest turned to alarm and pain as the knife began to slice, then the squawk was cut short and all that remained was a bloody froth of bubbles. The blood dripped into a plastic bag as the man held the thrashing legs and wings firmly. Finally he dropped the bird to the ground and it flapped and kicked in the mess of blood and dirt.

"Can you put some vinegar with that," Madam Fan said as he tied the top of the bag. "I don't want it all to congeal."

He nodded again and nudged the chicken with his toe to see if it was dead. Madam Fan looked away and rubbed her hands against the chill. In her head she went through the list of dishes she was going to cook. She didn't want to wait here while he plucked and gutted it, she still had all the other shopping to do!

"I'm going to buy some vegetables," Madam Fan told the man. He didn't take any notice. "Heh!" Madam Fan shouted. "I'm going to buy some vegetables."

"All right, all right," the man said through his cigarette stub, "I'll be here." He picked the limp chicken up by one leg and dropped it into a clear pot of water, staining it red. "I'm not going anywhere."

The only people who visited Liu Bei's house were lost and looking for somewhere else, so the sudden knock on her door disturbed her. She dropped the clothes back into the tub and dried her hands as the knocking continued.

"I'm coming!" she shouted.

"It's me!"

"Mother?"

"Yes!"

Liu Bei unlocked the door and turned back to the washtub as her mother came in and put her bag of shopping down on the table. "I've bought some pork," her mother said. "Where's Little Dragon?"

"He's out playing."

"Who with?"

"His friends," Liu Bei said, picking up the pork. "Why have you brought this?" she asked.

"He's looking too thin. You don't feed him enough. You should be a better mother."

Liu Bei didn't answer, pulled the clothes out of the water and started rubbing them against the board.

"Look at yourself!"

"Mother," Liu Bei warned.

Her mother began to cry, but stifled the tears as they came out, and bit her lip. "Your father and I were so proud, and now look at you," she said.

Liu Bei rubbed.

"What have you done with your life?"

Liu Bei rubbed.

"Why did you get involved?"

And then rinsed the clothes one by one.

"Didn't I tell you?"

"Yes, you did."

"But would you listen?"

"No, I didn't."

"And now look at you."

Liu Bei sat up and wiped her hair back from her face with her shoulder, keeping her dripping hands away from her.

"Mother, why did you come here?" she asked.

"I wanted to tell you."

"What?"

"Before anyone else told you. I wasn't going to — but there you go."

Liu Bei looked away and said with exasperation, "Mother — what are you talking about?"

"I wanted to tell you," Liu Bei's mother trailed off into silence, unable to bring herself to tell Liu Bei her news. "I wanted to tell you," she repeated, wriggling closer to the point of her visit, "I wanted to tell you — Old Zhu's son is back in town."

Liu Bei stopped and looked up. "Da Shan?"

"Yes."

She dropped the washing and pushed the hair from her face. "How do you know?"

"I saw him," she said. "He came to the house." Liu Bei searched her mother's face, but it was set firm.

"And?"

Liu Bei's mother struggled with the words. "He wanted to know where you were," she said at last.

"Did you tell him?"

"Of course I didn't."

"Why not?"

"Because he abandoned you!" Liu Bei's mother said, mining an old vein of anger.

Liu Bei swore as she dumped the clothes into a basket and took them out to hang them out on the line. This was the last thing she needed. Shit.

Shit!

Liu Bei threw the clothes over the line, where they flapped in the gentle breeze. She pinned them to the line with wooden pegs, but they still waved arms and legs at one another in a childish dance. Liu Bei rested her head against the line for a moment. There was no point. What else could she do?

"Mother!" Liu Bei shouted through the door. "Can you look after Little Dragon when he comes back?"

Her mother's voice came back from inside, tinted with suspicion: "Why?"

"I'm going out."

Her mother's face appeared at the door, her hands smeared with minced pork and held up so as not to touch anything. "You're not going to see him, are you?"

"Yes," Liu Bei said, "I am."

Madam Fan's apartment was seething with activity all morning as meat was chopped and vegetables were sliced. Peach was in charge of gutting the chicken and chopping it into small pieces, while Madam Fan tried to keep herself calm as she talked and scurried around, checking that everything was going according to plan.

"How are you doing?" she fussed. "Where is your father? You did tell him the right time, didn't you?"

"Yes!" Peach said for the tenth time as she tipped the chopped-up chicken fragments into a bowl and sprinkled them with salt and soy sauce. "I told him."

Good, Madam Fan thought. She didn't want him letting her down today. He only had so many duties as a husband, and he wasn't very good at any of them.

Peach wiped the blood off the chopping board into the sink and used her arm to brush her hair back from her face. "What needs doing next?"

"The fish."

Peach sighed and rinsed her hands. "Where is it?"

"In the fridge," Madam Fan said.

The blue carp was wrapped in a plastic bag on the top shelf of the fridge, flicking its tail in a languid dream of rustling plastic. She took it out of its bag and rinsed it under the cold water tap and the fish revived a little. Its tail was beginning to flap in appreciation as she held it down on the chopping board and sliced off its head, then slashed open the stomach from gills to tail. She thought of Sun An's thing, squirting on her hands and clothes, as she pulled all the twisted entrails out and threw them into the bin. A dead fish and a slippery and stinking mess.

Madam Fan came back in a swirl of air. "How are you doing?" she asked over Peach's shoulder as she scaled the fish. "Have you finished?"

"I think so," Peach said, putting the fish down and wiping the side of the sink.

"Good. Leave that now. I'll do that. Go and get yourself washed and dressed. I want you to look pretty today."

Peach wasn't listening. She washed her hands, sniffed them to check they no longer smelled. Not only of fish, but also of Sun An.

Old Zhu's wife spent the morning fussing to hide her nervousness. Da Shan had gone out after breakfast and hadn't come back. He knows the time, Old Zhu's wife told herself, he won't be late. While she worried, Old Zhu gave his vegetable plot a quick tour of inspection, checked on the tomatoes and picked off some snow peas, then carried them upstairs.

"Look!" he announced to his wife, who looked. "The tomatoes are doing well too," he said. She smiled.

As his wife swept the floor and dusted the tabletop Old Zhu smoked on the balcony, admiring his chrysanthemum. There were two heavy white flowers, bobbing contentedly on the air. He tried to remember the line from Du Fu's poetry: when the flowers open they open my tears — or something like that; it sounded better when Du Fu said it. Something about the flower's precarious glory and the grieving wind. Or was that from a different poem? Old Zhu was still trying to remember when his wife came and stood on the balcony and stared down toward the factory gate. She looked for her son but saw only strangers coming and going and getting in each other's way. So many faces she didn't know: and no sign of Da Shan.

"Wah!" she said at last, and Old Zhu looked up.

"Hmm?" he asked.

"What time is it?"

"Eleven thirty."

"We'd better be going. Come on."

It wasn't Madam Fan who opened the door, but her husband. He didn't like it when his wife's friends came over and outnumbered him in his own house; but at least it gave him a chance to drink.

"Come in, come in," he said to the old couple, pulling them through the door. He dragged them across the room to the sofa, and he pushed them into it: "Don't be so shy!" he said. "Sit down!"

Old Zhu and his wife were relieved to see Madam Fan coming out of the kitchen wiping her hands. She stopped and looked at them and frowned. "What's happened to Da Shan?"

"He's coming," Old Zhu's wife said.

"Oh," Madam Fan said, and let out a long tense breath. "So," she started. "What can I get you?"

"Nothing."

"Are you sure?"

"Really."

"Tea?"

Old Zhu was about to agree to tea when his wife cut him short.

"Nothing," she said. "Nothing at all."

"You must have something," Madam Fan's husband insisted, and told Peach to go and get some tea for the guests. They sat stiffly as Peach pulled the stopper from the top of the thermos and then filled both their cups. The green tea leaves floated up and swirled in a miniature eddy, then slowly began to sink.

"Are you hot?" Madam Fan's husband demanded.

"No," Old Zhu and his wife insisted, but he was already on his feet, moving the fan and aiming it at his guests. He put it on setting number three and pressed the start button. The fan whirred to life and Old Zhu's wife shivered. "Is there anything else I can get you?" Madam Fan's husband asked.

"Nothing," she stated. "Thank you."

"Are you sure?" he called over the electric whirr of air.

"Yes."

Madam Fan's husband pushed through the bead curtains into the bedroom. The beads rattled against one another as they swung back in place, rippled gently. There was a couple of seconds when the beads hung still before he pushed back through them, a couple of ten-yuan notes in his hand.

"I'm just going to get some wine," he told his guests. "You sit there."

"Not for me," Old Zhu's wife told him, but the metal door swung shut and Old Zhu let out a sigh of relief.

They all sat in silence, the fan contentedly whirring away to itself. At last Peach spoke. "Well," she began, then stopped. "Well," she tried again, "I'm glad you've both come."

"Thank you," Old Zhu's wife said, and then the silence returned. Peach played with her fingers and concentrated on the sounds of her mother cooking in the kitchen; the hiss of spitting fat and the scrape of metal as her mother stirred the wok. She could still feel her cheeks warming. She didn't know what to say to the old pair.

Her father came back and held up the bottle: Open Your Mouth and Smile Wine. "Shaoyang's best!" he declared. It was good strong stuff, to get the guests drunk. As he unscrewed the top there was a knock on the door. Madam Fan came sweeping out of the kitchen, wiping her hands on a tea towel, and saw her daughter looking at her hands, acting dowdy. "Come on, Peach!" she said. "Don't just sit there — go answer the door!"

It was Da Shan. He came inside and stood in the middle of the room, everyone smiling at him, waiting for him to do something. "Well," he said, "it smells delicious — almost as good as my mother's cooking!"

Ha! Ha! Ha! they all laughed, even Madam Fan's husband, whose grinning teeth bit his cigarette as he took Da Shan's hand and pulled him across to a seat. "Come in, sit down," he said, "don't be shy." Da Shan resisted at first, but he didn't want to look too polite so he let Madam Fan's husband drag him across the room and push him back into his seat.

"Ah, Da Shan!" Madam Fan said, clapping her hands in excitement. "Welcome! Welcome!"

Da Shan saw the half-drunk cups of tea, could smell the cooked food. "I'm not late, am I?"

"The honored guest is never late," Madam Fan expounded. "Treat this as if it were your own home!" She pressed her hands together. "It's such an honor to have you come to our house today," she started, the beginnings of an impromptu speech. "I've never had the honor of such —" she stopped to think of such a what, and then laughed with embarrassment — "of such a rich young man!"

Old Zhu's wife cleared her throat. Madam Fan continued unabashed. "Peach!" she called, catching a glimpse of herself in a mirror and putting her hand to her face. "Why don't you sing us a song!" Peach's white cheeks went red. "My daughter has a very fine voice," Madam Fan told Da Shan, "like a songbird!" Peach bit her lip. "Come on, Peach," Madam Fan said, "why not sing us some opera?"

"I don't like opera."

"Oh," Madam Fan chuckled, "come on."

"You know, I'm not really in the mood for opera," Da Shan said, and Madam Fan's expression changed.

"Oh, but you must hear my daughter sing!"

"How about after lunch?"

"Yes." Madam Fan clapped her hands together. "What a good idea!" She stood for a moment, assessing the situation, then began to usher everyone back to their respective roles. "Please, please!" She shooed Old Zhu and his wife. "Sit down! Drink tea!" She picked out a large green apple from the fruit bowl and began to peel it. "Husband," she said, pointing toward Da Shan, "our honored guest needs tea." The green apple skin came off in one long curl and she handed it with two hands to Old Zhu, then she gave the knife to Peach. "Here," she said, "I'd better go back and cook." She put an apple in her daughter's other hand. "Peel an apple for Da Shan."

Peach blushed and Old Zhu's wife shuffled uncomfortably on the sofa.

L iu Bei walked all the way across town, pushing her way through the exhausting chaos and panic of the crowd. She walked till her feet were sore and she had to limp with her left foot to stop her patent shoes from rubbing. She came to the factory gate and looked up: there was the bent sapling clinging to the brickwork, and the once-bright paintwork was peeling and faded. The old signs had been taken down, the brickwork was a richer red where they had once been. The remains of the signs lay at the side of the road in a moldering pile. The Four Modernizations, one fragment said, Space Rocket Factory, said another. There was a new banner slung across the gateway: *"Embrace Reform — Accept the Challenges of the 21st Century,"* the words said, as the banner hung limp in the bright sunlight.

Liu Bei stopped and looked at the stripped factory gate. Stepping through it was like stepping into her past. Her mother had been one of the prostitutes who'd stayed on after reeducation. Stayed on, got married and tried to live a normal life. Liu Bei had been born here, grown up here as well, before her mother moved away. It was here that she'd found her hope for the future; and lost it as well. She looked down at herself, her clothes now looking tired and worn after the pulling and scrunching of the crowd. Before she'd left home she'd put on her best clothes and her best shoes, and she'd painted a gaudy red smile on her lips just in case.

Liu Bei walked to the side of the road and sat down where the taxi drivers sat while they waited for customers. She took off her shoes and massaged her feet, anticipation making her fingers shake. She sat with her chin in her palm, staring into the world but seeing nothing.

You're an idiot, Liu Bei told herself. Forget it all. It was a long time ago. We were young and naive. We were fools. She laughed to herself. We were all fools. A car passed in front of her and she looked to see if Da Shan was inside — just on the off chance — but it was a middle-aged woman in a black dress with short hair combed back in a bun. She took a long deep breath and shook her head. Liu Bei — you're the biggest fool of all.

Liu Bei remembered how enthusiastic she and Da Shan had been when they'd volunteered to organize the pro-student demonstrations in Shaoyang. The Party had supported them at first. Revolution is no crime, Rebellion is justified. They were following the example of the students in the past who had demonstrated against foreign imperialism. The May 4th Movement come back to life. They were on the local radio and in the newspapers, their calls for reforms were aired on Hunan TV; and then the Party changed its mind. To rebel is to show a lack of filial piety, they'd been cautioned, and people stopped supporting them then. One Chinese is like a dragon, ten Chinese are like worms. The worms had crawled back into their holes.

Liu Bei massaged her temples, tried to soothe the thoughts inside. Is it just me who remembers these things? she wondered.

The guests murmured in appreciation as Madam Fan brought the first few dishes out and laid them on the table in front of them: Sweet and Sour Cucumber, Five Spice Beef and Shredded Coriander sprinkled with MSG.

"Wine for our guests," she said to her husband, nudging him with the bottle. "Open Your Mouth and Smile Wine," she announced as her husband unscrewed the top, then crushed it in his hand. "Shaoyang's most famous wine!"

Old Zhu's wife turned her cup upside-down.

Madam Fan's husband brandished the bottle. "Have some!" he ordered.

"I don't drink," Old Zhu's wife stated.

"Go on!"

"No."

Madam Fan laughed nervously. "I'd better go and cook." She

clasped her fingers together and smiled at Peach, then Da Shan; then hurried back to the kitchen. As she heated more oil in the wok, the guests drank a toast to Long Life and Prosperity! Madam Fan's husband refilled all the men's cups, and looked at his daughter's glass: she had drunk half her cup. "Look! My daughter can drink," he announced. "In fact that's all she does do — eat and drink! You know the old saying about daughters." He chuckled. "I'd have made more money raising pigs!"

Old Zhu's wife scowled at him, but it didn't stop him from laughing. He announced another toast, Long Live Friendship! refilled the glasses, raised his glass again. To Returned Sons! he announced and they drank the third cup, then Madam Fan's husband picked up his chopsticks and waved them in the air. "Begin!" he declared, and helped himself to a chicken's foot that he dropped into his bowl. "Begin!"

As he chewed on a slice of cucumber Da Shan watched Peach. She must have been a schoolgirl when he'd gone away. Her black hair and eyes, jade-white skin. He had a feeling that he'd met her outside the factory, but he couldn't place the time or location.

He was still watching her when Madam Fan came sailing out with Red Star Fish. "Who is more beautiful," she called, "me or my daughter?" Da Shan's face went red, and Peach coughed. "I know, I know," Madam Fan said with practiced modesty, "she's much prettier than me, isn't she?"

Old Zhu's wife coughed as loudly and sternly as she possibly could. Madam Fan patted her back. "You're getting sick! Eat more!" she urged. "Don't be so polite!"

D a Shan and Old Zhu responded to the exhortations to eat by shoveling in the food and giving contented grunts from time to time. Madam Fan's husband kept their glasses filled with wine, made sure they didn't stop eating. "Mmm, thanks," Da Shan said when his cup was topped up again, the wine running over the side of the glass. "You didn't go to university?" he asked Madam Fan's daughter.

"I failed Math," she said.

Old Zhu looked up from his bowl in surprise. "And they wouldn't let you in?"

Peach shook her head.

"It's very difficult to get into college these days," Madam Fan shouted from the kitchen. "Even very intelligent students get turned down."

Old Zhu's wife clenched her teeth. She should never have agreed to this. The sooner it was over the better. Madam Fan's husband shook the bottle to see how much was left. It sounded nearly empty. He poured more for Da Shan and Old Zhu, then topped up his own glass till the wine ran freely down the side of the cup. "The problem with my daughter," he declared, "is that she's lazy."

Da Shan picked some coriander and put it into his bowl. "I never liked Math either."

"What did you like?"

"I liked everything but Math," Da Shan said. "But I guess I liked History best. I was in the History and Politics Department at Changsha University."

"You went to Changsha University?" Peach began, but her father cut her off.

"Eat!" he ordered, nudging his daughter and gesturing wildly across the table at Da Shan with his chopsticks. "Eat! Or it'll all go cold!"

Madam Fan kept coming with more dishes and each time she came she said or did something that made Old Zhu's wife scowl even harder. "Twice Cooked Pork Trotter! Good for the lonely heart," she announced, then disappeared and came back with another dish: "Ma Pu Tofu! Nice and spicy!" —

she winked at Da Shan — "just like Hunan girls!" In the end Old Zhu's wife took her hand and tried to pull her into a seat. "One more dish," Madam Fan said, escaping her grasp. "One more dish!"

As Da Shan drank more wine he found his gaze kept returning to Peach's face, and her black eyes. There was something about her. The way she caught his eye, half smiled and half looked away. He shook his head, sat back in his chair.

"I'm sure we've met," he said at last. "Before today, I mean."

"Yes," Peach said. "We did. On the hill."

"That's it — by the temple," Da Shan said. "You were flying a kite!"

"Yes," she said, "I couldn't get it to fly and . . ."

"Unbelievable!" Madam Fan's husband snorted. "My daughter can't even fly a kite without finding someone to do it for her!"

"There wasn't much wind."

"Pa!" Madam Fan's husband reached for the bottle and began to refill their cups. "Eat!" he shouted. "Drink!"

D o you want me to take you someplace?" the man said, tapping Liu Bei on the shoulder. She looked up and stammered. "No. No," she said. "Thanks."

"Are you OK?" he asked. "I have a taxi. I can take you somewhere. No charge."

"No. Really. I'm going to visit a friend. He lives here," she said.

The taxi driver stood a little way off and watched her stand up and walk into the factory.

A s she passed under the gateway, Liu Bei instinctively looked up the road toward the little garden where the wisteria used to grow. Years ago she had sat there with Da Shan to enjoy the spring. Nothing particularly special had happened that day, but she'd been happy. Just remembering it made her smile.

Of course the garden was no longer there. The whole area had been cleared away, and was now buried under a row of restaurants where no one came to eat anymore, now that the factory had closed. That's how life is, Liu Bei thought as she kicked a stone and watched it scuttle away like a crab.

She pushed the hair back from her face and turned up toward Number 6 block of apartments. At the entrance she stopped. The porch was cool and dark, sharp lines of sunlight and shadow drawn across the floor. She ran a hand through her hair and ran the tension out and took a deep breath.

Liu Bei took the stairs two at a time. In front of the right-hand door on the second floor she stopped. The doorway didn't appear to have changed. For an instant Liu Bei felt the exhilaration she had when she waited on the doorstep before: knowing she'd see Da Shan. It was sudden and sharp, and Liu Bei squeezed her eyes shut to escape it, then knocked. There was no response.

She waited, and knocked again.

Empty silence.

Liu Bei knocked a third time and a little girl peeked her face out of the neighbor's doorway. "They're out," she said in a child's lilting voice. "They've gone out."

"Oh," Liu Bei said. "Do you know when they'll be back?"

The little girl shook her head. "I don't know," she said carefully, and diligently shut the door.

Liu Bei stood on the landing, feeling stupid and not knowing why. She started down the stairs, her heels clipping the concrete steps. At the bottom she stood on the porch and looked out into the hot afternoon's sunshine. She looked out and felt alien: as if she'd come to the wrong place, at the wrong time. She laughed at herself and started back down toward the gate. She'd got the day off. She'd go to her mother. Pick up Little Dragon. Take him to the park.

Liu Bei thought of the Drink and Dream Teahouse and changed her mind. She was doing this for Little Dragon as well.

She ran her hand through her hair again, and paused at the gate, squinting in the sunlight.

When everyone had finished eating, Peach helped her mother clear away the food. Old Zhu's wife got up to join in as well and there was a tussle as Madam Fan tried to force her back into her seat, to keep her out of the kitchen. While the two women struggled noisily in the kitchen doorway Madam Fan's husband handed cigarettes out to Da Shan and Old Zhu. They sat and smoked in silence, then Old Zhu cleared his throat. "I think," he announced, "it's time for my afternoon sleep."

"Me too," said Da Shan. When Old Zhu's wife heard this she let out a sigh of relief and said she had to go as well. Madam Fan was horrified: Da Shan couldn't go so soon. She hadn't even begun to work on him. Not yet.

She rushed through to detain him, but her husband had gotten in there already. "You can't go so soon," Madam Fan's husband insisted, taking hold of Da Shan's arm and keeping him down. "Have another drink!"

Da Shan paused. He could see Peach glance at him as she piled up the dirty bowls. Could see Madam Fan's concerned face. "Please don't go," she was saying. "Peach was going to sing to you, remember!"

Old Zhu's wife saw her son hesitate. "Da Shan, don't you think you've had enough to drink?" she asked.

"OK," he announced with a smile, "I will stay a little longer."

Madam Fan's husband poured out two more glasses of wine and smirked at Da Shan. Half the second bottle was gone already, and they were drunk enough not to care. Peach sat with them, avoiding her mother's eye. Her mother was trying to get Peach to go and dress up in the opera costume. She was making frantic gestures, Peach could see out of the corner of her eye, but she kept her head down, pretended not to notice. Peach didn't like opera at the best of times, and certainly not now.

"Well," Madam Fan's husband said, "you've done well for yourself, haven't you! You know, getting all this money."

Da Shan shrugged.

"Heh — come on! Don't be so modest. You know what they say — even your shit is worth something!"

"I wish my parents had known," Da Shan said, and Peach kept her head down and sniggered.

"So what did you do to make so much money?" her father asked, face serious.

"Work."

"What work?"

"I worked in a factory."

"Making what?"

"Clothes."

"What type of clothes?"

"Expensive clothes."

"How much did they pay you?"

"Four thousand a month."

"For making clothes?"

"I was a manager."

"Hmm!" Madam Fan's husband sat back and drew on his cigarette till the end glowed bright, and he inhaled it all, and let it come back out in a long plume. "How come you got *so* much money then?"

"I got lucky," Da Shan said.

"Tell me all."

"Investments," he said. "Shares. Property. Whatever. If you had the right contacts you could do well."

Madam Fan's husband took another long drag. "I suppose you made a lot of good connections there?"

"Quite a few."

"Could you get me a job?"

"What can you do?"

"Anything."

"OK." Da Shan nodded. "You'd have to start at the bottom," he said.

"How much do you get at the bottom?"

"Not much."

"But if you talk to your friends then they could get me something better, no?"

"It doesn't work like that."

"How does it work?"

"It's not like here."

"I see." Madam Fan's husband laughed. "It's all clear to me now," he said, stubbing his cigarette out. "What's the saying about the man who climbs to the top of the tree?"

Da Shan didn't answer.

"You know what I'm wondering," Madam Fan's husband said, refilling the glasses, "is why you ever came back here, to Shaoyang?"

"It was time to move out."

"Oh yes, of course."

"Money's only money," Da Shan said. "It's just something for monkeys to play with."

"Well, yes, we're all still monkeys here." Madam Fan's husband smiled, then they both tipped their cups back and drained them. "If only we'd realized. Thank you, now I understand. So clever. So successful." Da Shan had stopped listening. His eyes flickered across to Peach. "Of course," Madam Fan's husband was saying, "with all your friends and connections, you had to work *so* hard." Da Shan let out a long sigh. He was bored of this conversation. He squeezed his eyes shut as Madam Fan's husband's voice kept on in his ears. "I know how you worked, if you couldn't get what you wanted through the back door, your father would make himself a back window."

Da Shan opened his eyes and put his hands down flat on the table. He was drunk, all Madam Fan's husband's comments annoyed him. "I'm going home."

Madam Fan's husband threw his arms up in innocence. "Heh! Come on! I'm learning so much. It's changing my life. Let's just finish this bottle." He poured the last of the wine out, raised his cup. "Da Shan," he said, "you have honored my house by coming to eat here today. You have entertained us all, and even taught me the secret of eternal happiness. Who'd have thought it — I mean, you told us all you were bringing in the fifth modernization — and look what happened — you got yourself in prison!"

Peach looked across to Da Shan in alarm as her father lifted up his cup and announced the last toast: "To 1989, and the suppression of the Counterrevolutionary Movement!"

Da Shan held his cup up in the air for a moment, but instead of drinking he threw the wine into the other man's face, and dropped his empty cup onto the floor. It clinked as it hit the tiles, scuttled off under the table as Madam Fan's husband rubbed wine from his eyes. "I'm not going to drink to that," Da Shan said.

"Aren't you!?" Madam Fan's husband blustered, knocking over his chair as he struggled to get up. "Aren't you indeed?"

Madam Fan heard the raised voices. She came running from the kitchen. Da Shan and her husband were shouting and pushing each other. "Stop!" she screeched, and Peach screamed. Madam Fan kicked her husband. "Get off him!" she screeched but the two men were shouting and pushing. "Peach," she shrieked, "get a pan!"

Peach ran to the kitchen. In the panic of the moment the

words bounced in her head, devoid of meaning. She could barely remember what a pan was, or where they were. "Pan — pan — where's the pan?" There was the deep roar of a man's voice, and her mother screaming again.

"Peach!"

Peach grabbed a teapot and came running back. Madam Fan snatched it from her hands and jiggled it to get a good grip.

"Get off him!" she shouted, giving him no chance to respond before she brought the teapot down to smash against her husband's head. It didn't have any visible effect. She started crying, kicked her husband again. "Drunken — drunken — shitty — shit!" she sobbed, punctuating each word with another kick as Peach pulled Da Shan away. She helped him up and he swayed drunkenly. Madam Fan was panting, breathless.

"Peach, get him out of here. Go!"

The sunlight outside was sharp and hot. The cicadas were screaming in the trees. In the distance Peach could hear her mother's shouts. She pulled Da Shan along, in her hurry she tripped him up, almost fell over herself.

Da Shan leaned against a wall and Peach looked back up toward the apartment, anxious her father might follow. She wanted to keep moving. To get Da Shan home and then disappear. She thought of Sun An. Yes, she'd go and see him. Come on! she tugged. Da Shan stood up again and Peach got him moving.

"Fuck," Da Shan said, his legs feeling the alcohol. "I'm sorry."

Peach didn't speak, but strained to keep him walking. He was so heavy, and he stank of wine — but it was Peach who felt humiliated. She was ashamed of her parents. Of her family. Of herself.

"I don't do this, usually," Da Shan said.

"I know."

"No." He swayed. "It's important. Listen — I love her, you see."

Peach stopped.

"I promised. But I broke my promise." Peach stepped back, Da Shan stayed on his feet — just. "Promised!" he said aggressively, then he fell forward, smothering her, her knees almost buckling beneath her. Da Shan started laughing. "I don't think so," he said, then he started crying and Peach didn't know what to do. "I don't know where she is anymore. She's gone to me now. Gone." Peach pulled back as his hands clutched her cheeks. "I love her. I can't love you. You understand."

Peach froze.

"You understand?"

She nodded.

"I want to love you. Your mother wants me to love you. Do you love me?"

"Please," Peach said, "you're drunk."

Liu Bei wandered slowly around the factory compound, past the old New Block — where the migrant workers were building the hotel; past the sports field where some boys were playing football, and around again to the front gate.

It seemed that her whole life had revolved around the Space Rocket Factory. Even after her mother had moved away to a new house Liu Bei had still come back here. Especially after she'd met Da Shan. There was the night she'd asked Da Shan for a dance; the day she passed her university exams, the night Da Shan had told her he loved her and she'd cried.

Liu Bei looked across to where her mother's house had been. It'd been knocked down, of course, all the old buildings had gone, just like the people. She kept wandering till she felt hungry and thought about going home and dinner. She was exhausted by the heat and the memories. There was no one she recognized anymore. All the faces were strange.

Liu Bei walked through the trees' shadow and started to feel lucky. You can't have bad luck all your life. Mistress Zhang always told the girls at the teahouse, you're just saving your good luck up for your old age. The feeling in her stomach grew more intense as she walked up the stairs to the second floor. Her stomach felt lighter, like cobwebs.

At the Zhu family door she stopped and ran her hand through her hair again, and took a deep breath. The door was flanked with inscriptions left over from Spring Festival, the red paper peeling off the wall. "The gods of wealth enter the home; Wealth, treasures and peace arrive," they said. The picture on the door was red and gold, showed the New Year Gods and a pot full of hundred-yuan notes. She licked her lips to make her red smile shine, then wished herself good luck and knocked.

Liu Bei shifted her weight onto her heels, heard the grind of grit under her shoes. When she heard footsteps come to the door she braced herself.

It was Da Shan's mother.

"Hello." Liu Bei smiled nervously. "Is Da Shan in?"

His mother looked at Liu Bei. Squinted back into her memory, and her face dropped.

"Is that you, Liu Bei?" she asked.

Liu Bei smiled and shifted weight onto the other leg. "Yes. Hello, Madam Zhu. I heard Da Shan was back in town."

"*Really?*" Old Zhu's wife said. "Who told you that?"

Liu Bei frowned. "He came to see my mother," she said, trying to explain. "A while ago."

"Well, he *was* back," Old Zhu's wife said. "But you've missed him, I'm afraid. He went to Beijing on business. I don't think he'll be back for a while. In fact I'm not sure he will come back. He was planning to go to Shanghai. We'll probably join him there, what with the factory closing and all."

"Yes, I heard it was closing."

They looked at each other. Old Zhu's wife didn't give an inch. Liu Bei could hear the cicadas screaming outside. She felt flustered. "Oh," she said at last, as Old Zhu's wife continued staring at her. "Oh well," she said, "it would have been nice to catch up. Talk about student days again."

Yes, Old Zhu's wife smiled: yes, it would have been nice.

"It's been such a long time."

"Eight years," Old Zhu's wife said, putting on a wistful smile.

"Yes," Liu Bei started. "Well, I'll be going then."

"Best wishes to your mother," Old Zhu's wife said as good-bye.

Liu Bei turned back. "Thank you," she said.

Old Zhu's wife watched her continue down the stairs, but then Liu Bei stopped again and looked up. "If I write a note, do you think you could pass it on to Da Shan?" she asked, and Old Zhu's wife nodded. Of course.

Liu Bei took a pen and paper out of her handbag and leaned against the wall. The cicadas went quiet as she wrote. She could hear the sounds of voices carry across the factory compound and even the soft, patient breathing of Da Shan's mother. Liu Bei frowned and scribbled out what she'd written, sucked the pen for a moment, then wrote again and folded the paper over, slid it into an envelope. She wrote "Da Shan" on the front and handed it to his mother.

Old Zhu's wife took it and smiled. There was a moment of quiet as they stared at each other.

"I know we've had our differences," Liu Bei said, "but thank you."

Old Zhu's wife smiled reassuringly, patted Liu Bei's hand.

"Thank you," Liu Bei said again, and Old Zhu's wife stood

leaning against the door post and listened to Liu Bei's heels tap-tapping down the stairs.

O ld Zhu's wife shut the door and let out a long breath. The sound of Da Shan's breathing came from his bedroom. She sat and listened to each breath going in and out, turning the envelope over and over in her hands. He was still asleep.

Old Zhu's wife sat for a long time. The sound of loud footsteps coming up the stairs pulled her back to reality. She jumped up and rushed to the door to let Old Zhu in.

"Guess who I've just seen!"

"Shut up, you drunken old fool!" she hissed, signaling him to speak quietly. "I know," she said. "I know! She came here!"

Old Zhu raised his eyebrows.

"He was asleep. I told her he'd gone away."

Old Zhu took a moment to catch his breath back. He nodded and stroked a hand through his old white hair. "Don't you think he should know?"

"No," his wife told him. "It'd only upset him. She's got a child, remember!"

Old Zhu nodded slowly.

"It's better for him if he doesn't find out," she continued. She looked into her husband's smooth baby face, saw liver spots she hadn't noticed before. "If he knew what she'd become it'd only upset him. Why put him through all that?"

Old Zhu sat down, pulled out a cigarette and lit it and began to smoke. His wife went into the kitchen and poured him a cup of tea, blew on it so it was cool enough to drink. Her husband seemed old to her for the first time. As if he had just that afternoon crossed some invisible line between the living and the dying. "Here," she said, handing him the tea, watching him drink.

"Are you sure this is right?" he asked.

"Of course I'm sure."

"I can't even remember why we thought she was such a bad match."

"She's not right for Da Shan," she told him. "Look what she led him to."

Old Zhu remembered and nodded slowly. He took a long drag, sucking the flame down to the stub, then he screwed out his cigarette in the ashtray and slurped his tea. He coughed and hawked up some phlegm, spat it out onto the balcony and then walked into their bedroom. His chrysanthemum was nodding to itself in the afternoon heat. He stopped to admire it, then went back inside, feeling calmed.

Old Zhu's wife took the tea back to the kitchen, cleaned the cup, wiped the surfaces down. After ten minutes she went to check on her husband and found him spreadeagled across the bed, mouth open, snoring. Poor old man. She went into Da Shan's room and he was fast asleep as well. Young and strong, like his father had been.

Old Zhu's wife felt for the envelope in her pocket. She pulled it out and looked at the handwriting. Da Shan, it said. She pursed her lips, the girl had fine handwriting. Da Shan murmured something in his sleep and his mother held her breath. She watched him brush his hand across his face, turn over, snuggle into the pillow. He was just dreaming, she reassured herself. She stepped softly out of the bedroom and shut the door behind her.

Old Zhu's wife held the envelope in her hand and wondered what to do with it. She was going to burn it but the temptation to open it was too strong to resist.

She got a knife from the kitchen, sliced the paper open and the letter dropped out, spun to the floor like a dead butterfly.

She picked it up and unfolded it.

Da Shan, it said:
I came to see you but you weren't in.
The ancients used to write poems about this.

There was a crossed-out sentence she couldn't make out.

I guess lots of things must have happened since we saw each other last. It would be nice to catch up.

At the bottom was her signature: two plain characters:

Liu Bei

And a couple of lines of poetry:

I looked for you, and didn't find you
and turned back home in vain.

Old Zhu's wife took the letter and twisted it into a curl. This was not going to happen. Not now. No way. The wrinkles in her face were hard and set in determination as she lit the gas stove, and held the paper in the blue flames. Dancing petals of yellow fire blossomed and moved up the paper, reducing it to black ash that flew upward, like prayers that rose on translucent convections; then slowly fell back down to the floor, unanswered.

*T*he week after the meal the old women in the Space Rocket Factory met under the trees to talk. They squatted on their bony haunches; listened to the latest tale and gave loud snorts of disapproval: Mrs. Cao's daughter had been seen with one of the migrant workers; one of the men from the President's Office was having an affair with the nurse from the clinic. The women shook their heads and tutted: "Wah!" It wouldn't have happened in their day.

One declared that she'd been told that the factory was going to be turned into a theme park for Shanghai businessmen, there would be a swimming pool and a sports complex. This provoked a round of disapproval: swimming pools were dangerous things, all those half-dressed people strutting around the factory! Another said she'd been told that the new leaders were going to start a football factory. Shaoyang footballs, she announced, would be famous worldwide.

"It's true," she said, "my son told me, and he knows the man in the Shaoyang Central Planning Office."

In the fields the rice crop was turning gold: ready for harvest, and for a while the old women sat remembering harvests from their childhood. Rice seemed more fragrant then, the summers were not so hot, that was a time when they could skip and run.

As they sat under the tree the occasional fly buzzed along and found them. It swirled around their heads and ears, landed on sensitive spots before they shooed it away. The heat was too much. They sat fanning themselves, felt the swelling in their old joints ease. As they sat they heard a rumble coming closer into focus, a large yellow digger that drove in through the factory gate. At first they stared at it in astonishment. Their surprise turned to glares: it could only mean change and change meant trouble.

The digger ignored their disapproving looks, gave a triumphant snort of diesel fumes and then juddered through the factory complex. The old women squinted after it, as it dragged a long tail of black smoke. They kept squinting in its general direction when it had long ago blurred away into the rest of the world. They listened to the crunch of its gears; the drone of its engine and shook their heads in disapproval. "Wah!"

The digger came to a stop at the site of the New Block, and the driver jumped down and went to talk to one of the workers. A small group of people had followed it and now they settled down to see what would happen. All that was left of the old New Block were stumps of walls and the concrete floors. No one could remember it as it had been six months before; with tall red walls and broken windows. They just remembered that it had looked old and backward. Thank Heaven it had been knocked down. Nobody wanted their factory to look poor — a swimming pool would be much better.

The onlookers stared as the driver ran back to the cab,

revved the engine and then drove the yellow digger around the stacked piles of bricks. It plowed up the remains of the New Block, pumping hydraulic cylinders titanium-bright in the sunlight, terrifying a couple of local thrushes, who took flight, landed on the top of Number 6 block of apartments, and watched from a safe distance.

The digger pushed the last heap of smashed concrete to the side and the driver climbed out and lit a cigarette, went off for his lunch. The crowd sat waiting. The whole job had only taken half an hour. The women traded snippets of conversation and waited for the driver to come back from his lunch. He didn't come. His digger just sat there, its yellow paintwork keeping the birds away.

Liu Bei stood at the entrance to the Drink and Dream Teahouse, took a deep breath and pushed the back door open, started up the stairs. The other girls were sitting playing cards. Cherry was winning, her voice was loud and excited. Liu Bei slipped inside the door and waited.

"Heh look!" Cherry shouted. "It's Pale Orchid — you're back, are you?"

"Did you get to see your man?" Water-Spirit Flower asked.

"No."

"Oh dear," Water-Spirit Flower simpered, and Cherry giggled behind her hand.

"Come on," she said, "come and play — I'm winning."

Liu Bei slipped into her chair and Cherry dealt four hands of cards, smiling all the while. Her winning streak continued all afternoon, she got louder and more excited while Liu Bei lost her bets with silent resignation. As the heat of afternoon passed, Mistress Zhang came upstairs, saw Liu Bei and nodded. "Back for good?"

"Yes."

"Good," she said without any expression. "Commander Pan is coming again this afternoon. I want you to be ready."

The late afternoon sunlight was stretching the shadows of the Space Rocket Factory along the ground when the old women woke from their dozings and swapped stories about the digger. Yes, that was where the swimming pool would be, one old lady insisted. Her hair had been dyed a glossy black, but the roots were growing out, leaving a furrow of white across her scalp. She put her hand to it as she talked, yes, a swimming pool to be sure, she said. With all sorts sitting around it.

As the sunlight began to cool to orange the old women returned to the subject of the fight between Old Zhu's son and Madam Fan's husband. It wasn't that anyone liked Madam Fan's husband — but for all his faults, he was one of them. Something they couldn't say about Old Zhu's son. He was the old bosses' son; he'd gone away, which was bad enough. But even worse, he'd come back.

Never go back home when you're rich, the saying said, people will never forgive you.

One old woman with a lopsided smile adjusted her teeth and then declared it was Madam Fan's husband's fault, because he was someone you could say anything about and people would believe it; but another reminded them all about all the trouble Da Shan had caused in 1989. What with his marches and demonstrations: all that hot air and chaos. A dangerous combination. There was nothing they disliked more than chaos. It turned their hearts to gray cement, set solid.

More uplifting was the news that Madam Fan had finally thrown her husband out. At last, most people thought privately, but still they made disapproving noises about the whole topic. Husbands weren't there to be thrown out, they were there to be endured. All things had their root in Heaven.

For their part, Madam Fan's husband's friends spread rumors over their games of mah-jongg that Madam Fan had fallen in love with Old Zhu's son; that she had become obsessed with his money; that she was going to sell her daughter, Peach. Long-forgotten events began to fester in people's minds again; the length of time and the summer heat made them smell worse. Madam Fan had quite a history herself, the old women remembered. She was hardly one of them, either. What with all her opera singing and airs and graces. Who did she think she was — the local diva?

Madam Fan was in the market when she found out from Autumn Cloud that stories about her were circulating again, and that many of them were at least half true. She endured the renewed rumors with the grace of a tragic actor.

At night she slept badly, but in the morning when it was time to sing she still stepped out onto her balcony with the elegance and grace of a heron. Hungry mosquitoes still waltzed in the predawn air. The cool made their dances slow, they were easy to swat. Madam Fan picked one off her hand and squashed it as she cleared her throat. It was the black-and-white-striped one: they itched the most. She wiped the blood off her fingers; took a deep breath and began to sing Concubine Ji's prologue:

> Following my king on his military campaigns,
> Enduring cold wind and hardship

The grinding sound of the digger's engine started up across the factory.

> I hate the tyrant who has plunged
> Our land into an abyss of misery.

The engine revved, so loud in the cool still air. Its loud rumble devoured her words, made the leaves shiver. Her voice faltered and stopped. The roar of the engine continued. Someone crunched it into first gear and the roar changed note.

Madam Fan could smell the diesel fumes from where she was. She finished the aria and felt like crying. Her fists clenched and then unclenched. At last she stepped back inside and slammed the door behind her. She wouldn't sing to a machine!

The next morning Madam Fan woke up at 6:15 in order to preempt the digger, and heard the sound of disco music playing outside her apartment. She rubbed her eyes and peered out of her bedroom window: she could make out a group of women, ballroom dancing. They were doing the two-step. Madam Fan went straight downstairs and complained, but the women said that the digger had demolished the spot where they used to dance, so now they had to come here.

"But I can't sing over all this music," Madam Fan complained.

"You can sing," a friend of her husband told her, "but no one will hear you."

When Peach came home she found her mother sitting by the balcony window. A bottle of Great Wall red wine on the table next to her, one hand absentmindedly stroking her neck as the other played with the bottle top. Peach sat down on the other side of the table, but Madam Fan continued staring out of the window. She turned the bottle top over and over in her hand.

Peach reached out across the table, but her mother's fist closed around the bottle top.

"Ma," Peach said, "are you still upset?"

Madam Fan smiled, then turned to look out of the window again. "Your father's behind this," she said. "I know."

Peach went out and didn't come back until after sunset. They ate a dinner of egg noodles in silence, watched episode a hundred and eight of *A Dream of Red Mansions*. Dai Yu was dying, her beautiful face drawn and faded, like an autumn flower. Peach couldn't stand to watch: it was too sad. She went into her bedroom and put on some American music. She sang along, words she didn't understand, but which reminded her of Chinese. She was still singing when there was a soft knock on her door.

Madam Fan came in.

Peach sat up and smiled as she slid onto the bed.

"Mother," Peach asked, "are you all right?"

Madam Fan nodded. Her dark eyes were bright. "I want to tell you something," she began, and Peach slid down into the bed. "Before anyone else does."

"Is it about Father?"

Madam Fan nodded.

"Is he coming back?"

"No," Madam Fan said.

Peach wanted to cry.

"I don't want him to come back. There's only me and you now."

Peach swallowed.

"Come now, we'll be all right because we love each other." Madam Fan stroked her daughter's hair. Long slow strokes. "Remember how I once told you," she said at last, "about your father and me — how we got married?"

Peach nodded.

"My family was starving. Remember?"

"Yes."

"It was 1968, during the hard times, when no one had anything to eat." Madam Fan stopped stroking Peach's hair. "I was assigned a job at a farm on the outskirts of town. Working on a farm meant I could send my parents some food," Madam Fan said. "That whole year I gave them everything I had. I kept them alive."

Peach nodded and Madam Fan took her daughter's hand. "There was a young man whose family were classed as Stinking Intellectuals. When it was his turn to be criticized he accepted all his faults. He never complained." Madam Fan forced a smile. "He looked after me," she said. "When the criticisms were very bad. He let them beat him. When he saw how thin I was he gave me some of his millet to make soup."

Madam Fan ran a hand through her hair. "We couldn't talk of love: only 'Love the Country!' 'Love the People!' Love between two people was forbidden."

Peach gave her mother's hand a squeeze.

"He didn't care that I was a landlord's daughter. He never said so, but I know he loved me. I am sure of that. Really!" Madam Fan stopped to take a deep breath. "We used to meet at night."

There was a heavy pause. Peach didn't want to hear any more.

"We met at night," Madam Fan faltered, her grip tightened on Peach's hand. "One night they *followed* us! He loved me," she said after a long pause. "He loved me," she repeated, then burst out crying.

Peach sat up and held her mother tight. Madam Fan's body shook for a while. Peach rubbed her mother's back, soothed away the sobs. Madam Fan wiped her eyes and nose. "They surrounded us," she said. "There were so many torches shining at us. They had guns. I thought they were going to shoot. He didn't want them to see, but they pulled him away." Madam Fan sniffed, wiped her nose on her arm. "They demanded why he had done that to me."

The scene played itself back in Madam Fan's mind, and she breathed deeply, wiped her nose on her arm. "They said I was a reformed character. That he was a counterrevolutionary. That he refused to forget his feudal ideas. They made me say it," she stated with great determination.

The slogans were still so clear in her head:

A good female comrade should devote her time to the revolution!

Maggots infesting the country will be squashed!

Peach wanted her mother to stop there, but Madam Fan took another breath.

"I thanked the Party for their protection, then I said what they had told me to say. They made me say it," Madam Fan asserted. She looked up and stared at Peach. "They asked me to speak louder so that everyone in the hall could hear, so I said it again:

"He raped me."

An overturned cart serves as a warning to others!

"Later my officer found out that I was pregnant. That's why I agreed to go with your father. We were both bad elements."

When two lepers fuck, they can't infect the clean.

"The baby was a boy. He was your brother." Madam Fan sniffed. "He was very thin. I had no milk. All he did was cry. We fed him on rice gruel. He got sick. There was no medicine. There was hardly any food. They took the body away in a box. We had to think about the living in those days. We were starving. I had no choice," Madam Fan said. "I had to marry your father for my baby. And then he died." As she spoke she played with a strand of Peach's hair. She tried to hold it back, but she started to cry again, her mouth curling up in tears.

Peach hugged her mother. "I love you," she said, but inside she felt cold. She didn't want to know what her mother had just told her. She shut her eyes and hugged her mother and tried to forget everything she'd just heard.

*A*t night everything in the Drink and Dream Teahouse slept, except for a single light bulb that burned in the darkness, searing the moths that came too close. A lone bird with a grudge started singing before daybreak and stopped Mistress Zhang from sleeping. She rose early into a gray morning; tried to fill all the empty rooms with her presence, but the daylight was dim and the rooms remained full of shadows. She turned the TV on and turned it up loud. There was a documentary about some Beijing journalists who'd gone to visit a country village: old men and women reminisced, the younger ones talked of going to the city, their parents talked of the difficulties of making ends meet in times like these.

"Isn't life better now?" they asked the old ones at the end of the program and they smiled their toothless smiles.

"Oh yes," they said, "oh yes — much better!"

Mistress Zhang was combing her gray hair when there was a knock on the back door. A young girl came in, stood hesitantly in the doorway. She had a round moon face, was plump like a village girl and her skin was a bit too dark.

"What do you want?" Mistress Zhang snapped.

"I want to come and work here."

Mistress Zhang didn't bother to hide her irritation. "The stream of men is an endless river!" she said severely. "You dip your toe in and get washed all the way to the sea."

"I want to come and work here," the girl repeated.

"Then come back next week," Mistress Zhang snapped, and the girl left.

Mistress Zhang had a couple of girls come to her each week: she didn't know why. They must be stupid. Maybe they read too many romantic novels, they wanted to be the girl who was discovered by a handsome lover and whisked away. Whatever it was they didn't come back. Not many of them, anyway. Mistress Zhang was even more formidable if they did. There was no turning back for a girl once she became a whore. Why become a used shoe when you could be a house slipper?

Cherry arrived first, tiptoeing over the paving stones so she didn't step on the green moss. Mistress Zhang sent her back out to fetch some lunch from the local restaurant. "I want Wugang Tofu!" she shouted. "And tell them not so much chili this time!"

Cherry swore as she went out, and Mistress Zhang bit back her anger. Stupid girl, she thought, if she didn't have a hole between her legs she'd be penniless.

Mistress Zhang checked her hair in the mirror. She had it curled up at the back, one of her clips had slipped. She could feel her hands begin to sweat as she fiddled to put it back into place. It made her swear.

"Shit!"

She'd have to start again.

The next morning Liu Bei pushed her mother's door open and stepped inside. Inside it was cool and dark, it took a moment for her eyes to adjust to the shadow.

"Mother?" she called. "Mother!" The room was empty except for a glass jar of wildflowers, wasting their smiles as they slowly wilted.

Liu Bei found her mother sitting in the backyard, peeling potatoes. She wiped a stray lock of hair back from her face and smiled, pulled a boiled sweet out of her pocket and gave it to Little Dragon. "Here you are!" she said. "You handsome young man!"

"Why don't you go and play outside?" Liu Bei said. "Go and see your friends!"

Little Dragon put the sweet in his pocket and refused to move.

"Go on!" Liu Bei said. "Off you go! Your friends will be waiting for you!"

Little Dragon reluctantly let go of Granny's hand and went back into the house and Liu Bei pulled up a stool and sat next to her mother.

"How are things?" her mother asked.

"Fine," she said, running her hand through her hair.

Liu Bei's mother studied her daughter's face. "What's wrong?" she asked.

"Nothing."

Mistress Zhang was still spraying her hair in place when Liu Bei arrived. She shouted a hello and went straight upstairs. Liu Bei wanted to be alone, but when she got upstairs the cleaner was there, spreading clean sheets on the beds, muttering to herself about the amount of dirt men brought in on their shoes.

Liu Bei went into the girls' room, which was in its usual state: makeup and clothes strewn all over the place. One of Cherry's magazines was on the table, Lotus's fluffy slippers had been kicked across the floor. Liu Bei sat at the table and flicked through the magazine. There was an article about a female officer in the People's Liberation Army: "Brave Girls Clamor to Protect Our Homeland," the title read. *"Wang Hao, twenty-five-year-old member of the Communist Youth League and officer in the People's Liberation Army talks of her life in the ranks."*

Liu Bei turned the page over. There was a piece about the boom in plastic surgery clinics in Shanghai. She skimmed the article over, then flipped over again. Ads. More ads. Buy this, buy that. Liu Bei put the magazine back and picked up the next one in the pile: *Liberation Army Daily,* one of the customers must have left it here. She flicked through, and there was a long line of articles she couldn't be bothered to read. On the back page was a picture of a phoenix and dragon entwined. "Green Bridge of Magpies," the title read.

The letter of the month was from a group of soldiers in Qinghai:

> . . . *we have high-quality clothes, new houses, and can watch TV or go to the cinema. We all enjoy our life very much. Our only regret is that we lack virtuous wives to follow our ideals of honesty and bravery. We ask any patriotic girls who want to help us to protect the Motherland to come and join us.*

Liu Bei shook her head. She scanned the lists of lonely hearts.

> *I'm a university graduate and lower-ranking officer who wants to meet a young girl, with degree in foreign languages, who can share my goals in life and share a long and meaningful marriage.*

I'm a retired army officer with good eyesight and a strong heart. Childless and divorced. Wants to meet healthy educated girl without children.

Are you a "True Man"?: Educated girl striving for the chance to live a meaningful and productive life wants to meet a man with similar ideals.

Liu Bei put the magazine down and then picked it up again. She scanned the list again and found the one she was looking for.

Lonely Widower. Wants companion not love. Women over thirty only.

Liu Bei tore off a corner of the page, took the address down, checked the PO Box number and then put the scrap of paper into her purse.

*P*each stood by the window, one hand on the cool glass pane, watching people move silently through the factory. The summer felt like it was fading already; soon autumn would strip the hills bare. Everyone seemed sad today; the world had never looked so bleak and dreary.

It felt like a year since her father had left, but it couldn't have been more than two weeks. In those two weeks he hadn't come back once. His relatives had come instead.

"He's very sorry. Why not let him come and apologize?" they asked, and Madam Fan listened.

"Think of the shame," Peach's great-uncle said.

"The gossip!" a distant cousin put in.

"Your daughter," the great-uncle continued. "She needs a father at home. What will her friends say if her parents get divorced?"

Yes, think of me, Peach thought. Nobody thinks of me.

"Peach does not need him back!" Madam Fan declared. "And nor do I!"

That had been the final word. There was nothing else to say. Peach listened as her mother showed them all to the door, the door closed with a metal *clang!* and their voices faded away into silence. Take me away from this, Peach thought, then tried to see how the sentence would fit with his name: "Da Shan, take me away from this," she whispered. It felt just right.

Peach looked through her music tapes for one that she wasn't bored of, but couldn't find any and let out a frustrated sigh. There was nothing new at all, nothing she had any interest in anymore. She collapsed onto the bed and it creaked. She shut her eyes and tried to sleep, but not being able to see only made the world of sounds more vivid. She turned over onto her side and pulled open the drawer on her bedside table. There was an irregular wad of photos from her middle-school days: one of her making a snowman with a couple of classmates, the picture blurred by falling snow; another of a spring day they'd climbed up to the temple with pots and pans, with jars of chopped vegetables and meat, and then they'd cooked a picnic; one of herself with thumbs up, and her friend doing rabbit ears behind her head; Peach smiled for a moment, then carried on turning the photos.

At the bottom of the pile was the photo her class had taken on the day they'd finished their high school exams. It was the last time they'd all been together. Peach went through the smiling, excited faces: maybe a third of her class had gone on to university in Xiangtan or Changsha, or even farther away to the big cities. Two of them had even gone to Beijing. Peach looked into her own grinning face, and looked back and couldn't think why she'd been so happy, but even school was better than this.

Of the other students in the photo who'd also failed their exams, Peach wasn't sure. She saw some of them around town occasionally. Two of the girls had gotten married, a few of the boys had gotten jobs in Shaoyang, but most of them had disappeared — gone back to farming in their villages or off to the big cities to look for work.

Peach put the photos back in the drawer and lay back on the bed. She just had to get out of the house. She wanted to be held and loved, and for the first time in days she thought of Sun An. What with everything that had happened she'd forgotten to go and collect his letters. It was his punishment, she decided, for making her touch his *thing*.

I'll go and see him, Peach told herself, and see if he's learned his lesson.

She listened at her bedroom door and when she was sure the coast was clear she dashed through the door before her mother could catch her. She ran down the steps into the late afternoon sunshine; giggling with the excitement of being discovered. For a moment she felt she was being watched and glanced over her shoulder, but there was no one there. Her walk speeded to a trot and then she ran down and out of the factory gate.

Sun An was sitting in the front porch of his shop, looking up the street just on the off chance that Peach would come. He'd sent letters daily, and at first they'd been collected, but then she'd stopped taking them. He thought that maybe she had stopped loving him. Yesterday he'd sent his sister with another letter to put under their secret stone, but again she'd come back saying, "The last one you wrote's still there, stupid!" so he had given up.

All Sun An's misery disappeared when he saw Peach walking quickly down the street. He sat and held his breath, making sure she was coming to his shop, then he stood up and waved, started jumping up as he called her name. Peach smiled and Sun An grinned and imagined her pace quickening toward him.

"Peach!" he said, coming out to her. "Where have you been? I've been so worried."

She looked at him as if she didn't care. "Why?"

Sun An swallowed and paused. "It's been quite a few days. I've missed you."

Peach gave him a look and he stopped. "I'm sorry," he said at last.

"For what?"

Sun An didn't answer, so Peach gave a little "Hmph!" and she sat down. She took the tea without speaking and gulped it down, held it out for a refill. She could feel the water sloshing inside her as she twiddled with a thread of cotton on the bottom of her T-shirt.

"Didn't you get my letters?" Sun An asked.

"I looked but there was nothing there."

"My sister said she put them there."

"Well, they weren't there," Peach stated.

"Oh," Sun An said. He looked at his feet, then saw the teapot. "More tea?"

Peach put her cup out, and he filled it up again. "Why don't you shut the shop?" she said. Sun An moved a chair back from out of the doorway, and then pulled the metal shutters down. They rattled as they plunged the room into evening; stripes of light shining through the slats. He slid the metal bolt into place and Peach put her cup down onto the desk. She swallowed the saliva in her mouth, but there was more, so she swallowed again as a tingling spread through her body. It made her shiver.

"Are you cold?"

"No."

He held out a hand and she put hers in it.

"Are you sure you're not cold?" he said, tugging at her hand.

"Yes."

He could feel her breath on his face, smell her skin. "I missed you, Peach," he said. "I really missed you. I thought you didn't love me."

Peach squeezed her eyes shut, fantasizing about being held close, about being loved.

"You won't leave me, will you?" he whispered.

"No," she whispered. "I won't."

Sun An gave her another bear hug, as if he could squeeze more love out of her. He moved his head so they were nose to nose, and then they began to kiss. Their tongues entwined, then Peach pulled away and cuddled her head against his chest. They stood like this for a long time, Sun An feeling the rise and fall of her breathing; Peach listening to the strange noises his stomach made.

"Let's go do something," Peach said at last.

"We could see a film."

"I'm bored of films."

"How about going to the park?"

"I'm bored of the park." Peach curled her lip in resignation. "I'm bored of everything about Shaoyang! Bored, bored, bored!"

Sun An tried to sound jolly. "We could go out for something to eat."

"Where?"

"How about the night market?"

"Have you got money?"

"Yeah, I've got loads. I've been saving up, you see!" Sun An smiled.

"OK," Peach began. "I know — they've got crayfish in the night market." She mimicked a crayfish with her hand. "Big spindly crayfish that jump on you and crawl all over!" She attacked him with her hand and he fought her off.

"So, we go out?"

"Only for crayfish!" she said, attacking him again.

He grinned. "Great!"

Rain fell in the night, heavy soaking rain pummeled the leaves dizzy and even dribbled into Madam Fan's deepest dream and filled it with the sound of splashing water. Despite the disturbance she woke feeling refreshed and excited. There was no music; this morning she would sing.

Madam Fan pulled the bolt back and stepped out onto the balcony. The rain had kept the ballroom dancers at home. The factory was deserted; just dripping leaves and random droplets hung out on the clotheslines to dry. The rain had washed all the dust off the trees and bamboo: now they were a perfect emerald, polished with water. She took in a deep breath, let it out and took another. She danced a few steps, in time with the music in her head, danced a few steps more:

> No one can count the bends in a river
> Or stalks in a rice field.

She sang so beautifully even the rain stopped to listen.

> I will always sing joyful songs.
> Though my heart is broken,
> I will always sing joyful songs.

From far away there was the hoot of a train — so faint it was almost an echo in the mind. It made Madam Fan want to cry. She sang out the last note, kept it going for as long as she had breath. People leaving; always leaving.

Peach got up while Madam Fan reboiled the mung bean and peanut soup. She put an extra spoonful of sugar in, stirred it around, but Peach ignored the food and went straight into the toilet. Madam Fan hummed to herself as she set the soup on the table, slid a metal spoon next to it.

Peach ate mouthful by deliberate mouthful while her

mother was humming opera. It irritated her. She was too sleepy to talk. She was too sleepy to taste the soup. She decided she'd go and see Sun An again today. She'd have to change her trousers. They'd get filthy in the rain.

"Why don't we go shopping?" Madam Fan asked suddenly.

"I'm busy."

"What do you mean, you're busy?"

"I told a friend I would go and visit them today."

"Who?"

"One of my classmates."

Madam Fan bit her lip and nodded. She stepped in close and stroked a stray lock of hair from Peach's face. "I'm sorry about all the trouble I've brought you," Madam Fan said and Peach half smiled. "I should have chosen a better father for you."

Peach picked her bowl up and took it to the kitchen.

"What's wrong?"

"Nothing," Peach said. "It's just that I don't want to be late."

Peach ran down the steps and through the rain, the water splashing dirt up her calves. In the market the peasants sat with plastic bags wrapped around their heads, sheltering from the rain. There was a line of umbrellas at the end of the road waiting for taxis. Peach dashed past them all, all the way to the shop where a man sold steamed buns.

The man was inside playing cards with his wife. Peach pointed at the bamboo steamer and shouted in at him "Have you got any more sweet buns?" and he came rushing over, lifted the top off the pot and a cloud of steam plumed into the air. He swirled it away with his hand and then pointed. "I've got date buns and sugar buns."

"Can I have one of each?" Peach said, then changed

her mind. "No, actually can I have two date buns and one sugar?"

The man used a translucent plastic bag like a glove to pick the buns out, then handed them to Peach. She gave him a one-yuan note and took a bite out of the top bun. It was filled with dark-brown date paste. Delicious!

Peach ate it quickly, then ran out into the rain and kept running all the way to Sun An's video shop.

I've brought you a bun," Peach told Sun An as she sat on his bed. "Do you like sugar or date?"

"I don't mind," he said.

"Well, I like date," Peach said, "so you have that one."

They sat and munched on mouthfuls of bread. Sun An slurped his tea; chewed with his mouth open.

"You look like a pig!"

Sun An snorted and Peach giggled. He snorted again and she started laughing. He kept snorting as he shuffled toward her and tickled her ribs, still snorting.

"Get off, you pig!" she screeched, but he tickled her all the more.

"Oww! Stop it!" she managed to squeal.

He snorted again, close up to her face.

"Stop it!" she said.

Snort.

Peach wiped her hair back and took a deep breath. "Stop it," she said. "It's not funny anymore."

Sun An tried to kiss her, but she cautioned him: "Not till you swallow!"

He swallowed.

"Is that everything?"

Sun An opened his mouth.

"Your teeth are all yellow, and they're covered with food!"

Sun An ran his tongue around his teeth, cleaning the bits of bun from around and between his teeth.

"Let me see! OK," she said at last, and then he kissed her.

Peach spent the afternoon flicking through Sun An's sister's copy of *Junior English for China* while Sun An washed his clothes in a bucket of cold water. At last she got bored and slapped the pages shut.

"Are you all right?"

"No." Peach pouted. "I don't think I am."

Sun An dried his hands and came and sat next to her on the bed. He pulled her across the bed, wrapped his arms around her as if he could protect her from sadness.

"Is it your mother?"

Peach nodded.

"Isn't your father going to come back?"

Peach shook her head and snuggled into Sun An's side. He stroked her hair, rocked her very slightly, as he thought about what to say. "Do you want him back?" he asked at last.

"I didn't at first," Peach said. Her voice trailed off, uncertain. "It's mother," she said after a long pause. "She's so strange now he's gone."

Sun An squeezed her again and kissed her cheek.

"Why?"

"I don't know. Actually, I don't think I want to talk about it."

Sun An stroked her hair and she nestled into him, resting her head on his chest. She lay for a long time listening to his heart beat slowly and deliberately, beat after beat. Her mind wandered. She thought of the meal, and Da Shan on the hill with the kite. His voice had been so kind. His fingers had been as well. They were reassuring.

Peach imagined what would happen if she married someone rich like Da Shan. They could both go abroad. In Hong Kong or Singapore. Then it wouldn't matter that her parents were divorced. She could have lots of children and they'd be happy together. And rich. She wouldn't have to lie on a bed in the back of a video shop, with a peasant.

She looked up and saw that Sun An had dropped off. His mouth was half open, his eyelids were closed and very still. He looked silly. For a moment she felt a stab of guilt, then snuggled back into his chest.

*T*he rain had passed by the time Liu Bei got to her mother's home. People didn't go out much when it rained, there had been no point in her staying at the Drink and Dream Teahouse all evening just to play cards. Little Dragon was jumping up and down in a puddle. He was trying to move the puddle to a new hole, but each time he jumped and splashed, the water trickled back home. It was so frustrating he laughed, squealed when he saw his mother, kept jumping.

Liu Bei picked him up in her arms and hugged him tight. "Who's my handsome son?"

"I am!"

Yes you are, she thought and felt a coldness in her heart. Yes, you are.

• • •

Liu Bei's mother was inside cutting Aunty Tang's toenails; using a set of paring scissors to trim the knobbly flesh and dig out an ingrown nail. Aunty Tang grunted with satisfied pain from time to time and Liu Bei curled her lip. She waited till her mother had finished and then cleared her throat.

"There's something I want to talk to you about, Mother," she said.

Her mother nodded.

"Alone."

Aunty Tang pretended not to hear. She squeezed out a fart, slowly limped across the room to the back door, swung it open, stepped out over the threshold. The door swung shut behind her and a few moments later they heard the toilet door creak open and bang shut. Liu Bei's mother cleared the nail and skin trimmings up in her palm, dropped them into the bin.

"Yes?"

"I've written a letter," Liu Bei said. "To a man in Shanghai."

Her mother heard a final tone in her daughter's voice. "What man?" she demanded, turning around.

"He's a retired army colonel," Liu Bei said. "He sounds kind and warmhearted. I saw his ad in a magazine."

Liu Bei's mother looked away, wiped an imaginary spot off the table.

"He asked to see my photo. I sent it."

Liu Bei's mother took a deep breath. "And?"

Liu Bei tried to smile, but her eyes were too heavy to sparkle. She looked away. "That's it."

"What about Little Dragon?"

Liu Bei opened her mouth to say something, but couldn't. She started to cry. Her mother stared, refused to be moved.

"What about Little Dragon?" she repeated. "He's your son. How can you think of leaving him?"

Liu Bei nodded: she'd tried to do her best, but it was so difficult. "I know," she said at last. "I know he's my son. Do you think I don't know that?"

Peach and Sun An sat on the sofa in the shop, their bodies curled up against each other like two silkworms. The rain had stopped, but the roads were still wet, in the gutters rubbish floated slowly to the sea.

"Why don't we ever do anything?" Peach huffed at last.

"What do you want to do?"

"I don't know."

Sun An frowned. It seemed a very difficult problem. "Why don't we go out for a meal?"

"OK! A really expensive meal."

"Like what?"

"Like — I don't know!"

Sun An frowned and thought for a moment. This hadn't gotten any easier. "How about we go back to the night market," he said at last.

Peach curled her lip.

"The Hundred Old Names Dumpling Shop?"

"I'm sick of dumplings."

Sun An sat down. "I don't know then."

"How about," Peach began slowly, her eyes lighting up as she said it, "the Shaoyang Hot Pot City!"

"You want to go there?"

"Yeah," she said. "I do."

"OK, we'll go."

"Are you sure?"

"Yeah."

"Can you afford it?"

"Of course."

"Great!" Peach jumped up and ran to the door. "Come on then!"

Sun An stood up and thought. "Right," he said, "I'll just get some money."

S un An's sister looked up from the television when he came into the back room. She watched him go across to the bed and fold the mattress back. He pulled the white plastic bag out and undid the knot at the top.

"That's supposed to be for Ma and Pa," she said severely.

"I'm just borrowing some."

"Why?"

Sun An counted out two hundred yuan, and slipped it in his pocket.

"You can't take that much!" she said, her voice full of emotion. "What about my school fees!"

He ignored her. "Get yourself some dinner," he said, giving her five yuan.

She refused to take it. "You can't take that money!" she insisted, and began to cry.

"Watch the shop," he said. "I'm going out."

S un An ordered a taxi and he and Peach sat in the back, holding hands. It was a ten-minute drive along the river and then over the Black Dragon Bridge into the center of town. Strange faces filled the streets, they passed a row of welding shops, incandescent flashes dispelled the evening gloom, disappeared, then flashed again. Peach shut her eyes, but the flashes were still there, etched into her eyeballs.

The driver pulled up across the road from Shaoyang Hot Pot

City, and Sun An looked up with alarm at the huge flashing neon sign that read: Shaoyang's Premier Five Star Restaurant.

At the door a girl in a blue silk cheongsam bowed to them as they walked past, and Peach giggled and said, "Isn't it exciting," as a waitress in a red velvet dress, high heels and flesh-tone pop-socks met them at the bottom of the stairs.

"Would you like to eat in the dining room or in a private room?" the waitress asked. She had a forced smile that held for a moment too long.

"How much is the private room?" Sun An asked.

"Thirty yuan."

"We'll eat in the lounge."

The Hot Pot Lounge was a large room. Round tables with white tablecloths were positioned around the room like frozen dancers. They were all empty. The waitress opened each menu and gave one to Sun An and one to Peach. Peach held her menu up high and imagined how jealous the waitress must feel to see her being taken out for dinner at the Hot Pot City.

"Would you like to order?" the waitress asked.

Peach kept the menu up high. "What's the most expensive meat?"

"Dog meat," the waitress replied.

"Let's have dog meat," Peach said, taking Sun An's hand. He nodded, and the waitress wrote it down.

"Dog Meat Hot Pot. Any cold dishes?"

Peach read off a couple of the most expensive ingredients and the waitress read them back: "Roast Cow Liver, Five Spice Roast Meat, Chicken Stomach with Sichuan Pepper Dressing."

She sat excitedly watching as the waitress put a bowl of melon seeds and a packet of paper napkins on the table in front of them, poured them both tea.

Peach pulled a paper towel from the packet and put it to her nose and sniffed.

"Mmm!" she said. "They smell lovely."

"I never knew they did smelly napkins," Sun An said.

"You're so silly!" Peach giggled.

The waitress asked them what they wanted to drink and Peach said beer.

"American or Chinese?"

"American!"

"One bottle or two?"

"Two!"

The beer came and they drank and toasted each other: "Future Wealth and Prosperity — gan bei!" Peach finished hers in four long gulps, burped and put her hand to her mouth in surprise. "Whoops!"

Sun An finished his and his eyes watered with surprise. "Too cold!" he said. Peach felt suddenly sad and reached across the table and took his hand.

"Do you love me?" she asked.

"I love you," Sun An said, wiping his eyes. He watched her. She looked so pretty with her hair tucked back behind one ear. Her pink cheeks making the rest of her skin look paler, her black eyes darker. "Do you love me?"

Peach stopped. She hadn't really thought about it. "I think so," she said.

When they'd finished the bill came to a hundred and ninety yuan. Sun An's face went white. "How come it's so much?" he asked the waitress, who put the menu on the table in front of them and pointed to everything they'd ordered.

"Seventy-five for the hot pot," she said, "fifteen each for the starters. Fifteen for the beer. Each. The paper napkins are twenty-five."

"These?" Peach asked in disgust, holding up her crumpled napkin.

The waitress nodded.

"That's ridiculous!"

Sun An's face was red as he put both hundred-yuan notes onto the table. Peach tried to get them back, but the waitress snatched them up and threw down a single ten-yuan note in return.

"She's robbed us!" Peach said, talking louder than she meant to. She wobbled and put both hands down flat on the tabletop to steady herself. "I think I'm a bit drunk," she said, and Sun An helped her up. He was drunk as well, but the cost of the meal had just sobered him up. He'd have nothing for his parents this month. He'd have to go without meat or tofu to try and save money.

They took a cab back to the Space Rocket Factory, the glare of streetlights speeding up and then disappearing behind them. Peach flopped across the back seats, started singing a pop tune to herself. It was all about being in love, about spring, a mountainside of blossoms. Sun An thought she sounded beautiful. The driver decided he'd charge a bit extra. If fate gives you a couple of drunks then it was a foolish man who refused to take advantage.

"That's fifteen yuan," he said when they'd arrived.

Sun An guiltily counted out his last few notes. He only had twelve yuan, five fen. He counted them again. They made a small wad of one- and two-yuan notes; but it was all the money he had. Parting with it made him feel like he'd just paid for the meal all over again.

"All right — don't worry," the driver said as he stuffed the notes into his pocket. "As you have a video shop I'll let you off."

Sun An felt guilty. "Thanks," he said.

"Give her a bit of fresh air!" the driver shouted as he pulled off. "She'll be more fun if she sobers up a bit."

Sun An fumbled with the lock, then pushed the door open.

"What did he mean?" Peach asked as he shushed her, pushed her inside the dark room.

"I don't want to wake my sister up," he whispered. "She's asleep."

Peach leaned on Sun An and let him feel the way across the room. He thought he ought to give her some food, maybe let her sleep, then take her back. "How are you feeling?" he asked, leading her to the bed to sit down.

"Fine."

"Are you sure?"

"Yes," she said, her fingers groping in the darkness and finding nothing. She stepped forward and felt his arm, draped her arms across his shoulders. Her body pressed up close. Sun An could feel his dick start to fill with blood. "Do you really love me?" Peach asked. She swayed a little, held up by his arms.

"Of course I love you," he said, still thinking of the cost of the meal. "And you love me?"

"Of course I love you." Peach giggled, and fell back onto the bed, bumped her head on the wall.

Sun An helped her back up, rubbed the spot where it hurt and pulled her into a hug. "Do you truly love me?"

Peach's face stared up at him. "Yes," she said. Her skin was pale in the darkness, her eyes were shadows. Sun An was going to say something back, but instead he kissed her. Pressed his mouth down onto hers. She lay back and let him kiss her, his kisses became more and more passionate. Sun An was so erect he had to move position, his balls started aching. Her breathing made him more excited. He clasped her breasts and groaned; pulled her T-shirt and bra up, let her breasts spill out. Her nipples were hard. He tweaked them between his fingers, started to knead, then bent down and sucked them both, one after the other.

Sun An could hear Peach mumble something as he pulled her T-shirt up over her head, and dropped it onto the floor. Their groins were against each other, and they started to rub. They kept rubbing, and Sun An's balls ached so much they hurt. He tilted to the side to relieve the pressure, reached down, started to undo her zipper. Inside her pants she was warm and damp. He could feel his palm pulling on her pubic hair, so he pushed the top of her trousers down, slipped his hand inside her.

Sun An moaned again. He was so in love as he knelt up and pulled her trousers off. He stroked the smooth flesh of her legs, tangled his fingers in her underwear, then pulled them off, dropped them onto the floor. He lay on top of her again and kissed her, thrust his tongue in and around her mouth. He rubbed himself against her. He moaned with pleasure, it was more love than he had ever known before. He reached down and fumbled with his belt; wriggled his own trousers down, pushed himself upright and got them down as far as his knees. His dick was as taut as a drawn bow. It wobbled precariously, like it was about to fall over. He smoothed his hands down her spread legs, down her thighs. "I love you," he said, the words catching in his throat as he pushed her up the bed.

Sun An stared at the dark patch between her legs, lined himself up and lowered himself down. He pushed for the hole but it wasn't there. His penis hurt as it thrust against her skin. He couldn't find the hole.

Sun An lifted his buttocks and reached down. He took hold of his penis, it felt like it was about to explode. He found the right bit and pushed. She was tight and it hurt, but he kept pushing. Peach's insides were warm and wet and intoxicating.

Sun An groaned.

He pulled back and slid in again.

Went farther this time.

Out and in again.

*I*t had taken a few weeks for Fat Pan to finalize the details of the investment with Da Shan's friends. After the contracts were signed, he decided he would have a celebratory meal with his officers. It was always good to keep morale up, he told himself.

Fat Pan drew up a list of people: the Shaoyang Communist Party Secretary, his superior officer, the local mayor. There was the man at the police vice squad, it always helped to keep him well disposed; and also the local government planning official. He penciled in two of his subordinates and then stopped. He couldn't not invite Da Shan. Da Shan had given him the contacts after all, and he was good at keeping everyone drinking. Yes, Fat Pan decided, Da Shan could be the entertainment.

*A*ll the guests met at a place called the Jia Family Restaurant. A special room was set aside, with a table, sofas and a karaoke machine. Fat Pan sang "The Girl Next Door," while the other men had a few rounds of drinks, played drinking games and toasted one another with formal enthusiasm. Da Shan managed to persuade the Mayor of Shaoyang, a little man with a big opinion of himself, to sing, and he sang a patriotic song about the return of Hong Kong to the Motherland, very badly. Everyone clapped enthusiastically when he'd finished, then the Shaoyang Communist Party Secretary decided he would have to sing as well. Soon they were all clamoring to sing, and their singing added to the tuneless clamor.

Da Shan encouraged each man and found that he was quite enjoying himself. More than just enjoying himself, actually having a good time. It was as if he had forgotten how simple a pleasure being drunk was. It was like being on vacation from yourself.

The waitresses were short and pretty members of the Jia family. They acted as if they were the reason the restaurant was so popular, and served the food with a sullen resignation. First came cold starters of spinach salad, boiled peanuts and fried egg-plant salad. This was followed by an assortment of fried dishes: Bitter Melon, Pork Stomach, Sweet and Sour Pig's Fat. No one really ate much of these dishes, because they were all waiting for the restaurant speciality: steamed carp seasoned with slices of ginger and spring onion and sesame-seed oil.

Fat Pan ordered three; they came each on a separate plate and were set down on the table, one of the girls spilling a little of the juice over Fat Pan's left leg.

"Excuse me," the girl said as she left, as if it were Fat Pan's fault. His face was pink with the wine, and he pointed at the wet trail across his thigh. "Excuse me!" he repeated, and all the men laughed. "Excuse *me!*"

It was decided by popular agreement that anyone who had a fish's head pointing in his direction had to drink three cups. Those who had a tail had to drink four. The whole table burst into raucous shouting when Da Shan moved the table so that Fat Pan found that he had a head and a tail pointing in his direction.

"Whoa!" Da Shan clapped when Fat Pan finished his last cup and belched queasily. He gave him the thumbs up, joined in the chorus of shouting voices. "You're really strong! Good, very good!"

Another bottle of Open Your Mouth and Smile Wine was brought and opened.

"Open Your Mouth and Not Smile!" Da Shan cracked, and they roared with laughter. They were so drunk they'd laugh at anything.

When the carps had been picked down to their slender skeletons the waitresses cleared all the dishes away and brought in the fillers in case anyone was still hungry. There were three kinds of dumplings, steamed bread stuffed with minced tofu and spring onions, plain rice congee and a pile of mini-steamed breads that had red dots on top in the shape of the character for "Wealth."

The men fell upon them with the hunger of the drunk. Some called for vinegar while others called for chili paste, the waitresses brought neither. "How can we eat dumplings without sauce?" Fat Pan chastised the owner, Uncle Jia's eldest son, who apologized for his nieces and brought the vinegar and chili paste himself.

The men dipped their dumplings into the chili and vinegar, admired the delicacy of the fillings, the subtle blend of flavors. There was beef and mushroom; lamb and watermelon rind, pork and bamboo shoot.

"Crispy and soft!" Fat Pan announced. "Greasy and light!"

"A healthy combination," the Shaoyang Communist Party Secretary declared, and everyone agreed. Agreement and the Shaoyang Communist Party Secretary was another healthy combination.

The Mayor and Party Secretary left after the meal, but Fat Pan and the other army officers decided to go to a place in the center of town called the Joy Happiness Night Club. Da Shan said he was a bit too drunk, but they all insisted. "The wine would taste stale without you," they told him. "Come along, just for the company."

The Joy Happiness Night Club turned out to be another of the People's Liberation Army ventures, managed by Fat Pan's team. There was one girl for each man, to pour the drink and light the cigarettes. The minute Da Shan took a sip of his beer, his girl filled the glass up again till it dribbled down the side. Whenever he stubbed a cigarette out she pulled another one from the pack and lit it. She followed his thoughts before he even thought them. If he hadn't been so drunk it would have made him a little bit uneasy.

Fat Pan was so drunk he could barely keep himself upright. He had a feeling that everyone was laughing at him, which was made worse by the fact that he thought he had the ugliest girl. She said her name was Fragrant Beauty, but she had gap teeth and when she smiled it looked more like a leer. Da Shan was telling a story about Fat Pan when he was a student: how he'd gone out one night and got drunk and been sick in the dormitory — and Fat Pan could tell that she wanted to burst out laughing.

When Da Shan reached the punch line, "A real case of a fart turning into a bottle of perfume!" his girl couldn't stop herself, and joined in with everyone else, HAHAHA! She saw Fat Pan's glaring eyes and tried to smother her giggling behind her hand, but failed. Fat Pan saw the attempt to hide her amusement and wasn't sure which annoyed him most — the laughter or the poor attempt to hide it. It was all Da Shan's fault, he thought, he shouldn't have invited him.

Fat Pan rubbed his eyebrows, tried to keep himself awake. He shouldn't have invited Da Shan just to have him tell stories about him. If it wasn't for him Da Shan would still be in prison. If it wasn't for him; he was an important person, he was Vice-

Commander Pan of the People's Liberation Army! Why the fuck did he have to have this stupid ugly girl?

Fat Pan tried to visualize Liu Bei lying on the bed, wearing the dress he'd given her. The pleasure of knowing what Da Shan didn't know, the power it gave him over him.

"Oh we had fun," Da Shan was saying, "we really did."

Fat Pan raised his beer for a toast and the men all joined in. "To having fun with old friends!" he shouted, and they all drank.

When Fat Pan passed out in his chair Da Shan and the army officers decided enough was enough. There was a ten-minute fight over who should pay, two men holding Fat Pan upright and stopping him from going and joining in. He squinted at the row, hardly understanding what was happening, till he saw Da Shan paying, when he felt he was being upstaged at his own wedding.

"Heh! Let me pay," he slurred but no one was listening to him, they were all laughing and he didn't know why. "Fuck you!" he said and lunged, and they all started laughing more.

Fat Pan and the army officers climbed into a taxi and Da Shan waved them off. The camp gates were shut, but when the guards saw the men's uniforms they let them inside. One of the officers helped Fat Pan to his front door, then left him there, still swearing and cursing.

Fat Pan stepped inside his house and leaned against the wall as he took his shoes off and changed into his wife's slippers. His house was bent — the floors sloped, the walls moved away or up close without warning — and his slippers seemed to have shrunk five sizes.

He needed water.

Fat Pan walked through to the kitchen and turned on the light. His wife had demanded the kitchen be retiled and now all the surfaces gleamed newly back at him, dazzling for a moment and making him wobble even more. He poured himself a bowl of warm water and carried it through to the sitting room, spilling it down his front. There were karaoke videos scattered over the floor. Fat Pan kicked them out of the way, cursed his wife and her friends, and then hung his head over the steaming bowl.

He sat and inhaled, cleaning his nostrils and then taking a long deep slurp. He sat back and blinked his eyes. His mind was so slow with drink all he could think about was the meal, that girl's leer and the perfume-bottle joke. They kept jostling around in his head; clamoring for attention.

Fuckers.

Fat Pan took another slurp, closed his eyes, tried to silence Da Shan's voice, to stop the world from spinning.

Fuckers, he thought again, and got up, steadied himself for a moment, then staggered across to the bookshelf. His hands scrambled around for some writing paper and an envelope, then he staggered back to the sofa, which suddenly jumped out at him and made him fall over into it. His face pressed hard against the cushions. Fucking fuckers, as he pushed his body upright. He put the paper on the table and smeared a droplet of ink across the envelope. He strained to keep the table steady as he leaned his body weight on his elbows and began, very carefully, to write a letter that explained to Da Shan exactly where his old lover now worked, and how much it cost to fuck her.

D a Shan's taxi driver was a middle-aged woman who liked to talk. She rambled on about the number of nightclubs there were in Shaoyang now, and Da Shan lay back into the back seat, shut his eyes and grunted in the appropriate places. There hadn't been any nightclubs when she was young, all there was were demonstrations and political meetings.

Da Shan could feel the world spinning underneath him and blinked his eyes open. This car trip was going to end badly if he didn't get out, very soon.

Da Shan stopped the taxi by the Black Dragon Bridge, paid the woman and climbed out. The river was black and bottomless and deadly still. All rivers reach the sea at last, Da Shan thought, except the Shaoshui, which doesn't go anywhere.

Da Shan got to the other side of the river and turned left, along the riverside path. The rotting river mud smelled so bad that he crossed the road, walked along the pavement, past the long file of closed shop shutters.

He was walking along the deserted street when he heard the sound of shouting and saw a girl run into the street. He thought it was Peach, but he was drunk and sober enough to know it. Da Shan started walking a little faster, then the drunken half of him took control and he shouted out, "Heh!"

The girl didn't even turn.

"Heh! Stop!" Da Shan shouted but she didn't stop and Da Shan was already starting to break into a trot. The patter of footsteps made her turn. Peach saw Da Shan and recognized him, and tried to run faster.

Peach fell as he caught her up and Da Shan looked down in surprise. "It is you," Da Shan said, not really sure why he'd run to catch her up now that he'd done it. "I thought it was you." He was conscious he must stink of alcohol. "Have you hurt yourself?"

"No. I'm fine," Peach said, wiping her eyes. "Thank you. Really."

Da Shan's mind tried to assess everything that had happened: but it was all a bit confusing. He walked alongside her the short way to the factory gate, still trying to work out what was happening.

"Are you sure you're all right?" he asked at last.

"I'm fine."

"You don't look fine," he said, and she tried to laugh, but then her laugh changed to a sniff and he thought she might start crying again.

"Please," she said. "I just want to go home."

Peach looked up at her mother's bedroom window, and all the lights were still on. She felt sick, didn't know if she would be able to go and face her mother. She paused at the bottom of the stairs to rearrange her clothes. She undid her trousers, tucked her T-shirt in, checked that her bra was on properly. As she wriggled to get comfortable she could feel more of Sun An's stuff dribble down her inner thigh. She fought back a wave of nausea and stood very still as it trickled down her skin. She suddenly realized she had forgotten to put on her underwear she'd left in such a hurry.

Peach squeezed her legs together and then thought it might leave a wet mark. She wanted to cry. Wanted to go to bed.

Madam Fan had spent the evening watching Beijing Opera, getting up occasionally to stand in front of the mirror to copy a line or gesture. At the sad moments she felt weepy, told herself that her daughter had left home, was never coming back. She sniffed to herself, started knitting and waited for her daughter to never return.

Peach could hear the music as she came up the stairs and saw the line of light at the bottom of the door. She sniffed and wiped her eyes on her sleeves, took a deep breath and then knocked. There was a long wait before the door latch was pulled back and swung open.

"Peach." Madam Fan sniffed. Peach let out a sob and rushed in. She hugged her mother and started crying. "I'm sorry," Peach tried to say through her tears, but Madam Fan started crying as well. They cried and hugged and words didn't seem important anymore.

*D*a Shan lay in bed for a long while, trying to decide how much his head hurt. He winced when he remembered some of the things he'd said the night before, and laughed when he remembered telling the story about Fat Pan. It took a long time before he dared to open his eyes, even longer before he tried to stand up. When he did his heart fluttered, his head was disoriented, and he could feel gravity pull on his queasy stomach.

His mother and father were both out. On the stove there was a pot of lukewarm rice and peanut congee. He started heating it up, and got the shakes as he stood there watching it. His brain moved slower than the rest of his head, when he turned or looked up he could feel it pressing against the inside of his skull. Never again, he swore. Never ever again.

Da Shan sat at the table and slurped his congee down. He couldn't taste a thing, his skin started to sweat as he ate. He rested his head on the table surface until his green tea had cooled, then he slurped it down and refilled the cup. When Da Shan had drunk three more cups of tea he brushed his teeth and felt a little bit better. He needed ginseng, he decided, and checked to see if his mother had any. He picked through a bundle of unmarked brown paper bags in the cupboard and found some neatly sliced root with the familiar smell and glossy brown surface. He shook out a couple of pieces and began to chew them back to life.

It was time for a walk. He would rest his eyes in the green countryside, find a quiet spot and sleep. Maybe even dream.

Old Zhu's wife had gone to visit Autumn Cloud and Da Shan was out so Old Zhu locked the front door and set off down the lane toward his allotment. It was reassuring to plant seeds, watch them grow. It was something the young could never understand, all they did was knock buildings down to build hotels and swimming pools.

He squashed a few green flies, picked dead leaves off his tomatoes. He told himself his plants had done well this year as he pulled a weed out by the roots, then he stood up and stretched his back. It was time to go and see what was left of the New Block. See what was happening in the world.

They'd built the New Block in 1978, celebrating the end of the Cultural Revolution and the end of the Gang of Four and their extremist policies. It was their fault that he and Party Secretary Li had been kept in a broom shed for a year. The Red Guards called their home "the cow shed." They slept on straw and shat in a bucket. He'd gotten to know everything there was to know about Party Secretary Li in that year: and much of it he admired. Party Secretary Li had been a real comrade: stern and devout to the cause. When they'd been let out for meetings or struggle sessions they'd been led on leashes, like dogs.

Leniency for those who confess,

Severity for those who resist! they'd shouted.

Mrs. Cao was one of the worst. Her gang loved to beat up any others. "Plead guilty!" she'd ordered, and Old Zhu had pleaded. After his spirit had been broken he'd said anything they'd wanted him to. The first time he'd felt such shame he'd refused to eat their meal of rice gruel. Party Secretary Li had eaten his half and left the other half by Old Zhu. Party Secretary Li had had such integrity.

After the first time accusing others became much easier. Old Zhu would sign anything they gave him; he even made up stuff. He made up crimes to make up for all the ones he hadn't realized he'd done. How can we know all the effects of things we do in our lives? If they said he'd done it, he'd done it.

Old Zhu bit his lip. The first time was always the worst, that was what the whores had said. He'd done it just to stay alive. A voice told him that Party Secretary Li hadn't been broken: but Old Zhu refused to listen: Party Secretary Li was dead.

But the People remember Party Secretary Li didn't break, the voice continued, and *he* protested about the factory.

So what? Old Zhu retorted, and the voice had an answer ready: He'll be remembered, that's what! He'll be praised long after they've forgotten about you!

All praise after death is hollow, Old Zhu declared in his head. History is never written by the dead man.

No, the voice replied, but it's written *about* him.

Old Zhu's eyes started watering. He used the corner of his shirt to wipe the water away. Virtue's a luxury for the dead, Old Zhu told himself, being human was the lot of the living.

When Old Zhu turned the corner at the bottom of the road he let out a sad sigh: where the New Block had been there was black earth striped with track marks; heaps of smashed concrete flooring had been cleared to both sides; towers of stacked bricks stood guard over the workers who dug trenches between the string markers that had been stretched across the ground.

"Whoa!" Old Zhu called out, but none of them looked up. "Whoa there!" he called again, but they just kept on digging. Old Zhu was about to shout again when the man next to him told him not to bother.

"They're from Sichuan," he grunted. "Can't understand a word you say."

"I spoke to a boy here after Spring Festival," Old Zhu said. "He was from Shanxi, I think."

"They've gone."

Old Zhu looked at the men working: copper-brown skin, short cropped hair, eyes thin slits high in their faces. Their quiet conversation strange and alien.

"So what are they doing?"

"Digging," the man said.

Old Zhu squatted down next to him. He offered the other man a cigarette. They sat together and smoked. Watched the workers dig trenches just as they had years before. When the future seemed to be so good.

Old Zhu sat and thought: he still had his health and his wife, his son was at home, the Shaoyang streets were full of cars and motorbikes — the future has been good. The only problem, he thought, is that it hasn't been as good as they'd all expected it to be.

Late in the afternoon Da Shan also went down to the New Block and joined the crowd watching the workers. The sun cooled to red as it slipped down to the horizon, it cast the world in a strange half light that made the people around Da Shan seem unreal. The trenches were about a foot deep now, when one team of workers stopped another began. Picks and shovels and baskets of earth. And strong Sichuan accents.

"Why don't they hire Shaoyang builders?" someone next to him muttered. "It's not as if there's no one here who can dig holes."

Da Shan kept watching the workers. "Sichuan holes are much cheaper," he said.

It didn't look as if it was going to be a swimming pool. Da Shan wondered what they were going to build, then he decided it didn't really matter. As long as they were building something. As he stood he felt someone stand next to him, and turned to look who it was. It was Party Secretary Li's widow. She was trying to peer over heads to see what was going on. Da Shan moved to let her in front of him.

"What are they doing?" she asked.

"They've dug up the New Building and now they're digging foundation trenches."

Autumn Cloud nodded. The sunlight broke into yellow spokes as it slipped behind a cloud. It was good they had pulled the New Building down. If there had never been a Space Rocket Factory then her children wouldn't have left home, and her husband wouldn't have killed himself. But such was fate. It was all decided by Heaven.

"Did my mother come and see you this afternoon?" Da Shan asked.

"No," Autumn Cloud said, looking worried. "Why?"

"Oh, she just said she was going to visit you. That's all."

"Did she have something to talk about?"

"No, I don't think so."

"I was out," Autumn Cloud said with a worried face.

"Oh," Da Shan said.

The crowd stood in silence, watching as if their futures de-pended on it. There wasn't much to see; it was essentially the same as any other building site. Whatever they were building would appear overnight.

"Are you heading back?" Da Shan asked Autumn Cloud. She nodded and he tried to take her bags.

"No!" Autumn Cloud insisted, but after three attempts she promptly gave up and Da Shan walked with her back to her apartment. "You're a good son," she told him. "To come back and look after your parents in their old age."

Da Shan half laughed. He wasn't sure he'd be in Shaoyang permanently. Staying in Shaoyang was like falling asleep; you grew old quickly and quietly in places like this.

"You're divorced, aren't you?" Autumn Cloud broke his line of thought.

"Yeah."

"You should get married again," Autumn Cloud tutted. "Have a child."

"I have one."

"Where is he?"

"She. She's with her mother."

Autumn Cloud shook her head. "No wonder your parents are looking so old. They need to have children around them. It keeps them young."

Da Shan looked at the old woman and laughed.

"It's true," she insisted.

Madam Fan had been to Old Zhu's house but there had been no one at home. She sat on her doorstep all afternoon, waiting. When she saw Da Shan she jumped up and called his name, waved her hands to make sure he stopped.

"Da Shan, Da Shan," she panted in her excitement, "I'm so glad to see you!"

She didn't look glad at all. Da Shan could feel his hangover return a little as she flapped like a bat. She led him by the elbow off the path, still flustering as she began to talk to him in a confidential tone. "My daughter says that you walked her home last night," Madam Fan began.

"Yes," Da Shan said cautiously.

"How was she — I mean — did she seem strange to you at all?"

Da Shan stood still and thought. It was hard to say. Above his head the leaves vibrated on the cicada's single note. A mosquito buzzed in his ear and made him feel nervous. "I think she fell over." Da Shan nodded at last. "I remember that. She was crying."

"Oh." Madam Fan patted Da Shan's arm. "Thank you," she said, and then hurried home, her heart bubbling with excitement. Da Shan had seemed very reticent. Maybe something had *happened,* she thought. Something to make Peach so emotional. What a clever daughter!

What a very clever daughter indeed!

*T*he foundation trenches got deeper and deeper as the summer heat continued. At night the men used spotlights and continued working in the dark; as the pale yellow dawn spread, the men changed shifts and slept. Day and night pickaxes swung, baskets of dirt were carried up and tipped out at the side of the site. The men worked so hard that even the rats felt weary as they chewed through the piles of rubbish behind the kitchens.

One day one of the workers got hit on the head with a pick-axe and he made a strange gurgling sound as the other workers pressed in close to have a look. There was blood on the floor and a strange white goo that made some people feel sick. A crowd of workers and onlookers carried him to the meal tent while a boy ran off to get a taxi.

The taxi pulled up five minutes later, screeched to a halt and was instantly caught up by the cloud of dust that had chased it up the road. The driver jumped out, coughed out the dirt and asked what had happened. When he saw the man's head he refused point blank to have a bleeding man in his car. The other workers started shouting in their harsh Sichuan accents, they gesticulated wildly and became so threatening that in the end the driver gave up arguing.

"It's all right for you to make noises," he shouted at them all as he pulled off, "but it's my car that gets covered in blood!"

A crowd watched the taxi screech down the road, its horn blaring as people jumped out of its way. The red brake lights came on as the car hit the market, and the horn sounded again, for a long time, then it disappeared out of sight. The trauma of the event kept the crowd chained to the spot, as if something else had to happen; but the workers went back to their holes and one by one the other people dispersed.

The next day the workers were wearing blue plastic hard hats. They didn't stop to answer any questions, just dug and shoveled and carried baskets of earth and tipped them over the side. One rumor said the man had died; another said he'd lived but he had lost the power of speech; someone who had a relative who worked at the hospital claimed he wasn't dead yet, but that he soon would be.

"We're all guests on earth," one of the old women's gossip club declared that afternoon as they all sat under their tree, "whether we outstay our welcome or not."

The others nodded and grunted in agreement but weren't sure exactly what she was implying.

Or who she was implying it to.

The next day Da Shan decided to visit the temple again. He pushed through the crowded pavements into the center of town and out the other side. At the gateway of Central

Park he stopped, there was a woman with a Guess Your Weight Machine that flashed red lights and said in a computerized voice, "Welcome — Melcome." Da Shan paused to have a go, but the lady was talking to a man who repaired watches and cigarette lighters and she didn't look up or notice him.

He kept going up to the park gate, bought a ticket and walked up the steps that led to the East Pagoda. There were tombs along the way in the shape of mini-pagodas, for virtuous nuns who had lived here. There used to be a nunnery at the top of the hill. The nuns had all been beaten up and married off when he was a boy. He remembered laughing at them as their faces were painted and they were dressed like brides and made to marry the monks. Everyone laughed then, whether they found it funny or not.

The nunnery had been reopened in 1985: an official government license was framed on the wall next to the entrance. Official Site of Buddhist Worship, it said, by Authority of the Government of Shaoyang Prefecture. And a red official stamp.

Da Shan read the notice then stepped inside. A grizzled old man with a silver cataract in one eye sat by the door. He stuck out his hand and demanded money for a ticket.

"I've got one," Da Shan said.

"You have to get another one," the man declared. His cheeks were hollow, his left ear had a tear in it and his surplus-issue army coat was patched and ragged. He reminded Da Shan of a shaggy old dog as he gave him a one-yuan note. The man smoothed the note out with a callused thumb, put it in his drawer. He carefully tore off a ticket, handed it over to Da Shan, who handed it back.

"You haven't torn off the stub."

The dog-man took the ticket back and folded along the perforations, broke into a fit of coughing that ended with a gobbet being spat out of the door. The green lump rolled itself in the dirt and lay inside its jacket of fine dust. Da Shan waited as the man tore away the stub, then held out his hand.

"Thanks."

The temple had been smashed up in 1966. They'd piled the statues on a bonfire and burned everything they could find: clothes, books, religious hangings. The new statues were made of papier-mâché, their arms were too long, their elbows bent in the wrong direction. Guanyin had a severe look, her clothes were painted with red gloss paint that had dripped onto her knees. She had three double chins, and her left eye had a definite squint.

"For another yuan you can have your fortune read," the man offered, his blind eye disconcerting.

"No thanks."

Da Shan stared at the offerings in front of the statue for a while, then sat in the shadows. He had a jam jar full of tea in his bag, and a cold steamed bread bun. He chewed slowly, took a mouthful of tea, then chewed again. The first time he'd come here was with Liu Bei a few years after the temple had been reopened. The quiet hillside was a place where lovers would meet. They'd held hands and talked here. He half expected to see himself and Liu Bei sitting in a corner, laughing; but all there was was a half-blind old man, three burning incense sticks and a ludicrous statue.

Da Shan took a book of local history and flicked through the pages. It had been written in the Ming Dynasty and listed twelve natural scenic spots in Shaoyang. There was a poem for each.

One summer he and Liu Bei had tried to find them all, but of the twelve now only five remained. The last one they'd been to was White Cloud Temple. It'd been early on a Sunday morning and they'd arrived so early that the blind beggars were still asleep along the path. They turned around a bend to a cleft in the mountain where there was a forested hillside, a stream, and a Buddhist nunnery with a gray tiled roof furred with moss and lichen.

All the others were just names without places, existing only in memory. There was Shehu Mountain, which was more lovely in snow as the sun congealed from the mist; Celestial's Cave; and the Mysterious Sands Ferry, which he and Liu Bei had guessed must be down by the Black Dragon Bridge. The poets said the sight of red pavilions reflected in green water was the most lovely of all Shaoyang's scenic spots.

> Twilight colors fade in the mist (the poem went),
> The oar's splash shattered the water.

Da Shan remembered something Liu Bei had told him over a meal of mutton dumplings, that China wasn't mapped by lines on maps but by lines of verse. Dig under the concrete, the factories and endless high-rises and you didn't find pottery, but poetry.

He shut the book and looked around the temple. It was here that he and Liu Bei had come for their last night together; before they gave themselves up to the police. It was a day after the tanks had driven into Tiananmen Square. The demonstrations Da Shan and Liu Bei had organized had dissolved when the news from the capital spread. They'd gone into hiding, waited to see what would happen. The news was bad. Counterrevolutionaries were being rounded up and arrested. The same would happen to them.

They hadn't made love, they'd been too tired and frightened to kiss. Liu Bei had cried because of what she'd seen on the television and Da Shan had held her through the night. He hadn't cried. He thought he was being strong. "Whatever happens," he'd told her, "I'll be waiting for you." And he'd squeezed her tight. She believed him; and he meant it. He meant it even after he'd gotten out of prison and left. Even after he'd married he'd still meant it.

Da Shan shut his book. He stood up and walked out into the light. The old man was sitting on the steps, sunning himself and spitting more gobbets of phlegm into the dust. He grunted something as he left, but Da Shan kept on walking.

Liu Bei got up early and carried a sleeping Little Dragon through the winding streets of the old town. The sun was still a pale orange, the air felt damp and cool. There was smoke coming from her mother's chimney. The door was open and Liu Bei pushed inside, kicked the door shut behind her. Her mother was making dough for dumpling skins, her sleeves were rolled up and her hands were crusted in white flour. Liu Bei's arms ached more now that she was finally able to put Little Dragon down.

"He's still sleepy," she whispered. "I'll let him rest for a bit."

Liu Bei's mother nodded as her daughter lay Little Dragon on the bed next to Aunty Tang. The bed was cold, seemed to get colder the nearer to the other woman you went. Aunty Tang was sleeping more and more these days. It was as if she wasn't dying so much as drifting away. About time too, Liu Bei thought as she smoothed the hair from Little Dragon's face and folded the blanket over him, tucking it in under his chin. The sooner the better, she thought as she shook the blood back into her hands.

"Will you be OK?" Liu Bei asked her mother and her mother nodded. "I've got to go to town. I'll probably go straight to work. I won't be back until late."

Liu Bei's mother nodded again. She had long ago stopped asking questions. Questions were useless things unless they had answers to go with them.

The sun rose and the streets got busier and busier the nearer the center of town Liu Bei got. She checked she had the list in her pocket, and then she checked for the letter from Shanghai in the other pocket, just in case.

Liu Bei pushed past the confused mess of sellers and shoppers. She had to cross the road to avoid a market stall selling packaged shirts, where men shouted at the crowd through megaphones. There was a new row of glitzy shops with air conditioning and loud music and the occasional groups of bewildered peasants who were trying to find their way home. Across the street a new supermarket was being opened. Shaoyang's First Supermarket, the banner proclaimed, and there was a poster of a smiling pretty young shop assistant with the caption that read: *I'm enthusiastic and fair — I hope to serve you every day.*

Liu Bei decided she would go and have a look. Outside the doorway was a line of flower bouquets, each with a red ribbon and yellow calligraphy that named the principal investors. The Fourth Army, Fifth Division, People's Liberation Army, one of them read; Liu Bei curled her lip. Bastards, she thought.

Inside the shop there were lots of shop assistants standing and smiling like those on the posters outside; wary shoppers investigating the long aisles. There were twenty types of washing powder; two whole sections devoted to toothpaste, and an entire aisle of foreign brands of milk powder. Liu Bei stopped to look at a rack of toothbrushes. The colors were beautiful. They had toothbrushes with smiling faces and colored bristles, with free mini-tubes of toothpaste, brushes with stripes in red and white and blue. On an impulse she picked one out to give to Little Dragon as a present, but then she saw the price and put it back in shock. Seven yuan! Too much. Better not come at all than be made to feel like a pauper.

It wasn't far to the central rotary where the statues of large-breasted Dunhuang fairies waited for the fountain to be repaired to wash the dirt from their concrete armpits. Liu Bei walked up and down the streets, looking for the right place, but it was hard to find. She thought she might be too early so she slipped into a streetside restaurant and had a bowl of wonton soup. The pork was too fatty, but the green broth was good, and there was a sauce of crushed peanuts that Liu Bei spooned in. Peanuts were good for your heart.

Liu Bei drank the soup then stood up and paid the man three yuan. She walked around the rotary a couple of times till she saw what she was looking for: a piece of laminated paper propped up between two stones, and leaning against a streetlight.

Diplomas, degrees, driving licenses, other miscellany: FOR SALE, it said. The writing wasn't very good.

Liu Bei stood by the sign and waited. Three men who'd been posing as passersby came rushing over — clamoring for her attention. "What do you want? What do you want?" they demanded, and she told them. "No problem," they insisted and led her away by the elbow. "No problem, good, come with us."

The moon was gleaming from the hilltop when Liu Bei got back from the Drink and Dream Teahouse. In her mother's house Little Dragon was just as she'd left him, except that he was dressed in his panda pajamas, and his hair had been messed up by the pillow.

"He's asleep," her mother called from the toilet, and Liu Bei sat down at the table and waited for her to come out. Aunty Tang sat in the corner on a footstool, smoking a roll-up. The butt of the cigarette was wet with saliva, stained brown by the nicotine. The tobacco had a bitter smell, like it was mixed with twigs. The old woman was silent as she sucked the smoke in, breathed it out again like a toothless old dragon.

"I wanted to ask you," Liu Bei said, when her mother had washed her hands and come and sat down with her, "if I could borrow some money."

"Where do you think I could get money from?" Liu Bei's mother asked.

Liu Bei nodded. Her mother was always like this about money. "I just thought you might have some. Don't we have any relatives we can ask?"

"Relatives?" her mother snorted. "You don't expect me to go and beg at their door, do you?"

Liu Bei stopped. Maybe this was the wrong time. They sat in silence. The light bulb swung above their heads and made the shadows sway from side to side in a slow and predictable dance. Liu Bei thought of another way to bring up the subject, but couldn't. She had no idea what she needed would be so expensive, but everyone she'd asked had quoted the same prices. They were in league, she was sure. The whole world seemed to be in league against her sometimes.

L iu Bei was working late the next few days, and Little Dragon stayed over at his grandmother's. On her next full day off she went over to see him. She was excited at the prospect, but when Little Dragon saw his mother he looked away and carried on playing with his friends.

"Little Dragon!" Liu Bei called, but he ignored her. She waited, but he kept on playing so she pretended it didn't matter and went inside, sat down at the table. The event made up her mind for her: a whore couldn't bring a son up. It would be better for Little Dragon and better for her. And maybe she could come back and collect him when she had some money.

Aunty Tang refused to get up for lunch and Little Dragon cried because he wanted to keep on playing. Liu Bei's mother picked him up and he cuddled into her breasts, and sucked his thumb. Liu Bei watched and ate in silence. The old crone lay on the bed and stared at them through her blurry old eyes, started singing an old song to herself. Her voice was old and crackly, so tuneless it was hard to tell she was singing at all.

The noise started to grate on Liu Bei's nerves. She clenched her jaw shut, wanted to scream. Aunty Tang carried on regardless and Liu Bei began to feel the song was directed at her; as if the old woman was enjoying some obscure private joke. Liu Bei thought about how she would have escaped all this if she and Da Shan had settled down quietly together — but they would have to have been different people to do that, and she didn't want to be anyone but herself. No, that wasn't really true: they would have settled down if he'd kept his promise. She could have settled down with someone else if she hadn't waited for him; or if she hadn't had Little Dragon. Maybe she'd passed lots of other Da Shans in the streets or in the market: passed her ideal lover in the street, and never known. The thought made her feel cold and hopeless. Aunty Tang continued singing.

Liu Bei stood up and started to clear the table, carried dishes to the side ready to wash. She filled a kettle, lit the stove with a match, and set the water to boil. Little Dragon sat on his grandmother's lap and wanted to play peek-a-boo.

"Peek-a-boo!" Liu Bei's mother was saying, "peek — a — boo!" and Little Dragon burst out into laughter.

"Can you write your name yet?" Liu Bei called across with a smile, but Little Dragon took no notice.

"Peek-a-boo!" Liu Bei's mother said, and Little Dragon burst out laughing again. He was still laughing when she gave him a pencil and a piece of paper and said, "Come on — write your name for your mother."

Little Dragon held the pencil in his fist and carved the words onto the paper. He was pressing so hard the paper tore and he had to begin again, in the corner. Liu Bei's mother went to the bed and pulled up the mattress, took an old leather envelope and carried it into the light. She opened it up and took the money out, put it on the table. Little Dragon's eyes peered at it as he carried on writing the strokes of "Dragon" like his grandmother had taught him. "Little" was easy, it only had three strokes, but "Dragon" was difficult. He finished carving it into the paper, and counted how many strokes it had: "little" had three and "dragon" had one, two, three, four, five — six strokes! He checked his strokes, tried to make them look more like they should, then held it up.

"Look!" he shouted, but no one looked. His mother and grandmother were talking.

"Look!" he said again, and carried the paper over to them. "I wrote my name."

"Very good," Liu Bei's mother said. "Now why don't you go and sit down and write your mother's name."

Liu Bei's mother counted out the money Da Shan had given her in front of her daughter. There was more than seven thousand yuan. "Don't ask me where it came from, but I've saved it for you and Little Dragon," she said. "For emergencies."

Liu Bei stared at the money. With this much she wouldn't

have to go marry the man in the ad. She could do something: set up a business or something. Her mind raced as she reached and took the money. This was her second chance. She could put this with the money she'd saved and — Liu Bei felt a sudden terror. What if she did go to Shanghai and start a business, what then?

The summer had been so hot it dried great cracks into the yellow earth. Autumn Cloud noticed one had cut across the path as she walked up the hill to the Temple of Harmonious Virtue. There were good views out into the countryside, and there was usually a breeze up at the temple, even when the rest of the world was still. She climbed up one day each week, paid a monk to chant his rosary. While he chanted she would light three sticks of incense and stick them into the copper bowl at the feet of Guanyin. Let them carry her blessings to her husband.

Today she lit the incense as normal and puffed out the yellow flames. The tips glowed red then retreated slowly under long hats of ash. Autumn Cloud whispered her prayers and the monk started to cough. Guanyin's half-moon eyes looked on, unmoved, but Autumn Cloud turned in alarm. The monk wheezed a little more and then held his hand up to her not to worry, took a sip of tea from his jam jar, blinked his eyes. "It's OK," he said recovering his composure, using the disturbance to skip a couple of beads.

Outside the spring sun was scattering pale shadows across the floor and a light breeze was dancing with the sunlight. It ruffled Autumn Cloud's hair and sent gray wisps flickering across her forehead. She put her hand to her head, stroked a long strand, pulled it down and let it fly back again. From here she could see all across Shaoyang, she could even hear the clatter of machines on the building sites.

It had looked much more beautiful when she'd first come here in 1959. There had been so many villages and bamboo forests dotted through the fields. Now they were all buried under concrete and pavement. Autumn Cloud thought back to the time she'd been released from the reeducation camp, and shivered. How long ago was that? she thought. Ten, fifteen — no, it must be over twenty years ago now. She must have been released in 1973, she thought, and her husband in 1975.

Autumn Cloud let out a long sigh. What terrible days.

She and Party Secretary Li had worked hard to build China. Even though they were newlyweds they hardly saw each other for days or sometimes weeks. He'd been in charge of the Prostitute Reeducation Center, and she'd been working in the Political Press Office. Dreams of modernizing the country had driven them on. It was as if they'd been married to the country.

Autumn Cloud shivered again, and tried to wipe the tangled threads of hair from her face as the wind wrapped itself around her. She remembered reading about widows in Old China, maybe in the time of the Qing Dynasty. She'd always thought that she had nothing in common with people so far away, but now she wasn't so sure. Look at the worker who got killed last week: he was as dead as her husband. What did time matter: it was all in the mind. We all got washed away in the end and the muddy stream soon ran clear again.

It took a half an hour for Autumn Cloud to get back into town. She usually went to the man in the factory compound, the one by the office block, but there would be so much fuss — and anyway, it didn't matter where she went.

The first hairdresser's she found was a concrete box with a metal garage door open to the street. A teenage girl in a miniskirt was sitting in the doorway filing the nails of her right hand down to neatly curved blades. Her slim legs were folded over each other, her feet slipped carelessly into a pair of fluffy slippers that were made in the shape of dogs' faces with two flappy ears on either side. Autumn Cloud stood waiting, but the girl kept working on her nails. On the walls were pages neatly torn from magazines and stuck onto the wall with thumbtacks. Autumn Cloud peered into the beautiful faces with white smiles and gorgeous hair. She studied them for a moment and turned to look at the girl, who was still grinding her nails, then she cleared her throat and said, "Hello?"

The girl looked up and sniffed.

"I want a haircut," Autumn Cloud said.

The girl turned back to her nails.

"I want a haircut," Autumn Cloud repeated.

The girl let out a long bored sigh and stood up. Her doggy slippers dragged lazily along the floor as she walked to the back of a battered metal chair. She pulled the chair out and the metal legs scraped noisily across the bare concrete, then she pulled a dirty towel off a peg and flapped it in the air — creating a dust cloud of black hairs that fell toward the floor.

Autumn Cloud shuffled her bottom to get comfortable, and looked up into the mirror and her reflection gazed back.

"How do you want it?" the girl asked.

"Shaving."

"Shaving?"

"Yes."

"Completely shaving?"

"Yes."

The girl raised an eyebrow and reached forward to pick up the electric shaver, turned it on. The blades rattled together with excitement. Autumn Cloud felt the cool metal touch the nape of her neck, and the tone of the metal changed as they began to cut, and then strands of gray hair fell to the floor; one by one.

Autumn Cloud walked back to the factory and walked through the gate and up the stairs to her block of apartments. No one recognized her at all; it was as if she wasn't there anymore. Not even her neighbor's child, who was playing with a toy airplane and who just looked straight through her.

Autumn Cloud made herself a cup of tea and then sat down at the table and put her plastic bag down in front of her. It rustled as she unknotted the top and pulled it open, and looked down at the tangled strands of gray hair. She put her hand in and felt them, expecting it to feel reassuringly familiar, but it felt cold instead — cold and lifeless.

Autumn Cloud took a deep breath and unlocked the bedroom door, pushed it open. She didn't like to go back in there, it made her apprehensive. She quickly went over to the bed and smoothed the sheets down, and then knelt down and pulled the box out from under the bed. The ashes moved inside the box as she picked it up and carried it out into the living room. She shut the door behind her, and lifted the box onto the table. As she did so the box rattled again and Autumn Cloud shuddered. Her left hand began to shake and she bit her lip, but it wouldn't stop. She put the box on the table and clenched both fists, forced herself not to cry and took a deep breath. She was all right so far.

Autumn Cloud opened the flaps of the box. She didn't want to look inside, but couldn't help smelling damp ashes and seeing the irregular pattern of gray-black remains. She stared for a long moment at the jumble of ash and charred fragments of bone, and a wave of cold drenched her insides. The entirety of her husband's life reduced to a box full of ashes.

Tears blurred the world as she fumbled for the bag of hair and tipped the mess of hairs into the box. She found the box flaps and pushed them down again, and carried the box back into the bedroom. She left the box on the bed, and closed the door behind her, and locked it.

Old Zhu's wife was bargaining over the price of eggplant when she overheard someone say something about Party Secretary Li's widow. She piled up more than a kilo, bargained the price down to a pittance, then marched under the factory gate and up toward Party Secretary Li's apartment. Her feet tramped loudly on the stairs; she was breathless when she got to the top and knocked loudly on the door. There was no answer. She listened and thought she could hear the voices inside. She knocked again, louder this time. Still nothing.

Old Zhu's wife took in a deep and angry breath. She tried the door and pushed it open, and saw a figure sitting at the table: a shaven-headed Autumn Cloud.

"Oh heavens! Look at you!" Old Zhu's wife shouted. "What have you done?"

It took a while for Autumn Cloud to stop crying, and Old Zhu's wife felt guilty for being so forthright, but then her hand brushed against the bristles on Autumn Cloud's head and she started. A shaven head looked so unnatural: especially a woman's.

"Wah! You look like a nun!" she chided and Autumn Cloud smiled weakly. "There, there, that's better!" Old Zhu's wife said, then gave the woman a severe look. "Imagine how I felt this morning when a peasant told me you'd become a nun! I started telling them off for spreading tales and then I come here and find it's true. How do you think I feel — people will laugh at me."

"I've been thinking about doing it for a while." Autumn Cloud shrugged. "It felt right."

"But you look terrible."

"I got a cold head last night," Autumn Cloud admitted, and then let out a long sigh. "I get so lonely sometimes," she said. "My children are so far away. My husband is dead. It's not right," she said, her voice cracking with emotion, "everything he did for the country. Everything he did for this factory. All the work he put in. Everything he did for these people — and what do they care? They're building a swimming pool!"

Old Zhu's wife remembered what she had had to suffer in the labor camps: the hunger, the shame, the indignation. The night they came to take Old Zhu, and when they came to take her. Admit your sins! they demanded, but she had no sins that would satisfy them. The cold fear at night when the Red Guards would come to struggle against her. The terror when she heard that one of the male prisoners had hanged himself in his cell, and she'd been convinced it was her husband. The hours she had worried about her child: and what would happen to him without his mother and father. Whether they would punish him too. She thought about the years of his life she'd missed. Her own years wasted, the years she and Old Zhu could have spent together. The other children they might have had.

Old Zhu's wife wiped her eyes, the anger inside her was so strong she was afraid to let it out. She took a deep breath and tried to calm herself down. At least she'd come out of it with her mind intact, she told herself, which was more than could be said for Autumn Cloud. Autumn Cloud's mind wasn't strong enough. She'd lost her mind. They'd sent her for electric shock therapy. She'd never been the same after that.

Old Zhu's wife stroked Autumn Cloud's bristly scalp. At least Old Zhu and she were still here, she told herself, it was a victory of sorts. And Da Shan was here with them as well. She ought to be grateful. She looked down at Autumn Cloud and her shaven head. It reminded Old Zhu's wife of a rice field full of stubble. Poor Autumn Cloud. Life had broken her and then she'd been stuck back together and forced to carry on. Party Secretary Li had never forgiven the country for what had happened to his wife in the labor camps. He'd always tried to understand how it had happened, but there was no understanding. The past just was: like the cold or the mountains, like the fact Autumn Cloud had shaved her head, like the fact Party Secretary Li had hanged himself.

Old Zhu came back for lunch and found his wife furiously mincing a piece of pork with her cleaver. She glared up at him. "Where have *you* been all morning?"

"I was gardening."

"I looked there!"

"Oh, I went down to the river," Old Zhu said, as if it had slipped his memory.

"Well, *I* went to see Autumn Cloud this morning!" Old Zhu's wife announced. "And guess what!"

"What?"

"She's become a nun!"

Old Zhu looked up.

"She's shaved her head."

Old Zhu shook his head. "Impossible!"

"It's true, the man who sells bean sprouts told me," Old Zhu's wife continued. "I didn't believe it until I went to see her."

"But why?"

"How should I know why?" she spat. "What do you think?"

Old Zhu looked out of the kitchen window. Green leaves were rippling in the sunshine, and his mind was caught in their gentle dance.

"Are you taking any notice of what I've said?!"

"Hmm? Yes," he said. "Of course."

"You ought to do something."

"What can I do?"

"You can do *something*," she said.

Old Zhu spent the afternoon behind Number 7 block of apartments looking at the weeds and smoking. It was too hot to do anything. He wiped the sweat from his head and sat for a while in the shade of a tree, looking around at the factory buildings and chimneys, thinking of Autumn Cloud and her shaven head. Just like the women they had cared for all those years ago when he and Party Secretary Li were assigned as leaders of the Number Two Reeducation Center for Shaoyang Prostitutes.

The first women arrived when the place was still half built. There was such a demand. Those women had had to help build the place during the day and taken part in sessions that taught them how the Old Society had abused them. That wasn't so hard: there weren't many high-class prostitutes in a place like Shaoyang. The first girls were cheap fucks: riddled with syphilis and addicted to heroin. Their clothes were burned and their heads were shaved. This was the hardest thing: they'd spat and bitten like cornered dogs. Old Zhu chuckled to himself — he'd been bitten at least three times. Liu Bei's mother had been one of them. Old Zhu remembered Liu Bei when she'd been a little girl: red ribbons in her black hair and a shy smirk. He'd been fond of her, and quite pleased that Da Shan had gotten together with her, but Old Zhu's wife had been furious. She didn't care about New China anymore. New China had sent her to a labor camp for six years. What mattered to Old Zhu's wife was that Liu Bei was a whore's daughter: and once a whore always a whore.

Old Zhu snuggled back into the tree trunk, and the niche of memories. There was the night in 1950 when a gang of young thugs surrounded the prostitute reeducation camp and demanded their favorite girls be set free. Most of the girls had tried to get out and join them. He smirked at the memory but he'd been furious at the time. He'd had to bar the door with his body as they clawed at his face and screamed for help. Old Zhu smiled. He'd been bitten then as well.

Old Zhu stretched his legs. One by one they cured the girls physically and mentally. They educated the illiterate ones, taught skills to the others, and one by one the girls were found jobs and husbands and let back into the community. They were washed clean of all the filth of Old China and given a second chance. Some stayed on at the center, and then they'd started the factory. It was a good feeling — to have worked so hard helping to change lives. It made up for everything else that had come after.

Old Zhu was enjoying the solitude of memory when he saw Mrs. Cao walk past. She looked over and saw him and started to tiptoe across his allotment.

"Whoa!" she called out as if he were stupid. "President Zhu!"

It was a long time since anyone had called him that. He'd been the factory president for years, but now the name had a strange sound to it. It no longer fit.

"President Zhu!" Mrs. Cao smiled, sugary sweet.

"Careful," he said as she stepped on a melon tendril and crushed it beneath her shoe.

"Oops!"

"What can I do for you?"

Mrs. Cao collected herself, cleared her throat. "Well," she began, "as you mention it, there is something." Mrs. Cao cleared her throat again, let a smile rise up to the surface and break like a bubble across her face before settling in her pale brown eyes. "It's about the factory. Haven't you heard?"

"What?"

"Terrible," Mrs. Cao said.

Old Zhu looked at her feet, which were straying too close to his melons. Mrs. Cao shifted her feet. "They're going to start charging everyone under fifty rent. Either that or we have to buy our apartments off them. For 80,000 yuan. How can we afford that?"

Old Zhu tutted and shook his head. The factory always looked after its own. It gave people housing, schools, clinics, jobs, even an old people's club. It was a basic part of a Communist country. "Yes!" Mrs. Cao continued. "The shame of it! After all our contributions to the Motherland. Treating us like strangers in our own homes. It wouldn't have happened in your day."

"No, it wouldn't," Old Zhu agreed. "But then lots of other things wouldn't have happened either."

This seemed to be going down the wrong track, so Mrs. Cao tried to steer the conversation her way again. "We went to talk to them."

Old Zhu gave a dry chuckle. "And?"

"They wouldn't listen. I thought they might listen to you."

Old Zhu nodded, no expression on his face. He sat quietly for a long while, looking at his allotment. "Do you know the poems of Ruan Ji?" he asked.

"Ming Dynasty?" she said, uncertain.

"End of the Han Dynasty," he told her quietly. "Third century."

"I'm too foolish," Mrs. Cao said, half embarrassed and half

proud of the fact that she didn't know. "You know my generation never got an education," she said, straightening up. "The Cultural Revolution got in the way. We were educated in the fields, with the peasants."

Old Zhu nodded. He knew all about that.

"Ruan Ji was forced to choose between two factions at court; so he chose neither and became one of the Seven Sages of the Bamboo Grove."

Mrs. Cao fidgeted. "I have no idea what you're saying."

Old Zhu carried on, talking patiently. "Well, have you heard of Wang Wei?"

"Of course," Mrs. Cao said, getting irritated with this foolish old man.

"And how he retired from office."

Mrs. Cao sighed loudly. "Yes."

"To live the simple life, in a thatched hut. And when men came to ask him to return to court he refused."

"Of course."

"Well," Old Zhu stated, "I have retired from office. And here is my thatched hut."

Mrs. Cao stood for a moment and regarded Old Zhu standing in front of her. "That's a fine way to be," she sneered. "Just because this doesn't affect you. Just because you have a son to act as your retirement policy." She struggled for another barb, then she shook her fist and spat, "Has your son's money corrupted you as well?"

Old Zhu quoted Zhuang Zi: "How can you discuss the size of the ocean with a frog who lives in a well?"

"How you ever came to be leader of this factory — I'll never know. You're nothing but a running dog of the capitalists!"

Old Zhu's gap-toothed smile opened wide into a loud laugh. "I think you said that to me in 1967," he said.

Mrs. Cao snarled, "And it was true! We should have left you in your cow shed!"

"Maybe you're right," Old Zhu said, smiling at Mrs. Cao, "and maybe not. Either way — why don't you go and read some Ruan Ji? A very fine poet."

"Indeed!" Mrs. Cao said as she turned and walked back to the path, crushing melon tendrils as she went. Old Zhu sat down and pulled out a cigarette, lit it and watched and waited, puffing out little clouds of cigarette smoke. He watched as one by one, and very slowly, the leaves she had trampled began to straighten themselves out.

*I*t was two weeks since the night at the Hot Pot City, but still Peach was too nervous to go outside the factory compound. Her mother had suggested they go shopping together, but each time Peach had made up some kind of excuse: the sun was too hot; it was too dusty; there were too many people in town; she had all the clothes she needed. Madam Fan thought her daughter's change a little strange at first, but as the days went on she got used to it: took it as normal. If Peach had gone out into town without her then she would have cried all over again.

One reason for Madam Fan's attitude was that the more time Peach spent in the Space Rocket Factory Compound the more chance she had to see Da Shan; or more important, *be seen* by Da Shan. Things had fallen into place quite nicely, Madam Fan thought, despite her husband's lies and behavior. She was sure that Peach was the prettiest and kindest girl in the whole of Shaoyang Prefecture; and she had a high opinion of Da Shan too. He was rich and intelligent. He had enough good sense to choose Peach as his wife.

The sun always rose in the east. Heaven was kind, if only you were patient enough.

Peach spent the whole week helping her mother: sweeping, washing, dusting, cleaning the toilet — but at random moments she felt Sun An was in the room watching her, or that stuff was dribbling down her thigh and she needed to cry. Then she gritted her teeth. Clean, clean, clean!

Madam Fan was surprised by her daughter's sudden desire to clean the house, but what with all the other changes in her daughter, she told herself that maybe Peach was maturing into a woman. It was natural for a girl to start keeping house: it was a sign she was ready to start one on her own. Peach would make a good wife after all.

Madam Fan watched her daughter with a swell of pride. If only she could sing opera as well she would be the perfect daughter. She put on a tape of opera greats and hummed to herself as she started knitting a red sweater: Peach would look beautiful in red, she thought to herself, and imagined the wedding day setting the whole factory on fire with gossip and excitement. Peach dressed from head to toe in dark red: her beautiful pale skin and black hair. How pretty she'd look. She would have the wedding Madam Fan never had. There'd be cars and motorbikes, firecrackers and a video. The Zhus would make sure it was a big occasion: Da Shan was their only son. They'd be looking forward to some grandchildren.

Madam Fan remembered that Da Shan was divorced and stopped for a moment, before starting her fantasy again. His wife was in Shenzhen — and that would take a couple of days by train. And anyway he'd had a girl. Who wanted a granddaughter when they could have a grandson? And he'd be *her* grandson as well.

Heaven was kind! Madam Fan told herself, despite everything.

As Madam Fan knitted the day outside got colder and colder. In the evening a mist rose off the river, milky tendrils wriggled up over the piles of rubbish and reed beds, then settled over the streets. Overhead stars began to glitter, and a waning moon lifted itself above the hills and crept nervously into the sky.

The mist was at its thickest in the old town, down by the river. It was so thick it condensed on the cold glass windowpanes and began to drip. Light from a carved window lit the mist up with a yellow halo, and from the window stared a woman's face. Liu Bei stared into the whiteness and shuddered. It'd be autumn soon, and autumn was the saddest time of year, when she resented being alone most of all.

Well, she wouldn't go through that again. She'd be gone before then.

Liu Bei shuffled through the forms she had collected this afternoon: they'd taken longer than expected, the men said, because of a government crackdown on corruption.

"But they're always having crackdowns."

"I know," the man responded, "it's good for their business. Means they can charge higher prices for what they should do anyway!"

At the top of the pile was a letter to say that Liu Bei was unmarried and childless. If she'd been in a work unit then they'd have written it; but she'd been thrown out after 1989. In a place like Shaoyang a person without a work unit was a nonperson. If you didn't belong to a village or a factory or school or hospital then you were on your own. She'd heard it was different in Shanghai: but you never knew.

At the bottom of the pile was the last form she had bought. A new birth certificate for Little Dragon. Liu Bei sniffed and bit her lip. It was the best thing she could do for him. He was getting older now, he needed a father.

Little Dragon, the writing read, born: January 9th, 1990. Mother: Liu Bei; Father: Zhu Da Shan.

She folded the papers up, put them in her pocket and

waited. There'd be a couple more customers if this night was like all the others. A few more men and then she'd go and see Little Dragon at his grandmother's house. Liu Bei could almost hear her son's breathing: faint but audible. If only Da Shan had written back. She thought of what might have been, then checked herself. Mistress Zhang was coming up the stairs. Liu Bei wiped her eyes and told herself to stop. A couple more customers and then she could go and forget this place.

The next morning Liu Bei was up early, before dawn. It was a long way to the train station, she had to walk to the Black Dragon Bridge before getting the Number 204 bus. As she walked through the early morning dark, it seemed that Shaoyang had never looked so beautiful: the moonlight cleaned the river to a glimmering silver; through the mist she could hear the hoot of a car horn.

Liu Bei turned a corner and saw a soybean-milk seller starting the fire on his mobile restaurant. She hadn't even left and she was feeling homesick already.

The minibus to the train station cost two yuan. It was full of people with faces still puffy with sleep. No one spoke except the ticket collector, who crammed people in two to a seat; called for the people at the back to pay their money.

Liu Bei nodded off to the rhythm of the potholes, woke again when they pulled up outside the train station. The sky had turned a pale turquoise and the sun had begun to glow. She walked up the street, past all the restaurants that lined the road, and past the men shouting out the prices for a bowl of dumplings or steamed buns. The ticket office didn't open until 7 A.M., but already there was a crowd of people milling around in confusion, looking for the right counter. Liu Bei looked up at the signs and tried to work out which counter she should line up at. Eastbound trains. Numbers 22–27.

The longest lines were for tickets south, to Shenzhen and Guangdong — but there were about a hundred people waiting to go east as well. Most of them were peasants, tanned a deep amber from the weeks of harvest, now going away till the planting season came again. They shuffled sacks at their feet, gathered into uneasy clumps, or just gave up and sat on the floor. There was an old woman with bowed legs who didn't seem to know whether she was going north, south, east or west. She walked from the hips, swinging around on her bent legs, and kept trying to push to the front of each line. The peasants let her past, but the city folk shouted and pushed: told her to get to the back and stop causing trouble. Liu Bei joined a line and waited. At seven o'clock there was a bustle of activity behind the screens and everyone shuffled forward in expectation. Ticket touts started going around offering tickets anywhere for a price.

"Where are you going?" one girl asked Liu Bei.

"Shanghai."

"There aren't any tickets for Shanghai left," the girl said.

"Then I'll go to Beijing."

She left Liu Bei alone and moved on to someone else. Another tout had captured the old woman and he was taking her outside. "Wherever you want to go I'll get you a ticket," the man was saying, and the old lady was hobbling after. At that moment a shutter snapped open and ticket sales began.

It took forty minutes for Liu Bei to get to the front of the line. All the time large confident men in shades pushed to the front and no one dared to stop them. Anyone who didn't look rich and confident was cursed and pushed to the back of the line.

Liu Bei stayed tightly crammed into her space in the crush. She couldn't stop anyone from pushing in five spaces ahead, but she could stop anyone from getting in front of her. If someone pushed in behind she didn't even turn: that was for someone else to worry about.

When at last the push of bodies left her at the front Liu Bei bent down to the small hole and shouted. "Ticket to Shanghai!"

"Hard seat or hard sleeper?"

"Hard seat."

"There's nothing for a week."

"OK."

Liu Bei could just see the woman's face: she was flicking the beads up and down an abacus and adding up the cost. "A hundred and forty-seven yuan."

Liu Bei counted out the money and shoved it into the hole. She could hear more clicking as the woman checked the sum, then flicked a small cardboard ticket at her. Liu Bei grabbed it and squeezed out from the press of people, clutching it in her hand. It was a small thing to cost so much.

The day was sunny and warm all morning, but in the afternoon a wind rose and blew clouds in from the coast. Sun An sat in the doorway of his shop and watched them grow steadily more gray and foreboding. In the bamboo grass at the side of the shop the wind whistled a sad tune. Sun An decided he wouldn't wait this time. He would go and see Peach and find out why she hadn't come to see him. She'd said that she loved him. Didn't that mean anything to her?

Sun An hadn't been inside the factory compound before. As he walked under the gateway he bit his lip and thought what he'd have to tell his parents about the missing money. He wouldn't go, he decided, not until he had some more money.

Then he would go and see them and take Peach as well. They'd be happy their son had a girlfriend from the city. An educated and pretty mother for their grandchildren. They'd be too happy to say anything about the money. He wondered what he could do to pay for his sister's school fees. He would go and visit his relatives and see if they would loan him the money. Some of them didn't approve of educating girls in the family so he'd tell them it was for the shop.

Sun An's mind jumped ahead and he imagined himself with the biggest video shop in town; with Peach as his wife and his sister at university in Xiangtan or even Changsha. He would take his parents to see the village that Chairman Mao was born in. His father would like that. He respected Chairman Mao, thought Mao was a strong leader.

Sun An stopped thinking when he got to the blocks of apartments. He didn't know which one Peach lived in so he went to one door and knocked. He could hear a TV inside, the shouts of a family: husband, wife, mother-in-law, child.

"Who is it?" a man shouted.

"I'm looking for someone," Sun An shouted back.

"Who is it?"

"I only want directions," Sun An tried again.

"It's a beggar," he heard a woman say. "Don't open the door."

"Go away!" the man shouted.

Sun An knocked again but there was no answer, just the random chatter of a television, so he kicked the door and went.

The wind was damp, the evening chill made Sun An's skin pimple. He'd have to get some more coal bricks in, he thought as he sat on a doorstep and waited. At last someone came walking along the path. Sun An asked the man where Peach, Madam Fan's daughter, lived.

"Madam Fan, the opera singer?" Da Shan double checked.

"Yes."

"Up there. Fifth block, third floor, on the right."

Sun An counted the blocks of apartments and stopped at the fifth. Fifth block, third floor, on the right, he repeated to himself as he paced up the steps. Fifth block, third floor, on the right. Fifth block, third floor, on the right.

Sun An's mantra became so hypnotic that he missed the right door and carried on up the stairs, still chanting. He was halfway up to the fourth floor when he realized his mistake and turned to go back down. On the third floor landing there were two doorways. Fifth block, third floor, on the right.

Sun An shuffled uncomfortably, third floor, on the right, he reassured himself as he lifted his fist and knocked.

Peach had soon learned that there was only so much housework any single house could provide. A cockroach couldn't even fart without her finding it and scrubbing the floor where it had been. After she'd scrubbed the toilet floor she sat down and stood up and sat down again; paced around the apartment, sat down again. She was so bored that the idea of learning opera began to seem more and more appealing. When her mother played tapes of music she started to learn the words, when the videos were brought out she stayed sitting on the sofa and didn't go straight to her bedroom.

Madam Fan turned to her daughter and was going to ask, but stopped herself at the last minute.

"What?" Peach asked.

"Nothing."

"I can tell you wanted to say something," Peach said.

"I was just wondering," her mother began, "I just thought how nice it'd be if we could sing opera together, that's all."

Peach didn't say anything. "Do you want me to sing?" she asked at last.

"You know I do."

"OK," Peach said. "We can start tomorrow if you like."

M adam Fan had begun to worry about her little plan because Peach was spending so much time inside, but now that she'd agreed to learn opera she was more delighted than she'd ever been. If Peach sang opera in the mornings no man's heart would be safe! The whole of Shaoyang Prefecture would be coming to her door. Maybe she'd even get a better man than Da Shan. One who was rich and not divorced. Someone high up in the Party.

They spent the evening going through the basic dance steps of Beijing Opera. Madam Fan clapped when her daughter got it wrong and laughed when she got it right. "Very good! Very good!" she shouted. "Good good!"

Madam Fan told herself that the change in her daughter had come about because of the things she'd told her about her own past. Peach had learned the lessons she'd meant to teach her. It wouldn't be long till Peach and Da Shan started meeting in the parks for secret liaisons, holding hands and looking bashful when people walked past. Madam Fan imagined walking through the park and finding them both together! How clever.

Madam Fan gave her daughter two tea towels so she could practice flipping her long sleeves over her arms when she wore the proper opera gown, and stepped in to adjust the angle of Peach's fingers. Peach repeated the steps with the tea towels, Madam Fan stood back and gave her the thumbs-up — "Good, very good," she announced. "How about singing?"

Peach's shoulders sagged, although her feet remained in place. "I'm tired."

"OK," Madam Fan said. "Singing tomorrow," and then went into the kitchen and boiled a kettle for tea. The flames were blue and yellow, they wafted in an unseen draft. Where they caught the soot on the kettle bottom they sparkled red. As she stood and watched, the glass panes rattled in the window frames. The wind was up. The autumn winds would strip the hillsides bare, comb the leaves off the trees.

Madam Fan was drifting off when she heard a knock at the door. It was a slow definite knock, like a warning. What could be the worst thing that could happen now, she thought, and imagined it to be her husband, come back. I'll let him know if he can come back, she said to herself as she strode to the door. I'll let him know what I think of all the things he's been saying about me!

Madam Fan marched to the door and swung it open. Her body was tense and her lungs were full and ready — but it wasn't her husband, it was a young man in cheap clothes.

"Yes?" she said, in a condescending manner, still ready to slam the door shut.

"I want to see Peach," the man said.

Madam Fan looked at him. The man spoke with a country accent and there was something about him: he didn't look like one of Peach's old classmates and he didn't live at the factory, she was sure. "Who are you?" Madam Fan demanded after she'd made this summary conclusion.

"I just want to see Peach," the man repeated. His movements were nervous, he was only a little bit taller than Madam Fan herself. She drew herself up and looked at him, almost straight into the eyes. His eyes would have been handsome if he'd had some presence about him, instead they looked shifty.

"Peach," she called out imperiously, "there's someone here to see you."

Peach came out of her bedroom while Madam Fan stood at the door, on guard. Peach peered around her mother and there was a long pause. Madam Fan began to realize her daughter knew this man after all. When Peach spoke her voice was sullen. "I don't want to see you," she said simply.

Sun An stepped forward and started to speak. Madam Fan had had enough of this, the boy sounded like a peasant; he was probably a worker down on the building site, she had no idea how he had gotten her daughter's name and address — but she was going to make sure he never came back. She stopped him in his tracks and gave him some choice words. "I don't know how you know my daughter's name," Madam Fan declared, "but she doesn't want to see you!"

Sun An tried to push past Madam Fan, which made her red with anger. Spots appeared on her cheeks, prickled her skin, intimidating the man into silence. "Get out of here, you filthy beggar!" she screamed. "Stop molesting my daughter or I'll call the police!"

"But she loves me," he protested.

Madam Fan was cold with fury. "What do you mean she 'loves' you?"

"We love each other," he repeated.

One of Madam Fan's neighbors opened their door and asked if they could keep the noise down.

Madam Fan tried to close the door on the impudent wretch, but he put his hand out and stopped her. "Peach!" he called out, but Peach was helping her mother push the door closed. They managed to shove hard enough to get the latch to click and Sun An was left standing in darkness on the concrete stair landing. He couldn't understand how she could stop loving him so quickly, after all the money he'd spent on her, after what had happened between them. He sat down in despair, but after a few minutes the neighbor opened his door again to check that the noise had gone and saw him there.

"Piss off!" The man tried to kick him. Sun An leaped out of the way. "We don't want any beggars around here!"

Sun An stumbled down the steps to the next landing, kept going down till he was out of the factory and down to the river.

For a whole week the cold wind kept blowing summer from the world. It blew over the dead reeds by the river, carried the mournful cry of geese that woke the residents of Shaoyang Number Two Space Rocket Factory from their dreams and made them shiver. Blankets were snatched from wardrobes and cupboards; they snuggled up under them, shut their eyes and wished they could pick up their dreams from where they'd left off. In the mornings they heard the wind and stayed curled up under their sheets, decided not to get up just yet, but to stay and enjoy the warmth a little bit longer.

As the cold wind kept blowing, the club of ballroom dancers started to thin and then fail altogether. It got to the point when only one middle-aged woman turned up with her tape recorder and waited, but no one else came. She put the music on, as if the noise would summon the others out into the crisp morning air: but none came. She would have to dance on her own.

The next morning even this last dancer decided to stay in

bed, and Madam Fan was out on her balcony to revel in their absence, but after what had happened with her daughter it felt like a hollow victory. Madam Fan took a deep breath and she found she was starting to cry, tears slithering down her cheeks like icy slugs.

The morning after the boy had come to the apartment Peach had denied knowing anything about him, but Madam Fan could not believe it. Who'd ever heard a single hand clapping? The neighbors said they'd seen Peach with a boy who had a shop along the road into town. Armed with a sense of betrayal and righteous indignation Madam Fan had persisted till Peach's defenses had crumbled and the whole story had come out. The meal, how he'd gotten her drunk, how he'd taken her back to his shop. How he'd had sex with her. Madam Fan listened and the anger against her daughter began to channel itself back toward the boy.

"He forced you?" Madam Fan gasped, feeling the cold weight of the past drain through her.

Peach wiped her nose, and looked inconclusive.

"Did he or didn't he?" Madam Fan demanded.

Peach mumbled something and Madam Fan said she couldn't hear.

"Yes," Peach said at last, "he forced me."

Oh heavens, Madam Fan had thought. Oh heavens.

Madam Fan still couldn't understand how her daughter could have had a boyfriend who was a peasant. As if there weren't enough boys in the factory for her. She tried to stop the sadness constricting her throat, but its grip tightened. She leaned onto the balcony and cried for all the opportunities she'd missed in her life. Cried because her daughter was about to make the same mistakes. Cried because it felt so good to let it all out.

She would have to do something. She couldn't let this ruin her daughter's life as it had hers. The boy might start telling tales: no one would marry Peach if they knew she'd slept with a peasant. Her beautiful daughter would end up with an uneducated man like Madam Fan had done. She'd end up with a wife beater.

Madam Fan wiped her tears away: Peach would get the husband she deserved. She would make sure of that.

Now that the cool weather had arrived Fat Pan found he could sleep again, but his wife tossed and turned. Her period had started in the night and after she'd gotten up and put a tampon in she knew she would never be able to get back to sleep again. She didn't particularly want to go back to bed anyway: her husband was no great lure anymore.

Fat Pan's wife filled a kettle and switched it on, then she yawned so hard she had to stand still and wait until it had finished. She'd cleaned the kitchen the day before, she may as well clean the living room. She could get it all nice and tidy before her husband got up. It was easier when he wasn't around.

Fat Pan's wife put all the videos back into their cases and stacked them by the side of the TV. She tried to find the TV remote control, but it always seemed to disappear whenever needed. At last she found it down the side of one of the cushions on the sofa and put it back in its proper place on top of the TV. If only people could put things back where they belonged, she thought, then things wouldn't get lost.

She gave an irritated sigh as she saw a piece of paper under the sofa and bent to pick it up. She'd assumed it was a scrap of some kind, but as she picked it up she realized it was an envelope. There was an address on the front: Zhu Da Shan, Shaoyang Number Two Space Rocket Factory, Shaoyang, 422000 and a smear of ink. Her husband must have forgotten to post it. She put

it on the coffee table where he could see it, let him sort it out.
She wasn't his secretary.

The same morning Old Zhu got up and threw the blankets off and went down to his allotment. A cold autumn shower had dyed the leaves red. His last melon had been withered by the frost, the tomato plants were just withered stalks now, but at least his beans were still cropping. It seemed no time at all since it was Spring Festival, hardly a week since he'd planted his seeds, and now — here he was, in the autumn already.

Year by year old age comes closer.

Old Zhu bent to pick up a yellow leaf that had not survived the night. It'll soon be time to start raking up leaves again, he thought.

The wind yanked at her clothes as Madam Fan caught a motorbike-taxi to her brother's house. The man was going too fast so she tapped him on the arm and shouted at him to go slower. She didn't like motorbike-taxis at all. They wobbled and leaned to the side when they went around corners — but she told herself she was doing this for her daughter. Madam Fan liked to imagine that she'd give her life for her daughter.

Her brother was still at work, but his wife was in. Madam Fan sat uneasy on her sofa while she waited for her brother to come home. After a few minutes she couldn't wait any longer. "It's about Peach," she began, and her sister-in-law patted her hand in encouragement.

"Yes?"

Madam Fan looked down at her hands. "I had no idea," she said. "Really — I had no idea." She sniffed. "She didn't tell me — her own mother."

"What?" her sister-in-law said.

"That she had a *boyfriend*," Madam Fan hissed.

"Isn't that good?"

"No!" Madam Fan said. "It isn't."

"Oh. Why not?"

"He's a peasant."

"Oh dear."

"She showed me some poems he wrote to her. His hand-writing is terrible." Madam Fan rubbed her nose and sniffed. "I had no idea. But he took her out to an expensive restaurant . . . and he gave her beer to drink."

Madam Fan's sister-in-law sat forward.

"He got her drunk. He took her back to his shop."

There was a moment of breathless silence.

"He took her back to his shop," Madam Fan said, "and he forced her!"

"No!"

"Yes!" Madam Fan said. "People will gossip so! It'll destroy her. It happened to me — *I* know."

When Madam Fan's brother came home he saw his sister sitting there. He sensed the chill in the room and put his police cap down on the table. "What's wrong?" he said, sitting on the chair opposite his wife and sister. "What is it?" he said again. "What's happened?"

Madam Fan sprinkled tears like seasoning; sniffed as she retold the story, more elaborately this time and her brother listened and nodded. He was a policeman, he heard this kind of story every day: but he still had a grave look on his face. This was family.

"Don't worry," he said, patting Madam Fan's arm, while his wife supplied her with another handkerchief: "I'll look after this."

After lunch Fat Pan went for his afternoon nap. He was snoring and his wife was irritatedly trying to not hear him. She let out a long sigh: wondered how she ever ended up with such a lazy husband. She tried to tell herself she couldn't remember why she'd married him in the first place: but it wasn't true. He lived in the city and she was desperate to leave her village. She'd married him because she thought he would be a good husband to have. And she supposed he was. It didn't really matter now anyway, she'd given him a child and he'd given her a bright new apartment.

Fat Pan's wife thought of asking Fat Pan for a new washing machine as she walked through the apartment. That letter was still on the table by the sofa. She picked it up and looked at it: he obviously wasn't very interested. His handwriting had an odd slant to it: his letters were careless, it looked like he'd written it on something soft. She took it back to the kitchen where she meant to leave it so she would remember to ask him what he wanted to do with it, but as she poured herself a cup of tea she spilled water over the front. She tried to dampen the water away, but the ink was smudged and the paper started to tear. Stupid thing! she thought as the tear got wider, then she thought, Damn it! and screwed it up and put it inside a plastic bag and put it in the bin.

Fat Pan's wife began to worry he might miss the letter, either that or he might see the bag and suspect something. She picked the bag out of the bin and took it outside to the rubbish chute. The metal shutter was smeared with dried grime; she kicked it open with her foot and threw the stupid bag away with its stupid letter inside.

On the hillside the cold pines were singing in the wind when the rain started. It rang out on the rooftops, slow, irregular droplets: sounded like it was going to be a downpour, but the cloudburst never came: just slow heavy drops and a whistling wind.

Liu Bei walked with Little Dragon through the drizzle. He kept falling behind and eventually she had to pick him up and carry him.

"I'm cold," he complained.

"Don't worry," she told him, "nearly there."

The evening streets of the old town were dark and unlit. The tightly packed roofs shut out the pale white glow of the clouds. She hurried past the turn for the Post Office and then took the next right, her feet feeling for the steps down, and then she walked quickly again, the path taking her up to her mother's house. A single pale yellow streetlight shone out, and a few moths flickered in a tireless and fruitless romance.

The door was bolted. Liu Bei banged and her mother opened it. Her mother didn't speak, Liu Bei pushed inside regardless.

"I've put all his things in here," she said in a businesslike manner. "All his clothes and toys. His shoes are in this bag."

Little Dragon was sitting on the stool, sleepily watching TV while Liu Bei's mother stood with her arms folded. Liu Bei looked up and saw her: stopped talking. She ran her hand through her hair and let out a long sigh. "And that's everything, I think."

Liu Bei's mother nodded. "Have you told him?"

"Yes."

"And?"

"I told him that Mother had to go away for a while. And he was going to stay with Granny."

Liu Bei's mother turned around and walked to where Little Dragon was sitting. She stood behind him and ruffled his hair. "Time for bed!" she said, and Little Dragon yawned. "Come on, say good night to Mother!"

Sun An and his sister slept in the same room when it was cold. He'd been silent for days, moving with a slow determined air: as if the whole world were against him. His sister watched him changing for bed: he'd stopped seeing that silly girl at least, she thought. She wasn't good enough for her brother. He was too honest for her.

"Night, little sister," he said and turned the light out.

"Night," she said.

Sun An's sister lay in the darkness and thought of which of her friends would make the best wife for her brother. It was a silly game that made her smile: she couldn't imagine him with any of them. He should marry a nice simple village girl, that's what he needed.

Sun An dreamed he was a fisherman who kept on catching the same fish. In the dream he kept saying no he didn't want to eat that fish and putting it back, but every time he put his line into the water the same stupid fish kept biting the food. His sister was dreaming about her school friends when a sudden battering on the front and back doors woke them both up. Sun An sat up in alarm.

"Who is it?"

"Police! Open the door!" came a voice. There was more banging as Sun An jumped out of bed in his vest and underpants and began to feel for his clothes on the floor.

"What do they want?" his sister asked. They heard the sound of a body barging the door. The door frame began to creak.

"I'm coming!" Sun An said as he pulled his trousers up. The door frame creaked again. "I'm coming!" he shouted. "Shit!" he muttered and hopped on one leg. "Coming!" he shouted as he fastened his belt and pulled the bolts open, and turned the key. The door flew open, and a number of flashlights dazzled him. Bodies came in, five or six, each with a flashlight, shining it in his face.

"What do you want?" Sun An asked.

"Who are you?" said a voice, a flashlight shining in his face.

"Sun An."

"You own this place?"

Sun An nodded, trying to move his face so the light wasn't shining in it. He couldn't, whichever way he turned was a shining light.

"You got any papers?"

Sun An nodded, eyes almost closed with tiredness. He reached to a bag on the wall, and rummaged through for his papers.

"Who's this?" A flashlight shone across the room.

"She's my sister."

"She got papers?"

He dug hers out and handed them over.

"What's your name?" another voice asked.

He repeated it.

"Date of birth?"

"Third day of the fifth month, 1972."

"You sure?"

Sun An nodded.

"I don't believe you," said a soft voice.

Sun An squinted into the light, shrugged with tiredness.

One of the policemen kicked him in the groin, and he grunted in alarm and pain and doubled over. "I said I don't believe you."

"It's true!" He winced.

His sister looked on in alarm, pulling the quilt up to her face, to smother her screams. There was another thud and another grunt, then another.

"Stop!" Sun An's sister screamed. "Stop!"

"I think you ought to come with us," one of the policemen said, and pulled Sun An up to his feet.

"It's true," Sun An said again.

"What are you doing?" his sister called out.

"Shall we take her too?"

"Yeah," another voice said. "Why not?"

A hand clamped around her forearm and dragged her out of bed, out into the cold night and into the back of the police van.

Sun An and his sister held each other's hands as they were driven over the potholed roads. He tried to speak but a flashlight was shone in his eyes and he was told to shut up.

They had hoods pulled over their heads before the back doors were opened, the cloth was rough and had a moldy smell to it. Sun An's hands were handcuffed behind his back and he was led down a corridor and thrown into a cell, his sister brought in a few minutes afterward.

"What's happening?" she asked him, and he shook his head. He didn't know.

Sun An's sister sat close to him, and he put his arm around her. "It'll be all right. Don't worry," he told her, but his voice sounded unconvincing.

It was late in the night when the men came back. Sun An and his sister were asleep on the bed, her arms wrapped protectively around her brother. The *clang!* of the door lock woke them, Sun An sat up and waited as his sister shielded her eyes from the light.

Sun An had never felt so frightened. He closed his eyes and waited for the blows — but they didn't come. Instead his sister started screaming as they pulled her off the bed and out the door. Sun An stood up and a voice said "Sit down," and he did. She'd be all right, he told himself. They must be letting her go. She had school tomorrow. He shouldn't fight, he'd just get beaten up. He had responsibilities. He had a video shop. He had to send his parents money.

They took Sun An's sister down the corridor to an empty cell where they threw her onto the bed. Two men held her hands down, pressed the metal frame into her flesh, stopped her struggling. Another tore her trousers off. She kicked and they chuckled to themselves.

"This is to teach your brother not to go around fucking city girls," one man said.

"Tell him to keep his peasant dick to himself!" another hissed. Sun An's sister stared at him, saw the stubble on his chin, the snarl on his face as time slowed down and twisted. His hands pulled the front of his trousers open and his penis was smooth and shiny and erect. Sun An's sister squeezed her eyes shut when they pulled her underwear off; started shouting. There were rough hands on her thighs and private parts. Fingers pushed her top over her breasts, the skin was rough, the fingers strong. When one of them pushed inside her she could feel the hairs on his legs rubbing against the skin on her inside thighs.

"Please!" she whimpered, but he pushed inside and she started crying. She opened her eyes. His face was twisted and angry. "Please no! Please!"

"If you talk any more you'll start singing opera," one of the men laughed, and she bit her lip but they didn't stop.

Sun An sat rigid on the bed listening to the screams drifting down the empty corridor. It wasn't his sister. They'd let her out. He pictured her back at the video shop, in bed. Too worried to sleep, then dozing off like she always did. It was good, he told himself, she'd get some sleep before she had to get up for class. The screams stopped and a door clanged. Sun An stood up. It's OK, he told himself. It's OK. She'll be home now in bed.

When the footsteps came back down the corridor Sun An sat up again on the bed: his eyes were so wide he could make out the dark gray walls and door through the darkness. They'd let her out and now they'd let him out. They'd have checked his details: he had all the necessary documents, his business license was in order. He would be OK. This was all a mistake. If they wanted money then maybe he could bribe them or something.

The policemen dragged Sun An's sister back through the door. Their flashlights dazzled him again, the door slammed shut. Sun An crawled. "Sis?" he said, and his hands touched bare skin. A leg. They felt halfway up her leg then stopped.

"Sis, are you all right?"

Her voice was quiet. "Go away," she said and pushed his hands away.

"Little Sister?"

"Please go away," she said, and started to cry.

Liu Bei didn't sleep that night either. Little Dragon's head was pillowed on her arm, her other arm was held protectively around him. She cried silently, sniffing only occasionally, and listened to his soft breaths. In the darkness her lower lip trembled, and the tears started flowing again.

There wasn't much time in the morning to get everything organized. Liu Bei had gotten up just after five, turned the stove on and started boiling a kettle. Her fingers smelled of kerosene, there was a black oily smear on one of her knuckles. She wiped it on her trousers, feeling the roughness of the fabric, moving the smear to her leg.

Liu Bei stood and waited. The noise of the warming water seemed so loud. She was frightened it might wake them all up. She turned the flame down to the lowest setting, let it boil slowly. She sat as the world outside the house began to wake up. Occasionally someone passed in the street, a hawk as someone cleared their throat and spat; or just the approaching tap-tap of footsteps coming close and fading away.

Liu Bei's mother grunted something in her sleep, turned over and lay still again. Little Dragon lay like the dead, unmoving. Aunty Tang's breathing was heavy, she snored then snuffled then snoozed silently. Liu Bei's train left at seven forty-five. She'd have to leave here at about six thirty to make sure she got there. She checked her watch, it was six twenty.

Liu Bei wanted to sit and watch her son sleep for the rest of her life: he looked so perfect and fragile, just as she wished she still was: not burdened down with memories and guilts, dreams and disappointments. She sniffed and blew her nose into a piece of toilet tissue. She'd promised to wake her mother before she left but now she couldn't bring herself to say good-bye. She would just sit and watch them and then slip away. They would wake and find she was gone: and it would be better that way.

Liu Bei turned the stove off, it'd still be warm when they got up, then she picked up her bag and put on her coat. She stopped at the door and looked back. Good-bye, she thought. Then stepped out into the waking world.

Liu Bei was so tired not even the motion of the Number 204 minibus could lull her to sleep. Her eyes ached but they couldn't close; she stared out of the window, through her own reflection, saw the sun rise over the hills and begin to burn brighter and brighter.

There was a bustle of people at the station: all pushing and shoving and getting nowhere. Liu Bei held her ticket in one hand and her bag in the other, pushed through to the entrance to the waiting room and showed the station attendant her ticket.

The waiting room was lit by naked electric bulbs that gave the room a sepia look. Most people were asleep, or sitting quietly, talking in low voices. 07:21. There was a smell of unwashed socks, a stench of cigarette smoke, the floors were thick with phlegm and grit. Liu Bei sat on the end of one of the benches and waited as the digital-clock display flashed on and off: the last digit changing every sixty seconds. Her eyes couldn't look away.

07:22

They were so tired. Every six hundred seconds the last two digits changed.

07:30

Liu Bei kept staring; stopped noticing after a while.

At 07:35 there was an announcement that the Shanghai train was approaching the station and half the waiting room jumped up and started to push for the exits. Liu Bei joined in the jostling crowd, kept pushing for the exit, through the gate where guards checked everyone had the right ticket, and then out onto the platform.

It was a fight to get onto the train: it was a slow train and over the miles it had filled up with peasants heading for the east. Liu Bei squeezed herself in by the door, struggled to turn around and sit on her bags. It was thirty-six hours to Shanghai: then she could begin again. After so long, thirty-six hours didn't seem so long to wait.

Guards marched up the train, ordering people to push up inside the train, then forcing the doors shut. Liu Bei peered past the man next to her; out of the window. If this was a film then Da Shan would come running onto the platform now. The thought made her smile. He'd come running onto the platform and she would force the door open and jump out, and then that would be THE END, and the names of all the actors would follow. She imagined what the happy ending would be like: something clean and simple. No loose ends to confuse matters. The train started with a jolt that made the man next to her lose his balance for an instant.

Liu Bei stared out as the gray Shaoyang platform began to move across the window. The train picked up speed, the platform and station disappeared altogether. The tower blocks and streets and cars and motorbikes flashed past in the window glass as they rolled through the town; out into the countryside.

Liu Bei stared out of the window: she was too overwhelmed to cry. She was leaving everything behind; even her son.

*T*here was one more week of hot humid weather, then autumn set in for good. It was Da Shan's favorite time of year: cool, clear days of blue skies and white clouds, a sense of wistfulness that got more intense as the year changed.

One day someone stopped Da Shan and said that there was a letter for him down at the factory office. It was from Shenzhen, the person said. Da Shan nodded. He took the fried dough sticks back home, ate them with a bowl of soybean milk, then walked down to the office, under the trees. The leaves that'd survived the night clung desperately to their branches; the ones that had fallen scuttled hopelessly around looking for a way back up. He kicked them and they rattled.

The letter was from Da Shan's ex-wife. She said she'd met a man from Singapore and they were going to get married. They would go and live with his family. She was taking their daughter. She thought he ought to know. Yes, Da Shan thought, I guess

I ought. He read the letter again, and then put it into his pocket.

It was the kind of letter you'd expect in autumn: it made him feel disconnected, melancholic. Da Shan was walking back up to the blocks of apartments when he met his mother hurrying down the road.

"Have you heard?" she demanded.

"No."

"They've found a body," she said. "Down at the building site."

Da Shan remembered the man who'd been killed. "A worker?"

"No, it's in a coffin."

Together they walked down to the site of the old New Block; there was a dry putrid smell that kept getting stronger. "One of the old women saw it this morning," she told him. "At first they didn't know what it was. Then they realized it was a coffin."

There was a crowd gathered. The trenches were so deep now they had to stand at one end of the building site to see in. Da Shan and his mother pushed to the front and peered in. It was hard to see around the workers who were gathered there having a cigarette, so Da Shan took his mother's hand and pulled her out of the crowd.

"This way," he said and ducked under the rope. "Cigarette?" he offered the workers. They smiled and Da Shan passed them his lighter, then jumped down among them. Da Shan's mother was too old to jump, so she went back a bit and let herself down where the trench wasn't so deep.

The top of the coffin had been staved in and the putrid smell was very strong. The half-excavated casket was dry and crumbly, like driftwood. Through a hole Da Shan's mother could see something white and stringy.

Go and have a look, one of the men signaled with his hand, and Old Zhu's wife didn't know if she really wanted to look.

"Go on." Da Shan laughed. "She's still there."

Old Zhu's wife edged a little closer and saw that the white stuff was grass packing. Da Shan was with her — go and have a look, one of the workers signaled and she leaned forward. A few of them chuckled to themselves, sucked deeply on their cigarettes and Old Zhu's wife laughed nervously for a moment and took another step forward.

"Oh dear," she whispered as she peered straight down into the face of a dead woman. "Oh dear."

The news that the workers had dug up a grave set the Space Rocket Factory into a flurry of activity. The older members of the community shut their doors and windows in case the spirits brought bad luck: the younger residents were more concerned about the smell. Smell or not, everyone put their shoes on and hurried down to have a look. Items of news were traded in exchange for cigarettes: she was a whore who'd died from a drug overdose in 1950; it was the body of the video shop boy; the clothes dated from before liberation; she had bound feet; the workers had stripped her of rings and gold.

Wah! The people muttered as they saw the small frail body. It looked like the body of a small woman. Her hair was bound around her head, she wore a long flowing gown of silk; her skin was dry; her long fingernails were black. The corpse's hair had grown in the grave, there were whiskers on its chin, its jaws were open, its teeth were black. Both feet were bound, shorter than the man's palm, they were perfect "Three Inch Lilies."

The old women under the tree spat in disgust. They didn't approve of digging up dead bodies at all. Death and burial were supposed to be the end of the story. If you couldn't find peace in the grave then where could you? It was a subject close to many of them, getting closer day by day.

Old Zhu's wife went to tell Autumn Cloud the news while Da Shan stayed around for a bit longer then decided he ought to go and tell his father.

Old Zhu had caught a cold and was sitting in a scarf and a Russian hat, watching TV. The program was about a man in the Northeast border with Russia who had spent all his life cutting down trees, and who now spent his retirement replanting the areas he'd cleared. He was sorry he'd done so much damage; but it had seemed right at the time, now he dreamed of the forests there were in his childhood. He wanted to replant as many trees as he'd cut down; he reckoned he had another 8,345 seedlings to go. He was getting old. He didn't know if he would achieve his aim.

"Haven't you heard?" Da Shan cut in.

"Heard what?"

"They've found a dead body."

Old Zhu was suspicious of things other people knew before he did, as if being told them made them less true. He shuffled, pulled an uncomfortable face and winced. "Really?"

Da Shan wanted to laugh at his father, but instead he opened the window and let the smell into the house. Old Zhu shivered when he smelled the putrid stench of the grave, but at least he stopped asking questions. Only a dead body could smell that bad.

Old Zhu stayed out at the graveside all morning. He watched the man from the Public Utilities Bureau arrive to collect the body. The man parked his car next to the building site, pushed through the onlookers and began to shout orders. He got a couple of the workers to help him lift the body out of the coffin and up through the crowd, to his car. People were pushing in for a closer look or pushing out trying to escape the smell, and when a black fingernail caught one girl on the hand she screamed and there was a sudden panic because she claimed the old woman's hand had moved. Everyone stepped back, maybe she'd been cursed!

At first the man from the Public Utilities Bureau tried to get the body into the trunk, but her feet were a little bit too long.

"You could tie the trunk down with string," someone suggested, but the man from the Public Utilities Bureau said that that wouldn't do at all. They tried to put her across the back seat — but they had the same problem: the door wouldn't close. At last they ended up putting the corpse into the front seat, with the seat reclined as far back as it would go. The man from the Public Utilities Bureau climbed into the driver's seat and leaned across the corpse to get the seat belt. He pulled it across the body and clicked it into place. "There we go!" he said and started his car. The crowd all jostled around the car; he waved at them all to get out of the way, then pulled around onto the road and out of the factory.

Old Zhu watched the car go and shook his head. The face of the dead woman had looked familiar. It was impossible, he knew, but still he had a feeling of recognition in him that he couldn't dislocate. He shut his eyes and saw the corpse's face: dried skin wrinkled and cracked, sunken eye sockets and leering teeth, and had a feeling that the dead woman had recognized him as well, even though its eyes had stayed shut.

The next day was colder than the first and the old ladies who sat under the trees said it was a curse for disturbing the dead. It wasn't right to dig graves up like that; once a family put you in the earth, there you should stay. A few of them, who'd been with the factory from the start, remembered that when they'd started building the place it was full of old graves.

"This was a south-facing hillside," one of them explained, "a very lucky place indeed!"

The others nodded. In spite of its faults the Space Rocket Factory had been good to them.

Old Zhu's wife found out from a neighbor that Old Zhu had spent the whole morning in the cold. She was furious he'd gone to look at dead bodies in his condition, kept silent about the fact that she'd gone to look as well. It was an unlucky thing to do, she snapped at her husband as he winced from his sore throat. What if the ghost of the dead woman came back to haunt him? He wasn't strong enough to fight her off, was he! First having dead bodies in the wardrobe, and now this!

When Old Zhu's cough didn't go away she claimed it was the least he deserved and called a doctor as a punishment. The first one insisted they take Old Zhu down to the clinic and put him on a drip. Old Zhu's wife refused: the clinic was too cold and drafty. The next was a short man with an open, frank look who felt Old Zhu's head and heart, looked at the color of his tongue and then prescribed a course of traditional Chinese medicine, combined with a chest massage twice a day with Tiger Balm. Da Shan went to the medicine shop just outside the factory gate and gave them the prescription. He sat and had a cigarette while they opened all manner of wooden drawers and took out what they needed: powders, twigs, roots, lumps, dried shredded leaves. Each was weighed out in a daily amount, and then poured into a row of white paper bags that the pharmacist stapled shut.

"How much?"

The man used an abacus and a piece of paper. "Thirteen yuan," he said.

Old Zhu's wife insisted on boiling up the first course as soon as it arrived, even though the doctor's instructions said "morning" and "nights."

"It is morning," she snapped when Old Zhu said he shouldn't be taking anything yet. "And how come you have the energy to argue if you're so ill?"

She boiled the stuff for two hours and the smell it gave off got worse and worse, till Old Zhu curled his lip and refused to take it. It was the same stuff his mother used to give him when he was a child. It was a black-purple liquid that tasted worse than he remembered. He put the bowl down and winced.

"Drink!" his wife ordered, and refused to go away.

Old Zhu was worse than a child, she decided as she sat down and flicked through the *Shaoyang Daily*.

Old Zhu was sipping the last few drops, making sure he didn't drink the lumps at the bottom when his wife sat up. "Wah!" she exclaimed, and leaned forward to read again.

"What is it?" Old Zhu asked, but she didn't respond until she'd read the whole article. "It's about the body they found," she said. "She was buried a hundred years ago."

Old Zhu raised his eyebrows. "What happened to it?"

"They burned it."

"Didn't they find anything on her?"

"Yes, it says she was from the landlord class," Old Zhu's wife read, scanning the article and picking out snippets that might interest Old Zhu. "She had no family still living in the area, the body was well preserved, dry conditions of the soil. That's it."

Old Zhu nodded then let out a long sigh that turned into a cough. The feeling of recognition stayed with him. The Zhu family had once had a graveyard on a hill outside Shaoyang, he remembered. Maybe it was a Zhu family woman.

As the days went by Old Zhu tried to pin down every body he could remember being accidentally dug up when they'd built the factory. When he slept the faces haunted him, and when he was awake he became more and more convinced that Shaoyang Number Two Space Rocket Factory had been built on a Zhu Family graveyard. All the bad things that had happened were because his ancestors had cursed him. All those years in the "cow shed" were part of his punishment. The man who'd shared the cow shed with them in the winter of 1967 hanged himself because the ghosts were angry. Even the fact that Old Zhu only had a single son was a curse: he'd been given just enough to ensure the Zhu bloodline would not die out and no more.

Old Zhu fretted. He thought about the man in the cow shed and bit his fingernails. He and Party Secretary Li had woken and found him swinging from his belt. He was a cadre from another work unit. They didn't even know his name. But what was strange was that Party Secretary Li had mentioned the man a few weeks before his death. Maybe it was a warning. Maybe this was a sign. Even when he was asleep his face was tight and nervous. Old Zhu's wife sat over him and thought he looked in pain.

Illnesses came in all varieties, but all after each man's nature, the doctor had said. This illness didn't seem to be in Old Zhu's nature at all: it was vicious and malevolent. Imagine all the disease and germs bottled up in that coffin for all those years. It was a wonder that half the factory hadn't been wiped out.

Have you finished your medicine?" Old Zhu's wife demanded that evening as Old Zhu coughed and he held up the empty bowl for her to see. "Hmm," she said and then left him to his illness.

Old Zhu dozed and dreamed of Party Secretary Li hanging still in the room, the ink drying on the wall. Party Secretary Li opened his eyes and smiled. "It's easy," he said. "We could have done it a long time ago. It could have happened to us anytime." Old Zhu didn't understand and Party Secretary Li explained, but the explanation made no sense. Old Zhu turned and saw the old woman in her grave. She got up and pulled the death mask off and he saw it was his wife in elaborate makeup. "It's easy to let go," she told him. "I've been here waiting. For you." "I've just got to check on my tomatoes," Old Zhu had told them, and then he'd woken up.

The next morning there was a gray hammered sky and Old Zhu lay in bed strangely quiet. He didn't even complain when his wife came to give him his medicine. He lay and thought about Autumn Cloud, about his wife, what they'd all been through in the last forty years. "You know," he said in a quiet voice, "all these years — you've been a good wife."

Old Zhu's wife looked at him in alarm. She saw the old man's tired face and thought of the young Communist Party visionary she'd fallen in love with all those years before. He didn't complain when she made him drink the medicine and she felt a rush of panic: Where's Da Shan?

"He's stopped complaining," she said. "I'm worried."

Da Shan went in to see his father. Old Zhu's skin sagged, his eyes had lost their sparkle. He saw Da Shan let out a long, deep breath. He looked at his fingers and shook his head, lay silent for a long time, thinking about what he had to say.

"Nineteen twenty-four," he said at last. "Nineteen twenty-four was the year I was born."

Da Shan gave half a smile.

"In a village near Dongkou. The youngest of my mother's three children. She died when I was five. I never saw my father." Old Zhu coughed. "He smoked opium. Even when he was there he was somewhere else. Each year there was less than before. Those were bad years. Bad years."

Da Shan adjusted the pillow behind his father's back and Old Zhu forced a smile. "Too many cigarettes," he said. Da Shan watched his father as he recovered, drew in a clear breath. "That's what it was like before liberation. We changed all that. Whatever we got wrong, China is a better place." Old Zhu nodded to himself. His mind kept on wandering. "Those girls we took in, they were in a terrible state. Terrible. Some of them were only girls." Da Shan held his father's hand and absentmindedly stroked a vein on the back of his father's palm. "We fed them and cured them. Gave them skills, found them husbands. And one of them bit me!"

Old Zhu dozed for a while and Da Shan sat by his bed listening to his rattling breath. Old Zhu was sleeping and Da Shan could hear his mother in the kitchen, chopping. He walked to the window and looked out. The factory hadn't even outlasted its founders. They'd lived to see it grow and decay and finally close. He let out a deep breath and Old Zhu stirred. There was a rustle of bedsheets and then the old man croaked, "Water!"

When Da Shan brought him his cup of tea Old Zhu slurped and coughed, put the cup down on the bedside table. He shut his eyes and breathed heavily, Da Shan sitting by the bed, just in case.

At six o'clock Old Zhu's wife stood in the dining room and shouted, "Dinner!"

Da Shan didn't move.

Old Zhu's wife stood in the doorway. "Come on!" she snapped. "If you're not careful the food'll get bored and walk away!"

Old Zhu patted his son's hand as if to say, go on, I'll still be here when you come back.

The winds got more and more ferocious the deeper they went into autumn. Old Zhu sipped his medicine every morning and night and refused to get better. Some days he started telling Da Shan about the Zhu Family Clan, but then he'd get confused and sit scowling out of the window. Other days he refused to understand why he had to stay in bed. One night he got up and was stumbling toward the door when his wife saw him, woke up and had to drag him back to bed.

The next morning he was unapologetic. "If I wasn't drinking that stuff I'd be fine," he told his wife, and she silenced him by tilting the bowl up again and forcing him to drink, making him pull a sour face.

Over the next week Old Zhu's wife kept a close eye on her patient. He wanted to go and check on his chrysanthemum, but she wouldn't let him out of bed for more than a few minutes, and he certainly was not allowed to go out onto the balcony. One night he wouldn't let her sleep till she had promised to go and sweep up all the leaves for him. She ignored him for as long as she could then turned and told him to go to sleep.

"But all the leaves," he said and broke into another coughing fit. His chest sounded raw and painful, full of phlegm and bile. She sat up, put her hand on his arm to reassure him, rubbed his back with the other.

"OK, I'll burn the leaves," she said. "Tomorrow."

"Promise?" he managed to wheeze.

"Promise."

The next morning Old Zhu's wife put on a padded great coat and went down to the allotment while his medicine boiled. The square of earth was buried under a carpet of brown rustling leaves: it seemed all the leaves in Shaoyang came here to shelter from the wind. Old Zhu's wife went back and got his rake, then began to rake them all into a pile. So many leaves, she half thought, half reprimanded them, if only you'd clung on I wouldn't be here sweeping you up. If you'd held on then you'd still be in the trees!

The leaves rustled in reply, but Old Zhu's wife wasn't listening. She was thinking about the medicine that was still on the stove, on a low blue flame.

When the smell of burning leaves drifted up to Old Zhu in his bed he slept more peacefully, and dreamed again of Party Secretary Li and the dead old woman they'd dug up. He dreamed that the ghosts, so many ghosts, of the Space Rocket Factory all came to welcome him to the Yellow Halls of the Dead, but Old Zhu kept on telling them he had some leaves to burn, and they all smiled:

We know you won't burn leaves again, they said, and Old Zhu insisted that he would. They were *his* leaves.

Old Zhu took his food in bed, his wife sitting with him and feeding him as if he were a child. "Come on!" she told him. "Open your mouth properly!"

Da Shan poked his head around the door. "I'm just going out," he said. "Is there anything I can get you?"

"Some decent food!" Old Zhu snapped, and his wife thrust a sliver of tofu in to shut him up.

"No?"

"No," she said.

Da Shan picked up his bag and walked down through the factory to the file of taxis. The first driver was asleep so Da Shan knocked on the window.

"Yeah?"

"To the Post Office."

They pulled out into the road and turned left, cruised alongside the river.

"Haven't I met you before?" the taxi driver asked, yawning.

"Probably."

"You're a businessman, right?"

Da Shan smiled. "Yeah."

"You used to work in Shenzhen, didn't you. I remember your mother. I knew it was you!" The driver slapped his steering wheel as he swung the car across a T-junction. "So are you here for good?"

"Maybe."

"You know what?" The driver grinned. "I've just come back from Shanghai. So beautiful and modern, not like here."

The lights at the crossroads were red. The taxi lurched to a stop. "Cigarette?"

"Thanks."

They smoked and exhaled out of the window while they waited for the lights to change. Da Shan looked out of the window at the row of deaf shoe-shine men sitting in the cold. They spoke to each other with their hands, tapped each other on the back when they wanted to say something. Da Shan took a drag, and exhaled; watched a middle-aged woman come and sit down to have her red high heels polished. The man at her feet signed something to the man next to him and they both laughed: a strange sound, like croaking frogs.

"You know I was in prison once," Da Shan said, shaking his head.

"Yeah?" The driver smiled. "So was I."

"Really?"

"Yeah. I've been out three years now. Three years today."

"Congratulations."

The lights changed. "I killed someone," the driver said as he hugged the back of the car in front.

"Why?"

The driver shrugged. "I didn't mean to do it. But I've done my time." The driver pulled into the center of the road and waited for a gap in the traffic. It had snarled up somewhere, a policeman was blowing his whistle. Someone beeped behind and the driver beeped back. "Fuckers," the cab driver cursed. "Can't they learn some fucking patience!" There was a moment of silence, then the driver turned to Da Shan. "So what were you in for?"

"Nineteen eighty-nine," Da Shan said.

The driver spat out of the window. "You were one of those guys causing trouble, huh?"

"I guess."

At last the traffic cleared and they turned right, pulled up on the other side of the road from the Post Office. "Well, we're both out now," the driver said. "Free men!"

Da Shan smiled, paid him and climbed out. "Go slowly!" he called to the driver as the taxi pulled away from the curb. "Go slowly!"

D a Shan walked past a stall that sold telephone beepers and outdated glossy calendars and into the Post Office. The counter staff were sitting shouting up and down the line to one another in a long and complicated conversation that kept on being interrupted by people trying to post letters or buy stamps. Da Shan walked to the desk that said "Inland Letters and Parcels" and the girl sitting at that desk turned to serve him, and smiled. She had a sweet voice as she took the parcel from his hand.

"What is in it?"

"A book," Da Shan said.

"Printed paper?"

"No, I wrote it myself. It's for my daughter."

"She's in Shenzhen?"

Da Shan nodded. The woman had a nice smile. "You must miss her," she said.

"I do."

The woman smiled again, then looked down at the parcel. "First or second class?"

"First, please," Da Shan said.

She weighed the parcel, put a couple more layers of masking tape along its seals, then used a wooden lollipop stick to smear glue across the back of the stamps.

"That's seven yuan fifty."

Da Shan watched the woman stamp the parcel with a first-class stamp, stamped it with a carved chop that said "Shaoyang Post Office," and then handed it back.

"Can you write your address on the back please."

Da Shan handed her the parcel back, she handed him the

forms that had to be filled out. He wrote them out as quickly as possible, and then she stamped them all again, added her own personal stamp, and smiled. "OK."

"That's it?"

"That's it."

When Da Shan got a telephone call from the factory office to say he had a parcel he imagined that his ex-wife had sent back the book he had sent his daughter. So, she won't even give me that, he thought, and wondered whether he ought to go and collect it or not. He smoked a cigarette, stared at the curling blue smoke as if it were some kind of divination. When he finished it he popped his head to check his father was OK, then walked down the stairs into the cool crisp mid-morning sunlight.

Dead leaves covered the path to the office, there were a couple of boys playing basketball against the wall, Da Shan kicked the leaves that rattled with the cold. The office had a deserted feel to it: no one worked here anymore, there was just the postman and a couple of the older men who came to sit and smoke and play chess. The postman was sifting the week's supply of newspapers into piles for people to come and collect when he saw Da Shan and waved. He brandished a neat brown parcel. "It's for you!" he said. "Look!"

Da Shan looked. It wasn't the parcel he'd sent.

"Sign here," the postman said, and Da Shan wrote the date in his book and signed.

Old Zhu was having another coughing fit when Da Shan got back home, his mother was sitting next to Old Zhu on the bed, rubbing his back. Get some tea! she signaled and Da

Shan went and poured out a cup from the thermos and gave it to his mother, who held it ready.

"Is he OK?" Da Shan asked.

"A bit better." She smiled and Da Shan nodded.

D a Shan went into his bedroom to open the parcel. Inside there was a thick envelope that had been folded in two; he pulled this free of the wrapping, flattened it against the bed. There was no name, so he ripped one end open, pulled out the paper inside. It was an official form: he had another look.

A birth certificate. It had Liu Bei's name on it, and his own, a son.

The sound of Old Zhu's coughing started up from the room next door, and Da Shan looked at the form again. He shook his head. All this time. Why hadn't she written to him or anything?

Da Shan checked inside the envelope and found a note that was in her writing.

> *I looked for you, and didn't find you*
> *and turned back home in vain.*

On the day Sun An and his sister caught a bus back to their village a cold wind blew down from the north and made everyone in the bus station shiver. His sister was quiet, Sun An tried to comfort her even despite the layers of clothing she'd wrapped herself up in. She didn't speak all the way back, and Sun An didn't feel like talking either, but the bus conductor wanted too much for the ticket and he argued the price down to ten yuan each.

"My sister's a student!" he protested, but the bus conductor took no notice.

"Students weigh as much as nonstudents," she said. "And they take up just as much room!"

Sun An and his sister stared out of the window as the bus took them farther and farther away from the city. All around were snowy hills, more snowy hills and over them loomed wintry clouds. After six hours Sun An shouted to the driver and they got out at the side of the road. It was a long walk from the main road to their village. They caught a lift on the back of a farmer's truck that was returning from the local market. It bounced over the earth track, splashing frozen puddles into the fields, bouncing Sun An and his sister on top of each other. At the top of the rise they looked down on their village: they could see their parents' home with its single light bulb: a pale lantern glimmering in the late-afternoon twilight.

"Don't worry," Sun An said without looking at his sister. She didn't look up, so he pressed his lips together and stayed quiet.

"I suppose they'll marry me off now," she said as she stared down the hill at their snow-clad village. The fields were full of broken rice stubble, a patchwork blanket of snow covered the ground.

Sun An bit his lip. He'd written home and told them something serious had happened. How his sister had been involved. She would need to get married. Maybe it would be a good man: someone who'd let her carry on her education.

The Sun family graves were treeless in the biting wind. "I'm cold," she said, and started down the tiny black path that slanted back home.

Winter moved into Shaoyang overnight; quietly and ruthlessly, like an invading army. Old Zhu's chrysanthemum was the first casualty: the petals curled and faded, they went brown and fell to the floor. One fell over the side of the balcony and drifted into a muddy puddle, where it floated for a while then drowned. Next the cicadas began to fall out of the trees and were swept up with the leaves. The few birds that hadn't left gathered in great flocks that vanished. All that was left was the north wind and the chattering clumps of bamboo.

For over a week the winds were northerly, bringing cold to the river. They smelled of the steppes, the lands beyond the far

Great Wall. Snow fell one night, and the wild geese slanted away across the sky, disappearing at a cloud's edge. The sprinkling of white melted in the sunlight, and then froze again at night. On the hills the temple courtyards were empty, the monks sat deep in silence, shivering with cold. The market was full of tired old men who sat selling their turnips and potatoes, while the rich went out to have dog hot pot to keep their blood warm.

It was a cold night, with a black sky and a white river shivering with ice, when Old Zhu died. The windows were rattling in their frames as he fell asleep and then forgot to wake up. His wife went out to light a brazier of coals to keep the room warm. She was poking at the coals and stirring up old memories, when she came back she found him cooling in the bed. Cold drafts wafted the curtains. Outside an eddy of air made the leaves dance to welcome his ghost.

Old Zhu's widow called Da Shan and he checked his father's corpse for signs of the living: but there weren't any. He stood and looked around his parents' bedroom; the neat tabletop, the rows of photos; his father's body lying in the bed. The room was very quiet, as if no one was breathing, he stepped forward and heard the creak of his shoe. He half expected his father to open his eyes or cough: but he did neither. Da Shan touched his hand, it was cold.

"Father?" he whispered, and patted the hand as he repeated a bit louder. "Father?"

But there was no response. Old Zhu lay still.

Old Zhu's widow and Da Shan sat silently as friends and neighbors came over to fuss and wail. Their sobs rose and fell in a discordant stereo — as they filled in for one another, took over the lead, then handed it on: red eyes; dripping noses and wailing voices.

Da Shan went into the kitchen and Autumn Cloud followed.

"Your father was a good man," she said, "a very good man."

"Yes, he was."

"He was very kind."

Da Shan nodded. He felt his dry eyes were some kind of affront, and looked out of the window, pretended to wipe a tear away.

"You be strong for your mother," Autumn Cloud said.

"Yes."

"She'll need you now. More than ever."

Da Shan spent the afternoon making promises to each of the women who came up to him: yes, he'd look after his mother; he'd be strong; he'd look after her; he wouldn't go back to Shenzhen. At last there were no more promises left to make and he slipped through the doorway and outside. The air in the apartment had become stuffy with all those tears, stifling with all the noise and sniffing and snuffles.

Da Shan set off walking, down through the market and along the river where an old man sat with his fishing rod waiting for the fish to come back, and into the old town. Da Shan had recently found a new shortcut to Liu Bei's mother's house: that led him around a cake shop and past a man who sold mutton.

There was a sheep tethered outside the shop waiting for slaughter, while another one was being cut into sections on a wooden chopping board. Da Shan continued around the corner and saw his son, playing in the dirt with a bird someone had caught for him. The bird had a string tied around one of its legs, and it was flapping in the dust as Little Dragon pulled it along.

"Heh!" Da Shan shouted, and his son looked up and then ran over.

"Have you seen my bird?"

Da Shan pulled the bird to him with the string. Its wings flapped as he pulled it closer and closer. "It's a big bird," he said. "Did you catch it yourself?"

"No," Little Dragon said, "the man next door gave it to me. It made his daughter cry."

Da Shan laughed. "Come on," he said, "let's go see Grandma."

Liu Bei's mother was gutting a fish she'd bought at market when Da Shan came in. From the way she looked at him he thought she'd heard about Old Zhu, but she didn't say anything.

"We're going kite flying today," Little Dragon said, and Liu Bei's mother's eyes looked at Little Dragon.

"Are you?"

"Yes!" Little Dragon said.

"Maybe," Da Shan began, "we could let the bird go." Little Dragon looked like he was going to cry, but Da Shan continued, "then he can go and fly with the kite. How's that?"

Da Shan walked through the streets with Little Dragon trailing by his side, one arm raised high to hold his father's hand. His mother had always said that his father would come, and that his father would take him kite flying. Little Dragon tried to remember his mother, he remembered the smell and the feeling of being wrapped in her arms. When his grandma showed him her photo it didn't seem to be the same person. That wasn't his mother.

"Where has Mother gone?" Little Dragon asked Da Shan as they began to walk up the hill to the temple.

"She's gone a long way away."

"Why?"

"Because," Da Shan began to say, then stopped. "Because she wanted to live by the sea."

"Oh," Little Dragon said, as if that explained everything.

"Why doesn't she come back?"

Da Shan was distracted. He was thinking of Old Zhu, not Liu Bei. Little Dragon asked his father why Mother didn't come back and Da Shan pursed his lips. "Because," he started, but didn't know what else to say. Sometimes there weren't answers. "Because — I don't really know," he said.

Little Dragon nodded again.

Madam Fan joined the other mourners in Old Zhu's apartment, while Peach sat in her room and thought of the summer and her time with Sun An. She wondered what had happened to him: he seemed to have disappeared and his video shop had closed. She'd heard he'd gone back to his village, and she wondered why. She missed having him around, missed having someone to talk to. To listen when her mother was driving her mad.

Peach turned over the page of the magazine she was reading. It was said that Da Shan had found a son in the town. She wanted to cry when she thought of it: he was so lucky, it seemed he had everything. Except, of course, a father.

Peach had liked Old Zhu, he'd been a kind old man. She stood up with a sigh and wandered to the window. The moon was rising, its silvery polish was gleaming over the factory: polishing away all the dirt and grime: turning the world a beautiful silver.

Peach decided she'd go for a walk to enjoy the autumn moonlight, went to fetch her coat. The moon was at her saddest and most beautiful in the autumn.

Da Shan returned to the house and said hello to the women who were sitting with his mother. He sat with them for a while, but the sound of their monotonous sobbing drove him into his bedroom. He picked through a couple of his father's books, pulled out the *Ten Thousand Tang Dynasty Poems* and opened it to a random page. "Selling Tattered Peonies," by a woman called Yu Xuanji. He'd never heard of her. He started to read, but it was a sad poem so he shut the book and stretched his legs out. He didn't need sad poems tonight.

Da Shan shut his eyes and thought of the times his father would tell him stories. It must have been before 1966, Da Shan was too old for stories after that. It seemed that Old Zhu had been full of stories when he'd been a child. He knew so much about Old and New China. He could tell a folktale one day, and then a story from the revolution the next.

Da Shan told himself to ask his mother if she remembered any of them, when the time was right. Children needed stories. She would know some that he could tell Little Dragon.

Da Shan lay for a while, reached into his pocket and pulled out his cigarettes, but the packet was empty. He reached into the drawer, but there was none there either. He slammed the drawer shut and let out a long irritated sigh, then stood up and paced from wall to window. From the other room he could hear the women's wailing, and he thought of his mother, sitting there crying. He tried to imagine life without his father and couldn't.

Da Shan picked an old notebook from the chest of drawers and flicked it open. There was some scribbling on the first couple of pages. It was in his mother's handwriting, there were some numbers, like she'd used the book for doing accounts. He tore them out, threw them in the bin, found a pen in a pot on the bookshelf and then lay down on the bed. He stopped for a while and thought of what to write first; it was difficult to choose a single moment to begin; but all stories had to have beginnings.

"Your mother and I met under a wisteria bush on a summer's day in 1987," Da Shan wrote. "There were so many butterflies in the air and your mother was reading the poetry of Wang

Wei. I don't think it was love at first sight; that is too simple. It was slower than that, but, now, when I look back it all seems very sudden." He sat back and scratched his head. This was so much less than he wanted to say; words could be so inadequate.

"We were both teachers in the Teacher's College. She worked for the Youth League, I taught in the History and Politics Department. We were both patriotic, we wanted to help our Motherland." He pursed his lips and wasn't sure it was coming out in the right order. "The last time I saw her was in 1989. We'd organized the demonstrations in support of the students in Beijing, and we were arrested. Maybe we were wrong; we were trying to make the lives of the common people better. I do not think that was wrong."

Da Shan shut his eyes. The summer of 1989 was still vivid in his mind. He could still remember the excitement everyone had felt when they thought that things were going to change. Instead it had all gone wrong; it hadn't changed for the better.

"People say that it was good that the government stopped the pro-democracy demonstrations because the suppression stopped the country from falling into chaos. When you are fully grown and married, maybe people will think differently." Da Shan bit the end of the pen. "Now I sit here and try to imagine what China will be like when you are a man. When you have children of your own, but the future is a foreign country. When I was your age my father told me that the earth was round for a good reason: so that the future was always a mystery. It works the other way as well, we can never look back. All we see is what is in front of our eyes."

Da Shan read what he had written, and then nodded to himself. "One day there will be a time when what I and your mother did will be seen differently. Maybe there will also come a time when you have to act like we did. These opportunities only come once a life. I know your mother would agree with me when I tell you not to miss that chance."

D a Shan and Little Dragon turned down along the road to the factory and took a right turn into the old town, to his grandma's house. Little Dragon's legs were tired, so Da Shan lifted him up onto his shoulder and carried him along. But Little Dragon was so tired that even the kite felt heavy.

"I'll take the kite," his father said, bouncing him up to get a better grip.

Little Dragon liked being carried by his father. His father was so tall and strong.

"Do you think Mother will come back?" Little Dragon asked as they walked down the street.

"You know I don't know," Da Shan said. "Maybe we should ask Grandmother."

After lunch, Liu Bei's mother put Little Dragon to bed for a rest then made Da Shan a cup of green tea. She filled the cup while Aunty Tang sat in the shadows and wheezed.

"I'm sorry to hear about your father," Liu Bei's mother said as she put the cup down on the table. "He was a good man. I remember."

Da Shan nodded. He didn't really want to talk about it.

"There was something Little Dragon asked me this morning," Da Shan said, "about his mother. He wanted to know if she was going to come back or not."

Liu Bei's mother looked at him and put her knitting down. "No," she said. "I don't think she is."

Da Shan nodded. He let out a long sigh, looked away down at his trousers, picked a fleck of dust off them, scratched an old stain with his nail: it still refused to come off. "If she's not coming back," he said at last, "then I thought it would be easier for him if we told him his mother had died."

Liu Bei's mother looked at him across the table. In the corner Aunty Tang lit her pipe and coughed. "Yes," she said, "you're right."

That evening after supper, Da Shan sat with his son on his knee and cuddled him close. "Are you a brave boy?" he asked, and Little Dragon nodded. The child's face was grave. He could sense this was a serious question. "I want you to be brave," Da Shan said, "because I have something very sad to tell you."

Little Dragon nodded.

"It's about Mother."

"Is she coming back?" Little Dragon asked.

"No," Da Shan said. "She's not. She's dead."

Little Dragon nodded. His father was serious and he was serious too. If his father cried he'd cry. Little Dragon fiddled with his father's collar. He saw his granny washing the pots, her hands cut off at the wrists by white bubbles. She wiped the pots and put them to the side to dry. "Mother's dead?" he asked.

"Yes."

"But Grandma is here, isn't she?"

"Of course she is. And I'm here."

Little Dragon nodded. He started crying even though he didn't want to, tried to bring the picture of her face into his head but the image was starting to fade, her face was blurred. He wiped the water from his lashes and the snot from his nose, imagined him cuddling close as they lay in bed together. He could still feel her there.

"You haven't forgotten, have you?"

"No," Little Dragon said and his father gave him a squeeze.

Da Shan wished he'd brought his book so he could read it to Little Dragon. "How about," he began, "we go and visit the places that Mother used to go to?"

"OK," Little Dragon said. His tone was flat and sad. He didn't sound very enthusiastic. Da Shan bounced him on his knee.

"We'll go tomorrow — OK?"

"OK." Little Dragon nodded.

The old town had a quiet, thoughtful feel to it that morning. The streets were bathed in burning sunlight, the shadows looked deeper than they were. Da Shan held Little Dragon by the hand as they walked through the streets, following Liu Bei's mother's directions. They went confidently at first, but after a few minutes he wasn't so sure. This part of town didn't look so familiar. Maybe he'd taken the wrong turn. At the end of the road was a fork. Da Shan stopped and looked around him. Both directions looked the same. He screwed up his nose and decided that left felt right.

The big heavy cobbles had been smoothed down by the years, rickety wooden houses leaned in, their eaves almost touching in the middle. Each step felt more and more like he'd come the wrong way. It wasn't the look so much as the unbroken silence. Halfway down was a house with a red-painted doorway and a bamboo birdcage hanging from the eaves. Under the birdcage sat an old man with watery eyes, his thin bones poking out like knitting needles under a thick woolen sweater. The old man sat staring into nothing. He didn't seem to notice Da Shan approach, but the songbird cocked its head to one side and broke the totalitarian silence with a sudden trill: a tiny tune, like a fragment of a much longer piece.

"It's a fine bird," Da Shan said. Little Dragon stood silently by his side.

The old man didn't move.

"Is this the right way for Well Street, do you know?" Da Shan asked him.

Still no response.

Da Shan tried again: "Is this the right way for Well Street?"

Silence.

Da Shan looked back along the way he'd come and let out a frustrated sigh. A little girl came running out of the doorway. She stopped when she saw Da Shan and put her hand to her mouth.

"Hello."

The girl sucked her hand while she looked at him.

"Do you live here?"

She didn't answer.

A woman came out of a house opposite, locking the door behind her. "She don't speak," the woman said as she turned back up the way Da Shan had come. "Neither of them speak," she called over her shoulder. "No one speaks around here."

Da Shan kept going after all, walked down a few more empty streets and came to a little shack where a woman in a red dress and plastic slippers sold ice cream.

"Is there a teahouse near here?" Da Shan asked.

"A teahouse?"

"Yeah."

"I don't know any teahouse."

"It's called the Drink and Dream Teahouse."

She echoed the name and rubbed her chin. "Sounds familiar."

"It was near the old city wall."

"The Drink and Dream Teahouse," the woman repeated. Da Shan waited. "The Drink and Dream Teahouse, I know I know it, but I can't think now."

Da Shan waited and waited. After a while he wanted to shake the woman.

"Oh yes!" she said at last. "I know. I know the place. Wooden house — yes?"

"I'm not sure."

"It must be. It's off Yellow Willow Lane, I think. It must be the same place," she told him, and pointed down the street. "It's down to the bottom and on the left. Straight down."

"Thanks," Da Shan said.

The woman's directions weren't quite right, but the nearer Da Shan got the more he began to recognize where he was. Yellow Willow Lane was a narrow street, there was no pavement, the pavement was hemmed in close by rickety wooden houses, and at the end was one of the old city gates: a narrow arch of dressed stone.

Da Shan asked for directions for the Drink and Dream Teahouse and a man waved his hand in the direction of the gate. "Through the gate," he said. "On the right."

The gateway was thick, like a tunnel, and the air had a cool damp feel to it. On the other side was a patch of wasteland, halfway between a demolition and building site. There were a few peasant workers squatting in the shade eating lunch. To the left was a little alleyway, and Da Shan looked up to see if the sign was still there. The Drink and Dream Teahouse, it said across the top of the wooden gateway.

Da Shan lifted Little Dragon up into his arms, held him close. "There you go," he said. "That's where Mother used to work."

Little Dragon looked and stared. His mother was dead. She wasn't going to come back after all. He turned and cuddled his head into his father's shoulder, wrapped his little arms around his father's head.

"So when people die they can't come back?" Little Dragon checked.

"No, they can't," Da Shan said.

"So where do they go?"

"They used to go underground, but now they go to a special place in town," Da Shan said.

"Can we go there?"

Da Shan thought of the chaos and the smoke from the town's incinerator and shook his head. "Maybe when you're older," he said, and Little Dragon nodded. Da Shan watched tears trickle down his son's cheeks and tried to smile.

Old Zhu's funeral was a simple affair. The old women sat and discussed the poverty of the arrangements, the Zhu family didn't even hire a bus to take all the relatives to the Number Three Incinerator. It came and went and the ashes were collected, and it seemed to the old women that another link with the past had been severed.

One day Da Shan came to pick up his son and Liu Bei's mother drew him aside.

"I think it's time he went to go and live with you," she said. "He is your son, after all."

Da Shan nodded. He'd been wanting to suggest it himself, but had been waiting for the right moment.

When Old Zhu's widow heard that Da Shan's bastard was going to come and live with them she was so angry she went into the kitchen and looked for something to smash. She picked up a blue bowl and was about to throw it onto the floor when she remembered it was a bowl that Old Zhu had bought. She could picture him sitting at the table and dipping his spoon into it, or ladling soup. No, she couldn't smash that.

She looked around the kitchen for anything that wouldn't remind her of her husband but there was nothing. Everything had his touch imprinted on it: every chopstick, plate, bowl or cup. She held the cup she'd given Old Zhu medicine in and remembered his face as he swallowed the medicine. Silly old man, she thought, and then realized she was supposed to be angry.

When she met Little Dragon she tried to be cold and distant, but he was such a pretty little boy that she couldn't resist pinching his cheeks and speaking to him in baby-talk.

"So how old are you, little man?" she asked.

"Five," Little Dragon said.

"Six," Da Shan corrected, and tousled his hair. "You can't count, can you?"

"Six!" Little Dragon declared.

That evening Little Dragon and Da Shan sat on the balcony, and Da Shan took out his book and wrote on the inside cover "The Drink and Dream Teahouse," in neat brush strokes. Little Dragon watched wide-eyed. "Shall I tell you a story?" Da Shan asked and turned over to the first page, as if he were about to read a story. Little Dragon clapped his hands together and sat up, his eyes intent on his father's face.

"And did the President really go and drink there?" Little Dragon asked at the end.

"Of course. All the famous people went there. They all heard about your mother. She was so beautiful and her tea was the sweetest in all of China."

Little Dragon sat and thought. He tried to fit everything he could remember in with this new bit of information. They didn't really blend, but swam around together in a contradictory soup.

"Did you ever go to the Drink and Dream Teahouse?"

"Once," Da Shan said.

"Was Mother there?"

"No."

There was a pause as Little Dragon pursed his lips.

"Was that because she'd died?"

"Yes," Da Shan said, "it was."

Before Little Dragon went to bed Da Shan stood at the window and looked out, over the hill with the temple on it, where the best winds were. Little Dragon could see the moon rising. "Look, Father!" he said, and Da Shan looked.

"She's not shy anymore."

"Who?"

"The moon."

"No," Da Shan said, "she's not."

Da Shan and Little Dragon sat watching the moon cast long dark shadows across the factory yard, when Da Shan thought he could see movement in a window opposite.

A *clunk!* of a door bolt being drawn back startled two rooks from their sleep. They flapped through the dark and landed in the next tree, disappearing noisily in the mass of black branches. The door creaked as it was pulled back, then silence as a woman stepped out onto the balcony. She was dressed in a red robe embroidered with swirling phoenixes of turquoise blue and electric green: but all they could see were the shades of light and dark that moved around her body. The fringe of her robe billowed out from the concrete edge of the balcony. She had black hair, white skin and black eyes.

Madam Fan sat inside, listening in the shadows as her daughter began to sing:

> Sigh for a beautiful woman
> Born under an unlucky star

And Little Dragon fidgeted in Da Shan's lap.

> Beyond the mountains are still more mountains.
> A heartless lover sends no news.

Madam Fan mouthed the words as Peach sang them:

> I long to send a message
> But don't know where he is.

Peach danced a few steps, flapping her sleeves like the shadow that danced at her feet. Da Shan thought of Little Dragon and Liu Bei and wanted to cry.

> There's no cure for sleeping alone,
> No medicine to warm a half-cold bed.

Peach held her stance as she sang out the last notes: a breeze tugged at her robe, making the phoenixes dance and fly for a moment before they went still. She looked out across the factory, chill moonlight, blocks of apartments and gray rooftops; then looked across the yard toward Old Zhu's house. There was a light on and she could see his silhouette in the yellow square of the window. Da Shan and his son watching her.

Peach stared for a moment, then she turned her face down and stepped back inside, and the bolt slid back in place. Madam Fan's eyes were closed in silent contemplation. A long cold tear snaked down her cheek. She wiped it away.

"How was it?" Peach asked nervously.

Madam Fan opened her eyes, and looked at her daughter. "Beautiful," she said.